Lovers, Past & Never

Stories by

Donald Skiff

Donald Skiff

ISBN (Paperback): 978-0-9832003-4-5
ISBN (eBook): 978-0-9832003-5-2

Stories

Foreword

People don't exist, *as people*, except in relationship to other (usually) people. Our brains are wired to respond to each other, to learn who we are by interacting with others. The process doesn't always go well, leaving us wounded and, over time, scarred. When it does, however, we are made richer by it.

Much of who we grow up to be is profoundly affected by those around us as well as the happenstance experiences we encounter while young. Each moment in our lives alters the next experienced moment. We are never really "finished" until the moment of our death.

This is a collection of stories, mostly about relationships. Each of these stories became a puzzle to me. One appeared to me in the form of a dream, which I felt obliged to write down the next day, adding such details as seemed necessary to give it shape. One of the longer ones, "Where Never Lark," began as a simpler story of a flight in a home-built aircraft. When it was "finished," it kept nagging at me, insisting that it was not finished at all. The result was a different story than I had thought it to be in the beginning. "That ... Sense of History" had a similar life.

There is no sequence to these stories—you may read them in any order. The characters depicted in one are unrelated to characters in any other. They were written over a period of seven or eight years.

Personal essays, the usual products of my earlier writing, had been more deliberately fashioned from ideas that occurred to me in my reading or in my musings about day-to-day experiences. I've written five books of such essays, and have seldom felt any mystery involved in their genesis or development. The stories in this book affected me as I was writing them, at times profoundly.

I'm willing to accept the conundrum—for now.

"The Elevator" was incorporated into a novel, *Osmosis*, published in 2011. "Where Never Lark" and the first part of "That … Sense of History" were previously in a small book, *Where Never Lark*, published in a limited way in 2005.

Donald Skiff, October, 2012

Acknowledgements

Most of my writing in the past ten years or so has been in response to the writing groups I've been in, where I've read them aloud for comments and critiques. My current group, *Writers Unlimited*, led by Joy Rome, offers me the comments of a remarkable collection of writers, editors, poets and playwrights, and I am deeply indebted to these people: Alice Bingner, Bob Brill, Larry Nathan Burns, Charles Duncan, Mary Fancher, Ken Gaertner, Susan Hansen, Randi Hoffmann, Jim Kane, Don Lamphiear, Dorothy Mikat, and Edna Morris.

I also impose upon my friends, urging my writing on them in the hope that they will respond candidly. Some of these are Marjorie Lynn, Martha Kimball, Charlie Paul, Sara Tallaksen-Greene, Bill Lichtig, Karen Hamp, Mark Rycheck, Laura Namet and Debra Sachs. My gratitude to them is boundless.

And I must acknowledge the person who reads every piece I write before anyone else and has helped and encouraged me in this enterprise as well as in my life itself, my wife Judith.

Parsley, Sage, Rosemary and Time

One

His door was open a crack when someone knocked. Barely awake, he turned his head on the pillow to see who it was. A very young woman stuck her head around the door. "Mister James, it's time for you to get some air!" she said pleasantly.

He tried to smile. As she entered the room, he woke up more. Very pretty, she was wearing regular street clothes, not the boring white smocks most of his visitors wore. She opened his wheelchair that was standing just inside the door and moved it over next to the bed. Then she took his robe down from its hook and approached him. "You look like you're still asleep."

"Yes," he said. "What else is there to do in this place?"

"Well, that's why I came to get you outdoors!" She laughed and babbled as she helped him sit up in bed and put his arms through the sleeves of his robe. Then the two of them got him first onto his shaking legs, then sitting in the wheelchair. She hooked his oxygen canister onto the chair and straightened the tube to his nostrils. "Okay, ready?"

He nodded and settled into the chair. They rolled out into the hall and down to the back entrance of the hospital, where the sunshine greeted them on the lawn. He closed his eyes in the brightness, enjoying the warmth and the gentle breeze.

"Take a turn around the lake?" she asked.

"Thank you," he said, "what's your name?"

She put a hand on his shoulder. "Oh, I'm sorry! I didn't introduce myself—I'm Cyndi, and I'm an aide, and I can come and take you out just about every day, if you want."

"If the weather's like this, every day would be nice."

They moved in silence for a while. He could hear some ducks in the pond, but couldn't see them. There was traffic somewhere beyond trees in the opposite direction. He sighed deeply.

"Are you okay?" she asked, concerned, stretching around to see his face.

"I'm wonderful. Let's park over there by the bench."

"Do you want the shade or the sun?"

"The sun, at least for a few minutes."

She turned his chair so he faced the pond and set the brake.

He looked over at her. "Pretty girls always make me smile," he said.

She laughed. "Thank you!"

"I used to dread getting old," he said, "and then when I got here I didn't mind so much. It's nice not to have to work so hard just to live."

"You've earned your rest," she said.

"I'm not so sure of that. But here I am, however it happened. The worst part is the boredom."

"Do you spend any time in the lounges or in the television room?"

"I hate television," he said, "and most of those old bags in the lounge don't do anything but gossip."

Cyndi laughed again. "Well *you're* a sourpuss!"

"Yeah, I am. There's just nobody in this place who can carry on a conversation." He glanced over at her and smiled. "Does that put you on the spot?"

"Well," she said, "I don't know what you want to talk about, but I'll surely try."

He tilted his face to the sun. "I spent a summer in the Bay Area. Do you know where that is?"

"San Francisco Bay?"

He chuckled. "That wasn't a test. It's the only bay area I know of. I know there must be a lot of them."

"I've been there," she said. "It's a beautiful place."

"When were you there?"

"Three years ago. My boy friend and I drove out there. We wanted to see California. We drove down to Big Sur and LA, and then came back by the Grand Canyon."

"I thought you must have a boy friend," he said. "Pretty girl like you."

"He was my boy friend, but he's Back East in school now."

"You don't think he'll come back for you when he finishes?"

"Three more years—it's a long time to wait, for either of us."

"When I was your age, I felt that way, too. Three years is a long time when you're young. There are just so many things to experience."

"Tell me about when you were my age," she said, looking at him. "Did you have a girl?"

He laughed. "Several of them, actually, all at the same time."

"Oh! How was that?"

"We lived in a house near Golden Gate Park, on Cabrillo Street. We thought of ourselves as family. It was 'the summer of love,' they called it, 1967. We did our best to live up to that."

"How fun!"

"For a while," he said, and looked down at his hands. Veins showed through the thin skin on the backs of his hands, and his knuckles stuck out. "Later, it got bad, and a lot of evil people came into town, and people changed."

"That was a strange time," she said. "A lot of changes."

"You weren't even born then, were you?"

"Not for another ten or fifteen years."

"We thought we were changing the world."

"Tell me about it," she said, turning her body so she could see his face better.

"You must have heard Simon and Garfunkel."

"Of course. I think I've heard just about everything they did." She began to sing softly, *"Tell her to make me a chambray shirt ..."*

"Parsley, Sage, Rosemary and Thyme." He smiled. "I had all their songs memorized."

"The song was 'Scarborough Fair.' He was off to the war, and he wants to send his girl a message."

"You do know something about it, don't you?"

"It was a very romantic time," she said. "Not like these wars today."

"When people sing it, they usually leave out the sub-text, the other song that's mixed in with it. The song about the soldier cleaning his gun and going to fight in a war for a cause they've long ago forgotten. Just like today," he said. "Just like always."

He squeezed his eyes closed, but tears escaped anyway and ran down his cheeks. She put her arm across his shoulders. "Tell me," she said softly, "why the tears?"

He took a handkerchief from the pocket of his robe and wiped his eyes. "We lost the war," he said finally.

"It was the first war the United States ever lost," she said.

He turned and looked at her. "I don't mean Viet Nam," he said. "That was a tragedy for the country. The real war we lost was for humanity."

She shook her head. "I don't understand."

"We found a new way to live," he said, "where everybody had a chance to be who they wanted to be. We didn't need rules. We loved everybody."

"That must have been hard to give up."

"Martin Luther King made that great speech ..."

"I have a dream," she said. "You had a dream, too."

"We did."

"Do you still have that dream?"

He looked at her sharply, then dropped his eyes. "It died, years ago."

"I'm sorry."

Looking back at her, "What is your dream?" he asked.

She smiled. "I don't know. I guess everybody wants peace and justice. It's just so hard to accomplish."

They sat silently. The sun had moved enough that they were shaded by the big maple tree behind them.

"Why do you do this?" he asked suddenly. Turning toward her, he asked, "What is the objective you want to accomplish—for doing what you are doing right now?"

She seemed hurt by his question. When she spoke, her voice was broken. "I want to do something for other people. I want to make a difference in the world."

"I'm sorry," he said. "I guess I'm talking to myself. I remember how idealistic I was back in those days, wanting a better world, and then I just gave up. I became like everybody else. I never became who I wanted to be."

"Did you love anyone?" She tilted her head a little, as though her question was merely whimsical, but he felt the seriousness in it.

"I loved my family," he said. "My hippie family. But it didn't last."

"You moved on."

"We all moved on. I've been grieving ever since."

"That was forty years ago," she said. "No loves since then?"

"I was married—twice. I thought I loved them at the time."

"What happened to them?"

He shivered. "I'm getting cold."

She stood up. "Let's get you back inside," she said. "We can continue this conversation next time."

Neither spoke as she wheeled him back to his room. "I hope I didn't upset you," she said as she helped him back into his bed.

"No," he said. "My life upsets me."

"Oh!" she cried, and then she leaned over and hugged him. "I'm sorry!"

"Not your fault."

She turned away from him and wiped her eyes with a tissue. Then she turned back and smiled at him. "Can I come again?"

"Of course, Cyndi. You're sweet."

She blew him a kiss, and left, leaving the door slightly ajar, as she had found it.

Two

At the same time the next day, Cyndi appeared again at his door. This time, with a big smile, she held her phone close to him. "Listen," she said. He could hear the faint strains of Simon and Garfunkel singing "Scarborough Fair."

When the song was over, she laughed. "I've got the whole album, if you'd like to hear it," she said.

"I'm touched," he said. "Thank you. But I can barely hear it. My ears aren't very good."

"Maybe we can do something about that. But first, you need some fresh air."

She prepared him for their stroll on the grounds. "Maybe they can loan us a CD player," she said as they headed down the hall.

"I've been thinking about our talk yesterday," he said. "I've been looking forward to talking some more."

"Good!" she said. "So have I."

They stopped at the same bench facing the pond. He stared at the water for a few minutes, then said, "I said I spent the summer in San Francisco. That was only three months out of my long life. It's funny that those three months seem now such a big part of my life."

"How old were you?"

"Goin' on thirty. I was older than most of the kids there. It just seemed to be the place to be right then."

She pulled a strand of hair that had blown across her face back over her head. The rest of her hair was tied at the back, and he could see two small diamonds on the edge of her ear. "Where were you before that?" she asked.

"I was down south for a couple of years, trying not to get shot." He grinned.

"What do you mean?"

"I was in Selma in sixty-five, helping out some folks."

"Selma, Alabama?"

"Yeah. It was pretty dangerous down there for a Yankee boy."

She turned to look directly at him. "You mean the civil rights demonstrations?"

He shrugged. "I was trying to help out."

"Another Simon and Garfunkel song," she said, "He Was My Brother."

"A lot of people put their lives on the line."

She put her hand on his arm. "Did you see Martin Luther King?"

"Only from a distance."

She turned her face toward the pond, and was silent.

"What are you thinking?" he asked.

"You said, 'Only from a distance,' and I was thinking that's as close as most of us get to what's really important."

"Why is that, do you think?" He reached over and put his thin hand on her shoulder.

She turned to face him. "I do so little about the things I care about. You asked me yesterday what my dreams are, and all I could say was 'peace and justice,' as though they were real things."

"Peace and justice aren't real?"

"Sometimes," she said, looking away again, "they feel like just dreams. Smoke dreams."

"So you make do with pushing an old man around a lake in the sun." When she looked at him he was smiling. "I'm teasing," he said. You don't know how important this is to me."

"You must be very lonely." She was studying his face.

He suddenly wanted to cry, but he took a breath and smiled at her. "Not at this moment," he said.

"I'm so glad!"

"You see," he said, patting her hand, "you don't do 'so little' about things you care about."

She beamed at him. "I do care about you!"

"I know. It used to be that it'd take me a long time to care about somebody, because I didn't want to make a mistake." He smiled. "Even then, I still made mistakes. Now, I don't have time to wait until I'm sure."

"That's lovely!"

"It's also scary," he said.

Her face sobered. "We only have this moment."

"That's very astute. Thank you for reminding me." He closed his eyes and turned his face to the sun. "In more ways than one."

"What do you mean?" she asked, perplexed.

"Well, the easiest part is that we will soon go back inside and you'll go off to whatever else you do in your life and I'll go back to sleep."

She tilted her head and smiled. "And what else?"

He looked out across the lake. "That family of ducks over there is growing up."

Her brow furrowed as she studied his face.

"The little ones," he said, continuing to look across the lake, "are almost as big as their parents. Won't be long and they'll fly away."

"I ..." she began.

"There's another song from before you were born," he said. "Remember 'Turn, Turn, Turn'?"

She thought a moment. "You mean, '*For every season, turn turn turn* ...'?"

"You do know it," he said. "*A time to dance, a time to mourn.*"

She suddenly turned her face away from him. For a long moment she didn't move. Then she looked back at him. "That's mean," she said. "Of course I know we have just a little time. I don't need to be reminded. That's why I said we only have this moment—but then you had to throw it into my face!"

He could see tears running down her cheeks. For a minute, he didn't know what to say. Then, "Please forgive me. That was not intended to be mean."

She turned away again.

"A person my age," he began, "has to come to terms with his own death. The people in this place," and he gestured toward the building, "are all aware that any of us can go at any time—any moment—even if some can't face it yet. I forget that other people haven't had time to get comfortable with that. It was a thoughtless remark, and I hope you can forgive me."

She turned back to look at him with red-rimmed eyes. "I haven't lost anyone I've loved yet. My parents and grandparents are still living, and the only relatives I've known who have died I didn't know well enough to grieve over."

He reached for her hand. "When I was young like you, we talked about losing people we had come to love, but it wasn't usually through death. People used to move on when relationships cooled." He thought for a moment. "Somebody used to sing a song about 'Hello, hello, good bye, good bye.'"

She smiled at him, a sad, little smile. "I think it was your friend Paul Simon," she said, and began to sing softly, *"And the trees that are green turn to brown."*

He thought for a moment, then he also began to sing in a weak, raspy voice, *"Once my heart was filled with the love of a girl. I held her close, but she faded in the night, Like a poem I meant to write, And the leaves that are green turn to brown ..."*

The girl joined in, *"And they wither with the wind, And they crumble in your hand ..."*

"Hello hello hello hello, Goodbye goodbye goodbye goodbye."

"That's all there is, And the leaves that are green turn to brown."

She covered her face with her hands and sobbed. He touched her arm. "I'm sorry, Cyndi. I didn't mean to upset you."

She looked up at him, smiling through her tears. "You didn't. The song is so sad!"

Looking into her face, he asked, "How is it that you know all those old songs?"

She dabbed at her face. "My grandmother," she said. "She used to sing them all the time, and when I lived with her for a while she taught them to me. I have all the old LPs she collected."

"Sounds like you learned a lot from her."

"I worshipped her, I think. She was my role model. I wanted to be like her."

He sat back in his wheelchair and clasped his hands. "Tell me about this wonderful woman."

"I have pictures of her at Woodstock," she said. "She was a flower child."

"That was quite a gathering."

"You told me yesterday about thinking that you were building a new world, or something like that."

He nodded.

"Well, she thought that, too."

"Can I meet this wonderful lady?"

"No," she said softly. "She doesn't remember anything. She's got Alzheimer's."

He put his hand on her arm again, and she put her hand over his.

"I'm sorry," he said gently.

They sat in silence for a while. Then he said, "Now *you* are her memory, aren't you?"

"I guess I am." She sighed. Then she stood up and unlocked the brakes on his chair. Neither spoke on the way back to his room.

Three

The next day Cyndi didn't return for their outing, and he was despondent. When another aide, who had come in to straighten his room, asked him what was wrong, he said his "fresh air girl" hadn't come.

"Oh, Cyndi?"

"Yes."

"She doesn't come in on Thursdays," the woman said. "Other people have missed her, too."

"She's very sweet."

"Yes, she is. Her grandmother is here, too."

"Oh, I didn't know that."

He felt better after that, and read a couple of magazines.

The next day, when Cyndi tapped on his door and greeted him with her cheerful "Hi!" he smiled widely.

"It's a little chilly out today," she said. "You might need a jacket over your robe."

"The other girl—the one with black hair—said your grandmother was here."

Her face became sad. "Yes." As she helped him into his robe, she said, "I look in on her every time I come here, but she doesn't remember me."

He turned his face to look at her. "I'd been thinking," he said haltingly, "that you came just to see me. That's pretty selfish, isn't it?" He grinned, trying to let her know he was kidding her.

She gave him a hug. "I do see other people, but I think you're special," she said.

"It's okay," he said. "I guess I just want too much." His eyes misted over, and he wiped them on the sleeve of his robe.

She looked at him for a long time. "I want too much, too."

"I guess that's what people do, isn't it," he said gently. "Don't take it all on yourself. But I'd like to meet your grandmother—even if she can't remember anything."

She thought for a while. "Well, it's kinda chilly outside anyway," she said, and continued getting him settled in his wheelchair.

As they rolled down the hallway, she said, "Sometimes she seems to know where she is, but usually she just looks at you."

"That's okay," he said. "I'd just like to see this woman who taught you all those songs."

Cyndi laughed.

The door to the room was open. An old woman sat in a chair, her head drooping, asleep.

"Grandma," Cyndi said loudly as they entered, "I've brought you a visitor!"

The woman looked up blankly. "Is it lunch time?"

"No, it's Cyndi, and I've brought somebody with me who wants to meet you!" She spoke with emphasis and a forced cheerfulness.

Grandma looked at him blankly. "Who are you?" she demanded.

"Just another old man," he said. "You know Cyndi, your granddaughter, don't you?"

She looked up at the girl. "Of course I do," she said, "she takes me outside every damned day!"

In spite of the woman's tone of voice, Cyndi smiled. "You like it, Grandma, once we get out into the sunshine!"

"Sunshine girl. Waste of time."

"Tell me your name," injected Mister James.

"Celia," she answered immediately. "What's yours?"

"Oh, Grandma! You remember!"

"Make him tell me his name."

"It's Greg," he answered.

"Well, Greg," Celia said, "what's your business? Are you another doctor, come to poke me?"

"No, Grandma," Cyndi said, "he lives here, just like you!"

Celia looked at him for a moment. "Bet you can't remember shit, either."

"Oh, no, Grandma," the girl said, "he's been telling me about the old days!"

Greg said, "Cyndi said you were a flower child at Woodstock."

"Who told you that?"

"Cyndi, right here, your granddaughter."

"What's she know?"

Greg looked up at Cyndi, who had her hand over her mouth, her eyes filling with tears. "She knows everything you taught her," he said gently. "Show her your phone," he said. "Play Parsley, Sage for her."

Cyndi grinned at him and pulled her phone from her pocket. Holding it close to Celia's ear, she played the song. For a minute Celia listened blankly. Then she began singing along, her voice barely audible.

Greg looked at Cyndi. She was smiling gleefully.

"Do you have her song?" he asked.

For a moment she looked perplexed. Then she grinned. "You mean Cecilia?"

"Yes."

Her face sobered. "Not here, "she said.

"Bring it next time," he said. "Bet she'll remember it."

"Oh, that's wonderful!" Cyndi said, still holding the phone out to her grandmother.

"I have to pee," Celia said.

"Okay, Grandma, I'll get some help for you." Cyndi disappeared, and in a minute returned with another aide.

"Okay, Celia," said the aide, "let's get you into the bathroom. You two get lost."

Cyndi wheeled Greg out of the room and down toward the lounge. "Thank you, Mister James," she said. "That's the first time I've seen her recognize anything!"

"Stop calling me mister," he grumbled. "Everybody here calls me by my real name."

"All right, Greg," she answered with a laugh.

As they entered the lounge, he looked back at her. "What are we doing here?"

"Well, since it isn't so nice outside, I thought we could do something different."

He looked around. "Nothing here but a bunch of old gossips."

She held her face close to his. "We've got to get you out of your room, and I see somebody I think you'll like."

She steered his wheelchair over next to a white-haired woman sitting alone, reading a magazine. "Wanda," she said, "I brought somebody I want you to meet."

Wanda looked up from her magazine, first at Cyndi then at Greg. "I've seen you," she said to him.

"I'm Greg James," he said formally.

Wanda smiled at him. "I'm Wanda Evers."

"What are you in for?" he asked. Cyndi laughed.

"Probably like you," Wanda said, "I'm old."

"Greg was a hippie," Cyndi said.

Wanda's eyes brightened. "Were you in a commune?"

"No—well, sort of. I had a little family in San Francisco for a while."

Wanda gestured to Cyndi. "Pull up a chair, Honey." Then, to Greg, she said, "When was that?"

"The Summer of Love," he said, grinning.

"I was in school, in Berkeley," she said. "My folks were scared to death I'd get caught in a riot or something."

"What did you study?"

"Men," she said, then laughed. "I wasn't a serious student. I must have changed my major five times."

"Trying to figure out where you fit in?"

She looked at him. "Weren't we all?"

Cyndi said, "I don't think that's changed much in forty years."

Greg looked over at her. "You would have fit right in."

Wanda looked at Cyndi's arms. "You been tattooed?"

She blushed. "Just a little one, back here." She indicated her shoulder.

Wanda, without hesitating, pulled the top of her slacks down so they could see her hip and just the top of an elaborate, if faded, tattoo.

"Greg wore an earring," Cyndi said, pointing to his ear.

"Who told you that?" he asked.

She reached over and tugged at the lobe of his ear. Laughing, she said, "Look at this. The hole is still there!"

"You're feeling rambunctious today," he said, pulling his head away from her. Then, to Wanda he said, "Cyndi's grandmother taught her all the old songs—Simon and Garfunkel, everything."

"Peter, Paul and Mary were my favorites," Wanda said. "I loved the folk songs."

"Maybe we could organize a sing-along," Cyndi said. "I'd like to get Greg more involved in things here."

"Cyndi's grandmother was at Woodstock," Greg said to Wanda.

"Oh, I loved Crosby, Stills, and Nash! They were there!"

"Judy Blue Eyes!" Cyndi exclaimed.

"See, she knows them all!" said Greg.

Another aide came up to them. "Cyndi," she said, "Priscilla has been asking for you."

"Oh, I'm sorry! I lost track of time! Tell her I'll be right there."

The aide left, and Cyndi looked dejected. "I have to see somebody else," she said.

"Ah," said Greg, smiling. "Fickle young women!"

"Go," said Wanda. "We can get Greg back to his room when he's ready."

Cyndi stood up, leaned over Greg and kissed him on the forehead. "I'll see you next time," she said softly. Then she turned and left.

Wanda and Greg looked at each other, smiling uncertainly.

Four

Greg James was thoughtful as the aide wheeled him back to his room an hour later. He hadn't cared about anybody in a long time, and it hadn't seemed that anybody cared about him. All his relatives had either died or moved away. His only daughter, Leanne, from his first marriage, lived in California and rarely even wrote. He hadn't seen her in years. After nearly a year in the senior living center, he hadn't made any friends. He seldom left his room except to eat.

Meeting Cyndi, though, and Wanda, had stirred feelings in him. They both reminded him of things in his life from a long time ago and of people—especially women—that he had once loved.

The next day, Cyndi didn't come again. After fretting for awhile, he asked another aide to take him to the lounge. He hoped to see Wanda there. But there were only four other women playing cards in one corner. "Put me over there," he said to the aide, "by the magazine rack."

"I'll come back to take you to lunch," she said.

"Thank you." He watched her walk away, and realized that he had barely looked at her as she helped him. "I'm getting crotchety in my old age," he told himself.

Most of the magazines were for women. He found an old *National Geographic* and settled back in his wheelchair to read.

A few minutes later, out of the corner of his eye he saw Wanda coming slowly across the room toward him, limping with a cane. In the doorway, another aide stood watching her, then when she reached Greg, the aide turned and left.

"Your guard was watching you cross the room," he said to Wanda.

She turned and glanced at the door. "I made her leave me there," she said. "I'm not helpless!"

"You're pretty feisty for an old lady," he joked.

She smiled. "Always have been," she said, "even before I got old."

He watched her laboriously settle into a chair. "You got family close by?" he asked.

"My son lives up in Middletown," she said. "He doesn't come by very much."

"We're kinda put out to pasture, aren't we?"

She looked at him and smiled. "You feel that way, too?"

"I haven't been this bored since I was ten years old."

"Sometimes, " she said, laughing, "I envy the religious people here."

"How's that?"

"They can pray, at least, and feel there's some kind of future for them," she gestured toward the ceiling, "up there."

"You don't believe in heaven?"

"Hell, no!"

He laughed. "Feisty to the end."

"Do you?" She raised one eyebrow.

He shook his head. "There might be some higher power," he said, "but I'll never know. This old body is just going to quit one of these days, and they'll dump my ashes in the rose garden out front."

"Would be nice, though," she said, her face sobering, "to wake up in the morning and not think, 'Oh shit, another day to get through!'"

He laughed again, then forced his expression to sober. "I'm sorry—you are serious, but the way you said it was really funny."

'Look around," she said, "what's so interesting about this goddamn place? A few of the staff, and a very few of the inmates, are nice enough. I'm not mistreated, the way I've read they are in some of these places. It's just dull as hell here!"

"A fellow curmudgeon."

"Reminds me of George Bernard Shaw," she said. "His Don Juan in Hell spoke to me even when I was young."

Greg was intrigued with this woman. "For instance," he said.

"When the devil protested that Don Juan was being uncivil to the devil's friends, he said, 'Your friends are the dullest dogs I know. They are not beautiful, they are only decorated. They are not clean, they are only shaved and starched. They are not dignified, they are only fashionably dressed. They are not moral, they are only conventional.' He went on and on, but I can't remember any more."

He grinned. "That was a lot more than I could remember," he said. "So you think people are hypocrites and phonies?"

"Not so simple as that. Look up that play. Shaw was a lot deeper than that. When I first read it in college, I thought it was a riot. We read the play aloud in English Lit, and we were rolling in the aisles."

"You think they have a copy of it here?"

She shook her head. "I doubt it. But you can get it online. It's free—as it should be."

"Online—you mean with a computer?"

Wanda laughed loudly. "You don't use the computers here?"

He looked down at his magazine. "I never got into them," he said. "I wouldn't know where to begin."

She shook her head, still laughing. "And you're complaining about being bored!" She stood up slowly, with some effort. "Come on—I'll show you!" Motioning for him to follow her, she began limping toward the door.

He looked at her, incredulous. Then, realizing that she wasn't waiting for him, he unlocked his brakes and rolled after her. It didn't take much to catch up with her. "Should you be walking that much?" he asked.

She stopped and turned to face him. "I'll be in one of those things soon enough," she said, and continued across the room.

The computers were in a small room next to the lounge. No one else was there.

"Let's take this one, so you can get your chair close," she said, sitting down at one of the machines and moving the mouse back and forth. The screen lit up. Greg pulled his wheelchair as close to the desk as he could get, and watched closely.

"I'll keep this simple," she said. "All we want to do is get the text of Shaw's play, and print a copy. It's pretty short." She looked at him. "I'll show you how to do this, but right now, just watch."

"I'm at your mercy," he said.

"Baloney," she said. "You're smart enough to do this. I'm amazed you haven't learned this before. Now, I'm opening the browser. That's the program that gets you online."

"On the Internet," he guessed.

She laughed. "See, you know! Now, we want to search the Net for Shaw." She demonstrated. "Hit Return, and watch what happens!"

A listing of sorts filled the screen, each item containing the words "George Bernard Shaw," just as she had typed it.

Wanda did something then to make the list move upward on the screen, revealing other listings. Then she stopped it and pressed a button on the mouse. Instantly the material on the screen was replaced by text, at the top of which was the title, "Don Juan in Hell, a play by George Bernard Shaw."

"Now," she explained, "we click up here on this little icon of a printer."

He watched, trying to understand what she was doing, but feeling completely befuddled.

In a moment, another machine in the corner began making noises, and Wanda stood and hobbled over to it. "I hope it's not too many pages," she laughed. When the printer became quiet, she pulled out a handful of paper and turned to hand it to him. Then she lost her balance and fell among the chairs.

Greg rolled over to her, pulling chairs out of the way, and tried to help her up, but together they couldn't get her to her feet. "Stay there," he said, "I'll get help." He went to the door of the room and called, "Somebody? Somebody help us? She's fallen!"

In a moment, several nurses and aides rushed in, and helped Wanda into a chair. The nurse examined her carefully. "Are you hurt?" she asked, probing about on her arms and legs.

"No, just embarrassed," was the reply.

"You have to be careful of that hip—you don't have your strength back yet!"

An aide gathered up the papers scattered on the floor. "Are these yours?"

"She just printed them," Greg said, holding out his hand to take them. "Thank you."

Another aide appeared at the door with a wheelchair. She and the nurse helped Wanda into it. "You ought to go back to your room and rest," the nurse said. "You're going to be sore for a couple of days."

As they rolled out, Wanda turned to Greg. "Greg, you take that play and read it. We can talk about it tomorrow." He could see that she was shaken by the accident.

Subdued himself, he went back into the lounge, settled himself and began to read.

Five

The next day he asked the aide about Wanda.

"She's okay," the girl said, "but she's supposed to stay in bed for a while."

"How is she taking it?"

She grinned at him. "Fighting every step of the way!"

That made him feel better. "I haven't seen the aide Cyndi in a couple of days. Do you know anything about her?"

"No. She called in a couple of days ago, but I don't know anything more."

"I'd have to ask the nurse, I guess."

"Yeah."

In a little while, he called and had someone help him into his wheelchair, and then he went to the office. "What happened to Cyndi?" he asked the secretary.

She put on a sad face. "I don't think she's coming back— but wait, let me check." She went into the super's office, and when she came out the super came with her.

"Cyndi's gone," the super said. "She's got a boyfriend in college, and she decided to go there." She smiled. "Young love takes 'em all away from us."

"She didn't say goodbye to me," Greg said, dejected. "Wonder why she didn't say goodbye."

He returned to his room, and sat in his wheelchair reading the Shaw play. He had heard of it, back in college, but never read it before. In the part where Don Juan tells the devil that he doesn't like his friends, Greg had to smile, thinking about Wanda's comments. When he finished the short play, he went out again, down to Wanda's room.

Tapping on her closed door got no response, so he wheeled on to the lounge. He felt bereft. A magazine in the lounge didn't distract him, and he returned to his room.

The aides had instructed him to not try to get into or out of bed by himself, but he managed anyway, and lay there thinking about his feelings.

Before Cyndi had come, he'd been bored and grumpy most of the time. Now he felt a terrible loss, and it seemed intolerable. In the past, he had gone through this feeling a number of times, but eventually it went away. Now, bad as it felt to him, he didn't want it to stop. Somehow, feeling sad was at least *feeling something*. There was something precious about it, that allowed him to feel connected to the world. Last week he'd been dead—dead to feelings, except that residual annoyance at everything.

All the comparisons listed by Don Juan in his diatribe to the devil came back to him—"not kind, only sentimental, not moral, only conventional"—things he had been feeling for years. But his feelings had simply made him a recluse, distanced from everyone: *"Trusting no one, no one trusting me,"* as Paul Simon had put it in his song, "I Am a Rock." Shaw's Don Juan, however, had chosen to respond to something bigger, the "Life Force," he had called it. Greg wondered if he could come to that. No, he decided, it was too late for him. He was stuck in this hell of loneliness—vastly worse than boredom.

He fell asleep trying not to cry.

The next day an aide brought him an envelope. It was a letter from Cyndi, apologizing for not coming in to "at least say goodbye." But she was weak, she said. She didn't have the courage to face him.

She had decided to join her boyfriend in the East because she had become lonely for him. "You did that to me," she wrote. "You got me in touch with how wonderful it is to feel things about people. I'd been denying my feeling of loss when he went away to school. But I knew that I would leave you with that same loss, even as little as we knew each other. And I couldn't face you. I'm sorry."

Greg lay back on his pillow and let go. All the feelings he had been holding inside came welling up, and he sobbed into his pillow for a long time.

When an aide came to ask him whether he wanted his lunch in his room or go to the cafeteria, he thought for a while. He didn't feel like facing other people in his present state, but the idea of staying alone seemed worse. "I'll go to the cafeteria," he finally said.

The End

Pilose

He'd been driving all day, and the idea of checking into a crummy motel didn't appeal to him. There was a Hilton down the street that he'd passed, so he turned around and went there. On a Tuesday night, they had plenty of vacancies. He was halfway in a two-day trip to Denver, so he dropped his gear in his room and went down to the bar for a drink before thinking about dinner. His neck hurt from driving.

"Saphire Martini, no olives," he told the bartender, and looked around the dark room. A couple in the far corner, making out. A white-haired woman at the other end of the bar, facing away from him talking to a waiter. Long white hair. He watched her to see if she turned around. Don't see many older women with hair that long. Luxurious, actually.

Halfway through the drink he noticed something else. She had a figure. "Maybe," he thought, "she's bleached her hair." Some women do that—some women will do anything to be a little different. From her body, he judged her age at thirty or forty. Slim. Nice curves. Interesting.

The bartender wanted to talk about sports. He listened, but he wasn't interested. He ordered a sandwich and another martini.

"See that babe?" The bartender was leaning close to him. "Something strange about her."

She finally turned halfway around to order another drink, and he could see what the bartender meant. Her face was different. There was a kind of animal quality to it. The nose, especially, was not like most people's noses. By this time, he was feeling the gin and couldn't focus too well. He went back to his sandwich.

But she drew him, somehow. She was attractive, and wore the usual eye-centered makeup. Hard to see her lips. She glanced at him, then looked down at her drink. She wasn't on the make. Those eyes, though, were something else.

He put down his half-eaten sandwich and picked up his drink. Making his way—he wasn't too steady by this time—to the stool next to her, he said quietly, "Do you mind?"

She glanced at him, smiled (a strange kind of smile). "No."

"You from around here?"

"No, just passing through."

"I'm on my way to Denver," he said. "Family out there."

She smiled at him again, and the hair on the back of his neck stood up. He'd never seen anyone like her. Strange, she had a nice body, carried herself well, well-dressed. Only the face was odd.

"I'm on my way to the Coast," she said, her voice high, like a little kid's.

"Buy you another one?" he said, indicating her glass.

"If you like."

They talked for a while, about nothing, as most people do in a bar, and decided to go into the dining room for dinner. Across the table, even in the dim light, he studied her face. It was odd—there was a feline quality to it. But somehow he was attracted to her. She didn't have much to say, asking him about his trip and the family he was visiting. She seemed vaguely embarrassed, frequently blushing when she laughed, but she didn't offer much information about herself.

Both of them had had a lot to drink. They half-finished their dinners (she had ordered some kind of fish), and chose coffee instead of dessert.

As he followed her out of the restaurant, he was aware of her body. Very nicely proportioned. In the lobby, he propositioned her.

She blushed, hung her head, and said, "I've had way too much to drink. I think I should go up to my room and sleep it off."

"Okay," he said, smiling. "I've had a lot myself. I'd probably not be very good company."

"Thanks for dinner. I hope you have a good trip," she said, touching his hand.

"You, too." As she turned away, he said, "Wait." He dug his card out of a pocket and wrote his room number on the back. "If you feel better later."

She blushed again and took the card without responding. Catching his eye briefly, she smiled and went down the hall.

Vaguely disappointed, he went to his room, showered and sprawled across his bed. That face haunted him. So unusual. Something vaguely wild about it. Very quickly, he was asleep. At some point, he was aware of being cold and pulling the bedspread over him.

The tap on his door woke him confused. A light tap, repeated.

Stumbling from the bed, he tried to orient himself. *Oh yes, Iowa City. Who's at the door?* He didn't even think to look through the peephole. Stark naked, he opened the door.

She laughed out loud, a high-pitched laugh that had music in it.

"Sorry!" he said, half-hiding behind the door.

"You were sleeping," she said. "I'm sorry."

He mumbled something, and opened the door farther. She was wearing the same dress, and his eyes were drawn to her cleavage.

"I sobered up," she said. "I'm sorry. You were asleep."

"No problem," he said, grabbing the spread from the bed and wrapping it around him. "I was hoping ..."

She had been holding a bottle of gin behind her, and held it up. "You have some ice?"

He opened the mini-fridge. "And some tonic water."

She was enjoying his embarrassment. "You weren't expecting me to take you up on your offer, were you?" Her large blue eyes slowly closed and opened, the way a cat's do when they're comfortable with you.

He grinned. "I'm glad you did."

"There's probably a robe on the back of the bathroom door," she said, laughing, "if you want it."

He found the robe, and mixed them drinks. They sat opposite each other at the little table, and he moved his computer off to the side.

After a few minutes of small talk, he began to relax. "Tell me what you're going to the Coast for," he said. "California?"

She smiled. "I'm drawn there," she said. "I think I might fit in there better than where I live now."

"How is that? You want to get into movies?"

She blushed. "I'm different," she said simply.

"Yes," he agreed. "Is your hair naturally white? You're sure not that old!"

"Oh, the hair—I could dye that."

He was just high enough to be bold enough to say it. "You have very strange features."

"Yes. Weird."

"No, not weird. Really different, though." He liked her eyes—light blue—and he liked the way she had outlined them. Her lips, though, seemed almost non-existent. And there was a glow on her cheeks, like the peach fuzz he'd seen on new babies. Touchable.

Things progressed as things do under such circumstances, and they found themselves in bed together. When he looked into her eyes, her irises had disappeared, leaving huge, black pupils. The one disconcerting thing he found about her was that she didn't want to kiss him. Actually, although he had the inclination, he wasn't quite sure how to go about it. Her mouth was the most different feature in her face. Since he had shaved in the shower, he caressed her cheek with his—and noticed that the peach fuzz was real. Soft, fine hair covered her face.

And, it turned out, everything else. Not much on her breasts, which he enjoyed immensely, but when his hands found her thighs, he was startled by ... thick fur.

He threw the covers back and looked at her. Her whole body was covered in a fine white fur. When he found her eyes, she looked disconcerted. "I'm sorry!" she said.

He didn't say anything, but stroked those legs with his hands. "I love it," he said finally. And he did. It was as soft as down, and felt to his hands like the softest baby toy.

Afterward, he spent hours feeling her fur with his face and lips. Never had a woman affected him so much. She kept apologizing, and he kept stopping her. "It's wonderful!" he said.

"I always shave," she said, "before I do this. But ..." she smiled shyly, "I had a lot to drink, and I didn't."

"You should never shave it off!" he exclaimed. "It's delightful."

"People get freaked out. That's what they call me—a freak." She began to cry.

"You shave your whole body?"

"Yes."

"And your face?"

"Yes. If I didn't, it would be two inches long, all over."

"Holy shit!"

"I even wore a hijab for a while, and a veil over my face. People thought I was Muslim."

"I think it's lovely," he said honestly. "But it must be difficult around people. Is it some kind of congenital thing? Your DNA?"

"I guess it is," she said. "My mother made me shave all over, from as far back as I can remember. She wouldn't let me go out if I hadn't shaved."

He smiled at her in the dim light, his hands caressing her body. "You're beautiful," he said.

"Weird."

"Not weird!"

"I could show you photographs," she said, "with my full coat."

"I'd love to see them."

She put her arms around his neck and pulled him to her. He felt her tears run down between their cheeks.

The next morning, they had breakfast together in the coffee shop. She had shaved her face and arms, so that no trace of her fur showed. She pulled a photograph from her purse. "This is what it looks like—full coat," she said. In the photo, she stood nude—except that she wasn't. White fur covered her body. On her breasts it was thinner, revealing soft curves. Even her feet were fur-covered.

He studied the picture. "How long does it take to grow that long?"

"About three months."

He smiled at her. "Not weird. Not a freak. You're just one of a kind."

"You're probably the only human being who thinks that."

They ate their eggs mostly in silence.

Finally, he said, "I don't even know your name."

"Celia."

"I'm Frank."

She smiled. "I know. You gave me your card last night, remember?"

"And you're going to California because ...?"

"I have some friends out there. They said people are more tolerant there."

He shook his head. "I wouldn't count on it."

"Somebody back home tried to talk me into going into a circus."

"Oh, no! Then you *would* be a freak."

"But I have to hide," she said, "all the time!"

He took her hand. "You shouldn't have to hide."

She turned her hand over. A fine glow of hair covered the back of her hand. "This is just since last night," she said.

"Nobody could see it, if you didn't point it out."

"I'm lucky it's a light color," she said, and touched her cheek.

"It must be hard for you."

She nodded.

He squeezed her hand gently. "Can we stay in touch?"

She looked at him with those cat eyes. "Let me think about it."

"Okay."

"You're sweet," she said. "Thank you."

As they prepared to leave the coffee shop, he asked, "Are you on a schedule? Could you stay over here until tomorrow?"

She looked down "I don't think so."

"I'd love to have more time with you," he said.

"I'm on a tight budget," she said.

"We can share a room," he said. "Let me tell the desk I'm staying on."

"I'd like that," she said.

"So would I."

"I'll get my things."

He headed for the desk while she went toward the elevator.

Pulling his phone from his pocket, he called his sister in Denver. "I'm delayed by one day," he told her. "And I may have someone with me when I get there."

"Why am I not surprised?" she answered. "Wearing cowboy boots?"

"You'll never guess."

"Long hair?" she asked. "You always have liked long hair."

The desk clerk smiled at him when he asked to hold his room over.

The End

Élan

One

A waft of perfume made him open his eyes. The woman lay beside him, her head propped by her elbow, watching him. She smiled. "Good morning."

He managed a weak smile. The very top of his head hurt slightly. "I drank too much, didn't I?"

"Just enough, I'd say." She continued to watch him silently, the knowing smile that rested on her face a living thing, seeming to metamorphose slowly, almost imperceptibly, from one meaning to another. The bedcover was down to her waist. When she saw his eyes drift to her breasts, she said softly, "Ah, he lives!"

The faculty party had been boring, and he had been ready to leave, to go home to his book, his fantasy world populated with interesting people. He had approached the host to say good night, standing a few feet away as she talked with a couple of people, waiting to be acknowledged, when the woman had spoken to him from just out of his line of vision. He couldn't even remember, this morning, what she had said. But he had turned his face into the glow of that smile.

At least an hour later, they had left the party together.

"Now that we've become acquainted," she now said, letting her head sink down onto the pillow, "tell me about yourself. What is this book you're writing?"

He grinned. "I can't remember."

She leaned over to kiss him gently on the cheek, and lay back on her pillow again. Without makeup, she looked the part of an eighteenth century model in a museum painting, her skin seeming to glow from inside.

"My mind," he said, "gave up control to my endocrine system some hours ago. It seems yours has recovered."

"It never left. It was totally aware all the time."

"I think you're more evolved than I am," he said, turning on his side to face her and propping his head with his elbow, mirroring her previous pose.

"You said last night that you were writing a novel. Tell me about it."

He fumbled for words. "It's about some people," he said finally, "but it's really about how hard it is to communicate."

"As someone else said, we live in our separate little worlds, wrapped in skin, fearfully peeking out at each other."

He smiled and shook his head slightly. "You should be writing the book instead of me."

"No." She pulled away a lock of hair that had drifted over her cheek. "No. I want to read *your* book."

He reached over and returned the lock to its rightful place. "I have no idea when it will be finished." Then he added, "Maybe never."

"Just like us, isn't it? Just like everybody."

"You don't consider yourself at least a little bit finished?"

"Oh, God no!" she laughed.

"Isn't that what adulthood means? We've graduated from childhood, and now we're ready to start living?"

"Excuse me." She threw the covers off and got out of bed. He watched her body glide across the room to the bathroom. "Adulthood is overrated," she called back just before closing the door.

He lay back and thought about his graduation to adulthood. It was a long time ago. Maybe the first time somebody called him "mister." Now, nobody does that anymore. Maybe it was when they stopped carding him in bars. It certainly wasn't the first time he had sex.

He listened to the shower running, and thought about how good her soapy skin would feel to his hands.

That part of so-called adulthood came several years before he could drink legally. "Judgment," he thought aloud. "It's when the hippocampus develops common sense about sex and drinking and driving."

"Wait! I can't hear you!" she called through the door. The shower had stopped. She opened the door and came out, drying her hair with a towel. "You want to shower? There are towels on the shelf. Take any of them."

As they passed on his way to the bathroom, she playfully dodged his hand.

While he showered, he thought how easy she was to be with, even though they had met only a few hours ago. He'd gone from being bored in a room full of high-functioning people to being as enchanted as a teenager.

If he'd written that in his novel, of course, everybody would protest. "Cliché!"

"Cliché only means it's overused," he said, suddenly aware how much he talked to himself lately. "Doesn't mean it isn't true." He dried himself and went into the bedroom to retrieve his clothes. She wasn't there. Vaguely disappointed, he dressed and made his way to the kitchen, where she was busy at the range. "I hope you like eggs," she said without turning around. "I don't usually cook breakfast. You're *visiting royalty*."

"Eggs are great. Royalty?"

She turned to look at him. "I don't *usually* bring people home like that." She was wearing white slacks and a pale green tank top. Bare feet. Earrings.

He smiled, but said nothing.

"I have no place to go until lunchtime," she said. "We can continue our conversation." She gestured with her spatula. "Help yourself to coffee."

The toaster popped its contents, and he retrieved the brown slices just as she handed him a dish for them. Then she spooned out the scrambled eggs and added a couple of small sausage links to each plate.

"Coffee for you?" he asked as he poured his cup.

"Please."

They sat opposite each other at the small table. "You were saying," she began, taking a bite of food, "something about adulthood."

"It's like there's two classes of humans—children and adults. It's reasonable to restrict the behavior of children until their brains have developed the ability to make good judgments."

"Sure," she said. "But you were talking before about adults being 'finished.'"

"I was? Well, I guess we never stop growing in some way. But as a class, adults are all considered alike."

"Finished?" She propped her chin on her hand, elbow on the table. Her other hand held her fork, poised to stab at eggs.

"Since you grew up and left home, haven't your parents always thought of you the way you were then—I'm assuming a lot here, I know—and then were surprised when you changed? When you actually grew up?"

She laughed. "My father thought I was sixteen until last year."

He ate the last of his eggs, leaving the sausage, and moved the plate aside.

Glancing at the plate, she asked, "You don't like sausage?"

"Sorry. I don't eat meat."

"Oh."

"I know," he continued, "my head tells me, at least, that maturation is a never-ending process."

"Okay." It was a tentative agreement, waiting for the "but."

"But I'm the same guy who began writing erotic garbage at sixteen and hiding it from my parents."

She grinned. "I'd love to read some of it."

He frowned. "Why, for God's sake?"

"Because I like sixteen-year-old boys! I like their enthusiasm, even if they can't spell."

His eyebrows went up. "Is that your father's sixteen-year-old daughter talking?"

She ignored the question. "You said your head knows that maturation never ends, *but* ..."

"I feel like the same person I was when I wrote that stuff. I've learned how to express things better, but the implicit memory is still the same."

"Wait," she said, "implicit memory."

"The stuff that lives in our guts all our lives. The emotional hang-ups, the automatic responses that our mature minds never learn how to control. What Michael Polanyi called tacit knowledge, that which we know but cannot say."

"The lurking beast in all of us."

"Yeah."

She pulled her hair back over her ears. "I'm picking up something," she said, "that I'd like to check out."

"Shoot."

"Does all this have anything to do with last night?" She looked straight at him.

He rubbed his temples with his thumbs. "I couldn't ask for anything better than that. I just remember being rather— impulsive."

"That horny sixteen-year-old?" She was grinning again.

"No finesse," he answered.

"Sure hooked into *my* sixteen-year-old."

"I don't want you to think that's all I am."

"Nor am I," she said. "Your book isn't finished yet, and maybe you're not finished yet either?" Her last word rose, making it into a question.

He got up and picked up both coffee cups. "I hope *we* are not finished yet."

One eyebrow went up. After he had poured the coffee and returned to the table she said, "Is that what I'm picking up? You're afraid last night was a fluke?"

"I'm afraid I'm out of my depth. My class."

She got up from her chair and circled around the table, extending a hand toward him. "Stand up."

When he stood, she moved close to him. "See how much bigger you are than I am?"

He put his arms around her waist. "I feel like ... like Tom Hanks."

"In 'Big.' You mean you're pretending? You're sixteen, pretending to be forty-something?"

"You know that old Simon and Garfunkel song, 'Fakin' It?'"

She sang, *"Girl does what she wants to do, and I know I'm fakin' it."*

"'Not really makin' it.' Yeah, that one."

"You spend a lot of time in your own head, don't you?" She ran her fingertips through his hair just over his left ear.

"Yeah, I guess I do."

"All the more reason I want to read your book, so I can find out who you really are."

"The sixteen-year-old is dying to show it to you. The mature adult is not so sure."

"Why not?"

He smiled. "As I said, I'm afraid I'm out of my depth."

She shook her head, and her hair tumbled off her ears. "Am I that intimidating?"

"I'm that insecure when it comes to my writing."

Easing out of his grasp, "Okay." she said, "I can wait."

"You're very direct."

"She laughed. "I've been called worse."

He noticed her glance at the clock on the wall, and took his phone out of his pocket. "Can we exchange phone numbers while we have time? You know, I don't even know your last name."

She laughed. "Let's do. I'll get mine."

She disappeared into another room and reappeared a moment later with her phone. Handing it to him, she said, "I'm very happy we ran into each other."

"Me, too."

They entered their own names and numbers into each other's device. "It's Taylor," she said, "Heather Taylor."

"And I'm Rich Williams. At home I'm Rich, but at work I'm Richard."

"Where is home? No, where *was* home?"

"Tiffin, Ohio. I left there a long time ago, but my mom is still there."

Heather handed him his phone. "We both have a lot to learn about each other."

"I'm looking forward to it." He turned toward the door. "Thank you for breakfast."

"I enjoyed it. All of it," she said, standing on tiptoes to kiss him quickly on the lips.

Two

Hunched over in front of his computer, supporting his chin with one fist, Rich stared at the screen and remembered Heather. She had told him at the party that she had just arrived on campus, one of the new president's staff. It was his lucky night, he knew. She was way out of his league socially and professionally. And she had nailed his doubt—fluke, it was. She could have enchanted any number of other males in that room.

Two days later, she was now haunting his book. All those struggling characters he had come to feel were his friends and kept hidden in his computer—suddenly they all seemed shallow and uninteresting.

It was spring break, and he had taken advantage of the students being gone to work harder on his novel. Several chapters into the story, he had begun to deal with the theme—how relationships change people, virtually rewiring their brains. One of his characters was named Heather, and he did a global search-and-replace to change it. "She just doesn't fit 'Heather,'" he said to himself of the character. "She isn't special enough." Smiling at his decision, he muttered, "Ever the sixteen-year-old." The character's name was now Patty. He wondered if the decision would change his story. How much of a character's personality is bound up with their name? "How much of *my* personality is tied to *my* name?"

He couldn't remember giving the story's character the name 'Heather,' and he thought about what that name had meant to him. Whatever it had meant, of course, it now meant something entirely different. Exciting. Sensual. Gorgeous. Ethereal—no, that wasn't her; she wasn't delicate. Only out of reach. "I am wasting my energy!" he exclaimed, then slumped in his chair. "Shit!"

The book was suddenly a sodden blob in his computer. He logged off, closed the computer and left his office. His footsteps echoed in the empty hallway as he headed for fresh air.

His phone vibrated in his pocket. Taking it out, he saw the caller's name, HEATHER.

"Hello?"

"Testing," she said, her voice a musical instrument. "Can you hear me now?"

He laughed. "I was just thinking about you."

"Wonderful! Got time for lunch?"

"I'd cancel an appointment with God—if I had one."

"If you had an appointment, or if you had a God?"

"Whatever," he replied, wondering if she had meant something more by the question.

"How about Barney's? Does a vegetarian eat pizza?"

"They have a great gourmet vegetarian there," he said.

"And with the kids gone to Daytona, we can actually hear each other in that place."

He was already outside in the sunshine. He turned down one of those long, diagonal sidewalks through campus that were paved after several years of students' feet had worn the path to show the grounds people where to pour the concrete. "Like habit," he thought. "Neurons that fire often, fire stronger, so that their paths become beaten like the grass across this lawn. What was once a new experience becomes familiar and comfortable. The problem is that comfort begets, eventually, yawn."

The air was clear, the sun was warm, and his heart was beating in time with his footsteps. "Maybe," he thought, "maybe this time."

"It's marvelous," he said to himself a moment later, "this body, this walking bag full of garbage, that can *feel* delight and anticipation flooding up from its depths, soaking mere words into shapeless irrelevancies." He liked those last two words; he'd file them away for the book.

When his eyes accommodated to the darkness in Barney's, he saw her sitting in a booth toward the back. He was surprised to see that she was dressed in a business suit. Sliding into the booth opposite her, he said, breathlessly, "Hi."

"You're out of breath," she said. A frosted mug of beer, half full, sat in front of her. "I didn't order one for you because I didn't want it to get warm."

"Thank you. You're all dressed up."

"You academic types can let yourself go. I have to meet important people sometimes." She laughed and touched his hand. "I'm kidding."

"Administration doesn't take spring break?"

"Unfortunately, no."

A young man in an apron came out of the kitchen toward them. Heather lifted her mug to signal him, and showed two fingers. He nodded, and returned a minute later with two mugs of beer. "Ready to order?"

"My friend says you have a fabulous gourmet vegetarian pizza. Medium?" She was used to handling things. Turning to Rich, she raised her eyebrows. "Okay?"

He smiled and nodded. The waiter left.

She paused and cocked her head slightly. "Was that okay, really?"

"Of course. You are very—what?—*proactive*? Is that the word?"

Heather covered her face with her hands for a moment, then said, "Oh. Too much? I'm sorry!"

"Male ego," he said, then laughed. "No, it's okay."

"Really okay?"

"Really okay. I'm a little off balance, is all."

She looked at him steadily. "I guess that should please me, but it doesn't."

He lifted his mug. "To new experiences. New paths to trod."

She touched his mug with hers and they both quaffed the cold beer. "Truth is," she said, "I'm a little giddy myself. I've been thinking about you for two days."

"Likewise," he grinned.

"And when I get nervous, I get obnoxious and bold to cover it up." She laughed. "You've probably noticed."

"And I pretend to be grown up," he admitted.

She looked at him for a minute with that knowing smile, that kept changing subtly. "I'm dressed like this because we had a staff meeting this morning. I'm not usually so formal."

"Your power suit."

"You got it."

"You haven't told me much about yourself," he said. "Harvard Business School?"

"No, as a matter of fact. That probably would have gotten me further. I was in the psych department at the University of

Minnesota when I got tapped for this job. Somebody told somebody that I'd be a good fit."

"Teacher?"

She shook her head. "I was in research. Did my dissertation on interdisciplinary research practices."

"Sounds impressive."

"Boring, actually. I was in love with my advisor, and he thought it would be good for his career."

Their pizza arrived at the table.

"Smells wonderful!" she said. "Look! Broccoli and cauliflower and onions and mushrooms ..."

"Even carrots."

They ate eagerly and ordered another round of beer.

"Besides writing a novel," she said, finishing her nearly-empty one, "do you teach?"

"Mmm, yes. Philosophy."

She wiped her mouth on her napkin. "A philosopher. I should have guessed. You had mentioned Michael Polanyi."

"He and Thomas Kuhn wrote on the philosophy of science."

"I've read Thomas Kuhn," she said and laughed. "All I remember is 'paradigm shift.'"

"Yes. He stirred up some controversy with that because some people said he had plagiarized from Polanyi. They eventually settled their differences."

"Oh, and I remember something about science not being as objective as we like to assume."

"Yes. 'The Tacit Dimension.' That's the knowledge we have but cannot tell."

"I wonder why we didn't study such ideas in my undergraduate years. It sounds like it should be as much psychology as philosophy."

Rich took another slice of pizza. "Sometimes the distinction is very fuzzy."

Heather looked at him with an amused smile. "Your novel about communication—is it psychology or philosophy?"

"Sometimes the distinction ..."

". . . is very fuzzy," she finished, nodding.

They laughed.

Rich was feeling the alcohol. "How many of these have we had?"

"To hell with work!" she said, grinning at him.

He leaned his elbows on the table. "You know," he began, "I am just smashed enough to tell you that you're messing with my novel."

"Oh?" she laughed.

"I even had to change the name of one of my characters, because of you!"

"You had a 'Heather' in your book?"

"Yes, and she was a cardboard cutout. I could not name her Heather!"

Heather blushed. "I'm flattered!"

His words came slowly and laboriously. "I grew up in a Baptist family," he said, "and drink was from the devil. My grandmother told me one time, 'Alcohol makes you do things you wouldn't ordinarily do.' She thought that was an awful thing."

"But you had a different idea about it." Her eyes were dark pools.

"I understand her position," he said. "Her father used to come home drunk and beat her mother."

"That *was* an awful thing." She leaned toward him, her arms crossed on the table, outlining her breasts through her jacket. "Have you been married?"

"Yes. I'm not now."

"Me, too."

"Good to have that question out of the way."

"Very good."

"Want another beer?"

"No. Yes. Then I will have reached—*passed* my limit."

"I think neither of us should drive for a while."

"No."

"No." He laughed. "We're reduced to monosyllables."

"I'm okay," she said, "with just sitting here and talking all afternoon."

"To get better acquainted."

"Are you still intimidated by my pro-act-ivity?" She stumbled over the word.

"Not a bit. You're just as funny when you're smashed as I am."

"We're back to being sixteen again." She giggled.

"If we were sixteen, we couldn't buy beer."

"We did manage in Saint Paul."

They sat there talking and laughing. The waiter had taken their dishes away, and Rich could see him glancing occasionally at them. There were no other customers in the place.

"Good thing the students have all gone south," he said.

"To get drunk and get laid."

"An admirable pursuit, if one is careful."

"You know," she said, smiling at him, "you have a way with words."

A couple of hours passed. They had ordered coffee and made several trips to the restrooms. Finally, she said, "I think I can get home now. I need to get out of this monkey suit."

He grinned. "The power does seem to have gone out of it," he said.

"Thank you. I need to catch a quick nap and put myself back together for a dinner tonight with some people."

"You have a busy social life."

"*This* was the high point of my day."

"Mine, too," he said.

"Are you okay for driving?"

"By the time I walk to the other side of campus to my car, I will be."

"Please be careful."

"I will walk the straight and narrow." He stood up.

"Maybe not that careful," she laughed, standing beside him.

They left Barney's together, just a little shy of sober. Heather turned one way, he another, and as he walked he watched his shadow precede him, looking younger than it had seemed in a long time.

Three

Rich wanted to connect with Heather again that evening, but he remembered that she had plans for dinner. Better not to seem too eager anyway, he thought. Wait a couple of days.

He sat at his computer, browsing through what he had written already. Why does it seem that communicating with other people—really communicating—is so hard? Heather makes it feel so easy!

Perhaps it's hormonal. Sexual arousal takes away the inhibitions. So does alcohol. When you lose that uncertainty, that self-consciousness, words come effortlessly. They don't seem so *important* because the atmosphere is redolent of something *more* important. Daniel Siegel writes of 'resonance' when two people are attuned to each other, when all the non-verbal cues just swim from one to the other, mirroring each other in that security of connecting in a warm bath of mutual comfort.

"We live in our separate little worlds," Heather had said, "wrapped in skin, fearfully peeking out at each other." Yet she was the antithesis of her words. She didn't seem to work at it. The other evening at the party, at least, he'd had enough to drink that all his walls were down when she spoke to him. He was defenseless to her smile. And she chose him.

But what could he do without the balm of sex or alcohol? She was so sure of herself, so competent in her social skills—how could he hope to keep her interested in him? His brain contained tons of facts. He knew that he had to relax into her, pay attention to her instead of to his own awkwardness. Awe does not belong in dialog, not in the give and take of conversation. Awe is reserved for dealing with gods. It interferes with the process, because the process has to be mutual, a sharing of intimacies.

Twenty years ago, he'd had that kind of sharing. At first, Becky had looked up to him because she thought he had some answers for her. He'd responded to her beauty and her intuitive nature, and he had welcomed the kind of role she saw for him. After they had finished school and the parenting stage, however, she seemed to need something he couldn't supply. He began to divide his energy between the competing routines of work and home life, until gradually the divide moved more and more to one side. His master's degree seemed inadequate, so he embarked on his doctorate, leaving him less and less time at home, more and more separated from his family. Finally, she had taken their son Keith and moved away, closer to the security and comfort of her mother.

He'd buried himself in his work, and for years it was enough—or it seemed enough. Writing was easy for him, and he contributed many papers to the journals, leaning on his grad students for the research.

Then, one day he'd written a story, a short story about people. It wasn't very good, but it gave him a feeling of release. He'd written more, until he discovered that the characters were somehow becoming real to him. He remembered his sister, when they were children, creating little worlds for her dolls, imagining their lives. He guessed that writing stories was like that, and he indulged the pull.

It was obvious to him, now, that his imaginary world of story telling didn't enhance his effort to actually *be* with others.

Especially with Heather. But she had insisted that she wanted to read his novel. He agonized over the quandary.

Four

He waited until Friday morning to call her.

"Rich! Good to hear your voice!"

"I've been wondering if you have an open evening this weekend."

"For you? Of course!"

"I'd love to fix dinner for you. What evening would be best?" He cringed inside at the stiffness he felt in the words.

"You name it," she said.

"Okay, then, can you be at my place about six this evening?"

"If I know where your place is," she said slowly. He felt her laughing at his awkwardness.

Plunging on, he gave her directions to his apartment. "It won't be fancy."

"I grew up on red beans and rice," she replied, chuckling.

"In Minnesota?"

"Lots of Latinos in Minnesota," she said. "Especially in our neighborhood."

"Do you have a Kindle or something like that?"

"I have an iPad. Will that do?"

"I think so. You said you wanted to read my book—or the part that is written."

"You can put it on my iPad? Wonderful!"

"I think so. Bring it along."

Rich stopped at the grocery on his way home. He planned to fix Italian risotto with mushrooms and vegetables, and a salad, but he thought he needed something that a meat eater might enjoy, without his actually having to cook meat. He found what he wanted in the deli section: a recipe for lentil loaf. Roaming the aisles, he bought his supplies and a couple of bottles of wine, and headed home.

Somehow, cooking for a guest gave him confidence. While the food he planned didn't take a lot of skill to prepare, it seemed to him to be out of the ordinary, an alternative to steak, potatoes and asparagus. When he read the recipe for the lentil loaf, he was surprised at the amount of time that it would take—a good two hours. The risotto, ordinarily the most time consuming dish he usually made, took only a half-hour, and that would have to be prepared after she arrived.

Eating a quick lunch of grilled cheese sandwich and lettuce salad, he took a part bottle of wine from the refrigerator and set to work. From the closet he pulled out a linen tablecloth and napkins that Becky had sent him for Christmas several years before. He set the little table with matching china, glassware and stainless tableware—the best he had. A pair of brass candlesticks finished it off. He stood back, smiled and said in his deepest god-like voice, "It is good."

He had almost forgotten, over the years, the good feelings that come from doing for others. Sure, he knew, it was an ego boost. He wanted other people to have positive feelings toward him, and as long as he could manage it without becoming too stressed (the first few times he and Becky had entertained friends after they had set up their home together were not fun until they were over). But it was more than ego, just as it is more than ego or lust that makes one gently stroke a lover. There is a sharing of feelings that both enjoy. Even a smile creates positive effects in both parties. The mirror neurons we all carry in our brains link us together and create single, interpersonal states of mind.

He washed spinach, carefully removing the stems, crumbled feta cheese and added dried cranberries for small salads, sprinkled them with slivered almonds and put them into the refrigerator.

In separate pots, he started brown lentils and bulgur wheat boiling. Sipping wine from the now-nearly empty bottle of Pinot Grigio, he collected his other ingredients. For the lentil loaf and the risotto, he took out cremini mushrooms and cleaned them with a special mushroom brush—another gift that had lain unused in the drawer for years. Garlic cloves peeled by hand. Broccoli, red bell peppers and white onion, all chopped and set aside. Fresh thyme, rosemary and parsley finely chopped for the lentil loaf and gravy.

Some people simply love to cook. Rich seldom prepared anything special for himself, and at this moment he wondered why. There was something about this meal that went beyond chopping vegetables and boiling beans. It was a kind of celebration of a relationship, a work of art in honor of the feelings he'd been experiencing for the past few days.

When the lentils and bulgur were tender, he drained them and set them aside while he sautéed mushrooms and onions in a small amount of apple cider with seasonings. When these were tender, he transferred them to the food processor and pulsed them to a fine chop. Then they were mixed in a bowl with the lentils, bulgur, rolled oats, red pepper and parsley.

He turned on the oven for the lentil loaf, and began sautéing onion, garlic, mushrooms, rosemary and thyme in a little vegetable broth. After they had cooked down, he added red wine and more broth. Meanwhile, he mixed yeast, tamari, and flour into a paste, and whisked it slowly into the skillet it to keep it from clumping. When the gravy was finished, he poured it into a small pot, covered it and set it on a warm burner on the back of the range. Even the odors of the cooking meal lifted his spirits.

Turning the lentil mixture into a loaf pan lined with parchment paper, he put it into the oven and set the timer for one hour. By that time the bottle of wine was gone, and he was satisfied with his work.

When Heather was due to arrive, he felt relaxed about being with her. The ingredients for the risotto were set out, the lentil loaf was in the oven and a half-hour from being done. "Get out the salads," he told himself, "and we'll eat at seven."

When the doorbell rang, he poured two glasses of Pinot Grigio from a fresh bottle and lit the candles. He opened the door, feeling like Santa Claus.

She was breathtaking. "Hi," he said cheerfully, taking her hand. "It's all ready except for the risotto, and you'll have to stand and talk with me while I make that."

"Smells wonderful!" she gushed.

He picked up the wine glasses and handed one to her. "Here's to new experiences," he said.

They clinked their glasses and smiled at each other. "I see you brought your iPad," he said.

"I hope you know how to move things into it," she said. "I've only downloaded from the Apple Web page."

"We'll figure it out." He turned on the stove burner under a heavy pot. "First things first—the food."

When the pot was heated, he threw a small bowl of chopped vegetables into it, and began to stir them. "In Italy," he said, "this is a task for the husband to keep him busy while the wife fixes the rest of the meal. It involves a half hour of constant attention."

She peered into the pot. "You're sautéing mushrooms and vegetables in olive oil?"

"Then," he said, dumping a cup of rice into the pot, "you sauté the rice."

"Really? I thought you had to boil rice."

"Browning it a little first gives it a toasted flavor." After stirring the rice into the oil and vegetables for a minute, he poured liquid from another pot into the mixture. "Vegetable stock, a cup at a time." He continued stirring.

Heather was watching his face. "You're having fun, aren't you?"

He grinned at her. "If I had to do this every day, I'd probably hate it."

"Well, you saw just about the limit of my cooking— scrambled eggs."

He looked into the pot. "When the stock is absorbed, you add more." He demonstrated, then picked up his wine glass.

"You are going to do this for a half hour?"

"No, I'm going to talk to you for a half hour, and while I'm doing that I'll keep my hands busy by stirring the rice."

She laughed, and touched his arm. "If I weren't so hungry, …"

"That's two of us!" He looked down at her blouse. "Nice color on you."

"I wonder," she said slyly, "what it would take to get you to stop stirring the rice."

He grinned. "Do you really want to find out?"

"Not now. But it's fun to think about." She put her wine glass down and moved close to his back, wrapping her arms around his waist.

"Careful," he said, laughing, "it's time for more stock."

She let go of him and picked up his wine glass. Touching it to his lips, she tilted it so he could drink from it. "Thank you," he said.

She laughed. "This is kinda fun at that. I get to feed you and tease you at the same time."

"You also like to watch me, very closely."

"Of course. Your face shows what's going on in your mind more than your words."

"You read me like a book?"

"Much better than a book."

"I've been reading about that recently," he said. "Daniel Siegel says that we learn to read people's faces when we're babies."

"We have mirror neurons, just for that purpose."

"You've read about it too." He smiled at her.

"*Mindsight,* he calls it."

"People who are good at it are usually good at knowing what's going on in their own minds as well."

"Do you know what's going on in your own mind?" she asked.

He shook his head, poured another cup of stock, and continued to stir. "A lot of times I have to sit down and write in order to know what I'm feeling."

"So you keep a journal?" She drank the remaining wine in her glass.

"Off and on. Usually, it's just when I need to figure out what's going on inside my head." Rich dropped a large chunk of butter into the pot and stirred vigorously. "Almost done," he said.

"What can I do?"

"The lentil loaf in the oven should be done. Be careful—it's hot. The hot pads are there, and there's a platter for it. Just turn it over."

While she took the loaf from the oven, he dished up servings of risotto. Then he poured the sauce for the lentil loaf into a gravy boat and set it on the table. "Oh, the salads!"

As he set out the salads and dressing, he said, "Please sit."

Heather filled their wine glasses, handed one to him and raised hers. "Here's to new experiences."

Five

Heather dabbed at the corners of her mouth with her napkin, careful to avoid getting lipstick on the linen. "That was wonderful," she said.

"I didn't plan dessert other than the fruit," Rich said, "but if you'd like coffee, I can make it."

"Coffee sounds great."

"How about espresso? I could sweeten it with cognac."

"Oh? That would be perfect!"

He pushed his chair back from the table. "And then we can do something with your iPad."

She finished the wine in her glass and stood up. "Let me help clear the table."

"Okay. Leave the fruit." He took the espresso machine down from a cabinet. "Do you want decaf or regular?"

"Either would work for me, thank you." She began loading the dishwasher with the dishes from the table. "You must have been cooking all day!"

He grinned. "It was fun, actually. I haven't cooked for somebody else in a long time."

With the table cleared and their coffee cups in hand, they moved to the other end of the living-dining room.

"I found a Kindle application for your iPad," he said, "so you can read Kindle documents. Let me have your iPad, and I'll install it and load the document into it."

While Rich was occupied with transferring the files, Heather browsed his bookshelves. "You have five copies of this little book," she said, pulling out one of them titled *The Class*. "Who is Donald Skiff?" She turned the book over.

"It's one of mine. I wrote it a long time ago and used a pen name because I didn't want my students to know it was me."

" 'Between the past and the future,' " she read, " 'between the idea and the reality, between the finite and the infinite—" Reminds me of T.S. Eliot."

He laughed. "Just a little pretentious, isn't it?"

"Depends on what's inside, I'd say. What's the class about?"

"Epistemology. I published it myself."

"May I borrow a copy?" She leafed through the book.

"Keep it. It's kind of autobiographical."

She looked at him, smiling. "Thank you. I get to learn more about you!"

"Those other books on that shelf are mine, too."

"Truly! Why, I thought this novel you're working on now was your first."

"No, but it's the first in a long time."

"Are they all autobiographical?"

"No," he said, "That one with the plastic binding, 'The Magic' has a lot of me in it. I never published that one. It was a little too personal. That's my only copy. You can borrow it if you like."

"You really want me to know that much about you?" She smiled at him sideways as she withdrew the book.

He turned away from the computer to look at her. He shrugged. "Yes. I've spent the last week or so worrying about not being good enough, not smart enough, not sophisticated enough for you."

She looked surprised.

"But," he continued, "if I'm not, I don't want to pretend. You'd find out one way or another. You might as well find out now."

Heather crossed the room and sat down in a chair near him. "It's that important to you?"

"It's that important to me."

"C'mere," she said, moving her chair closer to him and leaning toward him. "You flatter me. I'm not as good or as smart or as sophisticated as you give me credit for. I know I'm a pushy broad, but I've got insides just like you. I don't know what we can be like together, but I'm truly interested."

She leaned toward him and kissed him on the cheek. "One thing you have going for you—in anyone's book—is that you're a great cook!"

He grinned and took her hand. "I did feel good doing that," he said. "Thank you."

"I've been very careful that you see the better side of me," she said. "I also have some warts, and sooner or later you're going to experience them, too."

They sat there, knees touching, looking at each other.

"I feel unfairly lucky," he said, "and a little tight."

She smiled. "Isn't it the nature of luck that it isn't fair? I'm just as lucky. Since I moved here, I've been wandering around feeling like a lost soul. A few people have been very kind to me, inviting me to gatherings where I might meet other people. Another few men have seen me as 'available,' and I've had to protect myself from them. I've spent a lot of time on my cell phone talking with friends back in Twin Cities."

"And then you just walked up to me at a party and said 'Hello.' "

"If I'd waited another five minutes, you'd have been gone. You know it took me twenty minutes to get up the courage to speak to you?"

He took her other hand. "Heather, I promise I will quit talking about feeling like I'm out of my depth with you."

"Good!"

He turned and picked up her iPad and handed it to her. "This icon is the Kindle app," he said, pointing to the display. "So far it has only one document in it—my novel—but you can add more. If you register with Amazon, you can download any Kindle book, but you don't have to. They have a lot of free books, mostly public domain, a number of classics. Some might cost a couple of dollars."

She touched the screen to display a kind of book shelf. "I've used this thing mainly to read the newspapers. The online versions are not as satisfying as the big, floppy paper ones, but I can get today's news today." She flicked through the icons on the display and brought up the front page of the *Saint Paul Pioneer Press*. "Besides, they give me a connection to home."

"I use my computer for the same thing—only to get *away* from the home town."

"*The New York Times,*" she guessed.

"You got it."

"For a while," she said, "I subscribed to the Sunday *Times,* just to submerge myself in it for a few hours. They delivered it to my door—five pounds of it." She smiled. "I felt like I had arrived, somehow."

"Minneapolis isn't exactly the boondocks," he said.

"Next to New York, *everywhere* is the boondocks—except maybe London."

"And yet you came here to this place. Why not New York?"

She pursed her lips. "I thought I'd drown there, and nobody would ever find me."

He shook his head and smiled at her. "I'm glad you used our little college as a stepping stone, at least."

She frowned. "I don't think of it that way."

"Sorry. It's more of what I just promised I wouldn't do, isn't it?"

She smiled, then turned her attention to the iPad and opened Rich's book, then skimmed through several pages. "I'm eager to get into this."

"By the time you get through that and those other books, you'll know more about me than I know about you."

She sat back in the chair. "What do you want to know?"

"Everything." He turned off the iPad and stood up. Leading her by the hand to the sofa, he said, "Let's get comfortable."

Before sitting down, she asked, "Do you have any more of that nice brandy?"

"Of course." He took their coffee cups to the kitchen and returned with two snifters and the bottle of cognac.

"This is a treat," she said when he handed her the drink.

They sat for a moment, sipping from their glasses.

"What do you usually drink?" he asked. "I didn't think to ask before, did I?"

She raised the snifter to her nose. "This is really good. Actually, I don't have a very sophisticated palate. I'll drink just about anything." She sipped the cognac and smiled at him.

"I usually buy cheap," he said, "although I really love good wine when I taste it."

"Sometimes I ask myself why I drink," she said. "Obviously, it's for the effect. I began drinking in high school, at parties and things."

"And 'things'?" He grinned.

"You know," she said, smiling back. "Only, sometimes it isn't fun. I get all emotional and blubbery."

"You fall in love too easily?"

She sang the next line, *"I fall in love too fast."*

"Somehow," he said, "I find it hard to see you falling in love too fast—or doing anything you didn't intend to do."

She put her glass down and turned toward him. "I learned a long time ago that I had to stay in control in order to stay out of trouble."

He sipped from his glass. "I'm sensing that there's more."

"You're very perceptive," she said.

He chuckled.

"Actually," she continued, "I've always been a sucker for a smooth talking man."

"And you feel safe with me, or you wouldn't say that." He grinned broadly.

Furrows appeared between her eyebrows, and then she smiled. "As a matter of fact," she said, "I do."

"Because I'm not a smooth talker?"

"No! Because you show yourself in your face."

He sighed. "I always wanted to be a little mysterious."

"Sorry, Charlie." She put her hand on his arm. "I've had enough mystery in my life."

"So your mirror neurons get you in trouble sometimes?"

"No, it's the words that get me in trouble."

"The smooth talking words."

"Yes. I don't know why that is." She folded one leg under her and picked up her glass. "Like right now, I'm sitting here perfectly relaxed with you, and I'm feeling safe, like I'm with a good friend."

"No mystery here, eh?"

She raised one eyebrow. "More male ego?" Her smile was impish.

"Yep. I always wanted to be able to sweep a woman off her feet." Rich was relaxed and enjoying the game. He no longer felt outclassed by this woman. Both of them, it seemed, were vulnerable—and at the moment for him—fearless.

Six

The next day Rich spent thinking about Heather, and about how she described herself—emotionally vulnerable, especially when drinking, but when challenged becoming assertive and powerful. She knew herself.

She also seemed sensitive to non-verbal signals from other people. She paid attention to the little clues about how others were relating to her. The mirror neurons.

And—and this was the thing that attracted him to her the most—she seemed to love living. She had a positive attitude toward her experience of the world. When she was engaged in something, she gave herself to it. Her love making was for him spectacular and freeing. She showed her own joy and physical intensity at the same time she seemed tuned in to his. It was as though they not only complemented each other physically and emotionally but built on each other's passion. She made him feel powerful without relinquishing her own.

Still, she admitted to doubts and weaknesses. Even those admissions revealed the inner strength that comes from self-knowledge.

None of the characters in his novel came close to her. Before he met her he would have expressed doubt that anyone could be that wonderful. He didn't know how to describe such a character, much less know what to do with one in a story.

He went to the last page of his book and plodded along with the plot, feeling more and more as though he were wasting his time. His characters spoke and reacted to each other but without any *juice*. The theme he was trying to reveal, the difficulty that people have in trying to communicate with each other, was actually being clearly revealed in the story itself. He was having trouble communicating any meaning to his reader.

Closing his computer, he dug out the student papers he had to read and mark before they all returned on Monday. After a half-hour, he slammed the folder closed. His students were no more motivated than the characters in his book. Or than he.

Rich went home, opened a bottle of nondescript white wine and dredged up an old movie to watch until he fell asleep in his chair.

Seven

His phone seemed to be ringing from a long distance off. Looking around, he discovered that he had slept all night in his chair. At some point he must have turned off the television, but he didn't remember anything.

Stumbling toward his phone lying on the dining table where he had dropped it the day before, he noticed irrelevantly the shaft of sunlight squinting through the kitchen window at a low angle and lighting up a photograph on the far wall.

"Hello," he said groggily. He didn't even look at the phone to see who might be calling.

"Have you eaten breakfast?" It was Heather.

"No, you woke me up."

"Are you still in bed?" she laughed.

"Never got there," he said. His mouth tasted of old, stale wine.

"You sound like you're hung over."

"A little bit."

"Well jump in the shower and meet me outside your apartment in fifteen minutes. It's a beautiful spring day and we're going for a ride!"

"Oh," he groaned.

"Your stomach upset?" Her voice lilted, as though she were singing.

He thought for a moment, then said, "No."

"Then chug exactly a half-ounce of vodka in a small glass of orange juice, get in the shower and get outside! I'm on my way."

He started to answer, then realized that she had hung up.

Her energy gave him a boost, and he followed her instructions, all the while grumbling and smiling in spite of himself.

Rich couldn't remember ever having seen her car—and the subject hadn't come up in their conversations. Just as he was walking out of his building, she drove up in an electric blue 1957 Thunderbird, top down, gleaming in the morning sun.

Dressed for the car, she sported sunglasses and a little tennis hat. "You made it!" she said, laughing. "You still look a little peaked."

"I feel more than a little, but better after the vodka," he said, opening the passenger door. "Where did you get this gem?"

"My father, of course. He restored it about a hundred years ago, and then didn't want to drive it because it might get scratched."

Rich settled into the bucket seat and fastened his seat belt. "It's in beautiful shape."

"The steering wheel feels too big," she said, pulling out from the curb. "But it has a nice response."

Rich felt better already. Just being in her presence buoyed him up, and he was stimulated by her gaiety and her radiance in the sunlight with the wind blowing her hair.

She punched an icon on the iPod sitting in a little bracket on the dashboard. The familiar trumpets and marimba of Tijuana Brass, music from the nineteen sixties, filled the space around their knees.

"You sure know," he shouted in her ear, "how to wake up the dead!"

She shot him a quick grin as she turned onto the highway. Saying nothing, she let the atmosphere of the moment lift him out of his stupor. He didn't even ask—he didn't want to know—where they were going. Destinations were beside the point.

Heather pointed to the glove box. He opened it and found a pair of sunglasses. He hadn't realized that he was squinting into the morning sun. Putting them on, he leaned back in the seat and breathed the country air. They exchanged smiles as "The Taste of Honey" filled their ears.

A few minutes later, she slowed the car and pulled into a highway restaurant. Even the sound of tires rolling over gravel added to his enjoyment of the moment.

The waitress brought them coffee without being asked. "Nice day out there, isn't it?" she said, handing them menus. "I'll bring water in a minute."

Rich looked at Heather, who had taken off her sunglasses. "You are something else," he said.

"I sure hope so," she said. "Now, why did you get soused last night? Or shouldn't I ask?" She raised one eyebrow.

"I'd been trying to work. Couldn't get into the novel, and then couldn't face papers I'm supposed to have graded by tomorrow."

"So you were bummed out. Why didn't you call?" Her eyes were squinting the slightest bit with her smile.

"I turned on the TV and drank a bottle of wine and went to sleep. That was my evening. I wouldn't have been good company for anybody."

"Well, today's a new day." She looked up at the waitress who had just arrived with her order pad at the ready.

"That your cute car out front?" the waitress asked.

"My dad thinks it's still his."

"Oh, oh. Better be good to it," the woman said. "What'll you have?"

Rich was busy looking at the menu.

"I'll have whatever he has," Heather said.

Rich frowned. "You don't have to ..."

She stared at him, her eyes pools of blue-black ink.

"Eggs over easy, hash browns, whole wheat toast," he said. "For both of us."

"Got it." The waitress grinned at them and left.

"So," he said, "where are we off to?"

"I don't know. Do you?"

He lifted his cup. "Here's to new experiences."

She laughed and touched his cup with hers. "All I know is that this road is smooth and lightly traveled. It goes up into the foothills."

"Our kind of road." He sighed, still smiling.

"What's the sigh for?"

"I am having fun. It's a new experience."

"We'll blow the cobwebs out, at least."

They ate breakfast leisurely, had more coffee, and walked arm and arm out of the restaurant. The waitress winked at them.

Outside, Heather dug her keys out of her purse and handed them to him. He looked surprised, but took them. "What would your father say?"

"He's dead," she said simply, walking around the car and getting in on the passenger side.

"Oh. Sorry."

She smiled at him. "Yeah. He was a prince."

"And you were his princess?"

She just nodded.

Rich started the engine. "The steering wheel does feel big," he said. As they started to move, the rear wheels threw gravel, and he eased up on the accelerator. "Sorry."

"Nice pickup, eh?" She was grinning at him.

A few miles down the highway, he began to relax. Heather dialed up some more music on her iPod. Glen Campbell sang "Galveston."

"Okay?" she asked him.

"Perfect," he said. "You like the old songs."

"Actually," she said, "It's all my dad's music. I copied hundreds of his records and tapes. Just seemed to go with the car."

"Nice not to have to cart around a bunch of eight-track tapes."

She pointed to the tape deck. "As a matter of fact, I had to play all his eight-track songs on this player in order to copy them."

Farms on both sides of the two-lane road were beginning to show the sprouts of spring crops. He slowed down for a town. "This car will attract attention," he said. "Don't want it to be the wrong kind of attention."

"I got stopped in Illinois on the way down here," she said. "The officer got so interested in the car that he forgot to write the ticket."

Rich grinned. "In the car *and* the driver."

Small towns on Sunday morning tend to be empty. Rich thought about how this town would have looked pretty much the same in 1957. A car and a pickup truck were diagonally parked outside the only open business, a family diner. A big square clock outside a jewelry store had stopped at 3:15 on an unknown earlier day. A blinking yellow signal marked the main intersection in town. He made a mental note to include such a town in his story.

He noticed that Heather was looking at him. "You're lost in thought," she said. "Memories?"

"Kind of," he said. "Thinking of a description of this town for my book."

"Is it like your home town?"

"Smaller. Tiffin is a city, compared with this."

"How big?"

"About fifteen thousand."

At the end of the business section, they passed a dozen large Victorian-era homes, each one immaculate with smooth lawns. Beyond that began the middle-class homes, of varying size and quality and condition. Recreational vehicles, some so large they dwarfed the homes next to them, were parked in driveways. "This is America," Rich said.

Heather took the iPod off its bracket and searched the song list. Soon, Paul Simon was singing, "America."

Counting the cars on the New Jersey Turnpike,
They've all come to look for America ...

When the song was over, she stopped the player. After a moment, she said, "It's odd, isn't it, how different America is to different people."

He glanced at her. "What's America for you?"

She gestured at the scenery they were passing. They had left the small town behind, and now on either side were fields of farms, homes and barns. "This is the place," she said, "but I don't know the people."

"But you grew up in the Midwest."

"I feel like I left that all behind," she said. "I've spent years in a university environment, where place didn't matter so much as the ideas from people—people all over the world. People who think and write and read. People who exchange ideas."

The wind noise made hearing her words difficult, so he slowed the car. The sun was higher and the air was noticeably warmer. At a place where there was room at the side of the road, he pulled off and stopped.

"I've been accused of being a snob," he said, turning toward her and taking off his sunglasses. "I teach in a small school in the middle of America, and I know the place and I think I know the people—I grew up here. But it's like I've outgrown them. It's awful to say that, I know."

"It isn't awful," she said. "We can't be all things to all people."

"Tell me," he said looking down at his hand, "what made you pick me out of that crowd at the party."

She reached out and lifted his chin so she could look into his eyes. "You're still feeling outclassed, aren't you?"

"What did you see?"

"A lonely man, wandering around with a glass in his hand, wanting to connect."

"Wow. Spot on. But why did you want to connect with someone like that?"

"My mirror neurons, I guess. Something in your eyes felt to me like what I was feeling inside."

"You, lonely?" He laughed.

"Rich, look at me." She removed her sunglasses.

Holding each other's eyes, neither spoke for a long while. A large truck sped by noisily. Then tears welled up in her eyes.

"Isn't everybody?" she asked, barely above a whisper. "You think my crack the other day about living in our separate little worlds was just my being flip? I meant every word."

Rich felt his own throat tightening. "Hard to imagine," he croaked.

"No it isn't," she said. "We just don't pay enough attention to each other."

"I thought I was paying attention to you. Was I just seeing your mask?"

"One of them," she said, smiling. "I have a whole closet full of masks."

"And here I am, trying to write about how hard it is for people to communicate with each other."

"We live in our separate little worlds, wrapped in skin, fearfully peeking out at each other."

"That's exactly what you said, that first morning!"

"I have a good memory." She smiled again. "And I've said that sentence a thousand times."

"Because you are the *we* in it."

"Yes."

"And so am I."

"Yes."

"That's why we are here, sitting in the middle of cornfields, staring into each other's eyes."

"What do you see when you look into my eyes?" she asked, holding his gaze.

"Back in the restaurant, I was enchanted by your eyes. They were like blue-black pools that I wanted to fall into."

"And now?"

"In this bright light, they are still blue, but your pupils are tiny."

"I've read recently that we unconsciously perceive very subtle changes in facial expressions, and adopt those changes from people who are important to us."

Rich laughed. "Here we were in an intimate exchange of feelings, and your rational brain suddenly engages."

"Interesting, isn't it? Maybe something about blue-black pools triggered a barrier to intimacy." She turned to look up the road and put her sunglasses back on.

"Okay." He started the engine and pulled back onto the road. "I'm disappointed, but not hurt."

Heather put a hand on his arm. "Good. I don't want to hurt you."

"Really," he said, "I do understand. I've had the exact same reaction, more than once in my life."

She dialed up Glen Campbell again, singing along with him the words to "Galveston."

I still hear your sea winds blowin'
I still see her dark eyes glowin'
She was 21 when I left Galveston

High clouds softened the bright sunlight as they began to enter rolling country and the straight road changed to curves along the banks of small streams. Rich liked the way the little car hugged the curves. He glanced occasionally at Heather, who was still singing. What he could see of her eyes behind the sunglasses, she seemed to be enjoying the music.

In the next town, he watched for service stations. The fuel gauge was showing the difference between cars from the 1950s and today—even in a small car, gas consumption was noticeably greater. "What do you have in this?" he asked as he pulled into a station, three hundred horsepower?"

Heather laughed. "More like two-fifty."

As he filled the tank, he looked up at the sky. "Clouding up."

"Think we should put the top up?"

"Getting a little chilly."

She reached over the center console and actuated the top mechanism, which slowly opened the cover behind the seats and installed the hard top. Rich thought the car looked even smaller with the top up.

"My dad thought they ruined the Thunderbird in 1958," she said when he climbed back in. "Going from a two-seater to a four-seater made it a completely different car."

"Didn't they go back to a two-seater?"

"Yes, but then they quit making them."

He looked around the interior. "Cozy."

Heather removed her sunglasses and turned to look at him. "Rich, are we okay?"

He took off his sunglasses. "Sure," he said. "Intimacy gets dangerous sometimes."

She continued to look at him. "Sorry," she said finally.

The mood inside the little car seemed different. As they continued up into the foothills, the sky became darker. Heather started the iPod again, with Glen Campbell still singing.

By the time I get to Phoenix, she'll be rising
She'll find the note I left hangin' on her door,
She'll laugh when she reads the part that says I'm leavin'
'Cause I've left that girl so many times before

Heather was not singing, and Rich glanced over at her. Her eyes were filled with tears as she looked straight ahead.

"Heather."

She turned her head and smiled at him through her tears. "A long time ago," she said.

"Tell me?"

She waited for the song to end, then stopped the player. "That was me," she said softly. "It wasn't working, and we both knew it. But I kept trying to leave, and he kept pulling me back."

"Your husband?"

"Yes. And my boss."

"The interdisciplinary research practices."

She snorted, then quickly grabbed a tissue from a box on the floor and dabbed at her nose. "Sorry."

"And you did make it to Oklahoma."

Heather laughed. "Yes."

"Did he finally believe you?"

"I had to take six months off. My father was ill, and I went home to take care of him."

"But the song still gets to you."

She smiled. "Actually, that took me by surprise."

They rode in silence for a while. As he slowed down for another small town, she said, "Are you getting hungry?"

"I could eat something."

A large family-style restaurant appeared at the edge of town, surrounded by cars. "Sunday after church," he said pulling in.

"Give me a minute to make myself presentable." She wiped her cheeks and applied lipstick. Smiling brightly at him, she said, "Better?" He leaned over and kissed her on the cheek.

The restaurant was filled with families, and the noise level was high. Waiters bustled around, dodging each other with full trays of food. They had to wait a few minutes for a table. When they were finally seated, Rich said, "Really different from breakfast, eh?"

Heather laughed. "You won't be peering into my blue-black pools."

"Nor whispering sweet nothings in your ear."

After a quick meal of waffles, they took their coffee in paper cups and left the noise behind. In the parking lot, he handed her the car keys. "Thanks, he said. "It was fun."

"You can keep driving if you want."

"No, that was enough. I'll hold your coffee for you."

Inside, she started the car. "You want to keep going, or turn around?"

"I'm loving this, but I do still have those papers to grade."

On the road again, they could see that their sunny morning had ended. To the west, the sky looked ominous. A few minutes later, raindrops began splattering on the windshield. They rode in silence.

Heather turned to Rich. "You got to experience some of my stuff around my ex-marriage. Willing to take your turn?"

He thought for a moment. "I don't have a song that tells my story," he said. "I was left."

"Oh."

"We'd been married almost ten years, had—have—a son."

"What's his name?"

"Keith. He's in high school now. I see him once in a while."

"Why'd she leave you?"

He smiled wryly. "We didn't work hard enough at it. We should have had counseling, but things got distant between us, and I buried my head in my work. She got tired of being alone, she said."

"The old story," said Heather. "father stays late at work, mother feels stuck at home with the babies."

"Not quite. She went for her teaching degree, and is now teaching back in her home town."

"Either of you have affairs?" Heather was smiling at him.

"Not really. There was one situation, though, that was hard for us for a while. She posed for a sculpture right after Keith was born. A woman sculptor, and there were some uncomfortable feelings. But nothing really happened between them. It was all my stuff."

"Might as well have been an affair, huh?"

"Hmmm," he said. "I was really jealous. But we all made up, and I thought it was over—my reaction, that is. But somehow, after that, it was different for us."

She nodded. "Those implicit feelings are hard to fight because they aren't rational. We can't explain them away."

"Yeah. They just pollute the relationship."

"Did you grieve? I mean, did you go through all the stages?"

"I thought I did. But a few years ago we met when Keith came to stay with me for a summer, and my heart broke all over again."

"Did you try to get her back?"

"No," he said. "She'd remarried, and our worlds were too far apart."

"You *think* that, or you *know* that?"

He grinned. "Yeah, it's over." He sighed. "I know a couple, back home, who dated in high school but then broke up. Twenty years later, they got back together after both of them had been married and divorced. It didn't last a month."

"All fantasy."

"All fantasy." He laughed.

"What's the laugh about?" she asked, glancing at him quickly.

"My fantasies go into my fiction."

"Safer than trying to revive a dead relationship."

"I hope so," he said.

"You're not sure?"

"I get emotionally involved in my characters."

Heather laughed. "The one named Heather?"

"Oh, no. She was a minor character. I just couldn't deal with her by that name after I met you."

Heather was silent for a while, staring ahead at the road. Rich finally looked at her and asked, "What's going on, Heather?"

She glanced at him, her eyes glistening. "This day started out so bright and sunny!" Light rain was still hitting the windshield, and the wipers slowly marked time.

"You're not talking about the weather, are you?" He turned in his seat to watch her face.

"We've been talking for an hour about old, torn relationships. Stuff comes up."

"The Way We Were. Barbra Streisand."

"You remember that?" she said, grinning, and pointed to the music player. "It's on there." He started to take the player down from its perch, but she said, "No! Don't play it. I don't want any more memories!"

"Our adventure did turn out a little soggy, didn't it?"

Heather pointed to the box of tissues, and he held the box for her to take one. "I feel like getting drunk," she said after wiping her eyes.

"Our timing is off," he said. "I did that last night. I *have* to grade papers tonight."

Heather suddenly slowed the car and pulled off the pavement and stopped. Laying her head on her arms on the steering wheel, she sobbed.

Rich put a hand on her back and waited. The metronome of the windshield wipers marked the minutes in dirge-time.

She lifted her head. "You see? I'm not always on top of things." She put the car in gear and pulled back onto the roadway. The rain became more intense, and she switched the wipers to high rate.

They rode through heavy rain all the way into town. Heather was clutching the steering wheel, occasionally wiping her face with the back of her hand. Her makeup was smeared.

When they approached his street, Rich said, "Don't go here. Let's go to your place instead. I'll feed you and hold you for a while, and then put you to bed. Okay?"

She stopped the car. "You have papers to grade."

"Fuck the papers. I need to take care of you."

She glanced at him gratefully, and turned toward her apartment.

They waited in the parking lot for the rain to let up a little, then dashed for the door. Even so, they were both soaked. As she fumbled with the outside lock, she looked at their reflection in the glass and laughed. "Drowned rats!" she said.

In her apartment, she said, "Drop our clothes on the tile in the kitchen. I'll get towels."

Standing naked and shivering, he took his wallet and keys and phone from his pockets and put them on the table. Heather appeared with towels, and they both dried off, still laughing. She picked up their clothing and took the bundle to the utility room. "Everything washable?" she called.

"Yes."

He heard the washing machine starting, and she returned, her towel slung over one shoulder. "No time for modesty," she said. "C'mon, lets get warm!" She led him into the bedroom.

Eight

He welcomed his classes back and said he hoped they had fun during spring break. Then he apologized for being late with their grades. "If that puts anybody in a tight spot, let me know," he said. That afternoon he graded papers and thought about Heather. She had dropped him off at his apartment on her way to work. Neither had said much.

They had lain in bed together all night, allowing their emotions to dissipate, drifting off to sleep and waking up to hug each other for a while. Rich was keenly aware of her body next to his, but he had promised her that sex was not what he wanted that night.

There was something she had not told him, and he didn't ask. She curled up against him in almost a fetal position. This competent, confident, bright woman became a girl in the throes of agony about something.

In the morning, she had put herself together as she had always appeared, but seemed subdued through their simple breakfast. By the time she dropped him at his place, she was smiling and cheerful again. He remembered her telling him at Barney's that when she felt nervous, she'd get obnoxious and bold to cover it up. "And well practiced at it," he thought.

He phoned her after dinner that evening and asked her if she wanted company. She said no, that she was going to do some paper work and get herself organized. They agreed to check in with each other in a day or so.

The more he thought about her the more he wondered about this remarkable woman. She had said she had a whole closet full of masks. He no longer felt outclassed by her, although he sometimes envied her ability to function in the face of what appeared to be desperate emotional circumstances.

Those moments in the car, when he had stopped alongside the road so they could talk more easily, seemed to be when her façade had begun to crack. She had spoken about being lonely—"Isn't everybody?" she had said—and then she began to talk about people not paying attention to each other. "What do you see when you look into my eyes?" she had asked, and then almost immediately said something completely different, as though turning a light switch to some academic thing.

At the time he'd had a thought that seemed irrelevant, that her eyes had somehow changed from the dark pools he saw in the restaurant to just pretty blue irises, pupils tiny in the bright light, as though the life had gone out of them. And then she was singing along with Glen Campbell.

When he called her a couple of days later, she put him off again gently, but they agreed to get together during the weekend. "Maybe not a drive," she said, "the weather forecast isn't great for the weekend."

"Cooking together could be fun," he offered.

"I don't know *anything* about cooking!"

"Gee, I thought women had this cooking gene," he laughed. "I won't make fun of you if you mess up the gravy."

That brought the lilt back into her voice, and they agreed to sit down on Saturday morning to plan their day together.

It was with a different kind of feeling that he anticipated seeing her again. He felt nervous and uneasy. This was no longer the professional Barbie Doll he had been enchanted by. There were more, and deeper, things going on in her, and he wasn't sure he knew how to handle them.

Working on the novel was out of the question. His characters, if not he, were totally out of their depth in relation to this woman, and he couldn't think of much besides her.

Perhaps, he wondered, she had read something in his books that she had taken home with her that night that had changed her perception of him. There was that thing about Becky and the sculptor that even made him uncomfortable at times, but he was the one who had actually gone through it. He couldn't imagine how others might react to it.

That's the problem with writing stories, he decided. A writer reveals a lot about himself beyond what he thinks he does. Every novelist needs a good editor, someone who can identify with the story and yet be able to point out what's *really* going on in it. Even better, one who knows the writer well enough to sense that he might not want to reveal that little bit of personal stuff, and not be timid about asking about it.

"My skin's too thin," he told himself. "My stories are just stories; they are not *me*. I've never been shy about telling people who I am in my essays. Some of those have been really open and frank. Why should my stories be *too revealing*?"

Left brain, right brain, he decided. His essays, even the ones that showed his weaknesses, have all been from his left brain, the part that puts words together, analyzes things, makes judgments. His stories just come out of his right brain without being censored or interpreted. It's like they *pour* onto the page right out of his gut.

He laughed at himself. He'd wondered if Heather had discovered something about him that she had a problem with, and here he was trying to explain, to justify what he writes. He pictured her reading his words on her iPad, reading glasses perched on her pretty nose, frowning at some phrase or image. He sighed. "Maybe that's why I can't write anything now," he said. "My left brain is judgmental and nervous. Our mirror neurons pick up clues from other people, and help us form impressions and even theories about what goes on in their minds. Society couldn't exist without this ability—indeed, this necessity—to know what others think and feel."

All this went into his computer—although not into the story. He kept a journal in another folder, and used it to try to figure out his middle-aged brain.

On Saturday morning, she showed up in her cute little sports car, she and it as bright as the morning sun. He was fixing breakfast for them, a puffy omelet with cream cheese, to be topped with powdered sugar and strawberries. Heather was dutifully appreciative. "You are so good!" she gushed, watching him take it from the oven.

"You can take off the sunglasses," he said. "You're indoors."

She complied, sighing. Her eyes were rimmed with red.

He served the omelet from a heavy cast-iron skillet, cutting it neatly in two, and they sat down at the table.

"Let's eat first," he said, "then let's talk. Okay?"

"Okay."

"I found this recipe in an old cookbook. Somebody told me that it is a 'boobala,' a traditional Jewish dish, but I don't know."

"It's so fluffy! Like a soufflé. Delicious!"

After breakfast and coffee, he led her to the sofa. He waited a minute before saying, "Something is going on, isn't it?"

She looked away and didn't respond. He reached for a box of tissues and placed it in front of her.

"You don't have to tell me," he said quietly, "but I hope you can talk to someone."

She glanced at him, smiling. "I'm the psychologist, right?"

"I'm sure not. All I can offer you is to hold your hand and feed you when you're hungry."

She laughed, still looking straight ahead. "You're sweet," she said, taking his hand. "It's old stuff."

"So it's not my aftershave."

Heather turned her face to him and kissed him on the cheek. "You don't use aftershave, and I'm glad."

Neither of them spoke for a long time. Then she said, "When I finally broke for good from Paul, ..."

"Paul's your ex?"

"Yes. I took a six-month leave, and went home to take care of my father. My mother died several years ago, and when Dad had a stroke, he needed someone with him. I thought it was a good time for me to get away from the university and think." She was speaking softly and slowly, her eyes down, as though she were not seeing anything. "At first, I thought it was a good chance to reconnect with my dad—we hadn't seen much of each other in years."

"He'd had a stroke," Rich said. "What effect did that have?"

"One side of his body was affected. He couldn't walk, his left arm was almost useless, and he couldn't pronounce words well because one side of his face was paralyzed. But his mind was there. We managed to talk together for hours, but he was frustrated and angry at his condition."

"I can imagine."

"His anger kept getting worse, and he started to take it out on me. He'd get furious with me when I couldn't understand what he was saying!" She dabbed at her eyes with a tissue.

Rich squeezed her hand.

"I finally couldn't take it anymore!"

"You used to be his princess."

She turned and buried her face against his shoulder and sobbed. A few moments later, she straightened up and wiped her face. "It felt as though he were blaming me for his stroke. I never could deal with his anger—I developed ways to get under his radar, to make him smile at me."

"And after his stroke, you couldn't do that anymore."

"I didn't want to! I grew up a long time ago!"

Rich looked down at her hands, which were twisting the tissue. "And you had just broken up with your husband."

"Paul used to yell at me when I made a mistake. And it was like I couldn't do anything right."

"And you finally stood up to him and left, and then found yourself right back in the same situation with your dad."

She looked at Rich. "So I left him, too!"

"Nobody could blame you."

"People did. Dad did. Paul did."

"What did you do?"

"I just holed up in my apartment. I didn't go out, I didn't see anybody. I just sat and watched daytime television."

"Yeah." Rich waited.

She looked at him again and laughed. "Yeah. Typical depressive response. All my anger got turned inside me."

"Until?"

"Until Dad died." She took a deep breath. "He'd had a live-in nurse, and one day he threw something at her, and she quit. Then he just quit, too. Refused to eat, and when they put him in the hospital he got hold of somebody else's medications and killed himself."

"You thought it was your fault?"

"Of course!"

"Then what did you do?"

She looked at him strangely, and then looked away. "I got a therapist." She looked back at him quickly. "Are you diagnosing me?"

Rich blushed. "Sorry. I'm trying to understand what you've been going through."

"I've had enough therapy!" She spat the words through clenched teeth."

He let go of her hand and pulled away.

Heather stood up, then whirled around to face him. "I know what's wrong with me! I don't need another therapist to tell me!"

He held up his hands in surrender. "I'm sorry, Heather."

She grabbed her purse from a chair and started for the door. Suddenly, she seemed to wilt. Turning around, she looked as though she were going to say something, and then stopped. She sank slowly to the floor, tears streaming down her face.

Rich went to her and sat on the floor next to her. He held out his arms, offering them to her, but didn't touch her. She looked at him briefly through tear-clouded eyes, then closed them again. He waited, his arms becoming heavy.

He felt defeated. The memory from years ago, of Becky crying, getting ready to leave him, looking at him as though she hated him, came back to haunt him once more. He didn't know what to do. He closed his eyes and let his hands fall limply to the floor.

Some time later—minutes?—an hour?—he had no idea, he heard her get up quietly and go through the door without saying anything. He lay back on the carpet and looked at the ceiling for a long time. His throat was sore and his head hurt.

Nine

That evening as he worked at home on his computer, his phone rang. "I'm sorry, Rich," she said when he answered, "You didn't deserve that."

Before he could respond, she hung up.

He knew that drinking wouldn't help him to feel better, but he went anyway to the refrigerator and made himself a very strong Bloody Mary. He turned on the television, then immediately turned it off. Instead, he connected his iPod to the stereo and played the first thing he came to, a Shostakovich symphony that he'd begun to listen to weeks before. The strong, militant chords felt like lashes across his back, but then softened into an incredible sadness matching his own.

One part of him wanted to scoop her up in his arms, kiss away her tears and make her whole again, just as she was on that first morning, smiling down at him in her bed, saying softly, "Ah, he lives!" He *had* begun to live then, after years of what now seemed to him sleepwalking.

Another part of him was furious with her for letting him think she was his angel, come to earth simply to make him happy, and then crumbling like a sand sculpture on the beach, just another fragile human like himself, no more able to figure out the tragedies of life than he was.

"What do you see when you look into my eyes?" she had said in the car, as though she knew what he'd see—not the blue-black pools that had kept him breathless, but the miotic pinpoint pupils he'd seen before only in people who had been smoking marijuana. He knew she hadn't been smoking anything that morning. Something had changed in her, and his new, fantasy relationship had simply begun to dissolve.

Rich couldn't face his novel again, not yet. He pulled books from the stacks in the library until he realized that he was taking psychology books, how-to-cope books about grieving and recovery. He returned those to the shelves, and instead looked for books on neurobiology. He was fascinated by recent scientific work in merging the fields of psychology and biology. The mind had gone in less than a decade from mystery to one more field of serious study. Neurology was suddenly opening up the mind to experimental science. Much of what was found was difficult to integrate with traditional thinking in ethics and culture. It felt to him the way it must have felt to people back in the Eighteenth Century, the new Enlightenment, when so much of what had been "known" was overturned and the former authorities of wisdom were eventually buried in new knowledge. Galileo's capitulation to Pope Urban didn't slow the advance of knowledge much.

Now, such holy concepts as free will and a separate entity known as the soul were increasingly coming under scrutiny. An actress (breathtakingly gorgeous Thandie Newton) told a live audience of her personal discovery that the self is but "a projection, based on other people's projections." She described her attempts to find out who she really was, as her repeatedly attempted selves became broken and destroyed. "And how many times," she said, "would my self have to die before I realized that it was never alive in the first place?" Heresies, that in 1600—or 1940, in some places—could have gotten her killed.

Had Heather's self become broken? In her anger at her husband and her father, had she lost a sense of who she was? Did she have a portrait of herself hidden in a closet slowly taking on the uncomfortable, shameful visage of a human who had failed her own values, while the mask (one of the masks, according to her) remained beautiful and flawless and powerful? *"What do you see when you look into my eyes?"*

Rich could do nothing but wait.

Ten

The following week he inquired discreetly and found that Heather had taken a "vacation" to visit friends in Minneapolis. She'd likely be back in a week. He resisted the impulse to try to find her—tracing a 1957 Thunderbird shouldn't be impossible, he thought, even in a metropolitan area of three million people. He remembered that her Minnesota license plate was "1OFAKIND."

Deciding not to chase after her and forgetting about her were not equivalent tasks. His memory kept playing back that day of their road trip to the foothills. It had started so well. He could still picture it—enfolded by the bucket seats of the Thunderbird, wind eddies blowing their hair, old music blaring from the speakers—and her smile. Peering in behind her sunglasses to watch her eyes was pure voyeurism, as sensuous as stroking her skin with the back of his hand.

His problem right now, he realized, was not Heather. Of course she was in serious trouble, and he had come to love her. His real problem, his more pressing problem, was his inability to detach enough to get through the day. He struggled through his classes and threw up his hands when young students failed to understand what he was trying to teach them, instead of grabbing those opportunities to *make a difference*. His mantra, from the beginning of grad school, had been that he wanted to make a difference, the way his first real teacher, Jack Garrison, had made a difference in him.

He wished for a friend, someone with whom he could let spill out all the crazy feelings he had to keep stuffed inside. Mentally listing the people he knew, searching for people he could talk with intimately, he came up blank.

One afternoon, Rich had given up on reading student papers and was simply sitting on a bench outside the LS&A building in the shade of a silver maple, letting the May breezes caress his face. He tried to meditate, eyes closed, simply feeling the touch of air on his face. He could hear young voices in the distance, no discernable words, just musical sounds. "Someone ought to compose a symphony of those sounds," he thought. Then just as suddenly they turned into Heather's voice, and he caught his breath. "No," he thought, "that's not the way life works."

He let the thought go, and counted his breath—in—out—in—out.

"Hello, Doctor Williams," said a young man's voice nearby.

He opened his eyes to see one of his students standing astraddle his bicycle on the path. "Ah, hello," he replied, trying to remember the student's name.

"You look like you're enjoying our beautiful day."

"Yes," Rich said. "I was practicing my meditation, just feeling the air against my face and hearing the distant laughter of children." He chuckled to let the student know he was making a little joke. Moving to one end of the bench, he gestured for him to sit.

The student laid his bicycle down and removed his backpack, then sat next to his teacher. "I've been thinking about something you said this morning in class, about how our knowledge of neurology and complex systems are making the concept of the self irrelevant."

"Did I say that?" Rich laughed. "Pretty arrogant, wasn't I?"

"I don't think so." The boy scratched his head, a symbolic gesture, and grinned.

"Ah, uh—George, isn't it? Tell me what you think."

George nudged his nose with a knuckle. "Well, I keep noticing that I change all the time, how I feel, what I think about certain things, how I relate to certain people—it's like I'm never the same person! Where's the self?"

"The same person couldn't simply be big enough to hold it all?"

"No, it's not that! Excuse me, sir, but I feel like I'm a different person!" George was aroused by his thoughts, energized by the act of speaking up to his teacher. Rich remembered that he seldom spoke in class.

Rich lifted an eyebrow. "You don't have multiple personalities, do you?"

"No, sir!" George laughed. "There's a little of me that carries over from day to day, but it's not always the important part of me."

"What's your major, George?"

"Psych. I get really turned on, sometimes. I hope I'm not making a fool of myself to you."

Rich smiled. "On the contrary, George. It looks like you're thinking for yourself—or yourselves, as the case may be. See if you can tell me—I'm not a psychologist, understand—tell me how this might work, your experience of sequential selves, that may or may not be real."

"Well, if the self is just a projection ..."

"Projection?" Rich broke in, remembering that lovely Thandie Newton, speaking at a TED gathering he had watched on his computer recently, using the same expression.

"A projection," began George, trying to explain a concept to someone out of the field, "is like when we're angry but can't express it, we see anger in other people. Does that make sense?"

Rich laughed. "Yes it does. You mean that you interpret different continuities in your day-to-day experiences as indicating that there's something 'real' there that holds them?"

George frowned. "Yeah, I think so."

Rich laughed again. "Sorry. I'm putting words in your mouth—not very good words. You tell me."

"Well, when we—no, when *I*—assume that 'this is me,' then I'm locking myself into a brick-and-mortar 'me.' Like, I'm a geek, and I can't do anything about it!"

"Because tomorrow, you'll be a scholar, not a geek."

George blushed. "Yeah."

"So," Rich said, "How would you describe this *thing*, whatever it is that you used to think is your self?"

The student scratched his head. "I don't know—it feels more like a—like a *song* than a thing, or an object."

"A song. That's good," Rich said. "I never thought of that. But I think you're right. The song can take almost any form, can't it? Didn't Walt Whitman or somebody write something like, I sing myself?"

"Uh, I wouldn't know," said George.

Another voice entered the conversation. "One's self I sing …"

They turned to see a young woman standing behind the bench. She blushed. "I'm sorry—I just happened to hear what you said. It's from 'Leaves of Grass.'"

"Thank you!" said Rich.

George laughed. "That's perfect! Maybe my real self has yet to be sung."

She began reciting, her voice sweet and strong:

> *One's-self I sing, a simple separate person,*
> *Yet utter the word Democratic, the word En-Masse.*
> *Of physiology from top to toe I sing,*
> *Not physiognomy alone nor brain alone is worthy for the Muse,*
> *I say the Form complete is worthier far,*
> *The Female equally with the Male I sing.*
> *Of Life immense in passion, pulse, and power,*
> *Cheerful, for freest action form'd under the laws divine,*
> *The Modern Man I sing.*

Rich spoke to her, "That's impressive! And does your real self have a name?"

"Candice," she said. "Candice Ross."

George looked at her. "Aren't we in the same class? I've seen you somewhere."

"Last year," said Candice. "English composition."

"I'm George Russell."

"I know."

Rich stood up. "Why don't you two get acquainted," he said. "I need to get back to work."

"Thank you, Doctor Williams," George said. The three of them shook hands, and Rich headed for his office. At the door to the building, he turned to see the two of them sitting together on the bench, deep in conversation. Even at that distance, he could see the wide grin on George's face. Rich felt better than he had in days.

Eleven

After three weeks, Rich had settled back into his routine, teaching three classes, supervising seven graduate students, and working occasionally on his novel. He had not heard a word from Heather; as far as he knew, she was still on a leave of absence, probably in Minnesota. He assumed that she was trying to get herself together; he hoped in therapy. She had said that she had seen a therapist before she left the Twin Cities, so he guessed that she would have returned there for more help.

Rich had considered therapy himself right after she left, but gradually the feeling of loss faded. His infatuation with her was not realistic anyway, he decided. They really had not had time to develop a permanent relationship. What he had felt was more like a teenager's crush, and he'd come a long way from his adolescence. At least he hoped he had.

Once in a while, however, when his phone rang, he looked at it with a feeling of anticipation, hoping for the word HEATHER to appear. Finally, he removed her number from his directory.

The fact was, he was lonely. It seemed to him that he'd always been lonely after he and Becky broke up. Rationally, he had let go of her. Deeper in his emotional system, he recognized that he might never truly let go. He still had a box of old photographs that he promised himself he would throw away, but then he thought that their son Keith might want them at some point.

His department head, Roger Trumble, held an outdoor barbecue for the department just before the end of the term. Faculty, staff and students were invited. Trumble lived on a farm outside of town, with a wide expanse of lawn behind the rather modest house, and he had set up tents, tables and chairs for the expected crowd. The weather was warm and sunny.

Rich wanted to attend; he always looked forward to such gatherings, even though he usually left them early because he had such difficulty connecting with people. Walking around with a glass that sometimes seemed to be part of his hand, he chatted with anyone who spoke to him.

George Russell was there with his new friend Candice, and the two of them made a point of greeting Rich.

"*One's self I sing,*" Rich quoted to her, smiling. She returned the smile, and turned to George. "Isn't he sweet?" she said, and Rich and George exchanged grins.

At the food table, laden with hamburgers and bratwursts, Rich picked around at the coleslaw and macaroni and cheese, not so much hungry as just needing something to do with his hands. He refilled his glass with gin and tonics until he thought he should ease up, and then simply left out the gin.

"Rich Williams!" The voice was vaguely familiar, but he couldn't quite place it. He turned, and Jack Garrison stuck out his hand. "It's been a long time!"

Jack was shockingly older. Rich's memory of him, from his undergraduate years, was young and tall, almost gangly. Jack had been his favorite instructor in his freshman year. Rich's sister had dated Jack for a while until their theological differences became too great for her. Jack had encouraged Rich in his personal efforts to find his own philosophical way, and had given him strong recommendations when he applied to grad school.

"Good to see you again!" Rich said. "I'm surprised to see you here, though."

"Roger was my mentor when I was in grad school," Jack said. "We've stayed in touch." He put a hand on Rich's shoulder. "Which is more than I can say for the two of us. I hear you are on a tenure track! Congratulations."

"Thanks," said Rich. "Are you still teaching?"

"Oh, come on, now! I'm not that old!"

Both men laughed, although Rich was slightly embarrassed. "Well," he said, "*I* feel that old."

Jack flicked the hair over Rich's ear. "Yes, there is a bit of gray there. How are you doing?"

Rich's face must have betrayed something, for Jack's expression changed. "C'mon, let's find a place to talk. We have some catching up to do."

They picked a couple of chairs that were by themselves in a corner of the lawn, under a huge oak tree.

"I've heard good things about you," Jack said, "but all professional. How's your life?"

"Becky and I split up a few years ago. My son, Keith is a junior in high school down in Indiana with Becky."

"Sorry to hear that," said Jack. "Stuff happens, doesn't it? How's Madeline?"

Rich smiled at the name. His sister was always "Maddie" to him. "She's out west somewhere. She teaches special ed to kids on a reservation."

"I believe that. She always had high ideals."

"How about you? Married?"

Jack tilted his head. "Married, and then some. Right now I'm sharing a house with an English teacher."

Rich wondered what "and then some" meant, but he didn't ask. "I wrote a book about you," he said, grinning.

"Oh? I hope it was all good."

"It's really about that first year in your epistemology class, about how you encouraged me to think for myself."

"Your sister wasn't so sure it was a good thing."

"She still doesn't."

"So when can I see this book you wrote?"

"Give me your address, and I'll mail it to you. It's not very thick. I self-published it as a kind of experiment."

"That would be great." Jack pulled out his wallet and handed Rich a business card. "Now, tell me how you are doing." Jack had, indeed, picked up something from Rich's manner when they met.

Rich smiled. "Well, I hadn't had any serious relationships since Becky and I split up, until a few weeks ago."

"From the looks of you, she must have swept you off your feet."

"As a matter of fact, she did."

"And then she vanished," Jack guessed. His eyebrows raised as he said it.

"As a matter of fact."

"Do you know why?"

Rich looked down. "She had problems. She just took off one day, I think to go back home to Minnesota."

"Tough. No goodbyes or anything?"

"No, just a quick apology on the phone. She didn't explain or anything."

"How long had you been seeing her?"

"Just a couple of weeks, actually." Rich picked up a small stick and drew a line in the earth next to his chair.

"You sound like you fell pretty hard for her."

"Yeah."

"Think she thought you were getting too close, too fast?"

"Maybe. I thought it was mutual, but maybe I came on too strong."

Jack grinned at him. "You romantic types tend to do that."

Rich was thoughtful. "She was so—polished, I guess was the word. She was straightforward with me, positive and yet not overbearing. She seemed so sophisticated! At first I was intimidated. I thought she was way out of my league, and she could have had any guy she wanted."

"But she chose you?"

"Yeah, it was fantastic!"

"And then what happened?" Jack looked at Rich over his glasses.

"Well, she called me up real early one Sunday morning, and said, 'Be outside in fifteen minutes. We're going for a ride.' And she was out front in this fifty-seven Thunderbird!"

"Wow."

"So we just took off out Route 23, top down, music playing really loud—Herb Alpert—and it was like a fantasy. We stopped for breakfast on the road, and then we got to talking pretty seriously. We pulled over to the side of the road, and we were there, sitting in the middle of cornfields, staring into each other's eyes. She said, 'What do you see when you look into my eyes?'"

"That's pretty direct," Jack said.

"I don't remember exactly what happened, but all of a sudden she seemed to change. It was like she pulled back." Rich drew some more lines with his stick. "And it went downhill from there. By the time we got home, she was upset and withdrawn."

"Maybe she was having second thoughts. Did you say anything that might have triggered that?"

Rich shook his head. "I don't think so."

"And then she just left town?"

"Yes. Just like that."

Jack looked down at his hands. "Bummer. Wish I could offer some advice, but I don't know what it would be."

"I guess I just have to get over it."

"You said that you and Becky split up. How did that go?"

Rich smiled at him. "Not quite the same thing, but close."

"Becky just picked up and left?"

"Yes."

"No warning?"

"Well," Rich said, "she did complain a lot toward the end, that we didn't seem to have much in common any more."

"The dangling conversation, eh?"

"Yeah, it was like that old song."

"You've had a string of bad luck, seems to me."

Rich laughed wryly, "And I was thinking I was uncommonly lucky when Heather came along."

Jack looked around at the lawn party. "Well, if I knew any of these charming ladies here, I'd be happy to introduce you. Do you know any of them?"

"No, not really." Rich looked up. "I haven't been very sociable around campus."

The two of them wandered back into the thick of the party, and got into separate conversations with different people. Rich had one more gin and tonic, and then stopped to thank the hosts before he got into his car and left.

It was good to talk with Jack, he thought, but not very satisfying. What he missed was intimacy, a connection deeper than the friendly and polite conversations he had at the party. Jack seemed the same as he'd remembered him, perceptive and thoughtful, but emotionally reserved. Most people, Rich guessed, were able to be sociable but not intimate. Maybe it's too much to ask, that level of vulnerability and trust. Rich himself yearned for intimacy but lacked even the skills to enjoy sociability.

The only person he could remember in his life who seemed to have it was Ray Fox, an old friend from his church years before. Ray and his wife lived trustingly and open to nearly everyone. Since then, Rich had yearned for that kind of relationship.

Intimacy was the thing he experienced with Heather, even, it seemed, when they were having a light conversation. There was a sense of authenticity between them, of seeing deeply into each other's self, of respecting that and responding in kind. She had spoken of the masks she wore, "a whole closet of masks," she said, but to him she felt open and whole—until that moment sitting in her Thunderbird. at the side of Route 23, when her eyes seemed to change.

After that, he tried in vain to guess what moved her. Her tears betrayed feelings that she could not share with him.

Twelve

Rich felt guarded. Heather's phone call had caught him by surprise. She wanted to meet him "for coffee" at a restaurant on the edge of town. It had been two months since he had last seen her. He thought he had seen her car in town, but he wasn't sure.

It was Friday evening, and the restaurant was crowded. Her car wasn't in the parking lot when he arrived, so he took a table in the back where he could watch the entrance, and ordered a gin and tonic. This wasn't a time for coffee, at least for him.

"Hi, Hon," she greeted him with when she arrived. It was an odd expression, he felt. She had never called him "Honey."

His chest and throat felt tight. He wasn't sure what to say to her. "Hi," was all he could manage. A part of him was suddenly angry at her, as though she had somehow betrayed him. He managed a weak smile.

She looked haggard. Gone was the enigmatic smile. "I was afraid you wouldn't meet me," she said.

"I couldn't not."

Heather smiled at that. "I'm glad." She looked around for a waiter. Rich signaled to the one who had brought his drink. When he arrived, Heather said, "I'll have whatever he's having."

"Gin and tonic," said the waiter, and left.

They sat looking at each other for a few moments, neither attempting to break the silence that had grown between them during the past weeks. Finally, she looked down. "I had to get help," she said softly.

"I'm sorry."

Then she looked up at him and smiled, just a hint of that old smile that had so captivated him. "I had left Minneapolis to come down here last winter without really dealing with things. I thought I was okay. As you know, I wasn't."

"It's okay, Heather. I could see you weren't doing well."

"I'm really sorry I didn't at least explain." Her eyes were beginning to fill up.

He felt himself softening, and had a thought that maybe the gin wasn't the best thing for him right then. He reached over and put his hand on hers.

The waiter brought her drink. "You want menus?" he asked.

Heather shook her head and the waiter left.

"How are you now?" Rich asked.

"Mostly okay. I'm still shaky sometimes." She smiled at him. "Like now."

"Tell me what you want." He said it as gently as he could, watching her face carefully.

"I've asked myself that same question a hundred times in the past week. I know you must have been terribly hurt, and I'm so sorry about that. That's the first thing I want, to let you know that."

"I guess you couldn't help it," he said. "I realized later that I had put you in a very special place in my life, and it was really too soon to do that. It was my own stuff I was dealing with. I got through it."

"Not without some scars." She said it simply, an acknowledgment.

"Not without some scars."

"You know what it was about?" she asked.

He shook his head, although he thought he had some idea.

"It was the car." She smiled again. "Dad's car. When he died, I was still angry at him, and I don't think I really dealt with our relationship. At first I felt the car was just a car, part of my inheritance, almost an apologetic gift from him for hurting me so much."

"He hurt you?" Rich felt his hand tighten on hers, almost imperceptibly.

Heather shook her head. "Not physically. Emotionally. And it wasn't his fault. His stroke made his life miserable, and so he made everyone else miserable."

"And the car?"

"I have to back up a bit," she said. "When I was a teenager, my dad was very jealous. He automatically hated any boy I got involved with. He demanded that I conform to his rules about how late I could stay out, where I could go, and all that. He never let me have a car while I was living at home. My dates had to come to the door for me, and he didn't make it pleasant for any of them."

Rich nodded. "I only have a son, and he's in high school. Sometimes I'm scared for him. I don't know how I'd feel if I had a daughter."

"Of course I resented my dad, at least until I was in college and no longer living at home. Then things smoothed out between us, and he began to treat me like his little princess again. That's when he promised me his car—his symbol of something or other, I'm not sure exactly. But I knew it was his pride and joy."

"His royal chariot?" Rich smiled.

Heather returned the smile. "Something like that. But that day you and I went for our Sunday drive, I began to feel guilty and ashamed. I guess it was a throwback to my adolescence. I tried to shake it off, but—well, you know how that day ended."

"It rained." Something in the back of Rich's mind noticed his answer. It was like something out of a novel. Layers of meaning summed up in two words.

It wasn't lost on Heather. She smiled, looking into his eyes. "It was on top of everything else—his death, that I felt partly at least responsible for, and a sense that I had abandoned Paul, too."

"A broken marriage dies a long time."

She nodded. "I was in a women's support group—a grief group, really—right after Dad died. My therapist had recommended it. Something that came to me, listening to those other women, was that our primary relationships, first with our parents and then with our lovers and spouses, are always with us, as long as we live. Our brains are rewired by them."

"Yeah, I can see that," he said.

"When I came down here from Minnesota, I thought I was starting over. One doesn't ever start over."

He smiled and squeezed her hand, this time deliberately. "True," he said.

She put her other hand on his. "It's a lot more complicated than what I've told you, but the rest can wait. I want to hear how you have been."

"Getting by," he said.

Heather laughed. "Sure you have. I can see it in your eyes."

Rich sighed. "Time for honesty, eh?"

"Yes. Please?"

"I've been a wreck. I went from wanting to follow you up to Minnesota, to hating you for deceiving me and then abandoning me, to grieving over some lost fantasy."

"You thought I deceived you?" There was something—almost horror—in her eyes.

"Heather, you *didn't* deceive me. It was my fantasy of you. You were like my angel, come to earth just for me." Rich felt his throat tightening.

She picked up his hand and held it against her cheek. "Oh, Rich," she said in a whisper.

"I thought it was women who dreamed of a knight in shining armor come to whisk them off." He grinned.

"But I did abandon you," she said. "I feel such shame about that!"

Rich leaned toward her. "Haven't you had enough shame in your life?"

Heather took a deep breath. "You're right. I'm doing it again. I am sorry I had to leave, but I had to."

"Of course you did. I didn't know how to help you. Did you go to your therapist?"

"Yes. I called her, and she said 'Come right now.' It took me five minutes to decide, and twelve hours to knock on her door."

Rich felt a lot more relaxed than he had when she arrived. Heather no longer had that super-competent, super-confident exterior that had intrigued him at the same time it intimidated him. But this vulnerable, wounded person in front of him was still the same person he had come to love, only stripped of her masks. "How is it," he said, "that a few weeks ago I would have slammed the door in your face, and right now I just want to hold you?"

Her face showed sadness, even as she smiled. "Let's go slowly, can we?" she said. "My work on myself isn't done, and maybe yours isn't, either."

"You remember that conversation we had the night we met and the next morning? About whether adults are ever 'finished?' It feels like we're in a whole new phase of that process."

"Yes," she said, "we each said that we didn't feel finished, but the world thinks we ought to be."

"You know what's incredible to me? How my emotional state can change so completely in a short time, when the so-called 'facts' of the situation are not altered in the least."

"Tell me what that means to you." Her eyes were just a little brighter.

"When you sat down," he said, "I was guarded and, frankly, not very hopeful about us, about our relationship. We've been talking for half an hour—just words passing between us—and now I feel as though I'm in a different world."

Heather smiled. "Just words? Have you not noticed all the other things, like gestures, facial expressions, tone of voice, even the timing of our speaking, that have been passing between us right along with the words? Excuse me for getting technical, but you've read 'Mindsight.' Our right hemispheres have been even busier talking to each other in the same half-hour."

Rich grinned. "You're the psychologist. You pay attention to such things."

"Come on, Rich. You do, too."

"That first morning we had together," he said, "I noticed that you were not only watching me, you were listening to me, too. I haven't had that experience much in my life. As someone put it, I felt *felt*."

"And I have been feeling felt right here, talking with you now."

They both finished their drinks.

"What was it like, Heather, that day when you walked out of my apartment? I kept reaching for you, and you weren't there."

She had that sad smile again. "I wasn't there, for me or for you. I felt overwhelmed, and I couldn't even describe what I was feeling."

"I'm glad you had the presence to call your therapist."

"So am I."

They looked at each other for a few minutes. Then Rich said, "When you first began to talk a little while ago, you said it was the car. I thought I understood, but I wonder if there is more."

"I said I thought the car was a symbol of something or other to him, but when it was mine I thought it was just a car. Talking with my therapist, I realized that it was a symbol to me, too, a symbol of my father, and he was criticizing me for having feelings for you. That's when I began to feel shame. It was on such an unconscious level that I couldn't see it at the time. All I felt was the shame, and it didn't make sense to me because you and I were not doing anything wrong."

"Wow," he said softly. "It really did rain that day, didn't it?"

"I sold the car," she said. "I couldn't bear to look at it any more. I sold it with the iPod and all the music we were listening to."

"It's kind of a shame," he said. "It was a nice car."

"To you, it was just a nice car. To you, my dad might have seemed just a nice guy."

"A prince, you said."

She smiled. "Yes. Sometimes I felt that. My adolescence was a difficult time for us."

"My adolescence was a difficult time for my mother and me, too."

"I remember," she said. "In your little book, you mentioned the difficulty she had with you. And then you brought that relationship along to college in your sister."

"In spades," he laughed. "I could tell my mother things, after I left home, that I didn't have the guts to tell my sister."

Heather took his hand again. "Rich, how are you, right now?"

"I feel like *we* are better. And that means that I'm better."

"Same here," she said. "I asked before if we could move slowly, you and I. Is that still okay with you?"

"My head says yes, but my heart says, 'Full speed ahead.'"

"Yeah, I know the feeling. But I'm trying to keep my head in charge, at least for a while. I'm no longer shaking, but way down deep there's still some fear."

Rich picked up the check and laid a couple of dollars on the table. He looked at Heather, and she nodded.

"Mirror neurons," he thought as they stood and walked toward the cashier.

Thirteen

When Rich awoke the next morning, he lay awake for a long while thinking about Heather and about who she had become to him. It was not that she was his female knight in shining armor or his angel, as he had supposed in his grief; she embodied the parts of himself *that he yearned to be*—to become. He saw himself as pure envy. She had all the qualities that he felt he lacked. He had enjoyed being with her as if she were himself fully developed. When she fell apart that day in his apartment, it was the personal renovation he had briefly experienced, crumbling, in the words he wrote in his journal, "like a sand sculpture on the beach, just another fragile human like himself, no more able to figure out the tragedies of life than he was." It was not only she but he who was so fragile.

He burst into tears. All the years he had spent wanting salvation, wanting to rise out of the ashes of his experiences like the Phoenix, to be able to look at himself—for once—as whole. All the tears he had not allowed himself to shed since his father had died and he was suddenly the man of the family; since Becky had left him, judging him inadequate as a husband and father. In the end, he was only *this*—this shell of a human being, hollow, *headpiece filled with straw*, as Eliot had put it, *alas*. He lay in his bed and sobbed and sobbed with grief.

He must have slept, for the sun was high overhead, lighting only the windowsill in his bedroom. He got out of bed and, shaking, made his way to the bathroom. In the shower he realized that he was no longer sodden with grief; there was almost no emotion left in him. His body felt the fatigue of it. His mind seemed strangely clear.

Words came back to him, of his student that day on campus, when Rich had asked him to "describe this *thing*, whatever it is that you used to think is your self?" George had replied, "It feels more like a *song* than a thing."

"I am not a thing," he said aloud as he dried his body, "I am a song—I am a song to be sung, along with Walt Whitman. I am not finished; I am not yet altogether *sung*."

Suddenly, it came to him, the old Simon and Garfunkel song Punky's Dilemma, and he sang: "*Wish I was a Kellogg's Cornflake, Floatin' in my bowl takin' movies, ...*"

"Does the cornflake have a self?" he asked the bathroom mirror, "or is it an illusion?" A ridiculous question, that seemed exactly the right question to ask. "I can play a knight in shining armor, or an angel, or a cornflake floating in a bowl of milk, taking movies."

He chuckled at the lame joke as he dressed and went into the kitchen for his breakfast. Glancing at the clock, he realized that it was late. Picking up his phone, he punched the speed-dial for his graduate assistant. "I'm running late," he said, "give them a question to work on together—something like, *Do I have a self?* And make them sing it."

"What?"

"Nothing. See you in a bit."

The End

The David

"Oh, my God!" Terry whispered to me as we followed the young man to the back of the house where our host was hanging some fresh photographic prints on a clothesline strung from a hanging lamp at one end and a drapery hook at the other.

Anthony Frisch had invited us to visit for a couple of days at his lakeside home early in October. He was busy, he had said, on a new book of photographs, but he needed some distractions from friends to keep the project from becoming a burden. We both thought he had another reason.

The photographs were, of course, of the beautiful young man who had met us at the door. Blond, evenly tanned in shorts and a tank top, Randy had a ready smile and an all-but-incomprehensible Scandinavian accent. Tony provided the necessary interpretation as we exchanged greetings. "Randy came to me as a model at the beginning of summer after school let out," Tony said, "but he's been so helpful I'm keeping him on as an assistant, as long as Immigration will let us."

Terry was obviously enchanted. "He's gorgeous!" she gushed, shaking the boy's hand and bestowing on him her widest smile. "A perfect David!"

"The original David probably didn't have blond hair," Tony said, "but he's got the body."

Randy blushed, and murmured something I didn't catch.

"You're still doing wet photography?" I asked, to tease Tony and shift the conversation, which was making me, as well as Randy, a little uncomfortable.

Tony smiled. He and I had traded friendly barbs about photographic processes for several years after I had made the move to digital. "The printer's lab," he said, "will scan these into their computerized system, and the result will be a lot cleaner than if I'd try to shoot them originally with your gigabyte so-called camera."

I browsed along the clothesline of prints, keeping my hands behind my back. "You do good work, my man."

"After forty years in the darkroom, I'm not about to change now," he said. "Thank you."

"Oh, I'd love to watch you do it," said Terry, following me along the line of prints.

"Sure, but let's have lunch first." Tony nodded to Randy, who disappeared into the kitchen. "This kid's a better cook than my old mother," Tony said.

Terry walked to the window wall overlooking the lake. Fall colors were near their peak, with golds and reds reflecting off the still water. "What a wonderful view," she said. "If I lived here, I'd be shooting those colors all the time."

"Actually, every morning I get up and sit in that chair right there and soak up the view. I'm so glad I picked the east side of the lake so I can see all the color in the morning."

Terry glanced at the kitchen, then in a stage whisper, asked, "How did you *find* him?"

Tony grinned. "Pure luck," he said. "I just put out a call at the art academy for a young male model, and he showed up."

"Tell me—did you decide on the title of the book before you saw him, or after?" She browsed along the line of hanging prints, examining each one closely.

"Well, I knew I wanted to do one of a young man, after the success of *Venus,*" he said, gesturing toward a folio book on the coffee table.

Just then, Randy appeared at the door. "*Frukost,*" he announced, "Lunch."

The three of us moved around the partition and took seats at the glass-topped table laden with an impressive assortment of foods—a fragrant quiche, sliced meats and cheeses, warm, crusty bread, fruits and wine. After filling our water glasses, Randy sat with us.

"Beautiful!" Terry said to him.

He grinned at her. "*Tack.*"

"He might have baked the bread," said Tony, "except we didn't get up soon enough."

"I presume you've put together a comp of your book." I said to Tony.

"Yes. It's in the studio. I'll get it out in a few minutes.

"You write the copy for it, too?" asked Terry.

"Of course he does," I said. He's a better writer than I am."

Tony chuckled. "I don't have to dream up a plot for my stories. I just follow the pictures."

"The *Venus* story is pretty solid," I said.

Terry smiled at Tony. "She was *so sensuous!*"

"She was another student at the academy. I'd worked with her before, and loved the way she projected herself. Judith was definitely the inspiration for that book."

I tasted the wine. "Wow," I said. "Wonderful!"

"My wine shop saved a case for me" said Tony. "He knew I'd like it. A lot of Chilean white is astringent for me, but this is the best."

We ate and chatted. I noticed that Tony often glanced at Randy, I supposed to make sure he was comfortable. It was difficult to include Randy in our conversation because his English was hard to understand, but Terry smiled at him a lot, whether she was speaking to him or not.

I remembered my father, who used to complain about his hearing difficulties isolating him from people. "It's like everybody else is speaking a foreign language," he had said. "I hear them, but can't translate the sounds into meaning." I thought of him now, watching Randy struggling to keep up with the conversation. He could understand the words we used, but not at the rate we spoke them. I kept reminding myself to slow down. Terry, on the other hand, habitually spoke so fast that a lot of times I had to ask her to repeat herself simply because my brain couldn't keep up. She said she had to speak quickly because that's how her words came to her, and if she slowed down she'd lose what she was trying to say.

Randy, poor fellow, had to translate each word of English from his native tongue before he could say it, and often he'd stop and shrug, embarrassed. Tony could follow him better than we could, and frequently translated a word in the middle of Randy's sentences. Terry, enchanted, hung on Randy's every word, and I couldn't tell if she understood what he was saying or simply wanted him to keep talking, in love with the sounds he made.

When we had finished our coffee—exceptional, of course— Tony asked Terry if she still wanted to watch him make a print.

"I'd love to."

Tony's darkroom was not very large, and the four of us gathered there in the dim yellow light, touching bodies as Tony readied a negative in the enlarger. At least, I was touching Terry, and she was between Randy and me. *Have fun, my love,* I thought.

"Your cover photos are always in color," I said to Tony, "but your stories are black and white."

"This print has to be in black and white," he explained, "or you wouldn't be able to watch me work. These two books, *Venus* and *David,* are in black and white because that conveys the idea of sculpture more. Color photographs give sculpture a false sense—in my estimation, anyway. And I'm trying to suggest sculpture in these two books. The only reason the cover shots are in color is because the publisher demands it."

"Yes, I've seen your other books, and most of them are in color," said Terry.

"The whole world is in color," Tony said. "We see black and white photographs as something from the past, just as we do old statuary. And there's a thematic simplicity to them, no matter how incredible the images—think of Ansel Adams and his photographs of Yosemite. I've shot those same scenes in color, and mine are just postcard pictures."

Terry, now engrossed in what Tony was doing, leaned over the edge of the sink to see the print gradually emerging in the developer. I could feel her muscles tighten. "Incredible!" she whispered.

"Yes, it is," said Randy, peering alongside Terry, his face almost touching hers, and then he said something in Swedish.

Tony turned and smiled at him. "*Tack*," he said, "thank you."

We all backed up to allow Tony to move the print from developer to stop bath. In a few minutes the print had gone through the row of trays and was washing in a large tray of running water. "Okay," Tony said, "that's the show. We can all get some fresh air."

It was noticeably cooler out of the darkroom. Tony picked up the book comp in the studio and Randy disappeared into the kitchen to clean up the dishes. The rest of us sat in the great room, now bright from the sunlight reflected off the lake outside.

"When we visited Florence," I said to Tony, "Terry went positively gaga over the David."

She laughed. "I did. It was like he reached out and grabbed my heart."

"Your heart," I echoed, smiling at her.

"Well, you know what I mean."

"Yes," said Tony, "we do."

"I was surprised at how big he is," I said. "Seventeen feet tall."

"Originally," said Tony, "he was supposed to be placed on the roof of the cathedral, along with some other statues, but when he was finished they didn't have a way to hoist him up there. He weighs something like six tons, so they put him in the middle of the square instead."

"They told us that's why his head is so large," added Terry, "because you were supposed to be looking at him from far down on the street."

"Tony," I asked, "are you distorting the perspective of Randy to get the same effect?"

Tony grinned. "No," he said, "most people don't see the original as distorted, but they would if my photographs showed that."

"You're not keeping him in the same positions as the original," Terry observed.

"No, that would get pretty boring. In each view, I altered his pose just enough to make that image seem real." Tony opened the comp book, a hand-made proof copy with pasted-in text blocks and rough prints on each page. Occasional bold marker notes directed the placement of elements on the page. Even at this stage, the book was impressive. Terry leafed through it, with me watching over her shoulder.

While we were paging through the comp, Tony disappeared into the studio and returned with a small camera. A true photographer, he shot a dozen views of us from different angles. It reminded me of many years before, when I had become enamored by photography, making hundreds of exposures during family gatherings and parties, and then wondering what to do with all the negatives. Usually, none were worth printing, but just the practice shooting probably made them worth the film I exposed. I'd long since moved away from photography into writing because I could make a better living at that, keeping my cameras for recreation. Tony never lost his passion for images. He'd been taking photographs since he was in high school, and had paid his way through college selling images to anyone he could persuade to pose for him. His portraits were stunning.

When I thought of taking portraits, it was always of women and children. To me the female body was as enticing to my camera as it was to my hands. Photographs of women and girls had fed my fantasies since adolescence. Tony didn't seem to have that bias. I admired his male portraits and nudes, but they didn't move me the way females did.

"Wonder what it is," I wondered aloud, "that makes that piece of stone so emotionally compelling."

"I wish I knew," laughed Terry. "If someone could bottle it, they could make a fortune. I'm usually drawn more by scent than visual beauty—it was like I could *smell that statue.*"

"I think it's because it's stone," said Tony. "A statue has an effect on us that's primal, no matter what the image. Something like the Grand Canyon or Half Dome at Yosemite— they just stun us the first time we see them. At least part of that, seems to me, is like somebody wrote, they are so beyond us, so uninvolved in our petty little lives. They live forever, and we are just these temporary little creatures running around for a while and then dying like the flowers. Beauty isn't really the word for that; it's more than beauty."

Randy was listening carefully to Tony, trying to hang onto his words, trying to understand the abstractions. When Tony paused, he looked at Randy and grinned. "Sorry, Randy. That was a lot to translate into Swedish, wasn't it?"

"Like maybe being up North," Randy ventured, "and being over—overwhelmed by nothing but white?"

Tony smiled at him. "Exactly. That's it, exactly."

"Impersonal. Like the Milky Way." said Randy.

"But the statue of David is not impersonal, is it?" I asked.

"Maybe it wasn't to Michelangelo," said Tony. "But to us, it's monumental—that's not personal."

"Why," Terry asked, "is my reaction so personal? There's nothing like *monumental* about it." She smiled at me.

"Unavailable?" I asked.

She shrugged.

Tony sat back in his chair. "Isn't most of this, what we're talking about, isn't most of it unconscious?"

"Non-verbal, at least," I said. "Terry's reaction to the David was right from her gut."

Terry made a little grunting sound.

I grinned at her. "See? Non-verbal."

She turned and punched me gently on my arm.

"But what you said about the Grand Canyon being *uninvolved*—that reminds me of somebody. Maybe it was Diane Ackerman."

"Bingo." Tony got up and went to his bookcase. He took an ebook reader off the shelf and searched through it. "Here it is," he said, and then read

> *Most of all, the canyon is so vastly uninvolved with us, with mercy or pity. ... we would like to keep the world as animate as it was for our ancestors. But that is difficult when facing a vision as rigidly dead as the Grand Canyon. It is beautiful and instructive and calming, but it is also the absolute, intractable "other" that human beings face from birth to death, the sharp counterpoint to our lives.*

He scanned ahead. "a vast, incomprehensible landform that both humbles and exalts."

"Like Randy said," I offered, "like the Milky Way."

Randy smiled at me. He was hanging on.

Terry was frowning. "I still don't get why the David is so visceral to me."

"Maybe that's just how you react to that *incomprehensible, that humbles and exalts*," I said. "Do you remember what you felt at the Grand Canyon last year?"

Her brow stayed knitted for a moment, then suddenly cleared. "Oh my god!" she whispered. I felt like I had solved the riddle of the universe. Tony grinned at me.

"I couldn't wait until we could get to our room and make love," she said to Tony. "That is weird."

That night in bed in Tony's guest room, Terry and I talked quietly about Tony and Randy. It was obvious to both of us that there was a strong connection between them, something we'd not anticipated. Tony had been married years before, a marriage that at the time seemed strong enough, but they had split up after a few years, and Tony had lived alone ever since. We'd met several of his models, and noticed what appeared to be affection between them. Terry had wondered when he was going to settle down with one of them.

Earlier, Tony had brought out a number of his reference books that he had used in planning this book. He had studied not only the existing photographs of the David and other contemporary sculptures, but the history of most of them.

"Maybe he has the same deep response to it that you do," I said to Terry. "It just comes out in a different way. He has to express it in his photographs."

"I felt really turned on in the darkroom," she said. "Watching that image emerge in the developer almost made me wet my pants."

I kissed her, gently. "I remember feeling that way in the darkroom when I was a kid."

"Why is that so erotic?"

"Because you are turned on so easily," I said, kissing her again.

She turned toward me and pressed against me.

I had been sound asleep. I hadn't even missed her presence until I woke to her scent next to me. She wasn't cuddled up to me as she usually slept, but lay still, breathing quietly. I knew where she had been. My heart was pounding; I was sure she must have felt it as well, but in a few minutes her breathing changed subtly, and I sensed she had fallen asleep. My body was charged, the blood in my temples throbbing, sweat forming on my forehead. I couldn't lie there any longer with the visions in my head of her with him. I finally slipped out of bed and, retrieving my robe from its hook on the door, went quietly out into the great room.

The only light there was from a heater in the fish tank, but it was enough to allow me to get around without bumping into furniture. I found a small lamp on the mahogany bar. The bottle of cognac still sat where we had left it after our nightcap. I poured a generous amount into a snifter and sat in the big overstuffed chair. The black windows revealed nothing outside. My body was still tense, my heart racing. I could hear the blood coursing through my ears.

It was inevitable, of course. I could tell, when we went to bed, that Terry was aroused by the David. It wasn't me she had wanted. Her lust had echoed the time in Florence five years earlier, after we had been to the museum where he stood, frozen in marble for five hundred years waiting just for her. Tonight, just as that night in Florence, she had made love to him, not me. I didn't blame her—I loved her passion, her wild enthusiasm, her feline grace. But it was hard knowing, sometimes, that I was less an object of her desire than a vehicle.

Ordinarily, Terry was the model of faithfulness. Most of the times we made love, she was completely with me. We could joke about her obsession with Michelangelo's statue. She had bought a tiny replica of it before we left Florence, and it still stood in a prominent place on a bookshelf at home. When Tony had written us about his latest project, a coffee-table book of photographs titled, "The David," Terry was exuberant. "I can't wait to see it!" she effused. I had that mixture of feelings that I felt sometimes when she and I were out in public. Men ogled her, understandably. She glowed with the awareness even as she avoided acknowledging their stares. I felt pride, jealousy and amusement all at the same time. It's the price I pay, I reasoned, for claiming such a creature as my own. One can't possess another, not really.

The brandy gradually took hold; I could feel my body relaxing, the images of Terry and Randy fading. Outside the great windows, dawn was approaching.

I awoke confused. There was blue-gray daylight outside, causing the little lamp on the bar to glow very yellow. Curled up on the sofa under an afghan, Terry was watching me, her face streaked with dried tears. We just looked at each other for a long time before she mouthed the word "sorry." Neither of us spoke; there seemed no need for words, nothing to be said, nothing to be done. When the others arose, we'd have breakfast together, and then we'd leave. Terry would avoid looking at Randy, and he'd likely avoid looking at either of us. Tony would undoubtedly catch it all.

Sunlight touched the very tops of the trees on the hills across the lake. Mists lay on the water over where springs that fed the lake changed the temperature. Terry stood up, carefully folded the afghan and placed it over the back of the sofa, and meeting my eyes once more, returned to our bedroom. I heard the shower running.

I watched the line of sunlight proceed down the gold, yellow and brown hillside in the distance, lighting up the room with the warmth of an autumn morning. I got up from the chair and went into the bedroom to wait for the shower.

The End

Beach Story

The lake was dead calm. Sounds carried clearly across the water—geese, maybe, splashing in the shallows, a boat motor, somewhere on the other side of the peninsula that divided the lake, throttled back and died. A dog far away barked twice, and a loon called in the distance.

The two women sat silently watching the clouds darkening over the trees on the far side of the lake. A few wisps of orange remained from the spectacular sunset that had drawn them to sit down a half-hour earlier as they had been preparing to leave. The air was still. The day had been warm, and scents from the shoreline—wild, earthy scents—drifted lazily past them. The only sound was a woman's voice from across the lake. They couldn't hear her words, but there was laughter. And then it was quiet again.

The sound of a splash startled them. A figure was pulling herself out of the water onto their dock. The two looked at each other—it was hard to see the expression on their faces, the light was so far gone. They turned and watched the swimmer stand, pick up a towel and dry herself, then slip into sandals and a light wrap, throw the towel across her shoulders, and come up from the dock toward them.

"She's not . . ." was cut off as the woman said something to them that they couldn't quite make out.

Then as she approached their chairs, "Water's warm," she said, "wonderful."

One of them laughed, but both were trying hard to make out the woman's face. She lifted a corner of the towel and fluffed her hair with it, tilting and tossing her head in a quick gesture that let her hair sweep across her face. She was a stranger to them, and younger.

Dolores waved, her hand just off her lap, and said, "Hi."

"This is my first dip in the lake," the woman said. "I just moved in Friday."

"Hi, I'm Jean, and this is Dolores. What unit are you in?"

She tilted her head again, reminding Dolores of her little Pomeranian, listening. "You know, I can't remember?" She laughed. "It's on Cambridge Court, down near the end. Ninety-seven something."

"Well, welcome to the co-op," said Dolores. "What's your name?"

"Oh, sorry. I'm Katherine Baker."

"You like to swim," said Jean. It wasn't a question.

"Oh, yes! I've been looking forward to getting into the lake."

"We didn't see you go in. We've been down here for over an hour."

Katherine turned and pointed toward a distant beach. "I have a friend who lives over there." She laughed, a light, charming laugh. "He didn't expect me to pop up on his dock!"

It was getting quite dark by then. Jean stood up. "We're all lucky the mosquitoes are not out yet."

She and Dolores prepared to walk up toward the parking lot. "Can we give you a lift? Doesn't look like you have a car here."

"Oh, thank you, but no. My place is right over there." She gestured again. "You can almost see it from here. I love to walk."

"If you go up through the field, watch your step. There are animal holes you can trip in."

The three of them walked to Jean's car. "Nice meeting you," said Katherine, continuing up the driveway.

"Yes. We'll see you again, I'm sure."

In the car, Jean turned to Dolores. "She swam all the way over there and back?"

"She's lucky she made it back before it was too dark to find our dock."

"You know, she wasn't wearing . . ." Jean reached toward the ignition and turned the key, and in that instant before the overhead light turned off, their eyes met.

"You have the nerve to do that?" murmured Dolores.

"I do if you do."

"You're on."

They stared at each other in the darkness, knowingly.

"Don't tell anyone."

"No."

The End

Perfection

He stood beside her, watching her in the mirror as she put on her makeup. "I thought you said you weren't creative," he said. "You create a painting every day."

She smiled at him. "I do, don't I?" She touched the thin brush repeatedly to the little lashes along the bottom of one eye. "I think about how to change it all the time."

"You never say, like God, 'It is good!'?"

"Don't be silly," she said. "It's never good enough. It's just the best I can do with what I've got."

He chuckled.

"And it's never as good—*I'm* never as beautiful as I once was."

"That's a matter of opinion," he said. "But I guess none of us are as good as we once were. Reminds me of an old cartoon I saw a long time ago—a guy is hovering over a woman, saying, "I'm not as good as I once was, but I'm as good once as I ever was."

She gave him a wry smile but said nothing as she leaned toward the mirror, working on the other eye.

"I hate to admit that I'm not as good even once as I once was."

"That's a matter of opinion," she said.

He looked at his watch.

"Can't hurry art," she said, lip-liner poised over her lips.

He patted her silk-covered behind and left the bathroom.

They'd been married twenty-five years, most of them good. And he still thought of Diane as attractive—more than most of the women in their circle of friends. It amused him, though, how much time she took applying makeup every day. And when they were going out in the evening, she took extra pains with it. He especially liked what she did with her eyes.

Waiting for her gave him time for a drink. He took the frosty bottle of Boodles from the freezer and poured a little into a glass. Leaning against the door frame in the bathroom, he sipped and watched her.

"Did you fix me a drink?" she asked.

"You want some of this?" He extended the glass toward her. She turned and carefully sipped—then made a face. "Oooh!"

"I didn't think so." He wiped lipstick off the rim of the glass and drank the rest of it. "Tell me what you want, and I'll fix it."

She gathered the tools of her beauty and stuffed them into a flowered bag. "We don't have time," she said, and pushed past him into the bedroom.

"I'll get the car out," he said, "unless you want to drive."

"I can't drive in these heels!"

At the door, he grabbed the keys to her Sonata. She wouldn't want to be seen in his old Corolla. Besides, her car was a lot more comfortable—and clean. She was as fastidious about her car as she was about her face. She had long ago given up suggesting to him that he get his car detailed. Or better, that he replace it with something more respectable. Rust was metastasizing all over it, but it ran well.

"I like that jacket," she said to him as he drove.

"You should—you bought it for me."

"I like to see you well dressed."

He grinned. "Am I another piece of your art?"

"Maybe an accessory."

"Your escort."

"Yes."

He glanced over at her. She had a pleasant, relaxed look on her face. "I'm kidding, Dennis," she said without turning her head.

He had mixed feelings right then. He knew she was gently teasing him, and that meant she felt good about the two of them. But something in his gut responded, a disappointment, perhaps. In all their years of marriage, only rarely did she actually complain about something personal in him. Sure, they had disagreements now and then, and issues that they had informally agreed to avoid, like politics. He was usually convinced that she genuinely liked him. Once in a while, though, he felt something in the way she spoke to him, something dark, and he was afraid to confront it, or her, in those moments.

"Sally tell you how many people would be there?" he asked, pushing the feeling away.

"She said twelve were all she could seat at the table."

There were a number of cars parked near the small but elegant home when they arrived. The hostess, in a flowing gown that went perfectly with the house, greeted them warmly.

"Sorry we're late," Diane said, kissing the air next to the woman's cheek.

"We're just relaxing with drinks," Sally said. "There's another couple still to come. How are you, Dennis?"

"I'm fine," he said. "You look stunning."

"Thank you. Jack is in the pantry mixing drinks."

"Dry white wine for me," his wife said to him as she followed the hostess into another room.

Jack mixed him a gigantic martini, and with a flourish thrust three big olives into it, impaled on a miniature sword. "Twist?"

"No, thanks. How's it going, Jack?"

"Great. How about you?"

"Great."

Jack gestured with his head. "Wait 'till you see who's here."

"Somebody I know?"

"You will, Dennis, you will."

Dennis took a sip. "Perfect," he said. "Diane wants white wine."

Another guest crowded into the little pantry. "Heard I could get a drink here," Randy said.

"You certainly can! What's your pleasure?" Jack pointed to Dennis's martini and raised his eyebrows.

"No, I can't handle those. Just a beer, please."

Jack opened a bottle of Corona and poured it into a frosted glass from the freezer. Dennis noticed that his face was just a little pink. It was clear that he had been sampling his wares, but his coordination was still good.

"We can join the others," Jack said. "I think we're all here." He handed Dennis the glass of wine for Diane.

In the parlor, Jack collected a couple of chairs from an adjoining room, and the assembly of friends sat cheerfully exchanging small talk. Jack caught Dennis's eye and nodded his head slightly toward the opposite side of the room.

He was right. She sat upright in the straight chair, her brown hair falling across bare shoulders, even a few strands finding their way into the cleavage revealed by her dress. Dennis's attention was taken away from her by Sally, the hostess, who began introducing people to each other. He knew most of them, but the goddess was a delightful surprise. As his eyes swept the line of guests, he saw Diane watching him intently, a faint smile around her mouth.

"Micci—spelled M-i-c-c-i—is a model," Sally told the others. "Isn't she gorgeous!"

"Sally has told me about you all—good friends," Micci said. "I feel honored to be here with you."

"Our company has been using Micci in a new advertising program," Sally said. "They brought her here all the way from California. And Rudy is her fiancé."

"Thank you for inviting us," said Rudy, sitting next to the goddess. His tan spoke of Southern California.

Everybody began talking at once, like a recording of a crowd that had been cued up by the audio engineer. Dennis heard a woman, apparently addressing Rudy, say something like 'bodyguard." Rudy just smiled and drained his glass.

"We're about ready to sit down," said Sally over the din. "Please sit boy-girl-boy-girl—and don't sit next to the one you came with!"

The long table was adorned with flowers, with four pairs of wine bottles, one red and one white, completing the decorations. Crystal—thin-edged, with brilliant, diamond-like catchlights—and tableware with gold handles sat beside elegant china place settings.

The martini had muddled Dennis's head, and he wasn't sure where he was supposed to sit. After making sure there were women on both sides of him, he took the first empty chair he came to. A whiff of expensive perfume from his right told him who his neighbor was, but he was afraid to look her way. Across the table, Diane was watching him. She wasn't smiling. Finally, picking up his napkin and spreading it in his lap, he turned and greeted both his neighbors.

Jack circled the table, pouring water. "Help yourselves to the wine," he said.

Dennis had enough presence of mind and (barely) enough steadiness of hand to pour wine for his neighbors and himself. The group was very noisy, and he felt as though he were just this side of "out of control."

Mildred, on his left, was talking across him with Micci. "How long are you going to be in town?" she asked.

Micci's voice was like honey. "Maybe a couple of weeks."

Dennis turned to her, noticing that his voice sounded strained. "Will these all be still photographs, or are they doing video, too?"

"I think there are a couple of sixty-second spots for television," she said, "but there will be a number of print ads."

"Did you always want to model?"

"My dream in the beginning was that it would be a step on a path to acting," she said, smiling at him. "Now tell me about *your* dreams."

He was flustered. "You mean ..."

"Not your night dreams, silly." She was obviously in her element, playing with him as a cat plays with a ball of yarn. Spectacular beauty is power, and his own batteries felt almost gone.

Maybe not quite. "In a minute," he replied, "but you said 'in the beginning'. Does that mean your dream has faded? Or been replaced?"

She smiled again. "I enjoy my work, but I'm conscious that time is passing." She pointed a perfectly shaped fingertip at the corner of her eye. "Any day, now, little crow's feet will appear here. Modeling feels very temporary."

"Crow's feet can be attractive on an actor."

"You're sweet," she said. Noticing that Mildred was following their conversation, Micci leaned in a little to see past Dennis. "Your husband is a smooth talker," she said.

Mildred laughed. "He's not my husband, but yes, he has talent."

"Oh, I'm sorry!"

Dennis glimpsed Diane, across the table, taking it all in. He smiled at her. "Our hostess forbad us to sit next to our spouses," he said.

Mildred gestured toward Diane. "That's his wife, Diane," she laughed.

Micci blushed, and spoke to Diane, "I've misplaced your husband!"

Diane laughed. "If he misbehaves, use a ruler across his knuckles."

"Not at all! He's been a perfect gentleman. You're a lucky woman."

"Yes," Diane said, but her smile seemed to Dennis to be less than enthusiastic.

There was that little tug again in his midsection. To deflect the feeling, he turned to Mildred—safe Mildred. "Weren't you involved in community theater?"

"For a while," she said. "I got sidetracked by children."

"Oh, that sounds like it would be great fun!" said Micci.

"It was."

Food was being passed to Mildred from the other direction, distracting her. Soon everyone at the table was busily dishing up food from the platters and bowls making their way around.

Dennis didn't want to look too carefully at Micci, but he was very curious. He tried to guess her age from her hands, smooth and beautifully groomed. Late twenties, he estimated. Diane took care of her hands, but there was no avoiding the tell-tale signs of middle age. He felt guilty for noticing that. After he had emptied the bottle of white wine into Micci's glass, he excused himself and took the empty to the pantry, where he was sure there would be fresh supplies.

While he was screwing the bottle opener into the cork, Jack came in, carrying a couple more empties. "What'd I tell you?" he said to Dennis. "Luscious!"

Dennis grinned at him. "I'm sitting next to her."

"I saw you! Crowded out Milton!" Jack laughed.

"An accident, really."

"Sure it was! Doesn't she smell good?"

"Takes your breath away."

"In deed." He made two words out of it. "Good luck with Diane later."

When Dennis returned with the fresh bottle of wine, Mildred had moved into his chair to talk with Micci. Seeing him approach, she started to move back, but he gestured to her to stay, and took her seat instead, sitting next to Milton.

Milton just looked at him and grinned.

"More white wine?" Dennis asked, holding the bottle over the other man's glass.

"Your hand is shaking," Milton observed, still grinning.

A while later, Jack tapped on his glass with a spoon. "This is the time when the men usually retire for brandy and cigars, but Sally won't allow smoking within twenty feet of the house. So the brandy and other sweet stuff are in the parlor, for everybody."

The guests noisily made their way into the parlor. After that big martini and a couple of glasses of wine, Dennis thought he should go easy on the liquor, so he filled a glass with ice and tonic water with a twist of lemon to disguise it. His head was still muzzy.

He saw an empty chair next to Diane, and sat there. "Get you a drink?" he asked her.

"No, thank you," his wife said to him, meeting his eyes. "Did you enjoy yourself?"

He glanced around to see if anyone were observing them. "I just took the first seat that was open!" he said. "I didn't even notice it was her next to it."

Diane didn't answer. She was watching someone across the room, and Dennis knew without looking who it was. He put his hand on her knee, where her silk gown divided and fell sensuously along her calf. She moved his hand away without looking at it.

"She's very sweet," said Mildred, who had appeared suddenly before them, holding a small glass of liqueur.

Diane looked up and smiled. "She seems to be," she said.

"She's interested in community theater."

Diane glanced around, then said quietly, "I hate her!"

Mildred laughed. "I know what you mean."

Dennis took a deep breath, trying to still the growing knot in his gut. Mildred moved away to talk to someone else.

Then She sat down on the other side of Diane. (There was also an empty chair next to him.) "We had begun to talk about our dreams," Micci said to Diane, but making eye contact with Dennis.

"You have dreams?" Diane was being polite.

"Acting, But Dennis didn't tell me his yet. We were interrupted." Micci and Diane held each other's eyes for a moment. "And I want to hear about yours."

Diane was flustered. The hardness that Dennis heard in her voice before was gone. "I think they are all around our children," she said. "Future grandchildren."

Micci laughed, and music played. "No, I mean for you," she said. "What dreams did you have before?"

Diane looked down at her hands. "Before children?"

"Yes."

"I wanted to dance," Diane said, looking up at Micci. Right at the end, her voice caught.

"Oh, wonderful! Ballet? Or what?"

A smile grew on Diane's face—the first smile Dennis had seen since before dinner. She nodded.

Micci turned to Dennis. "Now, your turn!" Laughter modulated the words.

It caught him off guard, and he stammered, "Well—I guess flying."

"In an airplane?"

He shrugged. "What other way is there?" When she laughed, he regretted his words. "Yes. I always wanted to fly."

Micci stood and turned to face them. "I hope you both get to have your dreams," she said, taking a hand of each. "Now, there are people here I haven't met yet. Please excuse me?"

As she moved away, Dennis looked at Diane. Her face was softer, and her eyes seemed to be looking at something far away.

Later, as they drove home in the dark, neither spoke for a long time. Then he said, "You okay?"

Diane gave a little laugh. "She's no stranger to Dale Carnegie."

"She's probably used to being among high-powered strangers."

"She makes me feel frumpy."

Dennis glanced at her. "She reminds me, too."

"Reminds you?"

"I'm not thirty any more, either." He watched the tail lights of the car ahead of them.

"Men have it so easy!" she said. "You age so gently."

"Is that why you've been gloomy tonight?" He smiled, trying to break the mood—his feeling as though he had been doing something wrong, and her feeling the ravages of comparison.

"I see these gorgeous young women on television and it doesn't bother me. It's meeting one in the flesh ..."

"Well, I have to deal with coming up against bronze beach gods like Rudy," he said.

"Oh, come on! I didn't see that you had even noticed him. He didn't bother you!"

He smiled again. "It's true. I felt guilty about not at least acknowledging him. Maybe we should have done the cigars and brandy thing after dinner. I could have asked him what his dreams are."

"That was so superficial!" Diane said. "She didn't really want to know!"

"Sure it was. But it pulled both of us in for a minute. I'll be honest—I was flattered."

"If I asked you what your dreams are, I would be sincere."

"You know what my dreams are—or were."

"She didn't care! She was just making small talk. Hollywood small talk!"

"Diane, are you put out because she touched something in you with her question, and then walked away?"

She looked at him. "Do I look like I could ever be a dancer?"

"Is that what's wrong?"

"I always wanted to be, but I always knew I wasn't built for it."

"To dream the impossible dream?" He suddenly felt her despair. Turning on the four-way blinkers, he pulled the car to the side of the road and stopped. He turned to face her.

She looked at him with a wry smile. "Something like that," she said quietly.

"I used to have a dream like that," he said. "I wanted to be a film maker. I wanted to make meaningful documentary films."

"What stopped you?"

"I realized that I couldn't compete with the kids just coming out of school. I should have started in my twenties."

"When we were busy raising kids of our own."

In the dim light he could see her face, her eyes looking at him softly. "You didn't mention that," she said, "when Micci asked you about your dreams."

He looked out through the windshield. "I said flying, because that wasn't my impossible dream." The last couple of words threatened to stick in his throat.

"You can always fly."

"Yes."

"Our lives are handed to us," she said, taking his hand, "and we do the best we can with what we've got. It's never perfection."

"I was part of that life handed to you," he said. "an ordinary man, with an ordinary weakness for feminine beauty." He smiled at her. "But utter devotion to one."

She smiled back. "Yes, I know," she said. "Let's go home."

.

The End

Audacity

He'd seen her in the gym a couple of times before, but he hadn't paid much attention until he happened to follow her on the overhead press machine and realized that she was pressing forty pounds more than he could. She didn't look that muscular. It was just that he was badly out of shape. Tickling the clit on his laptop all day didn't build muscles. She wiped the machine down and went on to the next one, not even glancing his way.

He moved the weights around, feeling like a carnival guy trying to confuse his mark about which shell the token lay under. There was nobody in the room other than her and him— why should he be self-conscious here? She sure wasn't paying any attention to him. Usually during the day there were only retirees in the gym, not working-age people. Today the place was nearly deserted.

He managed five extra counts on the press. His shoulders ached from the strain. Trying to ignore her, he made the rounds of the machines as he always did, and returned his log to the rack. He wiped his neck with a towel and headed for the drinking fountain, feeling righteous. Physical effort never appealed to him, and he wouldn't be here except that his doctor threatened him with physical therapy if he didn't begin regular workouts on his own. Finishing a workout gave him satisfaction—he'd show that doctor.

The cold water felt good in his throat.

"Place is quiet today," she said from behind him, waiting for him to finish at the fountain.

"Everybody has better things to do, I guess." He turned and stepped back so she could get a drink.

"You don't enjoy it?" When she bent over the fountain he caught a whiff of her woman scent. The back of her tank top was wet, and her shoulders glistened with perspiration. She stood up and grinned at him.

He grinned back. "I flunked gym all the way through high school," he said, "and avoided sports in college."

"But you're here, at least—that's a plus for you."

"For me this isn't fun. I have no discipline. I just know I have to do it."

"What would be fun for you?" She wiped her face with a towel.

He looked at her. "Truly?"

"Yes."

"Sitting in the cabin of a little Cessna at five thousand feet."

"Oh, you're a pilot?" A nice smile.

"No, just a dreamer. You asked what would be fun."

"I was in the Air Force," she said. "I love to fly, too."

"Oh? Where were you stationed?"

"Middle East, mostly. Were you in?" Her brown hair was tied back. There was a single diamond on the edge of her left ear.

"No," he said. "I thought about it a few times, but there was always some other priority." His other priority was staying as far away from military service as he could, but he didn't want to say that to her. "You've stayed in good shape."

"Thanks," she said, turning away. "I need to shower."

He wanted to wait for her to return, but that would have seemed eager. Grabbing his jacket from the rack by the door, he went home to his book. His muscles ached even though he hadn't broken a sweat.

Back home, thoughts of her interfered with his writing the rest of the day.

Two days later he was on his way to the gym again when his car dropped its muffler in the street. And the following day, he had to attend a meeting in Ann Arbor. And then it was the weekend, when the gym was only open until three. Besides, he hated to take up his weekends doing something that felt like work. On Monday, he managed to get back to his workout routine.

She wasn't there. Disappointed, he went through the whole program without logging any of it. He tried to remember what days he had seen her there, but couldn't. He was on his way out the door when she appeared, coming in.

"I thought you had disappeared!" she said brightly.

"I got side-tracked for a few days."

"You're just leaving?" She seemed disappointed.

"You wouldn't consider playing hooky and having a cup of coffee with me instead, would you?"

She paused, lifted her sports bag up and looked at it thoughtfully, then smiled. "I would consider it," she said.

"Starbucks?"

"It's close."

Together they walked the block to the coffee shop. "I was trying to remember what days I'd seen you at the gym," he said.

"I try to make it on Tuesdays, Thursdays and Saturdays. Sometimes I'm a little off because of work stuff."

The air was mild, so they sat at an outside table with their coffee. He felt slightly giddy from his exertion on the machines. "Those things wear me out," he said, leaning back in his chair.

"Stay with it," she said, grinning. "It'll get easier."

He sipped the hot coffee. "Did you work out regularly in the service?"

She laughed. "I was stationed in Kuwait, and they wouldn't let women off the base except under special circumstances. There was nothing to do but play cards or work out. I got into a contest lifting weights. I could bench-press a hundred eighty pounds when it was over."

"Wow. Bet nobody messed with you."

"Most of them were kids," she said, "I was like their den mother."

He looked at her bare arms. "You don't look like a body builder."

That laugh again. "I've gotten soft in six months."

"I've never been anything else," he said, lifting his arm and flexing his bicep. His embarrassment stayed hidden inside his jacket sleeve.

"What keeps you out of the fitness centers," she asked, "besides hating exercise?"

"I guess you're asking what I do with my time. I write books."

"Oh? Wonderful! What kind of books?" As she drank from the paper cup, her eyes never left his.

"Fiction, mostly," he said. "Novels."

"I think I'm supposed to ask next, are you published? But that's probably not so important, is it? Instead, tell me about your stories."

He pursed his lips. He really didn't want to tell this attractive woman the kinds of stories he wrote. He'd rather be able to tell her they were Hemmingway-type adventure stories, big-game hunters shooting tigers in Africa and rescuing beautiful women. *The Macomber Affair.* "Romance," he said finally.

She looked at him quizzically. "Really?"

"Well, that's not what I start out wanting to write," he said, "but they seem to end up that way."

"I want to read one of them," she said.

He laughed.

"Really. I'm serious." There was a hint of a frown between her eyebrows.

"Okay," he said, "but I want to hear about you. Something besides bench-pressing a hundred eighty pounds—that intimidates me."

She leaned to the side to look at his body. "Yep. Just about one-eighty." And then she laughed. "I'm a bookkeeper."

"Really?"

"Really."

He fingered his empty coffee cup. "Is that your passion?"

She laughed, long and loudly. And then, seriously, "It's a job. My passion is driving, very fast."

"Really?"

"Really."

"Now I'm *really* intimidated." He rubbed the back of his neck, which had begun to hurt.

"Tell you what," she said, chuckling, "you let me read one of your stories and I'll take you for a ride you'll never forget."

"Oh, my god."

"Come on," she said, "you said you love to fly, didn't you?"

"At five thousand feet."

She smiled out of one corner of her mouth. "You mean you want a couple of minutes to think before you die."

A tough lady, he thought. "In the Air Force—what'd you fly—F-Sixteens?"

She grinned. "Only once did I ride in a jet fighter. Scared the shit out of me."

"Whew," he said, wiping his brow. "I can relax a little bit."

He watched her drink the coffee. She held the cup lightly. Red nail polish, perfectly groomed nails. No rings.

"When did you discover this passion to drive fast?" he asked.

She put the cup down and smiled. "Probably on a roller coaster when I was nine."

"You like to be scared."

"I like the feeling of having the hair on the back of my neck stand up. Probably why I joined the Air Force. Pushing through the terror."

"Get into any combat over there?"

"No. I saw enough of the results, though." Her face became serious, and she was quiet for a moment. Then she looked up at him. Her voice was barely above a whisper. "Why do they have to do it?"

"It's romantic."

She seemed shocked. "That wasn't romantic," she said, shuddering slightly.

"No, I don't suppose the results are romantic," he said. "It's the anticipation. Putting yourself on the line."

"Pushing through the terror."

"That's probably it."

"I never wanted to fight," she said quietly. "Boot camp was a real mixed bag."

"You liked pushing through the terror part, but not pushing a bayonet through somebody's gut."

"We never had to do that. I couldn't do that."

"Me, either." He thought for a moment. "I ran into a quote the other day. 'Until we have created a romance of peace that will equal that of war, violence will not disappear from people's lives.' Harry Kessler, a German count, right after World War One."

She looked steadily at him. "Is that the romance you say you write about?"

"Pushing through the terror of interpersonal relationships—maybe."

She cocked her head. "Say more about that."

"It's maybe stronger than I mean. But the fear of losing something or someone you've attached yourself to, the uncertainty of the chase, wanting what you can't have. If you win, you feel euphoria. If you lose, you feel despair, desolation."

She shook her head. "That's not the kind of terror I'm attracted to."

"You want the physical, not the emotional."

She looked down at her cup and nodded.

"If this is too personal, you don't have to answer." He propped his chin on his hand, and he noticed his hand was shaking a little. "Ever been in love?"

She looked up at him, her face blank. "Physically," she said simply.

"I've never had the nerve, either." The admission made him smile.

She didn't smile. "I have to go," she said, standing up and taking her cup to the trash barrel. "Thanks for the coffee."

He sat there for a long while after she had left.

Two

Two days later he came to the gym with a story in a large envelope. She didn't show. *That's right*, he thought, *she said Tuesdays and Thursdays.* He gave the envelope to the receptionist. "There's a young woman who comes here on Tuesdays and Thursdays. Brown hair, well built," he said, blushing.

"Judy Blue Eyes," the woman said, smiling. "You want me to give her this?"

"Would you? Thanks."

He started away from the desk, and then went back. "Her name is Judy?"

"Without the Blue Eyes part. I'll leave it to her to give you the rest of her name."

"Thanks. What's the 'blue eyes' bit?"

She laughed. "The staff has nicknames for most of our regular customers."

"And I'm...?"

She ducked her head a little. Quietly, she said, "Mouse."

"Oh."

"Sorry."

He turned away without saying anything.

"Good luck," she said as he left.

He decided to come back the next day, and then changed his mind. *Let her read the story first,* he thought.

He was disappointed. *Why do I get myself into these situations? She's obviously not interested. I chased her away with that last remark about not having the nerve for a relationship, as if she doesn't, either. She probably sees me as needy. A woman like that doesn't need to get involved with somebody like me. Shit.*

The workout was a drag. He couldn't do as many repetitions as he had the last time. The word 'mouse' kept coming back to him.

On Saturday, he showed up without a lot of hope that she would be there, or would not speak to him if he were. *She sure won't have read the story,* he thought, *or not past the first page, anyway. Her idea of romance is not the same as mine.*

But she did come. And she smiled at him as he pushed himself on the leg extension machine. Soon, electric thrills shot through his shins from the effort, and he stopped.

"You were working hard," she said.

"This is the only machine that makes my legs feel like electricity is shooting through them."

"Some kind of nerve response."

He stopped and looked at her. "You left in a hurry the other day," he said. "Something I said?"

She frowned, thinking, then said, "No, I was anxious to get back here. I hadn't had my workout yet, remember?"

He wiped down his machine. "Time for coffee afterward?"

"Sure. I want to talk about your story."

"Okay." He felt a mixture of feelings. She had read his story, after all. *But if she wants to talk about it, does that mean she liked it? Or didn't?"*

He was done a while before she finished and showered, misgivings flooding through his brain as he waited. But she seemed to be unperturbed as they walked toward the coffee shop.

"You have a good sense of pace in the story," she said. "And I liked how you left the characters kinda hanging at the end. You didn't tie everything up in a neat little bow, the way some writers do."

"Thanks. Actually, when I got to the end I was searching for something to give it closure—and then I realized that maybe the reader doesn't need for me to 'tie everything up in a neat little bow,' as you put it. They can imagine the end, or ends, as they wish. So you think that works?"

"Definitely."

They were quiet for a while. Then he said, "I think too much."

She grinned at him. "That's one difference between us. I notice that you usually pause before speaking, as if you're composing in your head."

"The mark of a writer, I guess. It makes some people nervous."

"Some people—meaning you?" Mischief showed in her eyes.

He laughed. "A lot of the time I don't know what I think or feel until I've written it."

"I have a hard time grokking that. I think I understand, but it's just not the way I react to things."

"Oh, you've read Robert Heinlein."

She smiled. "A long time ago."

"I feel like that sometimes."

Her eyebrows arched a little. "Like what?"

"Stranger in a strange land. I may look like everybody else, but I've never fit in."

She smiled. "I think I do extreme things to justify being different."

"Like drive fast and lift weights?"

"Yeah. And other things."

He looked down at his coffee cup but didn't say anything.

She waited a moment, and then said, "What?"

"Other things that I will be intimidated by?"

"C'mon!" She reached over and put her hand on his arm. "Stop that shit!"

"Well?"

"So I lift weights. Big deal. So I drive fast—just means I'm nuts. Why should that intimidate you?"

He grinned at her. "Yeah, I know." He hesitated, then said, "You know what the people at the gym call me? 'Mouse.'"

That surprised her. "They call you names?"

"Their idea of humor, I guess."

"Why 'Mouse'? Wonder what they call me!"

"Judy Blue Eyes. I guess from that song by Crosby, Stills and Nash."

She thought a minute, then shook her head. "I don't get it."

He managed to sing, softly:

> *"I am yours, you are mine*
> *You are what you are*
> *You make it hard ..."*

She frowned. "Is that how you see me?"

"No," he lied. "That's just the song."

She looked at him steadily. "Do I make it hard for you to know me?"

"Probably no more than I make it hard for you to know me. Isn't that just the phase of our relationship?"

"Our *relationship*? We're just having coffee!"

He put his hand up. "A relationship begins when two people meet. Doesn't necessarily mean anything more."

"Christ!" she said. "You intellectuals!"

That stung. "Just because I write stories, I'm an intellectual?"

She burst out laughing. "Touché."

"I shouldn't have told you," he said. "They told me your name was Judy—Judy Blue Eyes. You do have blue eyes."

"Okay, then can we agree that I'm not from that song? I do know that you're not a mouse." She was smiling.

They were silent for a moment, then she said, "And I don't even know your name."

"Roger," he said, smiling back.

She put out her hand. "I'm Judy Taylor."

"Roger Burnes. Good to meet you."

They shook hands.

"Okay," he said, "you've read my story. When do I get my ride?"

She tipped her head down and looked at him under her eyebrows. "You sure?" Her smile was full of mischief.

"One time," he said, laughing, "I'll push through the terror."

She looked at him steadily for a moment. Then she said, "You're on."

Three

The next morning, just after sunrise, they met in the parking lot of the gym. He wasn't surprised to see her drive up in a late-model, red Corvette.

"I'm impressed," he said, getting into her car.

"You don't still use a Commodore computer for your writing, do you?"

He just grinned as he fastened his seat belt.

The ride out of town was very conservative. "This car attracts a lot of attention," she said over the throb of the engine.

Traffic was light. Judy held to the speed limit until they had cleared the small towns, and then she opened the car up. Roger felt pressed into the seat back, and for a moment struggled to catch his breath.

She looked at him and grinned. "And we're just loafing along," she shouted over the roar of the engine.

He realized that he was gripping the arm rest next to him, and made an effort to relax. He tried to glance at the speedometer, but he wasn't sure which of the gauges to look at.

Just then she pressed harder on the accelerator, and again he was pressed into the leather seat back. "They tell me that top speed is one-eighty," she said. "We aren't even close to that!"

His face must have been registering the terror he was feeling, because she let the car slow, glancing occasionally at him. "They post patrol cars along here," she said. "My radar detector hasn't gone off, but I'd rather not have to pay for the magistrate's weekend."

He tried to smile. His insides had been jounced around, and his fingers hurt from gripping the arm rest. He hadn't been this scared since his first flight in a light plane when he was eight years old. It felt to him that they were now crawling along the interstate, but when he found the speedometer with his eyes, it read a little under eighty miles an hour.

She was enjoying all this. She kept looking over at him, grinning. "There's a restaurant up here a little way, if you want to stop for breakfast. Or to use the rest room."

"Okay," he said, trying not to show his feelings.

She pulled off the freeway and into the parking lot of a restaurant. She stopped at the far end of the lot, away from other cars. "I like to avoid dings in my paint," she explained.

By the time they were seated in a booth, he was more relaxed. "It felt like the first time I left the ground in an old tail dragger," he said, laughing.

"I know," she said. "Like reaching the top of the first drop on a roller coaster—you look down and all you can think is, 'Oh, my god!'"

"Does it still feel like that to you?"

"It's different, if you have your own foot on the accelerator. You're in control. Maybe like being on the back of a big stallion you've just poked in the ribs. You think you're the boss, but there's always that little bit of doubt."

"You ride horses, too."

"Yes."

"It figures." He grinned at her. "One time I was driving an old Ford, and the floor mat got jammed up against the accelerator pedal. When I pressed down on it, it didn't come back up. I had to reach down and pull the mat away—while the car was roaring down the street. Since then I've always checked the play of the pedal."

She laughed.

"Is it hard to steer at high speed?" he asked.

"You have to get used to how fast it responds, and how fast *you* have to respond."

"I'll stick with my Corolla," he said.

"You're no sport."

After they had eaten, they walked back across the lot to the Corvette. "You had enough," she said, "or are you up for a little—a gentle little—ride in the country? It's too nice a day to sit in front of a computer, isn't it?"

"I've had my adrenalin jolt for the day," he said, "but I'd like to ride on with you."

She pulled out onto the blacktop road and turned away from the freeway. "I don't know where this goes," she said.

"You like uncertainty, don't you?"

"I do. Except, of course," she said, looking at him, "when I'm doing somebody's books."

He laughed. "That seems strange, for someone so physical and so in love with risk, to be a bookkeeper."

"I guess it keeps me in balance."

They drove for a while at moderate speeds, and he watched her shift gears expertly on the turns. She seemed to him a kind of female James Bond, and he was attracted to her as a moth is attracted to a candle flame. He'd been wondering about her combat experience, and finally got the nerve to ask. "You said you'd seen the results of war."

She looked quickly at him.

"I'm curious," he said. "You don't have to talk about it, if you don't want to."

She was quiet for a while. Then she said, "They brought some wounded in one day, right after I got to Kuwait. They were on their way to a hospital, but they had to patch them up for transport."

"You were a medic?"

"No. I was just a handy pair of hands to help get them to an aid station. There'd been a roadside bomb, and the guys were all torn up."

"Hard to imagine."

"I knew one of the kids. His face was almost gone. I had to swallow my puke so I could keep going."

"You said the other day, it was not very romantic."

"War is a sickness," she said. "All their flag-waving bullshit is just a way to keep the sickness going."

"So that German count—the one who talked about the romance of war—he missed something?"

"Maybe the officers, the ones who don't have to look at the wounded and dead, the ones who have never held a kid in their arms as he dies, maybe to them it's romantic."

After a few moments, as she turned off one blacktop road onto another, he asked, "That kid—the one you said you knew—did he die?"

She bit her lip. "In my arms."

He looked away to give her space for her memory. "Sorry."

"It hurts too much!" she said suddenly, wiping her cheek with her hand. When he didn't respond, she added, "Love is too painful."

There was nothing more to say, so they rode in silence for a long time.

"My grandmother was a nurse in World War Two," she said finally. "A frontline nurse in Europe. She watched kids die in her surgical tent, both American and German kids."

"Wow."

"She stood on a hill once, overlooking this little German town as American bombers destroyed it. The bombers were on eye level, opposite the hill they stood on. They were that close. She said she kept thinking about all the people down there, getting blown to bits as they watched. And the kids in the airplanes who were doing it were American boys, same as the cut and shot and bleeding boys she tried to save in her surgical tent."

He changed his mind about a female James Bond. Maybe she loved the thrill of driving fast, maybe she liked the exhilaration of terror, but she had a heart.

He had to say it, even as he knew this wasn't the time. "You have a heart, after all." He intended that last part to be a joke.

In response, she shifted down and pressed the accelerator. In a moment they were speeding along a narrow, winding road and he felt his stomach muscles tighten. "I'm sorry!" he shouted.

She slowed the car and found a place to turn off the pavement. They were next to a big maple tree with acres of farmland beyond. She stopped the car and sat staring ahead.

"I'm sorry," he said again. "I didn't mean that the way it came out. I was being flip."

After a few minutes she sighed deeply. "I am so angry at you right now," she said quietly, still looking straight ahead.

"I deserve it," he said. "It was a terrible thing to say, and it isn't true—the implication that you don't feel things."

She remained silent.

"I have just been trying to figure you out," he said. "You are so different from most people I know. I feel like this little kid watching a strong, confident ... *star* or something, somebody bigger than life. In my head I'd already thought you were like a female James Bond."

She glanced quickly at him out of the corner of her eye, then looked at her hands gripping the top of the steering wheel. She straightened her fingers, with their perfectly polished and shaped nails.

"But you're not," he said.

She looked at him, still angry. "What am I?"

"I don't know how to answer that," he said.

"How do you see me—really? Am I some kind of female jock that can bench press a hundred eighty pounds? Am I just a daredevil, an Evel Knievel?"

He thought for a while. "I guess I'm afraid to open my mouth. Give me a minute."

She opened and closed her hands around the steering wheel.

"When I first saw you," he said finally, "I was attracted to you. And yet you intimidated me."

"There's that word again."

"It's true. You could do things I could never do. I was in awe of you. And at the same time I felt this powerful attraction. I don't know why." He gave a little laugh. "Well, sure—you're a beautiful woman—and you were way out of my reach."

She laughed, but didn't look at him.

"Then when we talked, I got another picture of you, someone who feels things, but seems to keep them secret."

"I've never kept any secrets from anybody."

"Maybe it's just that this other part of you is so strong, I was afraid of you."

She shook her head slowly.

"I guess I was afraid of getting hurt."

Judy laughed. "So you come with me to fly down the highway at a hundred miles an hour?"

"I don't mean physically."

This time she looked at him. "I'm not afraid of much physically, either," she said. "Well, I am, but I've learned to use that fear—for the thrill of it."

"Maybe," he said, "that's how I wanted to use my fear of getting hurt emotionally. There's a thrill there, too."

She shook her head again, and looked at her hands.

"I don't know if this makes any sense," he said, "but the first time we had coffee I talked about the romance of pushing through the terror of interpersonal relationships. I write about it because it's so scary to me. And I've felt the reward, too."

"Your story—the one I read—never got to the reward."

He smiled. "You're right."

"That kind of losing," she said slowly, "is too painful to bear."

His throat was tight. "Judy—when I insulted you a few minutes ago—when I realized what I had said, I wanted to die. I'd been thinking about how seemingly impervious you were, and how I was beginning to see something else, a softness, and it just came out wrong. It's not what I meant, at all."

There was a little smile at the corner of her mouth. "And then you thought you'd lost."

"Exactly."

She wiped her hands on the legs of her slacks. "You're forgiven."

"I'm grateful."

"I've avoided this territory," she said. "This world you seem to live in. Or do you just look at it so you can write about it?"

He laughed. "It's the world I want to live in. I'm not sure I have the nerve."

"Me either."

She turned the key. The heart-throb of the engine ran from his feet into the center of his abdomen.

She turned in her seat to look at him, her eyes worried. After a long silence, he could barely hear her say, "Will you hold my hand?"

Taking her cool hand in his, he felt a faint thrill.

She smiled, very slightly. "Like you said, I'm very physical. Touch means more to me than words." She pulled the car out onto the pavement and withdrew her hand. They rode just a little fast down the road, a long, straight stretch of two-lane that undulated over low hills..

Suddenly, there was a car alongside them, another Corvette, bright yellow. The young driver was looking at them and gunning his engine. He wanted to race.

Roger tensed. He'd had enough speed. But Judy grinned— and pressed on the accelerator. The car leaped ahead.

For a couple of minutes, they stayed together on the road. She wasn't pushing it. They weren't going nearly as fast as they had been earlier on the freeway. He could tell that she was enjoying the race, but his heart was pounding.

On the approaches to the gentle hills, "Do Not Pass" signs appeared on the left shoulder, but the other driver ignored them. On the down slopes, he gained a little on them.

Roger could see another car far ahead, coming toward them, then disappearing behind the hills. "Judy," he said.

"I see him," she replied. "Our friend will have to yield in just a minute."

But he didn't. When the oncoming car suddenly appeared on the crest in front of them, the other Corvette nosed down, tires screeching. Judy speeded up to let him pull in behind her, but the young driver must have panicked. He swerved back and forth, his tires leaving curving black streaks in the roadway. The oncoming car swished past them, but the yellow Corvette dove off the road.

Judy screamed and applied her brakes. They stopped just over the crown of the hill. Both of them were breathing heavily, and trying to see behind them.

"I can't back up," she said, crying. "Other cars won't be able to see us!" She pulled off the pavement and stopped. Both got out of the car and began running back over the hill.

The oncoming car had stopped far down the road, its stop lights still on. They couldn't see the yellow Corvette, but kept running. Roger was completely out of breath, and had to stop. Judy kept going. He watched her suddenly turn and dash into the ditch alongside the road. Panting, he jogged as fast as he could.

The car had folded in two against a large tree, smoke and steam rising from it. By the time Roger reached the scene, Judy was tugging at the door of the car. Unable to open it, she turned to look at Roger, who was making his way across the ditch. Her face was a mask of agony.

Together, they pried the door open enough that she could reach in. She unbuckled the seat belt and pulled the limp driver out onto the grass. Blood covered his face. "Give me your sweater," she said to Roger. She took it and wiped at the young man's face. Crying, she lifted his head on her lap and gently stroked him. He appeared lifeless.

Someone shouted from the road. "I called 9-1-1." Roger could see several cars stopped. A man made his way through the tall grass to the wreck. "I thought we were all three going to pile up!" he said, his eyes wide.

Roger stooped down and put his hand on Judy's shoulder. His knees were shaking. She turned her tear-streaked face toward him, then without saying anything, turned back to the man in her lap.

"Is he dead?" someone asked. A small crowd had clustered around them. "Is anybody else in the car?" someone else asked.

Roger looked up and shook his head. "I don't think so," he said.

"Is he dead?" the voice repeated.

Judy looked up, horror on her face. She nodded very slightly.

They heard sirens approaching. In a minute, the emergency crew members were climbing down from the road, carrying gear. A uniformed man leaned over Judy and the young driver. He straightened up and turned to look back at the others in the crew. He shook his head.

Someone was spraying fire retardant into the engine compartment of the car. A stretcher was laid in the grass next to the body, and Judy gently lowered the man's head onto the grass and stood up. Her clothing was covered in blood. Roger led her to a little mound nearby and helped her sit down.

An officer approached with his clipboard.

Later, Roger drove the Corvette back to town. Judy, mute, stared straight ahead, not responding to him except to mumble directions to her apartment.

He helped her up the stairs and opened her door. Inside, she simply collapsed on the floor. He got her a glass of water from the kitchen. With wooden movements, she sat up, drank from the glass and handed it back to him.

"Let me help you into the bedroom," Roger said, extending his hands to her.

She looked up at him. "I can't get up," she said softly.

Moving behind her and reaching under her arms, he lifted her limp body. She managed to stand, and together they moved into the bedroom.

"You need to get out of those clothes," he said. She began to tug at her sweater, and between them they removed her bloodstained clothing. Then she simply collapsed again onto the bed.

Roger found a light spread and covered her. There were still a few blood stains on her arms.

She looked at him with round, red-rimmed eyes. "I killed him," she said softly.

"No you didn't. He lost control. He shouldn't have been on that side of the road."

"What did you tell the police?"

Roger touched her cheek. "That he was passing us in a no-passing zone. And that's what the other driver said, more or less."

"He was just a kid," she said, and began to cry again. Roger thought about the young soldier who had died in her arms in Kuwait, but said nothing. He found a box of tissues and gave it to her.

"I'll be back," he said, and went into the bathroom and returned with a wet washcloth. "Give me your arm."

She lifted her arm so that he could wipe the blood off, her eyes on his all the while.

"More water?"

She shook her head. "How could I have done such a stupid thing?"

"He challenged you."

"He was just a kid! I'm an adult!"

Roger sat on the edge of the bed and held her hand. He wondered what he could say to ease her torment. Whatever he thought of, he immediately dismissed. He could never blame her for what happened, but the events were so obvious—she rose to the kid's challenge, and the result was terrible.

They remained there on the bed, silently reliving the accident, trying to make sense of the tragedy.

After a while, she looked over at him. "Your car is at the gym," she said.

"I'll get it later."

"Take mine." She closed her eyes. "I'll never drive it again."

"Don't think about that right now," he said, squeezing her hand.

"I couldn't," she said. "Every time I got behind that wheel I'd see that poor kid's face, covered with blood." She turned her face to the pillow and sobbed. Then she curled her body into a fetal position.

Roger lay down behind her and wrapped his arms around her. For a long time, neither of them moved.

The End

Phone Call

"Hello," I said after looking at my phone to see who was calling me. I usually greet callers I know by name. I like that opportunity to make a connection with people. It's like a smile, I think, when approaching a friend on the street. Costs nothing, feels good to both of us.

I almost said, "Laura." I had hoped it was she. But there was only an unknown number displayed on the little screen. It wasn't Laura on the other end. I was wary. The words I was already forming in my mind slithered out of reach. "Hello."

"Hello," came the answer, a voice of unknown age, probably a male. "I have a request—just ten minutes of your time. Nothing more."

A sales call, obviously. I sighed. I don't get a lot of these, but the thing about them that I resent the most is that such callers not only don't know me, they don't *want* to know me. They just want to read me their pitch so they can get paid for the call. "About what?"

I would give him that courtesy, at least, before telling him that I wasn't interested in what he was selling. I was already rehearsing my "No thank you" and closing my phone. For some reason, I like that sound and that feeling of snapping shut my little old cell phone. It takes less attention than pressing a button and replacing a regular phone on its cradle. Snap, and stuff it back in my pocket. Situation handled.

"Well," he began, then stammered, "it's just about connecting. I don't want to sell you anything, and I'm not conducting a survey. I just want to talk with you for ten minutes. That's all. I promise."

The worst kind of pitch. It wasn't even an honest pitch. I sighed again. "Right," I said sarcastically.

I would have given anything to have *her* on the other end of the line. I wanted to apologize—for what, I wasn't sure. Our last words had been painful. "You don't know," she had said, "how to be intimate. You don't know how to be spontaneous!"

"Well," the fellow repeated, "you don't know me and I don't know you. I want to change that, just a little bit."

"After we know each other, *then* you'll try to sell me something, right?"

"No, honest. I'm not connected with any company. All I know about you is your phone number, and you don't have to tell me anything more."

"So, you're calling from—where? Where is the 778 Area Code?" You can never tell anymore where someone is calling from. People carry their phone numbers with them when they move, like I did. A phone number displayed on my phone may be just a connection point to somewhere, anywhere in the world. This fellow sounded American, at least.

"It's in Utah, actually. Near Salt Lake City. But it doesn't matter where I am or where you are. We are just connected right now, and I want that connection to mean something—to both of us."

"I don't understand. What is it you want it to mean?" I was getting annoyed.

"I don't know." He mumbled the words.

"Look," I said, my throat tight, "if I give you your ten minutes—and we've already used up a couple of them—where do you think we'll be when the time is up?"

He and I spoke at the same time. "I'm not good at playing games," I said, while I think he said, "I hope that we'll both feel something good happened." The only word I heard clearly was "good." I waited.

After a moment (another of his precious minutes), he said, "You know how you can be on an airplane sitting next to someone for five hours and neither of you speaks at all?"

"So we're sitting here next to each other on this phone connection, and you want to talk."

"Yes." He spoke slowly—not at all like a salesman. "Tell me something about yourself. What's your passion?"

That stumped me. I sighed again. This felt weird. "Look, what is my passion to you? What's *your* passion?" While I said it—with some force, I noticed—I was checking through my list of known passions. Writing, photography, Laura—this last not so much a current passion as one I used to have. Music. How did I forget music?

"Intimacy," he answered simply.

"Intimacy?" It wasn't so much a question as an expression of incredulity.

"Yes. I love intimacy. Not just physical—in fact, that's not even near the top of the list. I love that feeling that someone I'm with feels close to me."

It was sad. Here's this guy calling up a stranger thousands of miles away and wanting to feel close to them. Just like me. "You're lonely," I ventured. I hoped there wasn't an edge to my voice.

"Yeah, a little, but that's not the point."

"Look, I'm not a therapist, but it sure looks to me like that *is* the point."

"No." He paused. "I've told you my biggest passion, can you tell me yours? One of yours?" He sounded kinda young. Young and vulnerable.

"Okay, I love music. All kinds, but mostly classical."

"Awesome." He said. I love music, too."

"What's your favorite?"

"Oh, Rodriguez, I guess. He touches me."

"There's intimacy there, in some places." I was beginning to feel something about this young man.

"Yeah, especially his Aranjuez adagio."

"The guitar solo," I guessed.

"He wrote it about his honeymoon. I like Miles Davis's version, too."

"Never heard that." I couldn't imagine the Rodriguez coming from a trumpet.

"It's very Spanish. You can listen to it on YouTube."

"I'll do that," I lied.

"What's your favorite music?"

"It changes from time to time. Sebelius, right now."

"Somber," he said. "Lonely. Are you lonely, too?"

This conversation was teetering on the edge of weird. I was uncomfortable. *But what the hell?* I was a *lot* lonely. "Yeah, a little, sometimes."

"Sometimes. Right now?"

My voice was harsh. "What's this all about?" He couldn't have known that he hit so close to home.

"I stepped over the line, didn't I?"

"Yeah, you did." I thought of my old days in TORI and Trust Theory. Asking questions challenges people, and they don't like that. His question irritated me. "Maybe there's a way to this intimacy you're looking for that doesn't involve questioning them."

He was quiet for a moment. "I never thought about that. It's true, isn't it? A question can put the other person on the spot. But how do we get anywhere without asking questions?"

"I'm more apt to trust you if I sense your vulnerabilities." Right out of the book.

"Sounds like you're a therapist."

"My turn to step over the line?" I smiled.

"Maybe. It just sounded like something you know from school."

"Close enough. I've done it, though."

"Trusted someone?"

I had to laugh at that. "Touché. I admit, it's not one of my strong points."

"I guess getting a blind phone call like this from a stranger can put you on your guard."

"True." I noticed something, though. "It's interesting to me," I said, "that my guard has slowly come down a little."

"I'm glad."

"I keep wanting to ask you questions, though. And that's what I just said isn't good for intimacy."

"Fire away."

"Is this a grad school experiment?" I thought it was a reasonable question. I'd never had someone want to talk with me for no other reason.

He laughed. "It does sound like what they'd do, doesn't it? No, I'm not even in school. It's just something I've been wondering about for a long time—how do people connect, without living together for years."

"People I've connected with in a short time have been interested in what I'm interested in."

"Like music."

"Yeah." Laura loved music as much as I did, and I couldn't get rid of the memory of our lying in bed after making love and listening to Rachmaninov pour over us.

"But there's more, isn't there? It's not just sharing common interests." He paused. "I'm really struggling to understand this."

"It's emotional. Ever hear of Jack Gibb?"

"No."

"He had this theory about trust and intimacy."

"I was hoping it could happen just by rubbing two people together, without getting into theory."

I smiled at his imagery. "I 'spect it could, in time."

"Like getting stranded together on a desert island."

"Yeah," I said, "if you can't leave, you eventually knock the sharp corners off." I felt shame thinking about walking out on Laura. She kept pleading with me to stay and resolve our argument.

"A phone call, though, can be cut off instantly."

"You got it."

"Thank you for not hanging up."

"I came close, in the beginning."

"I could tell, and I was panicking."

"This is really important to you."

"Yeah, it's like I'm putting myself on the line for something."

"To prove something?"

"It felt like just curiosity before."

"Actually, the same here," I said. "My guard was up, but I didn't understand what you were trying to do, and I got curious."

"I don't know how to do it."

"Get intimacy?"

"Yeah."

"Maybe none of us do. We fumble a lot." I felt myself smiling.

"I heard someone say that two people meeting for the first time do like animals, 'circling,' she called it."

"Testing. Always testing." I thought of James Carse and his finite and infinite games. "Maybe it's a kind of game." *What kind of game are Laura and I playing?*

"When we're on guard, we're trying to learn the rules."

He's pretty smart, I thought. "Some games turn on winning or losing, but some games turn on keeping the game going."

"I'll have to think about that," he said.

"Okay. I admit, it's another theory."

"You know a lot about this."

I had to smile. "Sorry. I don't, really."

"It's okay. Only I don't know anything about games that don't have winners and losers."

"Sure you do. Flirting?" *When was the last time Laura and I flirted?*

He laughed. "Come to think of it, yeah. Sometimes."

"Maybe that's related to circling. That's what people do."

"Looking for connections."

"Sometimes."

"I got a lot to think about right now," he said. "Thanks. I think the ten minutes are up."

"You've got a lot of guts. I couldn't have called some stranger like you did."

"Did we . . ." He paused. "Did we make a connection?"

"I did. I went from trying to defend myself from you, and now I'm pulling for you. I hope you got what you wanted."

"Those theories—what was the name of the trust guy?"

"Jack Gibb. He's dead now, but you can probably find his book on Amazon dot com."

"And the other theory—about games?"

"James Carse. It's called Finite and Infinite Games."

"Is he dead, too?"

"He's retired, but the book is still in print."

He paused, apparently writing.

On impulse, I asked, "Tell me your first name."

"James."

"Mine's Don."

"Thank you, Don. I feel like I got to know you a little bit."

"Me, too. Good luck."

"You too. Bye."

"Bye."

I closed my cell phone gently and slipped it into my pocket. I sat there for a long time, thinking about what had just happened. *Good luck, James. Good luck, Laura. Good luck, Don.*

The End

Flashdance

One

"Daddy, you can't play Flashdance at a funeral!"

She put a hand on his shoulder as he sat, hunched and broken. He didn't look up at her, but just shook his head slowly. An old snapshot hung from his fingers: a woman, probably about seventy, obviously dancing alone on an outdoor deck in summertime, smiling into the camera as her body responded to music.

His daughter put her face down next to his. "We'll get through this, Daddy," and she kissed his cheek tenderly.

Someone touched her arm, and she stood up and moved away with them. He reached into his jacket pocket and pulled out a little music player. Removing his hearing aids from his ears, he inserted ear buds from the player in their place, and fiddled with the controls of the instrument.

Across the room, his daughter saw him smile for the first time in months.

Two

A little tipsy from the Cosmopolitan she'd been drinking, she got up from the table at the first few notes of "Flashdance" on the stereo, grinning broadly, and danced around the room—not for him, but for herself. "I just can't help myself. I *have* to move when I hear that music." Her dinner could wait.

He leaned back and watched her, sipping his drink. He'd suggested music with their meal, on one of those rare days when neither of them had outside obligations. He'd been thinking Albéniz, but she chose "What a Feeling," by Irene Cara, in the film starring Jennifer Beals.

It was a good sign—she wanted to let her hair down. Having chosen to continue working in her home business past retirement age, she often allowed her work to overwhelm her, and sometimes he felt guilty for sitting back and letting the commercial world go on without him. He wished that she could ease up and enjoy life before age took its inevitable toll.

At the end of the piece, she returned to her seat, breathless and glowing. After all their time together, he loved the way she looked and the way she charged into everything she undertook.

Finishing her Cosmo in a single gulp, she picked up her fork. "And I was hungry before!" she exclaimed.

"It's getting cold."

"I don't care." She took a bite of sweet potato. "It tastes wonderful."

Those eyes caressed him.

Three

She squeezed his fingers in the dark theater as the young woman on the screen nervously lowered the needle onto the phonograph record. His wife had seen the film "four times, at least!" she had told him when he said he wasn't familiar with it. "It's my fantasy," she gushed.

The music began slowly, as did the dancing, and the judges of the audition showed their boredom. Then it changed, the tempo becoming disco-like, the dancing likewise changing from classical ballet style to modern—and very athletic—movement. The on-screen judges perked up, and his wife's knee under his hand bounced to the music.

He looked over at her. She smiled back at him, and her knee bounced higher. She leaned over close to him and shouted above the music, "I can't *not* move with it! My body just takes over!"

Four

He'd been attracted to her from the first time he'd seen her at the club. Something about her hair, although mostly her eyes. She was always accompanied by another man, but it was a sociable club and switching dance partners was encouraged. Women sometimes danced together in groups. Acknowledging that he was a terrible dancer, he seldom initiated a dance. Standing on the sidelines, he watched her move gracefully to the music, obviously enjoying herself. There was always a smile on her face on the dance floor. Her partner performed adequately, but those eyes and that body took all of his attention.

When they finally met and began seeing each other, he hated to be reminded of how awkwardly he himself danced, and how much she enjoyed moving her body to music. It didn't seem fair. She deserved a better dance partner, whatever their other interests in common.

During the years of their marriage, he tried to encourage her passion for dancing. Often, he watched her dancing alone among other people on the dance floor, lost in the music and in the movement of her own body. He could join her in the slow dances and enjoy feeling that body move against his. For a few minutes he could forget how clumsy he was.

And remember how lucky.

.

The End

The Elevator

Meredith usually avoided having to take the elevator at rush hour. The crush of people and their smells, the feeling of being trapped, and hating to say, "Excuse me, please" six times as she pushed her way to the door always made her feel like an animal on its way to the slaughter house. But she had dawdled outside at lunch today, the first warm day of April.

She was near the back of the car. The man behind her, she could tell, was pressed against the wall. She hadn't noticed him when she got on, but now she felt how tall he was. Next to her a young woman was watching a video on her phone, and Meredith could barely hear music from the woman's ear piece. Another woman was in front of her, pressed against her breasts, squeezing the breath out of her.

The faint sound of an electric guitar drew her attention to the video. It was Eric Clapton, she recognized immediately, his eyes closed, drawing the music from "Concert for George" out of that glorious guitar—and Meredith was transported back to the night she had first watched that concert from her bed, sobbing uncontrollably over the loss—all the loss represented by the death of George Harrison, one of her idols in her youth. Paul had lain on top of her, kissing her tears, trying to bring her back to him, but the weight of his body was the weight of her loss, and Clapton's guitar solo in the middle of "Something" was her wail.

Tears welled up, but the press of bodies in the elevator kept her arms pinned and she couldn't reach inside her purse for a tissue. Her eyes were fastened on that little video screen. Her memory furnished the full resonance of the music. Her body was suddenly hot, and she tasted the saltiness of tears streaming down her face.

Then suddenly there was release; the pressure of bodies eased, and cool air wafted over her face from the open door. Several people left the car. Meredith managed to dig into her purse, but a woman's hand appeared beside her offering her a tissue. She murmured, "Thank you," and dabbed at her makeup.

A few minutes later she made her way to the doors and, dazed, exited the elevator. She never looked up to see who had given her the tissue, and she remembered nothing about the woman with the video except a mass of dark hair with a white wire trailing from under it. "Something" kept running through her head. At her desk all afternoon, she felt Paul's weight on her, holding her in the world that seemed to be flying away.

Memories of listening to the Beatles' music, lying stoned in a tangle of young bodies, smelling the sweet smoke mingling with incense and perfume, lips kissing her, all came flooding back. She had an impulse to go online and try to find that video, but she kept the entry form on her screen and pretended to work.

Finally it was after four o'clock, and she shut off her computer and looked over the wall of the cube, where Dolly was looking up at her. "I need a drink," she said fervently.

Dolly instantly closed her computer and grabbed her purse. "Yes, you do."

The End

Road Trip

"You must think I'm a real wuss," she said as he loaded her bags into the trunk of his car.

"Cause you don't want to fly?" He grinned at her, at the same time noticing, in just a small way, that she was cuter than he remembered.

She stood there with her head tilted down, looking at him sheepishly. "I flew once," she said, "and I was so scared I promised myself I'd never do that again."

"But you drive the freeways every day," he kidded, feeling ashamed even as he said it. Everybody has something they don't want to deal with.

"I know, it doesn't make any sense."

He closed the trunk and they got into the car. Neither spoke for a while as he maneuvered in the heavy traffic heading for the interstate.

They had agreed to drive cross-country to Portland for her father's memorial after the family had decided to put the ceremony off for a week to allow more members to attend. Most were flying in from various parts of the country. Mark and Tracey had been talking at an ad hoc family meeting on facebook about how far away it was for them, and when Tracey expressed her intention to drive, Mark offered to drive with her. No one else was interested in such a long trip. "When I was a kid," he had said, "my family drove to the Coast a number of times. I remember those trips as really fun."

"Gas was cheap in those days," his brother had reminded him.

"Driving with two people in the car isn't that much more expensive than flying," he said. "I'd be glad to drive."

"I'll go with you," Tracey had said. "I don't like flying."

"Okay, let's do it."

So he drove down to Bloomington to pick her up. They'd take I-70 across to Denver and cut north through Wyoming and Utah. Freeway almost all the way, an easy drive, maybe thirty-six hours on the road, four days. His Sonata was a good road car, comfortable.

He'd wondered, on the way down to pick her up, what it was going to be like. He didn't really know her all that well, even though they were cousins. They'd met a number of times when they were kids, but only once since they had left their family homes. Their email exchanges planning the trip had been light, almost flirting, and the only odd thing he'd noticed about her was her fear of flying.

"Tell me about your life," he said after they had gotten onto the freeway. "You've finished college, right?"

She looked over at him, smiling. "I'll never really finish," she said. "I love school. I'm starting my graduate work in three weeks."

"In what—biology, isn't it?"

"Neurobiology. I got a scholarship."

"Impressive."

"I couldn't afford it otherwise. What are you doing these days?"

"Writing."

"What kind of writing?"

"Commercial stuff, marketing copy, fluff pieces. But my real work is fiction, at night.

"Ah, the struggling novelist."

"Yeah."

She unbuckled her seatbelt and turned sideways to face him. "You always were a kind of introvert, weren't you?"

He shot her a grin, but didn't say anything.

"I remember when we were kids," she said, "you stayed in your room when we visited. I thought you didn't like us."

"You ought to keep buckled up," he said. "It wasn't that I didn't like you. Your family was always so ... loud."

"We were that."

"Your brother picked on me."

She tilted her head to see him better. "He was just trying to get you to open up. He's not mean."

"Yeah, I know." He thought of Doug, a couple years older than he, a true jock. Captain of the football team, all-round athlete. "You're not going to buckle up, are you?"

Laughing, she pulled the seat belt out from its slot, waved the buckle at him, then let it retract again. "My life is in your hands!" she said. "I don't like to be restricted."

"And you're the one who is afraid of flying?"

Her face changed. "That's different," she said.

"Tell me." He tried to watch her face, but kept looking ahead at the road. Traffic was light since they got out of town, and he was on cruise control.

"When I was a little girl, Mom took me on an elevator. It was a big office building, and the sensation of falling terrified me. I was sure we were going to die."

"I love elevators—and airplanes," he said. "I love that feeling in the pit of my stomach."

"You probably love roller coasters, too."

He laughed. "Haven't been on one in years, but yes—that feeling!"

Tracey shuddered. She was sitting sideways on the seat, with one foot tucked under her. Nice legs.

After a while, he said, "We can make Denver in two days, and another two days to Portland. Stop someplace in Kansas tonight, okay?"

"I'm in your hands, remember?"

"I just want this trip to be comfortable for both of us."

She put her hand, which had been resting on his seat back, on his shoulder. "Mark," she said, "if I'm uncomfortable, you'll know it."

"Okay."

"Okay now," she said, and he glimpsed a raised eyebrow, "will I know when *you're* uncomfortable?"

"It's not easy for me," he answered, "but I promise to try."

The rest of the day they chatted occasionally, were silent for stretches, both watching the Midwestern landscape pass by. Tracey turned the radio on for a while, but gave up looking for music she liked, and turned it off again. He was glad she didn't insist on having noise all the time.

"I can take the wheel whenever you get tired of driving," she said at one point.

"Thanks, I like to drive, but late in the day sometimes I get sleepy." He looked over at her. "That will be part of my promise. I know I tend to push myself, and I don't want to do that."

They stopped for gas and lunch, walked around the parking lot for a few minutes, then drove on.

Later, he said, "We haven't talked about sleeping arrangements. I assume you want your own room."

She looked at him for a minute before responding. "Not necessarily."

He wondered what she meant by that. Part of him wanted to be circumspect, but another part was curious, and even a little excited by the prospect of them sharing a room. He hadn't had a girl friend in a long time.

"One room is cheaper," she said, "but if you want separate rooms, I'm okay with that."

"One is cheaper," he agreed, without elaborating.

She was quiet for a while, looking out her window at the endless cornfields. Then she turned toward him again. "Mark," she began, "can I ask you a personal question?"

"Sure."

"Are you gay?" Then she held up her hand. "I'm sorry. You don't have to answer that."

"It's okay," he said. "And no, I'm not."

"It doesn't matter to me," she said, stammering slightly with embarrassment. "I just wondered."

He looked at her. "Where did you get that idea?"

"Now, I'm uncomfortable," she said. "I'm sorry I said anything. I just ..."

"Did you think I was?"

"No—well, a long time ago, we kind of wondered."

"Who's 'we'? Your brother Doug?"

She fidgeted with the hem of her shorts. "Well, he said one time that he thought you were."

"Cause I wasn't like him." Mark thought about the times Doug had teased him when they were young. He hadn't seen Doug in years, and hadn't wanted to.

"Mark, I'm sorry. I know he always seemed to get on your case."

Mark sighed. "He wasn't the only one."

They were quiet again for a long while. Mark was comfortable with silence. He spent a lot of his time thinking about people and how he felt with different ones. With Tracey, he didn't have his guard up, but he wondered about her the way he would in getting to know any young woman—what she was like when she let her hair down, could she really open up to him, could he really open up to her. He was attracted to her, but their familial relationship got in the way of anything like sex. They had known each other all their lives, and yet knew so little about each other.

As they approached the Kansas town of Salina, Mark pointed to a Super 8 hotel just off the freeway. "That look okay to you?"

"Yes," she said. "I'd love to take a dip in the pool before we go for dinner."

"Sounds good to me." He left the interstate and found the drive to the hotel. After checking in, they wheeled their luggage up to the room. Tracey opened her bag at once and took out her bathing suit. "You going in?" she said, heading for the bathroom.

"I didn't think to bring a bathing suit," he said. "I'll flop down while you go swim." Taking his shoes off, he sprawled on one of the beds. He didn't even look up when she came out of the bathroom, and was awakened from a sound sleep when she returned from the pool.

"Not an outdoor pool," she said cheerfully, "but refreshing!" She disappeared again into the bathroom, and emerged a few minutes later, back in her traveling clothes. Climbing onto the other bed, she lay facing him. "Are you ready to go, or do you want to sleep some more?"

"You look like you want to rest, too."

"I don't want to sleep, but lying here feels good. I'm still charged up from the cold water in the pool."

"We can ask at the desk where to go to eat," he said. "I think we're north of the town itself."

She rolled over onto her back. "This is a nice room. The pool smells like chlorine, but most of them do."

"When you came in, I got a whiff of chlorine."

"I rinsed off before I put my clothes back on. Smell anything now?"

"No."

She turned her head toward him, her face serious." Mark, I hope I didn't offend you."

"Hmmm?"

"About being gay."

"No," he said. "Maybe a little disappointed."

"Disappointed?"

"My ego gets a little sensitive sometimes."

"I'm sorry."

"S'okay. It's my thing."

"I like you, Mark." She propped her head with her elbow so she could see him better.

"I've been hit on," he said. "At first it was humiliating, having guys look at you like that. I got used to it."

"It's such a put-down!"

"Not always. To a gay man, it's just how they hook up."

"But if it were me I'd feel misjudged."

He grinned. "I guess that's why I felt humiliated at first. I had a strong judgment of homosexuals."

"And now you don't?"

He sighed. "I work on it. I don't want to, but it's like a gut reaction. Up here—" he pointed to his head, "I'm cool with them. I know a few, personally. I've been learning to let those old feelings go."

"I guess I have some of that, too. Where did we learn that stuff?"

"We just absorb it from people around us when we're young."

"Let's go eat," she said. "We can talk some more."

In the hallway on the way to the front desk, he asked, "You want a place that serves drinks?"

"Yes! I'm ready for that."

The clerk pointed out several restaurants in the area, and recommended a Mexican place. "They have great Margaritas."

Having ordered their meals and sipping the tangy cocktails, they began to let go of the tensions of the day on the road. "I'm feeling like we made the right choice," she said.

"This restaurant?"

"Driving to Oregon."

He smiled at her. "Gives us a chance to get to know each other, doesn't it?"

"Yeah, we've known each other since we were in diapers, but I really never got to know you. I kinda felt sorry for you because you didn't seem to have any fun."

"And you were always the instigator." He grinned at her. "I remember one time, when I was eight or nine, that you wanted all of us to go skinny dipping in our pool."

"Your mom sure put the kybosh on that!"

"Yeah, she knew the neighbors would complain."

"Well, I got my wish when I was in high school. You know, Bloomington is surrounded by limestone quarries, and almost all have water in them."

"So you went skinny dipping. This was in mixed company?"

She laughed. "It was *so much fun!*"

"I wouldn't have had the nerve."

"Poor Mark! You led such a sheltered life." She finished her drink and signaled to the waiter, holding up her glass.

"I guess I did. I was always bashful around girls."

She lowered her voice and smiled. "Tell me about your first time."

He felt his face get hot. While he was thinking about what to say, the waiter came with their drinks. "Food will be here in minute," he said in a strong Latino accent.

She was still waiting for Mark's reply, a half-grin on her face.

Mark stalled, emptying his first glass. Then the waiter returned with their food.

"Smells wonderful!" Tracey gushed.

After they had been eating for a few minutes, she looked up at him, still chewing. "Well?"

He laughed, embarrassed. "It was a disaster."

"Awww." Mischief played around her mouth.

"It was in the front seat of a car, and I couldn't get the condom on." He took another bite of refried beans.

"So then what?"

"She had to show me how to do it."

Tracey raised her glass. "Here's to learning how!"

Still embarrassed, he touched her glass and they both took large sips. She turned her attention to her dinner, and he felt relieved.

By the time they had finished eating, both were quite relaxed. He drove very carefully back to the hotel.

Back in the room, they both giggled as they went through the process of preparing for bed. After she had emerged from the bathroom, wearing modest pajamas, he took his turn, showering and shaving, still feeling the effects of the Margaritas and excited by the young woman in his room. When he finished, she seemed asleep in her bed. He crawled under the covers in his own bed, very much awake and aware of her.

"Did it turn out all right?" she said, suddenly breaking the silence. She hadn't been asleep, after all.

"I guess so. I never had another chance with her, though."

"Too bad. She wasn't very understanding."

"She had a lot of guys to choose from."

He heard her get out of bed, and in a moment felt her slip in beside him. They lay there for a moment, their hips touching, before she said, "I can talk better here."

He kept his hands away from her, filled with feeling. Finally, he said, "Tracey, I don't know if we should be doing this."

She turned her whole body to face him. "Why not, silly?"

"We're cousins."

She was silent for a moment. Then she said softly, "We're not going to make a baby, are we?"

He didn't know how to answer. "It's just ... "

"Okay," she whispered, moving away from him a few inches.

They were both silent for a long time, but he was far from sleepy, and he could tell she was awake as well. He wished he knew how to respond to her. His body was thoroughly aroused, but his mind was a whirlwind of conflicting thoughts.

She finally slipped quietly out of his bed and returned to her own.

It seemed a long time before he went to sleep.

Daylight was coming in around the heavy blinds when he awoke. He could hear the shower running, and then the hair dryer. He lay there until she came out. Smiling at him, she said easily, "Your turn."

They said little as they prepared to leave. Eating in the stark breakfast room of the hotel, they watched other guests silently filling their plates and sitting at the tiny tables. A television set on the wall blared the morning news. A small child was crying. The two filled plastic cups with coffee and went out to the car.

On I-70 again, Mark finally said, "I'm sorry if I disappointed you."

She turned to face him. "It's okay, Mark. I understand. I was thoughtless."

"It's not that," he said. "We'd both had a lot to drink. I didn't want us to regret anything."

There was a hint of anger in her voice. "What's the big goddamn deal?"

"Yeah, I know. There's nothing wrong, really." He glanced over at her. "I know I'm not very sophisticated."

"I'm not sophisticated! Do I look sophisticated? Jesus!" Now there was fury on her face.

He thought of pulling over and stopping so that they could talk, but an interstate highway is not a good place to stop, so he kept going, all the while trying to think of a way out of this. It was true that he felt naïve next to her; she seemed much more experienced, more worldly.

After a long while of silence between them, they began idly talking again, both avoiding the subject of sex. The sky was cloudy, but didn't seem to threaten rain. The terrain of western Kansas became flatter. Wheat, rather than corn, seemed the principle crop. There was prairie land as well, with cattle and horses grazing. In the distance he noticed little settlements, dominated by huge grain silos and connected by railroad tracks. At one point, where the tracks paralleled the interstate, a long train slowly overtook them, probably heading as they were, for Denver.

When they stopped for lunch and refueling, their mood was back almost to normal. He noticed that he was seeing her a little differently from the day before. She was no longer a stranger, mostly mystery, subtly exciting. They had touched, emotionally, and now felt familiar to each other even as the uncomfortable issue lay between them, unspoken but never disappearing. He wished it had not come up. It felt like a faint headache, distracting but not disabling.

"You want to drive a while?" he asked.

"I'd love to," she said. "I'd read or something, but I want us to stay connected."

That felt good to him. He recognized that he had been afraid she was regretting their joint adventure. So after they were again on the highway, he decided to risk. "Tracey, I want us to be okay with each other. I don't want something to sit here between us that we aren't saying."

She looked at him for a long moment, making him a little nervous about the highway. When she saw him glancing ahead on the road, she laughed. "You afraid of my driving, too?"

"Oh, shit!" he said, "This is what I don't want!"

"I'm teasing, Mark."

That made him relax a little, and he laughed. He reached across his body and unhooked his seatbelt.

"Hallelujah!" she laughed, and pressed on the accelerator pedal.

When their speed increased noticeably, he reached back and pulled his seatbelt out again, moving it toward the buckle. "Okay, okay, I hear you!" she laughed, slowing down again.

They both laughed until tears came to his eyes. He had released the seat belt again, and turned in his seat to face her. He touched her cheek with his fingertips. She smiled broadly, glanced quickly at him, and turned her attention to the highway.

In a few minutes, he said, "You're right. We don't have to be bound by what we learned in Sunday school."

"No."

"We absorb all those assumptions that probably were meaningful in another time or another situation."

"Cultural taboos."

"My family was very traditional," he said, looking off into the distance.

"We used to laugh at you," she said. "I'm sorry, but we did. Your mom was so straight laced. I remember hearing my mother say something like wondering how your mother could have ever gotten pregnant." Tracey smiled at him.

He looked down at his hands.

"Mark," she said, "look at me. It's okay. Your mom was a good person, and she raised a couple of good kids. You and your brother are fine people."

"Just a little bit ... "

"Just a little bit—a whole lot—*fine people!*"

"I wish we could have been a little looser." He chuckled. "My older brother was sometimes a tyrant."

She laughed. "At least he could have taught you how to put on a condom."

"Yeah."

"My brother ... " She stopped.

"He was a star," Mark said.

"Well—maybe."

"He was captain of his team."

"He laid every cheerleader in school." She gave him a wry smile.

Mark was about to add that Tracey was also a cheerleader, but stopped himself.

The rest of the afternoon they watched the dry prairie go by, and were excited when they got their first glimpse of the mountains in the distance. It was very hot outside the car, but they were comfortable. At the cutoff to I-25 east of Denver, he pulled out their map. "How tired are you of driving?" he asked.

"I could go for a while. I'm looking forward to a swim, though."

"Looks like about an hour to Fort Collins. Want to try for that?"

She thought for a moment. "We'd be out of this city traffic to start tomorrow."

"True. I'll see if I can find a hotel up there."

"And a bar."

He poured over his phone and finally said, "There's a Courtyard Inn in town, a couple of miles from I-25. One of the less expensive places."

"Do they have a pool?"

"Indoor pool. And a restaurant and a coffee shop. I guess that means no free breakfast."

She looked at him. "If we eat there tonight we don't have to drive afterward."

He laughed. "We can just stagger up to our room."

"Exactly."

Their eyes met, and The Question stirred in its slumber. He dialed the hotel and made a reservation.

When she returned from her dip in the pool, he wasn't asleep—and he didn't pretend to look away. Her miniscule, flame-red two-piece suit made his mouth water. The little nagging doubt in the back of his mind sparred with much deeper, more primitive, impulses.

They went hand-in-hand down in the elevator and over to the restaurant, which was dark and crowded. "Good sign," he said. "Must be a good restaurant."

"Two martinis," he said to the waitress, "one with gin and one with vodka. Olives in both."

When the waitress left, Tracey looked at him. "How did you know to order one with vodka?"

He grinned. "You don't remember last night, telling me that you liked vodka martinis?"

"When?"

"I was smashed, but I was paying attention."

She hung her head, pretending to pout. "I don't remember that at all!"

They both laughed, and when the drinks arrived, they toasted "To spontaneity!"

By the time the waitress took their food order, Mark had the confidence to order wine for them. Tracey's eyes sparkled in the soft candlelight. "You're full of surprises," she said softly.

After the meal, they walked arm-in-arm back to their room. As soon as the door was closed, Mark pulled her to him and kissed her passionately. They lay down on one of the beds and clung to each other, both breathing heavily. He pulled her blouse over her head and began working with the fastener on her bra. Neither spoke.

But by the time both of them had shed their clothes, it was evident that not everything was in their favor. She withdrew her hand from him and instead held his face between her hands. "Something wrong?" she whispered, looking into his eyes.

"I don't know," he said.

He rolled off of her and onto his side, his eyes closed.

"It's okay," she said softly. "It happens sometimes."

He remained silent.

"Is it about last night?"

"I don't know," he repeated.

She turned to face him. "Mark, talk to me!"

After a moment, he said, "I thought I was okay with this."

"But now you're not?"

"I don't know."

She slowly rolled away from him. He heard her begin to cry.

"Tracey, it's not your fault." He put his arm over her shoulders. She continued to sob into the pillow. Her body wrenched with the struggle. Pulling himself close to her, he tried to enfold her in his embrace. "I'm sorry," he said, over and over.

Suddenly, she turned toward him, but pulled away at the same time. Her face showed her agony. She opened her tearful eyes and looked at him. Taking a deep breath, she said hoarsely, "You didn't ask me about my first time."

Mark frowned. "I don't understand."

"It was with the captain of the football team."

Shock showed on his face.

"I was one of those cheer leaders."

"My god."

"He was my god, too," she said, barely able to get the words out between sobs.

"Oh, Tracey."

"Just once," she said. "Just one time, and then he left."

Mark tightened his embrace while she sobbed into his shoulder and clutching him. They lay there for a long time, until gradually he felt her body soften and her breathing become slow and even. He even thought she might have fallen asleep, but when he gently tried to ease away, she tightened her grasp on him. "Just hold me," she whispered.

His mind raced. It was beginning to make sense to him, even her anger from that morning. His doubts had triggered her old shame, and when he failed to maintain his erection, he was abandoning her, just as her brother had done. But none of this could he say to her. He lay beside her until they both fell asleep.

Sometime during the night, he awoke, chilled by the air conditioning, and managed to get up and retrieve the spread from the other bed. Laying it gently over her, he went to the bathroom. When he returned, she was awake. She held out her arms to him, and he gladly slipped into them. By that time, her body felt warm and soft to him, and he fell asleep almost at once.

In the morning, they lay together for a long time, neither talking. There seemed nothing to say, nothing important that had not already made itself known. Finally, she said, "I have to pee." With a little laugh, she emerged from their soft nest and went into the bathroom. Soon, he heard the shower. He got up and put on his clothes and packed his suitcase except for his shaving kit that was in the bathroom.

He was sitting on the edge of the bed, thinking about the night, when she emerged naked from the bathroom. She stood there before him, her face serious. Holding out her hands, she said, "This is me. Now you know the real me."

Mark started to say something, but she interrupted him. "You don't have to say anything. I'll understand if you want to stay at a distance from me. I can't change what I am—I'm soiled. It was a tough way for you to learn what I am, I know. I understand. If we can get through the next two days, I'll arrange to fly back home after the memorial."

He held out his arms to her. "C'mere," he said, and then, "Please come here."

She moved close enough for him to take her hands. She stifled a sob.

"I didn't know when we planned this trip how it was going to be, traveling with a near-stranger. I hoped, but I wasn't expecting, that we might become real to each other."

"This is about as real as I can imagine," she said, wiping her cheek and immediately grasping his hand again. "I've never told that to anyone before." Her lip quivered.

"I sure don't want to stay at a distance from you, as you put it. I feel closer to you than I have to anyone in a long time."

"Even—" She covered her face with both hands and moaned into them. *"I am so ashamed!"*

Mark stood up and pulled her hands from her face. "Tracey," he said, "I've never had that happen to me before, either." He held on to her hands, and spread his arms wide. "This is us. This is who we are, both of us. Now we can just be ourselves, and deal with what comes up. Okay?"

She giggled lamely. "Might be stronger if you took off all your clothes, too."

He started to unbutton his shirt.

"I'm kidding, Mark."

He laughed with her. "I don't know what's going to happen to us in the next two days, or even how we'll feel about each other by the time we get to Portland. But for sure, I won't let you fly back home."

The End

The Scar

He sat in his chair next to the window, watching the tree outside blowing in the wind. Not many leaves left on the branches. It looked cold.

A knock on the door, and the woman peered around, smiling. "I brought you something!" she said.

She had been here before, this woman, but this time she was wearing a coat. She carried a large box into the room and put it on his bed. He liked this woman, but he couldn't remember her name.

"We were cleaning out the house," she said, and suddenly stopped, as though she had said something wrong. "We were straightening up the house, and found this old box of photographs. I knew you'd love to see them."

She put an arm over his shoulder. "How are you doin'?"

He looked up into her face. "Good to see you," he said. "Won't you sit down for a while? That's a heavy box."

"I like to see you smile like that," she said, taking off her coat and sitting on the edge of the bed. "Come and look at the pictures."

He rose, then doubled over slightly as his bad hip reminded him again. Straightening up, he smiled. "It just hurts when I get up." Taking a place on the bed with the cardboard box between them, he peered inside.

"Wait, let me turn on the light so we can see better." She got up and flipped the light switch next to the door. Sitting back down on the bed, she took a photograph from the top of the pile in the box. "Who's this?"

He took the photograph from her and examined it. "I don't know."

"That's your house. It must be one of your many lady friends." She looked up at him and smiled. "Gretchen?"

He frowned, and put the picture back.

The woman dug deeply into the box and pulled out a picture from near the bottom. "Oh, my goodness!" she laughed as she handed it to him.

He looked at the photograph of a young woman lying nude on her back in the sand. Something inside him clutched up, and he felt as though he were going to cry. His fingers caressed the smooth surface of the picture.

"Who is it? Let me see!" She took the picture from him. "It's Mom! Oh, my goodness!" Her laughter shook the bed under him. "*That* was a long time ago."

He took the picture back and looked at it closely, moving his head up and down to get the picture into focus through his glasses. The woman in the picture had her eyes closed. There was a long, straight scar down her belly, all the way down from her navel to disappear in her pubic hair. He put the picture in his lap and closed his eyes. He was overcome. "I killed her," he said softly.

"What?" The woman reached across the box and put her hand on his arm. "Daddy! You didn't kill her! She died just last year!" She got off the bed and kneeled before him, taking his hands in hers. "You didn't kill her!"

She took the photograph from under his hands and looked at it. "She's just posing for you. Look, she's got her eyes closed because the sun is so bright. She's certainly not dead!"

He pointed to the scar.

"That's from her hysterectomy," the woman said. "She had a hysterectomy right after I was born." She touched the photograph with her fingertips. "That picture was taken not long afterward, because the scar is still prominent. I saw that scar one time just before Mom died, and it had nearly disappeared. She told me about how after I was born she kept bleeding, and they had to remove her uterus." She laughed. "She still blamed the doctors for keeping her from having any more babies."

"The doctor came in to see me and tell me that she was in trouble," he said, suddenly remembering that day. "They couldn't stop the bleeding. He said that she might die if they didn't do something immediately. I had to sign some papers."

"You remember!" She gripped his hand and peered into his face. "Tell me, tell me!"

"On the trip to the hospital, I got stopped by a cop," he said, smiling. "He took one look at me and at you and just waved us on."

She laughed. "He took one look at you and *Mom*," she said. "I wasn't there yet. Well, I was, but he didn't see me."

"I killed her."

"Daddy! You didn't!" She lived fifty years after that! You saved her life by signing that paper!" Tears streamed down her face as she looked up at him. "Look—look at her. She's sure not dead."

He looked down at the woman in the photograph. "We were out camping with Jack and Jeanie, way back in the woods in Indiana, on some property of a relative of Jeanie's."

"Tell me! And you were there with your camera, just like always." She sat next to him on the bed and put her arm around him. "Tell me about that time."

He looked at her, at this woman who came to see him sometimes. She was familiar, especially when she laughed. "We left you and Phil with your grandmother, and Jeanie got a babysitter."

She took a sudden breath. "You know me, Daddy!" Wiping tears from her cheeks, she smiled again. "You remember when you used to carry me on your shoulders so I could reach the leaves on the trees?" She leaned her head on his shoulder. "Oh, Daddy, I love you!"

He put his arm around her and squeezed as hard as he could. "And then you grew up and climbed your own trees."

"Yeah, I grew up. Eventually, anyway. Sometimes I think I still haven't grown up."

He looked at her. "Grown up into your mother."

She laughed. "No, not that. *Anything but that!*"

That made him laugh, too. "She was a good woman," he said.

"Yes, of course she was. But I'm not her." She took his hand again. "Daddy, I used to look at you and her and wonder how you two ever got together. You were so different!"

He looked at the picture again. "Not then. We never thought we'd ever be out of love."

"Daddy, what happened? It wasn't that scar. You stayed together for years after that. I was six when you divorced. Do you remember what happened to you?"

He sighed. "I messed up," he said simply.

She hit his arm gently with her fist. "It takes two, Daddy."

"She blamed me, too." When she looked at him quickly, he added, "I signed the papers so she couldn't have any more babies."

"She would have died otherwise!"

The two of them sat silently, thinking their own thoughts about the past. His thoughts were like occasional breezes on a summer evening. This woman sitting next to him was so familiar, like a part of him, but he couldn't even remember her name.

Almost as though she could hear his thoughts, she looked up at him suddenly and asked, "Daddy, who am I? What's my name?"

"Cookie. No, *Cynthia!*"

Cynthia burst into tears and buried her face in his shoulder. He held her as tightly as his weak arms would allow. After a while her sobs subsided, and she took a tissue from her pocket to wipe her nose.

"*She* was Cookie," she said. "Then she became Carrie. I don't know why."

"And you became Cyndi."

Her eyes glistened as she looked up at him again. "But you never stopped calling me Cynthia. And I loved it."

She stood up. "Daddy, I have to go. I'll come back tomorrow." She was holding back tears.

"Tell your mother I said hi."

She squeezed his hand and went out the door. He heard a sob just before the door closed. He went back to his chair next to the window.

Outside, another brown leaf separated from its branch and fluttered down out of sight.

.

The End

Pumping Gas

Routine. Pull into the bay, estimate where to stop so the gas nozzle is close to the tank in the car, get out, pull billfold from pocket, insert credit card into slot, unscrew gas tank cap, letting it dangle, pull pump nozzle from its socket and insert it into tank. Reach over to press the button to start the pump, and stand there thinking about something else as the gasoline pours into the tank.

How many times had he gone through this routine in the past twenty years? Once a week, at least, that's a thousand times. He glanced across to the other side of the pump island and saw that the car there was sitting unattended with the pump nozzle inserted in the tank. It bothered him a little, which made him smile at his own obsessive-compulsive tendencies. He obeyed the rules, followed the routines of his life for the most part, and true to type noticed nearly everything, counted strokes as he brushed his teeth, even "counting the cars on the New Jersey Turnpike," as the old song went (he laughed as he thought of this). Routine was comfortable. Routine was safe--it helped him to be sure he was doing all the things he had to do, especially the things he didn't really care about.

A woman's voice distracted him from his thoughts. She was on the other side of that car, talking loudly into her cell phone. She glanced over at him and, noticing that he was watching her, frowned and got into her car so he couldn't hear her continue what seemed to be an argument.

He finished filling his tank, replaced the pump nozzle and filler cap and closed the little door. Getting into his car, he pulled out the notebook from its compartment and entered in it the date, mileage, and number of gallons. He'd calculate his gas mileage at the end of the month, as he always did.

A loud noise from outside the car interrupted his routine. Looking out, he saw the woman's car stop suddenly, its brake lights continuing to shine as what happened registered in her mind. The pump nozzle lay on the pavement, leaking the small amount of gasoline that hadn't gone into her tank when the pump shut off.

He got out of his car and picked up the hose nozzle, noting that it didn't seem to be damaged. Returning it to its socket in the pump, he turned to see the woman, shock showing on her face, opening the door of her car.

"I'll get it," he said to her, retrieving her gas cap from the ground and replacing it, closing the door in a single, much-practiced movement. "No damage done."

She got out of her car and came to him. She seemed on the verge of tears. "How could I have done such a stupid thing?" she exclaimed. "Thank you!"

"I've done the same thing," he lied. He noticed that she was wearing sweat pants and a tank top, but her dark hair was well tended. Looked to be in her fifties. She held sunglasses in one hand and touched her forehead with the other in embarrassment.

"I was upset," she explained. "You probably noticed." A hint of smile dimpled one corner of her mouth.

"I've done that, too," he said.

"I'm shaking." She held out her hand to show him.

"I see that. I'll buy you a cup of coffee," he said, gesturing toward the service station store.

"I'd rather have a drink," she said, her smile widening. "I'd even buy."

He looked around and gestured. "That restaurant probably has drinks."

She put her hand on his arm. "Thank you. You've been kind. Do you have time?"

"I'm retired," he said. "I have nothing but time."

It was the middle of the afternoon, and the restaurant was deserted except for them. A waiter came over immediately.

"Martini," she said to him, "vodka, no olives, straight up."

He ordered a gin and tonic, and when the waiter left, the woman touched his hand and laughed. "I haven't picked up a man in years," she said.

"My name is Keith."

"Meridele."

"You're not shaking any more."

She grinned. "And I haven't even had the drink yet."

The waiter returned with their drinks. She lifted her glass. "To Sir Galahad."

He touched her glass with his and sipped the cold liquid. "I didn't do anything except put your gas cap back on."

"But you were so cool about it all. John Wayne cool."

"Wow. Never been compared to him before."

She took a long drink from her glass. "He was way before my time," she said, "but I've seen a lot of his movies on TV."

"Late night television."

"I'm up a lot at night. Haven't had a good night's sleep in years."

"Really?"

"A lot of tension at work—and at home," she said. "I try to catch a nap when I get home."

"Kids at home?" Then he raised his hand. "I'm sorry. Didn't mean to get personal."

"It's okay. No, no kids left at home. They're all gone, doing their own thing."

He took a drink, suddenly wanting to ask more but choosing discretion instead.

"Yes," she said in answer to his unasked question, "there's a husband—sort of."

"Mmmm," he said.

She laughed. "Okay, John Wayne, your turn." She drained her glass, set it down and stared at him.

It occurred to him to remark about how quickly she had finished the martini. Instead, "Actually, he was a hero of mine when I was a kid."

"And now?"

He cringed inwardly, but said it anyway, "I didn't like his politics."

"Ah, a bleeding heart liberal!" He could tell she was feeling the martini.

"Probably," he said. "But I voted for Ike."

Her face showed surprise. "You don't look that old."

"The second time, I voted for Stevenson." He laughed to cover his embarrassment. "You probably weren't even born then."

"No." She seemed amused.

He was carefully folding his cocktail napkin into a thin strip. "Been married for fifty-five years."

"That's wonderful."

He sipped his drink and looked at her over the top of the glass. "You said you hadn't picked up a man in years."

She laughed. "That's true," she said. "Scares me a little."

"Why is that?"

"I'm thinking of leaving my husband,"

"That who you were arguing with over there?" He gestured toward the gas station.

"Yes."

"That why you can't sleep?"

She looked at him levelly. "You are learning a lot about me."

He shrugged. "Just making conversation." He lifted his glass, which held only ice cubes. "Loosens the tongue."

"Doesn't it." It was a statement. "I still don't know anything about you. Do you often have drinks in the afternoon with strange women?"

"John Wayne's pretty much a loner."

"Like you."

"I guess."

"What's your wife's name?"

"Carol." He looked at his watch. "She'll be home from work soon."

"Okay," she said. "You need to be there." She reached for her purse.

He signaled the waiter.

"This is on me," she said, opening her wallet.

Awkwardly, he followed her as she paid the bill and they left the restaurant. Standing next to their cars, they shook hands. "You're a gentleman," she said, "thank you."

He smiled. "I hope you have better luck next time."

She had started to open her car door, but whirled to face him. "What's that supposed to mean?" Anger showed on her face.

He held up a hand. "I'm sorry. I only meant that if you're looking around, you'll have better luck meeting somebody ..."

"I wasn't looking!" She was furious. "I just wanted to acknowledge your kindness about the gas pump!"

He sighed. "I'm sorry."

She shook her head, then her shoulders slumped. "It's okay."

He sighed and went around his car to the driver's side.

"Keith." She was still standing by her open door, watching him. When he looked up, she said, "You're still a gentleman." But she didn't smile.

Smiling wanly, he ducked into his car and closed the door. He sat there until her car had backed out and left the parking lot.

Then he took his notebook from its compartment and finished entering the numbers for the gas purchase, slightly annoyed that he had not noted the odometer reading before he left the gas station. He pressed the button on the dashboard to zero the reading.

Driving home, he remembered her scent. Carol wouldn't mind, he thought.

The End

Guardian

Each of us has a kind of alter ego, a Jiminy Cricket, a little devil and/or angel sitting on our shoulder, or a mirror person in our imagination. Maybe it's our ideal self, the person we wish we were. A "What would Jesus do?" kind of persona, with balls.

Mine, of course, has straight teeth and big biceps, and can carry on a conversation. He has confidence, energy and skill in bed. He also reminds me (sometimes) when I'm not making sense or when I'm pontificating—"again!"

I carry on a continual dialog with him. His name is Frank.

He rode with me all the way to Ames. Actually, he was better company than the talk radio stations that were all I could get after I left the Chicago area. I was trying to get comfortable with the idea that I was driving three hundred miles for a blind date. I'd met her online a couple of months before, and we'd had some good conversations by email, and she'd invited me to "come on out."

"You're an arrogant wuss," Frank said.

"It has survival value," I reasoned.

"So does joining a convent." He stammered. "Well, maybe that's not a good example for a man—a *so-called* man. I should have said *monastery.*"

"We've been writing to each other for a long time, and if she didn't think I had possibilities, she wouldn't have invited me out."

"What's she have to lose? An evening, maybe—the dinner will be on you, you know."

"She's great-looking woman," I said.

"Yeah, if the picture was of her." He grunted. "Recently."

"She's a college professor, not the type who would deceive people."

"Hmmph," was all he answered, looking out the window at miles of cornfields.

I thought of all the emails she and I had exchanged since running into each other on facebook. I don't know how it happened that the program had suggested we might become friends. Maybe someone I knew knew her. Maybe it picked up on some kind of similarity in our backgrounds. Her writing was polished, in a spontaneous kind of way. "Elegant spontaneity." (I liked that. I'll have to remember it.) Sometimes we'd be online at the same time, and she'd answer my messages immediately, as though we were in a chat room. She had a sensuous, sophisticated style.

"I teach English composition," she had written. "I like that you take the time to express what you're saying, and you don't use all those Internet contractions."

I had admitted that I'd been writing since high school, even though I'd never published anything under my own byline. The crap I wrote for the agencies was not what I wanted to write. It was a living.

"What do you want to write?" she had asked.

"Stories about people. Real emotions."

"Would you send me something?"

I did, and she said she loved it. "It feels real," she said. "I wish I could get my students to write that well."

"Dream on," said Frank, sitting beside me in the car, filing his nails.

"Well," I replied, "I've got three or four days—enough time to find out if there is anything there for me."

"With the price of gas and the probability that this old car won't make it to Iowa and back," he said, "three or four days are not all you're risking."

"I can park it around the corner so she doesn't see it right away. It's a good, reliable car. Sensible."

"Wuss!"

"Fuck you."

"You're even wearing a tie!" Frank was obviously not impressed with me. He never was. He wears shirts with the top two buttons unbuttoned, so you can see the hair on his chest. Never wears an undershirt. When I try that, the sweat from my armpits runs down my side. "What are you paying me for?" he chided.

"I don't remember asking you for advice," I said.

"Ha!" he snorted. "Where would you be without me?"

"Without you always belittling me, I might have some confidence."

"Then you really would be an arrogant wuss. You're going seventy in a fifty-mile zone," he added.

I slowed down and looked in my rear-view mirror. No police cars behind me. I glanced over at him. He was good looking, a kind of Nick Nolte-type. No beard.

Overhearing my thoughts, as usual, he said, "That beard makes you look pompous. And seedy at the same time. At least the guys with the week-old whiskers you see on TV look virile."

"Yeah, like they just got back from a fishing trip in Canada, smelly and dirty."

"Flew out to a lake in a float plane. Pristine wilderness, no roads. Built campfires with a single match."

"Not the kind of guy Martha would go for."

"That ten-year-old photograph you sent her might be the kind she would go for. Wait until she sees the gray hair."

"Lay off, will you?"

"I'm just *sayin* ..."

"I'm trying to think of things she would like to talk about," I said. "Leave me alone."

He smiled that smug smile.

It was hard to tell from her photograph how old Martha was. Neither of us had brought up the subject of age. I'd thought of it, but decided that the relationship wouldn't depend that much on our ages. All I'd written to her should have given her some idea that I wasn't a kid. And I'd told her that the photo of me had been taken a few years before. She hadn't mentioned how old her photo was.

"I have to admit," I said to Frank fifty miles farther down the road, "I'm a little uneasy about this if it gets sexual."

"No kidding! You should be!"

"Fuck you!" I was aware I was repeating myself. Not something a writer wants to do a lot. "It's been a long time, though."

"Sitting at your computer at night, instead of getting out and circulating. There's stuff out there, who would be glad to help you practice."

"Nice girls don't do it," I said.

"Whoo-ey!" he whooped. "This ain't the nineteen fifties."

He had me there. I was just scared of rejection. I wasn't sure how to handle a woman who might take the initiative. All those wild scenes on television, backing them up against a wall or lifting them up on the kitchen counter—that's not something I'd be likely to do.

Frank grinned at my images. "Takes practice," he said. "And testosterone—something you ain't got much of."

I clammed up and just drove. By the time we crossed the Mississippi, I was bummed.

"Hey kid," he said finally, "You can do it. Don't think about it so much."

"Wonder if I should get a motel first."

"Hell, no! That sends her a message you don't want to send."

"What's that?" I asked.

"She may not be the kind who would go to a motel. She's a professor—she wouldn't want her students to see her go into a motel. Think, man!"

"But if I don't, won't that look like I'm expecting her to invite me to her place?"

"Aren't you? At least, wait until you're having dinner. And then you can casually ask her where's the best lodging in town. Don't say 'motel'."

I sighed. "After six o'clock is not a good time to find a motel. She'll think I'm not organized enough to think ahead. Or she'll think I'm hinting for an invite."

He shook his head. "Christ! If she invited you to come three hundred miles to see her, she had to know you'd be sleeping somewhere. If not her place, then she will have made arrangements already. She's the host, after all."

My stomach was already doing flip-flops.

"Watch that truck," he said, motioning ahead. "You're following too close."

"Yeah." I backed off.

"Pass 'im, for Christ sake!" he yelled. "You won't get to Ames before Wednesday!"

I checked my mirror and went into the left lane. I had to do eighty to pass the truck, and I kept looking for flashing lights behind me. "If you were driving," I said, "we'd be spending the night in jail."

"Like they used to say when you were a kid," he said, "if you asked a lot of girls, you might get slapped a few times, but you'd get a lot more tail."

"What's that got to do with speeding?"

"It's your attitude, stupid! You're a wuss!"

"I like to be considerate," I said.

"You're way over the top considerate," he said. "If she doesn't want you to be straightforward, she's a controlling bitch anyway."

"Knock it off! I just want to play this my way."

"You always do."

"I'm in unfamiliar territory," I said. "This is important to me."

"Well, you don't want to say all that to her. She wants you to be a man. Take charge, get a good table for dinner, and tip the maître d'. Then ask her if she wants you to order for her. They love that. And don't be ordering cheap wine!"

I sighed. Actually, I think I sighed a couple of times. Frank didn't say any more for a while.

"You don't think I should be wearing a tie." I looked over at him. He was sleeping. I nudged him. "Hey, wake up! I need you!"

Frank opened one eye. "No, you don't."

"Do you think I should take this tie off?"

"Are you asking my advice?"

"Yes. Yes. I admit, you're smarter than I am."

"Then, yes, take the stupid tie off. Open your shirt a little bit."

We were pulling off I-35 at Ames. I stopped alongside the road to look at her directions. She was on the other side of town.

"Frank," I said, "I got this now. Would you please hide?" My stomach was growling. I hadn't eaten since breakfast.

"Anything you say. You're the boss."

"Don't I wish," I said, and he was gone.

.

The End

The Funeral

The long line of cars parked along the curving drive, each one adorned by a little blue flag, was like one of those optical illusions—it could be seen as a conga line at a wild party, or a multicolored, jointed snake toy. No people were visible.

Inside the seventh car, a youngish middle-aged couple sat looking straight ahead, silently waiting, The woman leaned against the steering wheel to reach down and pull a tissue from her purse on the floor. She dabbed at her eyes. "He was kind enough to avoid her face," she said hoarsely.

"I can't imagine how they let it go so far without getting help," he said. "For God's sake, why didn't he say something to somebody?"

She glanced quickly at him, then turned back to face forward, watching the blank doors on the funeral home. "I should have guessed," she said. "I should have sensed that he was near the breaking point."

"How could you guess that? They were both so funny when we got together. Always laughing. Their banter was always light, even the little digs she made at him."

"Those 'little digs,' as you put it," she said, "were hurtful." She dabbed at her face again. "She knew how to hurt him. They were like rapier thrusts!"

"I never heard him complain," he said. "Even on our fishing trips—and we talked about everything—he never mentioned anything."

"No," she said, "he wouldn't. But she was so cruel to him!"

The doors to the funeral home opened, and a fastidiously dressed man came out to prop them open. A casket gurney appeared, pushed by two men, followed by another casket through the open doors. They were rolled to the matched pair of hearses parked at the head of the snake-shaped line of cars.

The couple saw little puffs of vapor between cars as people began starting their engines. The woman turned her ignition key.

"She was just bored," he said. "He didn't pay enough attention to her. All she wanted was to be made over once in a while."

The woman glanced at him again. "Well, you certainly did your part."

He looked directly at her. "What's that supposed to mean?"

"It means that you made over her every chance you got."

He turned to face forward again, frowning. He didn't respond.

"Wayne," she said, looking at him, 'admit it. You treated her like your own little princess."

His face reddened. "Bull shit," he said softly.

The funeral attendants had disappeared into their vehicles. The woman glanced ahead, waiting for the procession to begin, and then turned to study his face. "Were you sleeping with her?"

He was silent, and she suddenly laughed at him. "Look at you! You were, weren't you?"

"She just wanted to be touched. *He* never did. She was starved for affection!" He kept looking straight ahead. "We're moving," he said, gesturing toward the cars ahead of them.

"You bastard!" she said, angrily pulling the shift lever to Drive. "How long have you two been fucking?"

"Come on," he protested, "this isn't the time for this talk. They are both dead! Show some respect!"

She followed the line of cars out of the drive and into the street, where a motorcycle policeman was directing traffic. Once they were moving along the highway, she glanced at him again. "I knew it," she said quietly. "I knew she was fucking somebody. *It was you!*" Her last words were through clenched teeth.

He said nothing, and then looked over at her. "I'm sorry, Karen."

She drove on silently, looking straight ahead. Tears were streaming down her cheeks.

""I felt sorry for her at first," he said to the little flags fluttering on the line of cars ahead of them. "It just happened. I guess we had a lot to drink, and it just happened."

"When was that?" She glanced quickly at him. "When did it *'just happen'*?"

"Two years ago. It was that party at their house. She was so miserable. We went into a bedroom so we could talk. And it just happened."

"That fucking slut!" she spat.

"She wasn't a slut!" He sighed deeply. "He ignored her. He hadn't touched her in months."

"And so Mister Prince Charming, you took pity on her. So—how was it?" She glanced at him again. "Your tight little princess—how was it?"

He didn't answer.

Sarcastically, "Did she do nice things for you?" After a long silence, her voice changed. "Was she better than me?"

"Karen." He pulled out his handkerchief and blew his nose. "She's dead now, Karen."

They drove silently for a while, the procession moving through traffic like a railroad train, with vehicles on side roads waiting for them to pass. One could almost hear the crossing bells signaling at each intersection.

She stared ahead. "Wayne," she said quietly.

He glanced at her but didn't say anything.

"He and I were doing it, too." She cleared her throat.

When he looked at her she nodded. "About that long." Her voice was barely audible.

After a time, he said simply, "Jesus."

The procession entered the cemetery and slowly snaked along the curved drives.

"I had no idea," he said.

She looked at him with a faint smile. When she opened her mouth to say something, he interrupted her. "I don't think I want to know."

"All right."

She pulled to the curb behind the car ahead of them and turned off the ignition. They got out of the car and joined the other silent mourners moving toward the two open graves. The caskets were already in place over the openings. Green coverings were spread over the mounds of earth on either side.

High clouds reduced the sunlight to a bright ceiling over them. There was no tent over the gravesites, and only a light breeze stirred in the trees. Karen and Wayne stood among the others, occasionally nodding to someone but saying nothing to anyone. The minister droned on about the tragedy, never hinting at the violence that had brought them all together. When he was finished, someone threw a shovel of earth into each of the graves, and the group gradually disbursed.

On the path back to the cars, a woman spoke to them. "You were good friends of theirs, weren't you?"

Wayne nodded, but said nothing.

"Such an awful thing," the woman said. "How two such beautiful people could be in such turmoil that they would do this!"

Karen murmured something and turned away toward their car.

In the car, they watched the funeral cars move away, followed by other cars from the procession. Karen put the key in the ignition, but didn't turn it.

Wayne broke down and sobbed into his hands. Karen watched him silently, not moving. He finally pulled out his handkerchief and blew his nose. Looking up through the windshield at the trees, he blinked several times. "I can't help but wonder ...," he began.

"Maybe," she said, "we could have helped."

"*Sure!*" he said vehemently, "Maybe we could have helped them through it, if we had known!" His voice broke. "But I can't help but wonder—did we *do it?*"

"Do what?" She looked at him, wide-eyed. "Wayne!"

They stared at each other.

"I feel like," he moaned, "—like we helped pull that trigger."

She gave a little cry. "Wayne!" She looked at him, horror on her face.

Suddenly moved by her distress, he held out his arms to her. She collapsed into them, sobbing. They remained huddled there, in the quiet of the cemetery, long after the other cars had gone.

.

The End

The Director

Keeping her hands behind her back to avoid bumping the camera, Brianna leaned in and squinted at the little screen. "Okay," she said, "let's try it again. Janine, turn your head slowly toward him. That's it—don't take your eyes off his, just turn your head. Good! Now smile!"

Behind her, Sean laughed. "She's going to have a stiff neck."

"Shut up, Sean." Brianna straightened up and turned the camera off. "I'm the one that'll have a stiff neck, trying to see in that tiny viewfinder. Okay, you two, relax for a minute. I want to play that back. No, no! Don't move! Just relax."

Janine and Greg smiled at each other. "It's all I can do to keep from laughing at you," Janine said to Brianna. "You're like Drew What'sername, making this big Hollywood movie."

Brianna scowled, studying the moving image in the camera. "Well, this is how it's done," she said. "We have to pay attention to details."

"When do we get to do it?" Greg asked, stroking Janine's bare leg.

"Oh, my god!" Janine laughed. "You are ready!"

"Stop that!" Brianna said. "You'll get your chance. Now, let me move the camera for the next shot."

The four had been working hard for over an hour, and the strain was beginning to show. For the couple in front of the camera, it was great fun, and they were both turned on, anticipating the "big scene." Sean was standing behind Brianna, grinning all the while. The only serious one was Brianna, trying to make her story the way she had scripted it.

Her own excitement had been while she was writing the scene. It was all she could do to keep typing at the computer, thinking about what she was creating. Alone in her room, she closed her eyes and visualized the action, then typed furiously, breathing heavily.

She picked up her phone and called Sean. "I want you," she said.

He laughed in her ear. "You're writing the big scene," he said. "I can tell."

"I need you."

"You know I can't come over there now," he replied. "I have to finish this paper tonight."

Brianna clicked off and tossed the phone onto the desk. Turning back to the computer, she read over what she had been writing. It was a simple story—the same old story—boy meets girl, they make love, and he leaves her for some other girl. But the story is in the details, and at that point the details were carrying her away. She pictured Janine and Greg making love, and she wrote the details, her own body finally overwhelming her dedication to art. She slipped her hand inside her shorts.

The four of them had dreamed up the video the previous week, all of them lying on Brianna's living room floor downing shots of Absolut Citron with Red Bull. Brianna had been lying in Sean's arms feeling warm and comfortable, watching Janine and Greg feeling each other up. "We ought to be taping this!" she had said.

They had all become friends a few months before after meeting at a going away party for a classmate of Brianna, lying on the floor and talking for hours about movies and honesty and sex. "Why does it have to be such a big thing?" Janine had asked. "We all do it—that's how we're made!"

"But putting it up on the screen, you need to make it graceful," Brianna had said, "like music."

She had glanced over at Sean, whom she had noticed watching her earlier. "What do you think?"

"You're absolutely right!" he'd answered, slurring his words in a way that she found appealing. "Art has to mean something."

"But does sex?" Janine asked. "We're not back in Victorian times, when you couldn't even whisper the word."

"They had to make it a big thing then," said Greg. "There wasn't a pill then, or antibiotics."

Sean cleared his throat. "There were people even then, who wanted more openness, like Margaret Sanger."

The other three looked at him. "Margaret who?"

"Margaret Sanger. She was a nurse, who tried to get information about birth control out to people, and even got thrown in jail for it."

"No shit?" Greg asked.

Sean's face reddened, as though he were revealing some secret of his own. "It was against the law to tell people about birth control. Federal law. It was considered obscene."

Brianna said, "You're a history major, right?"

"Yeah," he said, looking down. Then he looked back up at her. "She knew Havelock Ellis, too. He was a psychologist who wrote a big book about sex. That was during those same Victorian years."

"So this openness about sex didn't start in 1970."

"The pill had a lot to do with it," Janine said.

"Yeah," said Brianna. "And condoms."

"We owe our parents," said Greg, laughing, "for making the world a better place to live."

The warmth of that evening on the carpet had led to more intimate talks among the four of them, and inevitably to less inhibited gatherings. Brianna, however, clung to her dream of doing bold video, "honest video."

"But it has to be good," she said, "not just screwing around."

"You think too much," Sean had said in her ear. It was true, she knew. Her imagination took her places no reality could go. When Sean made love to her, she drifted off into a different world, the sensations in her body transporting her far away from him. When she touched him at those times, she was touching someone else, and she could control that scene just the way she wanted, flying away in the embrace of—someone else.

Sean was a sweet man. He was gentle with her, sometimes too gentle. When he was inside her, it was only that part that she felt. The rest of him became almost irrelevant.

Watching Janine and Greg across the room, Brianna felt them both, their exploring hands, their moist skin touching her own, the sweetness of their lips touching hers even as they touched each other. She snuggled against Sean and basked in the warmth of his body. But her desire was her own imagining. And her imagining became a video that she wanted to make concrete.

"You mean," Janine said, frowning, "you want to put us up on YouTube fucking?" The word startled them all, the earthiness of it intruding.

"No, not if that makes you uncomfortable," Brianna said. "I just want to make the video. It doesn't have to go anywhere."

"Sounds like a lot of work," Greg said, grinning, "for you—not so much for us."

"I don't want to kid you," Brianna said. "acting in front of a camera is hard work. We might have to do take after take."

That brought laughter from all of them. "Well, maybe after nine or ten takes," Greg said, "I might have some difficulty getting it up."

Janine looked up at him, her eyes gleaming. "I wonder," she mused, "how many times you could do it."

Sean laughed. "Might go over budget."

"Whose budget?" asked Janine.

The four of them finally agreed. They would make the film, and it couldn't be sent to YouTube or anyplace else on the Internet. Brianna held up a flash drive. "Each of us will get a copy on one of these, and each copy will have a code to tell where it came from. So nobody has to worry."

"Do I get a part in this porn flick?" asked Sean.

"Sure," said Brianna. "And it's not a porn flick!"

"Whoa!" protested Greg.

"Don't sweat it," Brianna said, "I didn't mean he'd be part of your big scene."

Janine and Brianna exchanged looks. "There's always room in a video for bit parts," said Brianna.

"You going to be in it?" asked Sean.

"Okay, yeah, I'll be another bit part." But Brianna didn't know how all that would come about. When she thought about it later, some intriguing ideas came to her, but she set them aside. This video was to be her fantasy, but maybe not quite that much.

She spent most of the next week writing the script for the "big scene." She wouldn't show it to anyone, not even Sean. He teased her about it every time he saw her, but she was determined to keep it private until it was finished.

School was hard for her, not because she couldn't do the required work but because she kept dreaming of things beyond school, projects like this little video that she could never turn in for a grade. Class time usually bored her. She aced her exams, and read five times as many books as they were assigned. She wrote to directors and producers, begging for a chance at intern appointments. A few replies of encouragement, but no calls of, "Be here Tuesday morning!"

"You scare me sometimes," Sean told her. "Your mind goes like the Energizer Bunny."

"I just want to *do something!*" she said.

"You're doing something. You're getting your credentials in media. And you're making your little videos. You could relax once in a while."

She laughed and pressed her body against his. "You know you love my energy."

"So tell me how you're writing me into the script." He ran his hands under her loosely fitting top, feeling that back that was seldom encumbered by bra straps.

Brianna frowned. "I don't know. You and I will both come and go—the story is about them."

He withdrew his hands and leaned back against the sofa. "Brianna, what do you see when you look at me?"

"What d'you mean?"

"Am I just a convenient bit player?"

She frowned. "Do you mean in the video?"

"I mean in real life." He bent over to see her face.

"Sean! What a thing to say!" Little ridges showed between her eyebrows.

"Seriously."

"Of course not! You're in my heart!" She struck her chest with a fist.

"From one to ten," he said, still watching her face.

"Ten, Sean." Her voice was lower in pitch, warm, but not quite intimate. She gave him a quick kiss.

He dropped his arms to the floor, not touching her. "I was hoping for at least eleven." When she looked at his face, a slow smile was growing. She reached around and poked him in the ribs. Both of them laughed, and they embraced awkwardly, then rolled to the floor, where they enjoyed full-body contact.

Brianna sat at her computer, arms crossed, reading from the screen. Then she typed:

> She is standing by the copier, watching it churn out paper. He moves to her side and slips a hand down inside the back of her slacks. She—very slowly— looks up at him, smiling.

Picturing the familiar smile of her friend Janine, Brianna smiled herself. Janine was an excellent puppet for her story. In the script, in the story that was still forming in Brianna's imagination, she did what she was told. She could be molded like a clay figure on a kindergarten play table. She never objected; indeed, she was anything but inert clay. She spoke in a sultry voice, silky smooth, and her eyes always shined with excitement. All Brianna had to do was write down what the Janine in her head was doing and saying.

"That light is too bright," Brianna said. She moved from the camera to the light stand. To Sean, she said, "Watch the image. As I make it dimmer, when does the back light become noticeable?"

Janine and Greg watched them adjust the light, maintaining their tangled embrace on the fur rug. Greg whispered something to the woman in his arms, and both of them giggled quietly.

"Okay," Brianna said, returning to her position behind the camera, "Now, move your hips v-e-r-y slowly. That's perfect. Keep it up until I yell, 'cut!' Good! Keep going. Now, when I say 'cut,' be sure to stay in position. Cut."

Looking over at Sean, she said, "Help me move the camera over there." She nodded toward the right. "Careful we don't disturb the floor markers."

Shooting with a single camera was complicated. Brianna dreamed of the day when she could command two—better, three—cameras, and a half-dozen crew members to take care of the logistics of video. Now, she had to move the camera and the lights herself, and direct the actors while keeping the details of continuity in her head. "Janine," she said, "you moved your foot. Back more—that's it."

Behind the camera once more, she studied the scene in the viewfinder and made a small adjustment.

"You lost it," Janine told Greg. "Brianna, he's lost it."

"It won't show," Brianna said. "just keep your hips together."

"But ..."

"I can't help it," protested Greg. "I can't just stop and start."

"It'll be okay. Trust me. Okay?" She turned and looked at Sean, who was enjoying the situation. "Sean, check the script. What happens in this shot?"

"Looks like more of the same," he said. "It's only fifteen seconds long."

Janine frowned at Greg. "Can you get it back in?"

"I'm trying!"

"Stop that!" shouted Brianna. "You're moving out of position!"

Janine winced twice, then smiled. "Okay! Roll 'em!"

Brianna looked at Sean and shook her head. Sean was doubled over laughing.

"Come on, guys!" Brianna pleaded. "We only have two more shots."

"Looks good," Sean said.

"Rolling," said Brianna. "Janine, quit laughing! Now I have to cut that out."

A moment later, Greg was not laughing, but soaring in ecstasy. He groaned, then stiffened. Sean applauded.

"Oh, my god!" said Janine suddenly, arching her back. "Oh, my god!"

Brianna turned the camera off. "Cut," she said, discouraged. "That wasn't fifteen seconds." She walked over to the sideboard and picked up the vodka bottle. Taking a gulp from it, she said, "That's a wrap."

Janine, looking at the floor, said softly, "I'm sorry." Then she looked at Greg and smiled.

Later, after the two actors had left—they had all sampled the vodka and laughed at the shoot—Brianna and Sean shared a thawed mac and cheese from her refrigerator, washing it down with more Absolut Citron.

"You did good," Sean said to her.

"We'll never get the lighting the same," she said. "It's going to be obvious that the next shots were done at a different time."

"I'll make notes about the brightness of that key light. We don't have to move the light between now and then, do we?"

"But they won't be able to find that position again!"

"You've got the shot in the camera," he said. All you have to do is ... "

"I know," she interrupted. "I just wanted those shots today."

Sean stood up and held out his hand. "C'mere" he said. Brianna finally stood up and took his hand. He grinned at her. "You just need a rub down."

That night Brianna dreamed that the four of them were splashing naked in a shallow surf. Greg was casting a fishing line with his penis—adequately enlarged, bending just slightly as he whipped the bait back over his head. She woke to find Sean lying beside her, smiling at her.

"Good morning," he said. "You were sleeping soundly."

"I dreamed about you," she lied.

He kissed her tenderly. "I have a class in an hour." He slipped out of bed and headed for the bathroom. Brianna watched him go, remembering her dream.

A movie guides the viewer's eye to what the story wants you to see, just as a piece of music guides the ear. Neither are quite like a book, which allows you to stop and re-read when you have a question about what has happened or who it happened to. You can pause and think about the meaning of an event—or a possible meaning—before continuing. Watching a movie, if you don't keep up, your question just gets bigger.

Brianna typed as she thought, calling up pieces of action, breaking the story in her mind into bits that would direct attention to details of anatomy, of movement, of expression. Writing the details distracted her fantasy, but she knew that was the price of art. As she read over what she had written, her mind could race through the descriptions to connect the pieces together and recreate her fantasy.

It fascinated her, this process. Pure imagination, translated into words on a page, which would then be translated into actions by living puppets and captured on tape, which would in turn be translated into images—the imagined story made real.

They finished the crucial shots and took a number of cutaway shots for editing insurance. The Big Scene was in the can. Sitting on Brianna's balcony enjoying a mild September day, they talked about the video. "What's next?" Sean asked. "When do I get my turn?"

"Well," Brianna said, "I had originally thought that Greg would have another girl friend, and Janine would find out and leave him."

"And now?"

"Maybe she finds another boy friend, instead." Brianna looked off into the distance, thinking.

Greg frowned. "I don't think I like that," he said, looking at Janine, who simply smiled.

Brianna waved her hands. "No, we won't tape that—we'll just suggest it."

Greg looked at Sean. "No offense, Bro. That just feels shitty to me."

Sean shrugged. "No problem. I understand. I'd feel the same way."

"C'mon, guys!" Janine exclaimed. "We're all friends here."

"I hate feeling possessive," Greg said. He put his hand on Janine's arm.

Brianna turned to look at Sean. "Do you feel possessive?"

Sean, uncomfortable, glanced from one to another. "I wouldn't call it possessive," he said. "I have a hard time being so casual about who I'm making love to. I want to feel that she's totally into me. I've never had more than one sexual partner at a time."

"Isn't that possessive?" Brianna was watching Sean's face. A feeling grew in her chest, something she could not quite identify.

He looked directly at her. "Sometimes I wonder, when we're making love, where you are."

Brianna blushed and looked down.

"Oh, shit," said Greg softly, watching the two of them.

"I don't have a problem in the abstract," Sean said. "It's just a gut feeling."

"What do you mean," Brianna asked, "abstract?" The feeling grew more distinct, but still not nameable.

"Fucking is just fun," he said. "Like, I've been enjoying watching you two—" nodding toward Janine and Greg, "having fun, and that's cool."

Greg and Janine exchanged glances.

"But," Sean continued, looking at Brianna, "I have this feeling about you and me. Like it's just ours. I don't think I could watch you screwing somebody else."

Nobody spoke for a long time. Then Brianna said quietly, "Sean, when we are doing it, my mind just goes off in its own world. I can't help it."

"Then what am I doing there? Do you even need me there?"

Brianna looked down. In a small voice, "Yes, of course."

Janine put her hand on Brianna's arm. "Brianna, can I ask you a personal question?"

Greg laughed. "How much more personal can we get?"

Janine's voice was gentle. "Do you masturbate a lot?"

Brianna looked quickly at her, blushed, then nodded very slightly.

"I don't mean there's anything wrong with it," Janine said, "I used to—a lot. But then I discovered that it was kind of a habit, to fantasize, and I wasn't enjoying doing it with a man as much. It was like it took away the sharing of all that intensity."

"I get that," said Sean.

"I'm not all that into monogamy," Janine said, then looked at Greg. "I know you are, and I respect that. I won't cheat on you."

Greg's face was serious. "You mean you think about doing it with other guys?"

"Not when I'm with you! That's what I'm trying to say!" Janine took his hand in hers. "Sure, I like to fuck. And I'm attracted to other guys. But I wouldn't hurt you for anything!"

They sat in silence. Sean poured vodka into his glass, and held up the bottle to offer some to the others. They all shook their heads, and he tossed the liquor into his mouth.

"I'm here, Greg," Janine said, "I'm here with you. When we do it, I'm all yours. Nobody else is here." She pointed to her head.

Greg brooded, looking over the railing at the traffic in the street.

"Shit!" exclaimed Brianna. She slumped down in her chair. "Now I can't finish it!"

When the others all looked at her, she said, "I love stories. I love telling stories, and this was just a story I was telling. Now it's all screwed up. Like, it's *contaminated!*"

"What the hell does that mean?" asked Janine.

"If I have to deal with what's going on inside all of you, like, it's not my story anymore!"

"Brianna," said Sean, "I don't have a problem with you doing your videos. I don't have a problem with you going deep into your stories. This video has been fun for me, partly because I enjoy watching these two going at it, like I said, and partly because I like how your imagination works. But that little twist at the end, where they break up because one of them goes off with somebody else, it seems to make it more personal, and it brings up some stuff for me."

"But that's the drama!" Brianna said, her voice quavering.

Greg reached for the bottle and poured a generous amount into his glass. Janine held her glass out for him to fill it as well.

Looking up at them, Brianna's eyes filled. Her voice broke as she said, "I thought it would be fun for us—we're so into each other. We have always been cool with talking about sex, and doing it in the same room, even ..."

"In the same bed!" added Greg.

"I love you guys!" Brianna said. "I don't want this video to mess that up! But it's not finished—without the drama, it's just a porn flick."

Sean scooted his chair over closer to Brianna so their knees touched. "You know," he said, leaning toward her, "I wish we were taping *this*."

Brianna looked at him sharply.

"This, right now, feels so real to me," he said. "How much more drama could you want?"

Janine, her eyes glistening, said, "This is as real as we've ever gotten with each other."

Brianna put her face in her hands and cried. Janine reached an arm across her shoulders without saying anything.

Sean took her hand. "I'm sorry, Brianna," he said quietly.

The four of them sat for a long time without speaking. Then Brianna lifted her head and sniffed deeply. Greg went inside and returned with a box of tissues.

"Thanks," Brianna said softly, wiping her cheeks and her nose. Laughing, she said, "Writing this shit is so easy! It's living that's so hard." She looked at Sean and grasped his hand. "I'm sorry," she said. "I feel selfish. You don't deserve all this."

"All this?"

"When I write, I need to dig into my guts, and write from what I feel. But when I'm with you, you deserve my attention. Christ, I know I have yours!"

They all laughed.

"When I'm making love, I need to be making love to you— not to some fantasy. I need to keep the fantasy for my writing."

Greg and Janine looked at each other. She nodded.

Brianna squeezed Sean's hand, and in a small voice she said, "I promise to try."

He tilted her chin up and kissed her tenderly. "You know I love you?"

Brianna sat staring at the screen, running the video back and forth, snipping here and there to make it flow better. It was exciting, watching the story—her fantasy—unfold. Even without any sound (music would be added later), it worked for her.

Up to that point. The crescendo of form and movement, the big scene, satisfied her. The following scenes, though, she discarded.

Switching to the word processor, she eliminated everything after the big scene. It had to have consequences, and she struggled to imagine those. What should happen after that? What would those two people in her story do, afterward? It didn't come to her easily. Her fantasy met a blank wall.

She closed the computer and slumped back in her chair. What do puppets do, when they come alive?

The End

Reality TV

One

The three of us sat in the comfortable little screening room watching the huge LED monitor. Roger White operated the remote control, searching for a particular scene in the television episode. The images flipped past like snapshots until suddenly he stopped the scan and we were voyeurs, observing an elderly couple lying nude on a carpet before a huge stone fireplace and a dying fire. "This is the part I wanted you to see," Roger said quietly.

Roger had come into the Assisted Living Center where I worked, asking if someone there would come to his video production company and preview an episode of a new reality show they were doing about older people. I had agreed to view it, and on the way out the door we caught Grace, who was a recent widow living there, and invited her along.

He lowered the room lights until the edges of the monitor were all but invisible, and the video image seemed to be a live performance in the room before us. We could hear the whispers of the two people, murmuring, gasping, groaning softly, struggling to merge their bodies in the primal act. It was obvious that they were having difficulty. Grace's hand was on my arm, tightening her grip in response to the efforts of the actors.

My embarrassment diverted me from the action on the screen to visualize the three-camera setup of the scene, dissolving from one viewpoint to another in response to the changing positions of the couple. Occasionally there were two viewpoints at once blending the images into collages of skin, light and movement. The female actor seemed to be uncomfortable, but the scene went on. In my head, I imagined the set full of people standing silently off-camera, watching the actors, the director switching between cameras and gesturing to technicians. On the screen, it was only two old people trying to make love on the floor.

"Stop!" cried Grace suddenly. "Stop it!" She buried her face in my shoulder.

Roger stopped the tape and brought up the room lights a little. "What's wrong?"

I tried to put my arm around Grace, but she kept her face against my shoulder. Then she sat up and, reaching into her purse for a tissue, said hoarsely, "It's too much. I can't take that. You aren't going to air that, are you?"

"Sure we are," Roger said, "as soon as we get it timed for the slot. The whole episode has to run forty-two minutes, so with the commercials it will fit into the hour."

"But it's too personal! Those people will be humiliated!"

"Hey, Honey, that's reality TV," he replied. "They signed a contract. They are actors, getting paid."

"These are professional actors?" I asked.

"Well, they've never been on television or movies before— they can't be recognized, because then it wouldn't be reality TV. You should watch the online twittering going on while these episodes are being aired. We'd get creamed in real time if somebody recognized an actor."

I felt Grace shudder. "Why would you do that?" she demanded. "Why would you put those people through that? They are not young, beautiful bodies that everybody wants to look at. They are not skilled actors who can put across some dramatic situation to remind the audience of their own desires and fears. They are just ordinary, lumpy, clumsy human beings. What's the point?"

"It's entertainment, Grace," Roger responded. "People look at it, and they take from it what they can, and they buy the advertisers' products and services. That's the point."

She looked at me. "Paul, what do you think?"

I fumbled for an answer. I hadn't enjoyed the scene—it had clicked into my worst imaginings of lovemaking at my age. "When you told me about this," I said to Roger, "I thought it might be good for me, maybe give me a better feeling about my old body. I'm afraid it had just the opposite effect."

"When you described the series," said Grace, "I thought it was good that people our age were finally being portrayed realistically on TV. But this is repulsive!"

Roger gestured toward the screen with the remote. "Folks are watching this series! The ratings are going up as we introduce more intimate situations. Young folks are getting another idea about their parents and grandparents, more human. You should look at the comments on Facebook."

"I know that reality TV is profitable," I said. "People watch those extreme situations and get to experience fear and anxiety vicariously, like from the vampire movies that the kids love so much. But laughing at a couple of old people trying to relate to each other sexually seems perverse. Some day those kids will come to recognize how hard and how important it is. But they don't have a clue. A twenty-year-old male gets an erection just by thinking about a woman. The question at that age is about availability, not capability."

"I hear you," said Roger. "I know from experience that things change with age. It gets more complicated." He smiled at Grace. "It's like my mom used to say about me when I took big portions at the dinner table, 'Your eyes are bigger than your stomach.' I look at this scene as a kind of revelation. I can imagine myself at that age, and I'm less critical. It has to be seen with a little bit of humor."

"It's not funny!" she exclaimed. "It's sad! That's what you should be showing them!"

"Yeah," agreed Roger, "it's sad. When I watch this scene I feel sorry for those people. But at the same time, I have to smile—that's where I'll be in a few years. I laugh at myself already, trying to get a hard on after I've had a couple of drinks."

"You're what—fifty?" I asked, and Roger nodded and shrugged at the same time. "Women still look at you as having potential, at least."

Grace joined in. "You're still able to attract most women," she said. "Nobody thinks anything about a guy fifty being with a woman of thirty—even twenty. Unless it's his wife of thirty years who is seeing him with someone else."

I glanced at Grace, who had a wry smile on her face.

"Somebody like me, at seventy-five, is invisible," I said. Nobody—no female at any age even looks at me."

Grace laughed. "Bull. Excuse my language."

Roger chuckled. "Hell, that white hair just makes you look more distinguished."

"It's how I *feel inside* that matters most," I said, "and when I watch that scene, I cringe. I don't get a hard on." I touched Grace's arm. "Excuse my language."

"You know," she said, now more collected, "when I was young I wished I could have someone teach me about making love. I didn't have a clue what to expect or how to do it. Now, watching those poor souls, I wish there was a way to learn how to do it, all over again. The physical rules have changed!"

"Sex therapy for seniors?" Roger was grinning.

"Maybe," I said. "Barbara Robinson, our director, brought me into the Center to try out new ideas." I thought of Barbara, who had hired me out of retirement to help her in the Assisted Living Center. Mostly what I had accomplished was to get their computer system organized.

"With four women to each man there, that might be difficult to bring off," Grace said.

"Hey, but that sounds like a good idea!" Roger put the remote control back in its slot next to the video player and picked up his coat.

Grace and I collected our things and followed him out of the screening room. I watched her walk ahead of me out to the parking lot. *Maybe,* I thought, *maybe it's not too late for me.*

On the way back to the Center, Roger asked, "Well, do you think we can get a small focus group to watch a screening?"

"I don't think I could recommend it to people," I said. "I'm not saying no, because I'm only one person. It's just my opinion. But I will put the idea to Mrs. Robinson."

"I'd appreciate that," Roger said.

"I wouldn't want to watch it again," said Grace.

Roger glanced over at her. "I'm sorry if it offended you," he said.

She smiled at him. "Thank you. It shocked me, I guess."

"What if we made the scene darker, so you couldn't see as much?"

Well, I wouldn't have agreed to watch it the first time if the idea repelled me. It was just so *in your face!*"

"That's fair enough," he said.

When he dropped us off at the Center, I agreed to call him within a couple of days.

"I'm surprised you even said you'd consider it," Grace said. "Would you talk with me about it?" She gestured toward a couple of chairs in the foyer.

"Of course."

I'd chatted with Grace a number of times since I arrived at the Center three months previously. Her husband, who had been confined to a wheelchair for a long time, died shortly before I arrived. She was quite attractive, with carefully coiffed, almost white, hair. I had wondered why she stayed at the Center after her husband had died, since she obviously didn't need living assistance herself. "I like the people here," she had told me.

"Truthfully," she began now, "what was your reaction to the scene?"

I shrugged. "Pretty much as I told Roger. I cringed, because it reminded me of the way I'd look if I were that actor."

"They weren't married. Did that bother you?"

"No. Unmarried sex has become so common in our culture, especially on television, that I don't think about it much anymore. It's like smoking used to be."

Her eyebrows raised just a little.

"When I was young," I said, "everybody smoked. Nobody thought anything about it. Once in a while, someone would refer to cigarettes as 'coffin nails,' so there must have been some negative feeling about it. But the medical information about it wasn't as pervasive as the advertising."

"The pill changed everything," she said, then stopped. "I mean about sex, not smoking."

We laughed at that. "I can remember feeling pretty glad about the pill," I said, "even though at the time I was happily married and not inclined to wander."

"I asked the question about marriage to see where you were coming from about the video."

"You've been here longer than I have," I said. "How do you think the average resident here would react to it?"

She glanced around. "I think the average resident here is not likely to think much about sex."

"You seem pretty relaxed about it," I said, and then immediately regretted my words. "Sorry. That didn't come out right."

She smiled, but didn't answer.

"Okay," I stumbled on, "do you think there would be an uproar if Roger screened it in the recreation room—with clear warnings about the content?"

"I'm sure there would, especially if it preempted one of the programs they usually watch."

"True. But I'm wondering how much of my opinion comes from my personal reaction to it."

"You're trying very hard to be fair, aren't you?" She smiled again.

"Yeah," I said. "and maybe the fair thing is to let it happen—provided Barbara agrees—and let Roger take the heat, if there is any. After all, it's a test, and he needs to know if it will fly or bomb."

"I think most of the residents here watch a lot of television, including the rampant sex scenes."

"With the gorgeous bodies and uninhibited passion." I watched her eyes. Part of me knew I was looking for a sign of interest, and my face got hot.

"What would they do, ask people to fill out a questionnaire?" She was evading my reference.

"I don't know what Roger will do. Sometimes they give everybody a little thing like a remote control, with two buttons on it. If you have a positive reaction to something, you press the green button. If you have a negative reaction, you press the red button. A computer tallies up the button presses and keys them to the points on the program where they occur. Then the producers can see what parts get the most reactions, good or bad. It's like the old applause meters they used to have on talent shows."

"I'd have pressed my red button from one end of that scene to the other," she said, smiling at me. "One long RED!"

I laughed. "I don't know how they would count one long button press."

"I might have thrown my remote at the screen."

"That would count for many button presses," I said.

She was watching me. "So, what do you think you're going to do?"

"I'll talk to Barbara, first."

"Let me know?" When I nodded, she stood up. "I have to go—I'm in the first seating for lunch."

"Thanks for going with me."

She took my hand— for just a moment—smiled and walked down the hall.

Two

Barbara Robinson, it turned out, was not enthusiastic about the idea. "It's nonsense!" she said vehemently. "We're all beyond that!"

"It was Roger's idea," I said, "to take his video to seniors. At least he's aware of who his audience might be. I thought it might give him some valuable feedback, even if they run him out on a rail."

It was the next day, and I had pretty much lost the visceral reaction I had had to the video. "In fact, I'm curious," I said, "nobody talks much about sex among the elderly."

She looked straight at me for a moment, giving me the feeling I used to get as a small boy when I was caught in some mischief. Then she said, "I don't know. I'd have to see it first."

"He'd be happy to arrange that. And my guess is that if you didn't want to go to their screening room, he could arrange to bring it here in a laptop for you to see it."

"Even if it's good—maybe *especially* if it's good—there are a number of widows here who could get upset by it."

Barbara Robinson reminded me, perhaps unfairly, of what they used to call "spinsters"—older women, like some of my old school teachers, who never married for one reason or another. Seeming prim, even brittle, with a rare, thin smile. Barbara was nearing retirement age herself, and made a point in dealing with the residents of appearing to be "one of them." I thought she sincerely wanted the Center to offer a comfortable environment to these people who could no longer manage their own homes. The job kept her very busy, and it seemed that was what she wanted. She'd hired me to take some of the load off her shoulders, aware that she didn't have the energy she used to. At first I thought she was cold, but I detected, now and then, a hint of humor in her eyes. But it wasn't often.

"Should I call him?" I asked. "Would you prefer to go to his screening room, or see it here?"

"Not here. Too much chance for an interruption."

I took out my cell phone and called him. Roger was delighted.

"You name it," I relayed to Barbara. "I can take you, or he'll come and pick you up."

She was thoughtful. "You take me. We'll need to talk about it afterward."

"This afternoon?"

"Yes."

I passed it on to Roger, and hung up.

Barbara looked as though she were going to say something more, then waved me off. "After lunch."

I caught Grace's eye in the cafeteria, where she was at a table with several other women. She got up and came to me.

"Barbara wants to see the episode," I said.

She gave me a slight smile and returned to her table without saying anything.

I ate my lunch as I usually did, in a corner alone with my tablet, reading the Internet news sites. I watched the time, and left the cafeteria at one o'clock. Driving Barbara to the studio, I told her the little about the reality series that I knew. "It's not like the bachelor games or the *Millionaire Matchmaker*," I said, "but more like the shows where people mill around and interview each other, and sometimes hook up."

"How does it become a television program?" she asked.

"The cameras just nose into the conversations, and eventually follow the most, ah, *interesting* couples. It doesn't look staged, but there's probably some direction. Roger stressed that the people are actors, getting paid."

"Doesn't sound very interesting to me." I saw her glance over at me as I drove.

I laughed. "Nor to me. What I saw the other day, though, was pretty personal. I don't think I'd watch the whole series on television."

"You said some scenes were explicitly sexual."

"Yep."

"Who would watch such stuff?"

"Many of the channels, the cable channels at least, are moving more and more in that direction. It gets viewers."

"Disgusting."

We pulled up at the studio and Roger met us at the reception desk, graciously introduced himself to Barbara, and ushered us into the screening room. "Do you want to see the whole episode, or just the part that Paul and Grace saw the other day?"

Barbara looked at her watch. "How long does it last?"

"The whole thing is about forty-five minutes right now. It will be edited down to forty-two minutes for airing."

"We might as well see it all. We need the context, after all, don't we?" She looked at me, and I nodded.

I dislike reality television. To me it's all fake, and most of the drama is contrived and heavily edited for effect. So I endured the first half-hour. Barbara laughed occasionally. I noticed something that I didn't remember from my first viewing—a music track, very much in the background, that could have been perceived as part of the environment that the actors were in, but clearly it had been added, since it ran without obvious breaks through all the scene changes and cuts. It looked to me as though they were using at least three cameras most of the time, because the dialog was smoothly continuous within scenes. However questionable their taste, their technical skills were first-rate.

When the fireplace scene began, I sensed Barbara stiffening. I could hear her quick breathing throughout, as though she were trying to hold her breath. But she didn't utter a word.

They had darkened the scene, too, as Roger had suggested that they might. The fireplace lighting looked real. The faint music track, now a soft jazz guitar like the Wes Montgomery pieces I used to like, effectively masked most of the sounds the couple made. I also thought that they had edited the scene some, smoothing the action. I felt differently about it this time, maybe as a result of the changes. I no longer cringed, but even admired some of the shots of slowly moving limbs and torsos.

At the final fade-out, Barbara took several slow, deep breaths and let them out just as slowly. Roger stayed discreetly motionless. The three of us sat there silently for a long time.

"I don't understand," Barbara said finally, "how you can create such a superficial, ridiculous program, and then end it with such sensitivity."

I was shocked. I had expected this uptight, prim woman to explode.

Roger was good. He waited a long moment before saying, "We've tried to pace the program to the circumstances. As the people first come together, they are superficial and guarded with each other. They are all wearing their masks and their armor. That's what people do at first, don't they?"

I wanted to give Barbara some space and time to sort out her feelings, so I said to Roger, "You've smoothed it out a lot. You didn't have the music in it before, did you?"

He leaned forward and turned so that he could see past Barbara, and smiled at me. "You didn't cringe this time, did you?" He had been watching me, as well as Barbara.

"I don't think I cringed," said Barbara. "I was a little bit shocked at the beginning of that scene—I didn't know you could show such things on television."

"Things are changing," Roger said. "The culture is changing. They can't show things like that on the networks, but the cable channels are showing more and more. I think it's honest."

"I told Paul," she said, "that I didn't think older people would want to watch things like that. Whatever we did when we were young, we have left that all behind."

I stopped to wonder about what she said, whether it was true for me. I remembered what I had said to Roger and Grace at the first screening, about feeling invisible as a man.

Barbara went on, "Our bodies don't respond like they used to. I'm not titillated by things I might have before."

And I was getting a new impression of this "spinster school teacher." She seemed less prim, more human. Again I ducked behind a technical question, "If you screened this at the Center and asked for feedback, how would that work?"

Roger glanced first at me, then at Barbara—waiting for her—before answering. "We give each viewer a little box, like a TV remote, and ask them to respond to the program as they are moved to respond. No paperwork, no questions or answers. Just moment-to-moment gut reactions to what happens on the screen. In the end, we know for that audience what works and what doesn't."

"So nobody knows what anyone else thinks or feels," said Barbara.

"Totally anonymous."

I watched her, waiting for her to say something. She finally turned to me. "Paul, what do you think?"

"Most of the people in the Center could handle that, I suspect—provided they were interested in the first place."

To Roger, she said, "Why don't we try it. When would you be able to hold the session?"

"Some evening next week?"

"During the day—maybe an afternoon—would be better, I think, so it doesn't interfere with their regular television programs."

"Okay." He did some things to his phone. "How about Tuesday, say, two-thirty?"

I checked my calendar. "Looks good to me."

Barbara called her secretary at the Center. "Susie, can we schedule a video program for two-thirty Tuesday?" Then she hung up and smiled. "So it's set. A grand experiment. Paul, would you make up the flyers for it?"

Three

When I caught up with Grace later, she had been telling others about the program. "Most of them," she said, "weren't interested, and thought it was a bad idea."

"I was really surprised that Barbara bought into it," I said. "It's going to be next Tuesday, at two-thirty. They will set it up and provide those little response boxes. All responses will be completely anonymous."

She looked at me with a half-smile. "You going to furnish the popcorn?"

"Sure," I said. "Would you help me with the announcement?"

"As long as I don't have to watch it."

I touched her hand. "Grace," I said, fumbling for words, "Would you have dinner with me sometime?"

It surprised her. "Why—yes, I would like to."

"There is a little bistro near where I live. They have very good food, and it's fairly quiet, if we avoid the televisions in the bar."

"When?"

I thought for a moment, then said, "Well, how about tonight? We could work on the wording of the announcement over a glass of wine first."

I liked the sparkle in her eyes. "Okay. I have to tell the cooks I won't be here for dinner."

"They keep that close tabs on whether or not you'll be eating in?"

"I just like to be polite," she said. "They need to know how many servings to make."

"How about we meet here at four?"

"Perfect."

Back at my desk, I had a hard time not thinking about Grace. By ten to four I'd cleaned up all my inbox material and arranged for the maintenance crew to patch some plaster in the third-floor hallway, where someone had run into a wall with a motorized wheelchair.

Grace and I said little as we drove to my neighborhood. She had changed into an attractive aquamarine dress. It was the first "date" I'd had in a long time, and I was nervous.

As we got out of the car, she said, "Paul, I'm nervous. I haven't had a date in a long time."

I couldn't help bursting out laughing. "You know, I was thinking the same thing?"

We entered the bistro relaxed and laughing. The waiter showed us to a table in the rear, away from other customers. I laid my tablet on the table and we ordered wine.

"Are you one of those people who spend all your time online?" she asked playfully.

"I promise," I said, "I won't go online or answer any phone calls. This is my notebook, and I need your help to make up the announcement for the porn show."

At that, she laughed—a very nice, easy laugh. "Porn show! Is that what it is?"

"No, not really. The other day I wasn't so sure."

"What did Barbara say about it?"

"I was really surprised by her reaction," I said. "She called the fireplace scene 'sensitive.'"

"Really!"

"Well, they did smooth it out some in the editing, and put some soft jazz music over it, so you couldn't hear the sounds the couple were making—at least not very much. And it was noticeably darker. Made it look like the whole scene was lighted by the fireplace."

She took a sip from her wine glass. "When you and I saw it, you said you cringed. Did you not cringe this time?"

I laughed. "As a matter of fact, I didn't. Part of me was watching how they were shooting the scene—I was curious. And part of me was just watching something I don't usually see. A little uncomfortable, maybe, but not shocked, either."

"You'd seen it before, though," she said, "so you knew what was coming."

"Yes. And when you and I saw it first, you had him stop the tape before it was over."

"I was overwhelmed."

"The ending felt—complete, somehow."

"I still don't want to see it again."

"No." I opened a blank document in my tablet. "What do you think the headline should be?"

We drank some wine, and I watched her face. So different from my ex-wife, in so many ways.

"Well, it has to say 'reality TV program,' doesn't it?"

"And 'prescreening' will tell them that is isn't something they've seen before."

The waiter came to the table. "Ready to order?"

"We haven't looked at the menu," I said. Give us five minutes?"

"Of course. More wine?"

Grace nodded, and I said, "Yes."

When he'd left, Grace said, "It really has to be clear that there is explicit sex."

"One scene with explicit sex."

"And it's about older people."

I typed some things into the tablet and showed it to her.

"It also has to have a caveat," she said, "so people won't be shocked. "Like, 'This program contains adult material of a sexual nature.'"

I typed it in and make the sentence red. "I guess I'd better explain the situation more." I typed

The producers of this television series want to know our reactions to their program, and they will give us little devices to hold and register whatever reactions we have. All responses will be anonymous—no one but you will know what you register. There is no questionnaire to fill out.

Grace read what I had. "Tell them that they will not be expected to discuss the program afterward."

The waiter returned with more wine and took our dinner order. Both of us read over what we had composed. "Anything else?" I asked.

"I think that covers it."

"Thank you for your input. Sometimes I'm not sure what to say to our residents."

As we sat and sipped our wine, I noticed that the music coming from the bistro speakers sounded very much like what Roger's people had put over the top of the fireplace scene in the program. I laughed. "That music is like what they put in the fireplace scene!"

"I like it. So he has some taste, after all."

"I changed my mind about Roger, too," I said. "He handled Barbara very well. At first, I took him for an operator. But he was really good."

She smiled. "He seems to have handled you very well, too."

"Maybe."

"He did apologize for the scene offending me."

"Not just a circus barker?" I asked.

"Maybe."

The rest of the evening went well. We shared a bit of our life stories and how we felt about different things in the world. After our meal and coffee, I took her back to the Center and drove home thinking about how much I'd been missing from my life lately.

Four

In the next few days, word got around about the screening, and after I put up the announcements, everyone was talking about it. Barbara got more feedback about it than I did—she had more personal contact with the residents.

"From what I hear," she told me, "many people are eager to attend, but some of them flatly refuse—it's 'wicked,' they say. One woman—I won't say who—says she'll get her husband there if she has to drag him. Someone else says she will lock her husband in their room to keep him from going."

I laughed. "Any reactions from men?"

"They wouldn't tell me. Maybe you can keep your ears open at the poker games tonight."

I don't usually work evenings, but I made a point of wandering down to the poker club and sitting in on a couple of games. As expected, there was a lot of discussion about the upcoming screening.

One old fellow, known as Charliefish to the residents, always carried an oxygen tank around with him, but he joined in most of the men's activities. Charliefish was excited about watching the program. "Sal says she's going to lock me up that night. She says I'd get so excited I'd have a heart attack."

"You might," someone said to him. "How long's it been since they let you have sex?"

"Shit, son, I do it every night. Ask Sal, if you don't believe me!"

Another man said, "I go down to the TV room at night and watch the X-rated programs. This ain't going to be anything special."

"Maybe just the opposite," Charliefish said. "These are supposed to be senior citizens goin' at it."

"No shit? Who'd watch that? Some flabby old bag? Not me!"

"Paul, you seen this, right? What's it going to be?"

I held up my hands. "I can't say, 'cause it might affect the way some folks vote, and that would be bad."

"We're goin' to vote?"

"Well, it's like this—you will have like a remote control in your hand, and when something hits you in a good way you press one button. When something hits you in a bad way, you press a different button. That's all the voting there is. Nobody will know when you pushed what button."

There were scattered remarks about pushing buttons.

The next morning I told Barbara what I had heard. "Typical male reactions, I guess."

"As long as they don't get carried away at the screening," she said. There's always a few clowns. The serious ones don't get involved in the horseplay. I just hope there are some serious ones at the screening."

That surprised me. "You sound as though you have an investment in this."

She looked at me out of the corner of her eye. "I'm more invested in how it might affect the reputation of the Center."

"Maybe at the beginning I can suggest that they stay quiet until it's over."

"Or ask Roger to," she said. "He'll be giving them instructions."

"Good point."

When it was time for the screening, we had put thirty chairs in the room, but a number of late-comers brought in extra chairs. Roger had set up a larger monitor than the one we have in the room, and he asked me to tend the room lights. I counted nearly forty people by the time he was ready to start. Barbara was not present; neither, I noticed, was Grace.

The room was noisy until Roger held up his hand. "This is a program we plan to air on Channel 459 next month. It's part of a series called 'Senior Mix,' which shows senior citizens like yourselves in a social mixer. These folks come in and fill out a personal profile, and then the staff helps them to connect with people who have the same interests. They do all the work—the staff just helps them get comfortable. You'll see.

"As the series goes on, the mixing of the folks gets more and more personal. It's always up to the individuals how close and how personal they get with each other."

He paused. "This is real life, folks. What the participants say and do is always up to them. We just think it's interesting to see how real people interact when they are given the chance. We do not judge, nor do we interfere with what the participants do. The only thing they have to agree to in order to participate is that we be able to film their interactions. They sign a contract to that effect, and in the end we pay them a small honorarium for their time. None of them has ever been on television or in the movies—we didn't want professional actors."

Roger picked up one of the voting tools. "Each of you will get one of these," he said. "There are only two buttons on it, a red one and a green one. What we ask of you is that you record your honest reactions to what's happening at that moment on the screen. If you like it, you press the green button, and if you don't like it, press the red one." He demonstrated as he spoke.

"Now, we hope you enjoy our program—the producers have invested a lot of money in the idea, so it's serious business for us. And we sincerely want your reactions to it. Pushing the buttons will tell us a lot about how the series and this particular program are going to do when they are broadcast, and that allows us to tell our advertisers what they can expect to get for their support.

"Please," he said, seriously, "don't talk during the show, because that can affect how others will react to it. We can't ask you not to laugh, because sometimes you can't help that. We just ask that you respect our sincere effort to create television entertainment that people will enjoy."

He nodded to me, and I began distributing the voting tools. The room got noisy again until he held up his hand and said, "And please, folks, hold your remarks until the program is over. Then, if you want to ask questions or make comments, I'll stay here as long as you want me, to give you whatever information I have. Thank you, and let's have the lights, please, Paul!"

I lowered the room lights and he started the program. I heard a few muttered comments, and somebody laughed, but mostly the group was quiet.

As far as I could tell, the program had not changed since Barbara and I watched it. My own reaction to it this time was less than enthusiastic. It was boring to me. I watched for signs that the filming crew might be giving the actors directions, but I could see none. Ordinary people, behaving the way they do in strange settings, fumbling with their words, laughing with embarrassment at times and with genuine humor at others. Some of them were more outgoing and easy, some nearly mute. I noticed that the cameras tended to show more of the outgoing participants, as I would have expected. I couldn't say whether it was entertaining or not to most people. But I was aware that I was waiting for the fireplace scene.

The people in the room laughed a lot. I couldn't tell if there was any whispering going on because the soundtrack was loud enough to cover it up. In the dim light, I could see several people turn to look at their neighbors. There was no indication of how many buttons were pressed.

I was surprised to see something I had not noticed before; the program showed a clear build-up to the fireplace scene. The couple obviously "clicked" with each other early on, and the cameras followed them closely. By the time we saw them in front of the fireplace, we were familiar enough with both of them that their actions felt real and unstaged. Even their playfully slipping through the door into the room seemed spontaneous. The editing, I thought, was perfect.

On the final fade-to-black, I was about to bring the room lights back up when I saw Roger signal to me to wait. The audience was very quiet for what seemed a long time. Then a man laughed, and gradually the room noise increased. Roger nodded to me and I brought up the lights.

"Thank you," he shouted above the talking. "You were a perfect audience!" Clapping his hands over his head, he smiled broadly. Several people took up the clapping, and soon the room was full of applause. I stood near the door with the box for the voting tools as people began to leave. I thanked each one, and got a few wide smiles and several serious frowns.

Barbara came up behind me. "How did it go?" she asked.

"I thought it was great! They were very well behaved."

Roger was at the front of the room, surrounded by people asking him questions and in some cases, I could tell, making serious comments.

The two of us remained near the door to collect the voting tools—a couple of forgetful people almost walked away with theirs. I watched a cluster of people at one side of the room talking seriously. When they slowly moved toward the door, still engaged in their conversation, I collected their tools. One of them looked at Barbara and said, "We want to talk with you about something."

"Of course," she replied, "any time."

I glanced at her. Her face was a pleasant mask. I moved away, making my way through the people still in the room and taking their voting tools from them. Roger was still surrounded by people, so I began to disconnect the electronic gear he had set up.

Afterward, as the two of us loaded his equipment cart, I asked him how he thought it had gone.

"Wonderful!" he said. "Nobody was disruptive, and a lot of people took it seriously enough to ask questions at the end."

"When will you have the results of the voting?"

"Tomorrow. The editors will screen the program for us with a second screen set up to show the quantity of red and green responses in real time."

"I'd love to watch that, myself," I said, "if that's possible."

He shook his head. "Sorry. That will be top secret, with only the producers, directors and a few tech people present. Our television competitors would love to get their hands on that information!"

"Okay, I understand."

"I can pass on some highlights, if you want."

"I'd like that."

"I'd also like to take you to dinner, for all your help in this."

I waved it off. "Just doing my job," I said.

"Suppose I invite Barbara, too. I can fill both of you in on the results of the showing."

"You get her to accept, and I'll be happy to come."

Five

I was leaving the cafeteria the next day when Grace stopped me. "I hear your television program was a success," she said, smiling.

"It didn't cause a riot." I gestured toward a couple of chairs in the lounge. "Want to hear?"

"Of course." Grace always dressed elegantly, even in casual wear.

"First," I said, "you'll be pleased to know that they edited the program, and the fireplace scene was much more professional."

"You told me that. And you didn't cringe."

I laughed. "You remembered that remark, too! Actually, no, I didn't cringe. Some of it, of course, was because I was watching the audience. I was really afraid somebody would make a circus out of it."

"And Roger was satisfied with the showing?"

"He said it was wonderful. They will run the program for the bigwigs at the studio, with the real-time statistical results displayed on another screen."

She looked down at her hands. "One of the women told me that everything was genuine and unrehearsed."

"That's what Roger told us."

"You mean—those two people in the fireplace scene, who apparently just met, had sex on a rug with cameras trained on them?" She was looking at me, now, and I was uncomfortable.

"I guess I hadn't thought that out."

"Would *you* make love to a woman—any woman—in a room in which there were video cameras present?"

My face felt very hot. I tried to think of something to say that wouldn't make me into an idiot. "No," I finally said, "of course not."

"I didn't think so." She turned a little away from me in her chair. "I'm sure there are some people who would be able to do that, but I can't imagine ordinary people doing it. Did they show those two people earlier in the program?

"Yes," I said. "They were very charming, actually. I thought at the time that they would probably end up the stars of the program. But I knew what the end was going to be."

"Actually, that makes me feel better about the whole thing. The fumbling, seemingly vulnerable people that we watched in Roger's screening room were—if they were not professionals— probably hand picked for that scene before the rest of the program was filmed. They knew what they were getting into."

"Grace, you are very astute. Obviously, I didn't think about it very deeply."

"Maybe I'm cynical," she said, "but I never for a moment accepted Roger's claim that the actors were nonprofessionals."

I grinned, as much from embarrassment as from recognizing the humor of the situation.

"Paul," she said, putting a hand on my knee, "Please don't think I'm prudish. I'd blush to have to tell you some of the things I've done in my life. I just want it to be honest."

I put my hand on hers. "Thank you, Grace. You've given me some things to think about. Barbara and I are having dinner with Roger next week—his treat—and I hope I have the guts to bring that up to him."

She stood up. "I have a bridge game to go to. I'm glad we had a chance to talk. Let me know how it goes."

I managed to touch her hand as she turned to walk away.

Six

"Some of the women want to start a support group about sex," Barbara said when we next happened to be in the office at the same time. "They'd like to have a nurse or somebody there to give them good information."

"The men need one, too," I said, "but I doubt if they would actually do it."

"Don't men ever get *serious*?" She exclaimed, slamming a drawer closed.

I could only grin at her. "Sounds like there's some history behind that."

Barbara looked at me quickly, then smiled. "Yes, I guess there is. Forgive me, please."

"Anything you want to talk about?"

"No, it's ancient history." But she continued to smile as she went back to her work.

"I can ask around," I said. "See if there is any interest."

"If it feels good to you."

I was getting a glimpse of Barbara that I hadn't seen before. There was some softness there, some feeling, and some insight into what she was doing and feeling.

In the three months I had worked at the Center, I hadn't really made any friends, and sometimes I felt like an outsider. Barbara ran the place, and she connected well with many of the residents. I had been given the tasks she didn't want to be bothered with, those about the physical plant and the technical systems. It had suited me, for I tended to work alone anyway.

But in another way, I wanted to connect with people. Sometimes I just didn't know how. I looked forward to our dinner with Roger, as much as anything to be in a different environment with Barbara where I might taste who she really was.

We had agreed to meet Roger at the restaurant. I picked up Barbara at the Center, feeling a little as though I were having another date, and enjoying the tiny bit of personal adventure.

It was a first-class place, close to a major upscale hotel. Roger was waiting for us at the hostess desk. He was used to entertaining customers and investors—great smile, warm handshake, a hand gently guiding Barbara to our table. Fresh linen tablecloth, a pair of roses and a fern in an expensive-looking crystal vase, wine and water glasses, gleaming china and silverware. The chairs glided effortlessly on the carpet.

"I'm really glad you could do this," he said after seating Barbara. The hostess saw to it that fresh ice water was poured after we sat down, and then she handed Roger the wine menu.

Barbara, I noticed for the first time, was wearing much more makeup than I'd seen her with before. She looked ten years younger. Her dress was on the red side—I've never learned the names of colors beyond the Crayola Sixteen—with interesting reflective highlights. Some kind of metallic thread, I decided. I was glad I had chosen a business suit instead of the blazer I had first picked from the closet.

"You both drink wine?" Roger asked, looking at the wine list and glancing at each of us in turn. To our nods, he said, "I found this French Chablis the last time I was here, and it's exquisite. 'Louis Michel and Sons Grand Cru.' Comes from the village of Chablis, southeast from Paris." Nothing like the California Chablis I used to buy just because it was cheap."

I grinned. "Sounds like you know your wines."

"I'm also impressed," said Barbara. "I'll take your word for it."

The wine, when it came, was just as he had said, and the three of us touched glasses. "Good luck on your series," I said.

"I think it's going to do well. We had quite a mixed result from the voting at the senior center—some people hated the fireplace scene, but more people liked it, and altogether the program was liked by most. It was interesting to me to see the scoring at the very beginning of that scene," he said, "a big negative vote, followed within seconds by a big positive."

"Initial shock," I offered.

"I guess that's what it was," he said.

Barbara set her wine glass down. "I have a question about that scene."

"Shoot."

"What did it take to get that couple to make love in front of cameras? You said it was all unstaged, didn't you?"

Roger smiled at her. "I have a confession about that scene."

I saw Barbara smile and sit back in her chair, as if to say, "I thought so!"

"It did take a while for us to encourage them to do the scene. When we assured them that we would not judge them, they admitted that they would like to get intimate with each other—they were both attracted to each other, and both were really outgoing, adventurous types."

"So, how much was that scene edited?" I asked.

He dabbed at his chin with his napkin. "What you saw was just a fraction of what we had on tape."

"I thought you said it was all spontaneous," Barbara said.

"I never said we used everything we had—no reality show could do that!"

"I understand the need to select," I said, feeling a little pedantic. "Not only would it have been far too long, but it would have been full of junk. You have to choose what to include."

"But isn't that deceptive?" Barbara was still troubled.

"Look at it this way," he said, "if you were taking photographs at your daughter's wedding, ..."

"Granddaughter's wedding," she said, interrupting him.

"Okay, your granddaughter's wedding. You might take a dozen shots of the wedding party, but you would send only one or two to your relatives. You'd toss the rest because Uncle Ernie had his eyes closed, or somebody was yawning—right? Back when I was in school, they used to say that documentary films often had a shooting ratio of more than a hundred to one—a hundred feet of film through the camera to every foot finally projected on the movie screen. It didn't mean they were dishonest."

She was still frowning. "Have you screened it for the actors?"

"Of course.

He signaled the waiter, who brought our menus. As we browsed through them, Barbara persisted. "If they had had objections to the scene, would you have taken it out?"

"I can't answer that for sure," he said. "I wasn't at that particular screening. We do try to be sensitive to the feelings of the actors, even though they all signed releases."

"I suppose," she said, "I just have trouble imagining how ordinary people could put themselves on display like that."

He grinned. "Why don't we order, and then I'll give you my thoughts on that."

After the waiter had taken our order, Roger said, "You said you can't imagine how ordinary people could put themselves on display. Frankly, I can't either. I sure couldn't. But I don't have the temperament to be an actor. Those people in the program may not have been 'professional' before doing the series, but they can't claim that anymore. Nearly all of them have had ambitions in that direction. They *like* being in front of a camera. The two who did the fireplace scene thought it was *fun*. They enjoyed the attention, and all their actions were self-directed. We taped, and then we cut the tape to make the scene. We didn't tell them how to act."

I thought of something funny. "I guess it's one of those things that one learns how to perform rather quickly."

The others laughed.

That seemed to break the seriousness of the conversation, and Barbara laughed a lot more afterward.

The conversation went on from there, and all of us became more relaxed. More wine was poured—we were into red by this time, to go with our prime rib.

At one point, Roger asked Barbara, "Has the senior center always been your career?"

She smiled. "No. I was in hotel management for a long time. That was what I studied in college. But hotels are so impersonal!"

"How so?"

"You seldom get to know the people you serve. When this job came up I thought I would enjoy mixing with my charges—my customers."

"Still like it?"

"Yes."

"You know," I said to Barbara—and I was definitely feeling all the wine—"when I first came to the Center, I thought you were kinda stiff. Uptight."

She looked surprised.

"But I've changed my mind," I said.

"I'm glad of that!"

Roger looked at her, "Do you mind if I ask—married?"

"Not any longer. Not for a long time, actually."

He turned to me. "You, Paul?"

"Used to be."

"Hope I'm not being too personal," he said. "I am happily married myself, with three children, all still in school."

"My wife died, about ten years ago," I said.

Barbara looked at me, her face serious. "I'm sorry."

"Any kids?" Roger asked.

"No."

"What brought you to the senior center?"

"I don't know," I said, "I'd been retired for five years, and I got bored. Happened to see the ad Barbara put in the paper, and here I am."

"You probably answered this in your application, but I don't remember," she said. "What did you do before you retired?"

"Information systems. I was bored with that, too," I laughed.

"Sounds like you've been bored with your life a lot," Roger said. "What are you passionate about?"

I was surprised by his question. "Wow," I said, "I don't know. Let me think about that."

He turned to Barbara. "Okay, your turn. What's your passion?"

She blushed, but was silent.

I looked at him. "Looks like you have to go first."

He grinned. "I asked for that, didn't I? If I were a psychologist, I'd guess I'd asked the question just to get an opening to answer it myself."

"Good insight," said Barbara. "Okay, then ..."

"Filmmaking used to be my passion. I went to school and studied all aspects of production—not acting, more about all the other kinds of work involved—camera work, directing, scripting, lighting. It's a very complicated process, even making documentaries."

"What was your dream?" I asked.

"Oh, you know, creating something that had my name on it, something that would move people." His smile looked shy, and I liked him a little bit more.

"I wanted to be a dancer," said Barbara, making both Roger and me look up quickly. That was a surprise.

She blushed. "Since I was a little girl, I wanted to dance. I couldn't listen to music without my body moving."

"Ever do anything about it?" asked Roger.

"Not really. My family couldn't afford dance school for me, and my mother thought it was a waste of time. As a teen-ager, I learned steps from my girlfriends. But my heart kept saying, 'ballet.'"

"Do you attend the dances at the Center?" I asked.

"Of course. Mostly, I just do my thing—there aren't many men who go to those affairs."

"I've never gone," I admitted. "I'm not a good dancer, but maybe the next one ..."

She smiled at me. "Good place to meet people."

"Do it," laughed Roger. "Rub some of that nerdiness off of you."

"No, he's not a nerd!" Barbara exclaimed.

"Yes I am," I said.

Roger said, "Okay, then, what are you? You haven't told us about your passions."

It took me a minute to be able to speak. Something rose up in my throat. Finally, I said simply, "Music."

Barbara drank the last of her wine, then looked at me closely. My face was hot. "What kinds of music?" she asked, very softly.

"Most kinds," I said. "I've loved classical music since I was a kid, for some reason. I used to memorize all the popular songs, and sing when I was alone."

"You play an instrument?" Roger asked.

"No. I've tried, a number of times. I have a guitar hanging on a wall at home, collecting dust, and a little keyboard stuffed away in a closet."

"The guitar, I bet, is a classical one," said Barbara.

I smiled. "Yes. My finger tips are too fat, and my nails are too long."

Roger poured more wine. "So here we are, three unfulfilled artists." His eyes were a little glassy, and it made me notice how much I was feeling the wine. I looked over at Barbara, who was smiling sweetly at me. *Oh, shit*, I thought, *this is getting out of hand*. But I stayed in the game.

I looked at Roger to keep from returning Barbara's look, and asked, "What kind of films did you dream of making?"

He sipped his wine. "In school I saw a lot of documentary films, and some of them brought tears to my eyes. I wanted to make that kind of film."

"You wanted to move people, you said."

"Yes."

Barbara turned to him, allowing me to breathe easier, and asked, "Then how did you come to be involved in reality TV? That's a long way from films that move people."

"It's a job, and it's involved in film and video—not much film being made anymore—and who knows, maybe what I want will come along." He shrugged.

"Ever thought of grabbing a camera and a sound man and just going somewhere to do what you want?" I realized that I was putting him on the spot. "Wait," I said, "I don't mean to challenge you. You have to do what you have to do."

He gestured vaguely with his hand. "Yeah, I've thought about it. But I have a family to support. It's as simple as that."

"Paul." Her voice sounded like she was breathing into my ear. I turned, half-expecting to see her face inches away. She was still sitting across the table, but her eyes were locked on mine. "Paul, you know, don't you, that Grace Jamison used to teach music? And we keep both of our pianos tuned up."

I grinned at her challenge and shrunk down in my chair. Both of them laughed.

The waiters had cleared our table of dishes, and now one of them stood next to Roger. "Dessert, folks?"

He looked over at me, then at Barbara. She and I said, "Coffee" at the same time. Roger held up three fingers, and the waiter disappeared.

I realized that I should not drive, and I had seen both of my table mates drinking as much wine as I had. "I am not able to drive," I said. "I suggest we leave our cars here and get a cab together. That way all three of us will be alive tomorrow." I was trying to be funny, but my words were slurred, and I just felt stupid.

"I have a better idea," Roger said. "I'll call Ethel, my wife, who will be our taxi driver. She'd be happy to do it, I promise. It's not all that late, and the kids can be alone for an hour or two."

"That's sweet," Barbara said, her voice like honey.

It was true—Roger's wife was happy to chauffer us home. "I'd much rather do this," Ethel said, "than have Roger risk his life driving after one of these business dinners." She had picked us up in a big Lincoln Navigator, and made small talk with us as she drove. I noticed that Roger, in the front seat, dozed once or twice. Barbara reached for my hand in the darkness of the back seat, and we held hands while she and Ethel chatted about nothing. Fortunately, I thought, we were heading for my condo first. I wasn't sure that Barbara might not ask me in if we got to the Center first. I knew she had a very nice apartment on the top floor of the building.

And I had been here before. I have very little resistance when I've been drinking, and sometimes very little sense. But I knew that Barbara and I needed to keep our relationship straight. I recognized feelings that I hadn't had in a long time. I needed to be alone and wait for them to pass.

Roger woke up enough to shake my hand when I got out of the van, and Barbara kissed me lightly on the cheek. I thanked Ethel for her generosity and patience, and made my way into my cave. I slept for a brief time, but then lay awake longer, thinking about the evening.

Seven

My slight headache, when I got to the office the next morning, was not as bad as I thought I deserved. Barbara did not show up until two hours later. She nodded to me as she entered, carrying a handful of memos and other papers her secretary had handed her. We didn't speak to each other until lunchtime.

"I'm embarrassed," she said quietly. "I feel like a slut."

I managed a weak grin. "Nonsense," I said. "We both had a lot to drink. I hope I didn't make a fool of myself."

"Can we talk later?" she asked as she started out the door.

"I'd like that."

I had skipped breakfast, so I was hungry by then. I waited until Barbara had been gone for several minutes before heading for the cafeteria.

I had just sat down at an empty table with my tray when Grace came over, carrying her tray. I realized that she had been sitting at another table. "Mind if I join you?" she asked.

"Please do."

When she sat down, she looked at me. "You look a little peaked. Are you all right?"

I had to smile. "I wasn't a good boy last night."

"Oh?"

"Okay, I drank too much."

That prompted a grin from her. "Alcohol has its own built-in punishment, doesn't it?"

"I've read that."

"Was this your 'thank you' dinner with Roger?" Then she blushed. "I'm sorry. I shouldn't ask."

"No, it's okay. And yes, it was that dinner. We got to know Roger a lot better."

She smiled. "He's not just another pornographer."

"No, just a guy trying to make a living in his field."

"His field being what?" She seemed genuinely interested, despite her remark.

"Film and video. He went to school to learn documentary film. Had a dream of doing something meaningful."

"So reality TV is not his dream." She picked at her salad.

"No. It's a job."

"May he go on to better things."

I picked up my sandwich and sat there staring at it. "All three of us—we talked for a long time about our dreams."

"You have dreams, Paul?"

For some reason, I choked up. I supposed it was because I had opened up the night before, and some of that was still present. I thought about Barbara and me, how close we might have been to doing something we'd regret. Or maybe she wasn't that close—maybe it was all just me. But the talk about dreams was part of it. She had touched me, somehow, and as uncomfortable as it was for me, we'd connected in a way that I hadn't experienced in a long time.

I had to clear my throat to speak. "I grew up with a love of music that I never managed to—what—*consummate*?"

Grace looked at me for a long time. "That's strong language, Paul."

I laughed. "Sorry. I guess that didn't come out right."

"It came out perfectly. I felt what you meant."

"Barbara said you used to teach music."

"It was my life," she said quietly. "I met my husband in the college of music. He was one of my teachers, and we connected through music. He'd play cello along with my piano practice. After I graduated, I went off to play with several orchestras, but we stayed close. We even did a few recitals together—do you know the Franck Sonata for Piano and Violin?"

"I have always loved that piece—it's like a game, an intimate game between two people."

She smiled. "It was our favorite. Anyway, we eventually married, and had a wonderful life together. I was never at his level in performance, but we shared that passion, all those years."

"Sounds wonderful." For some reason, I wanted to hug her. I took a deep breath.

She dabbed at her eyes with her napkin, and smiled at me. "He hasn't been gone very long."

"No."

Straightening up in her chair, she picked up her fork and began eating. "Your sandwich is getting cold," she said quickly.

"It wasn't hot to begin with," I smiled.

"Right."

"I feel honored that you shared that with me," I said.

"Paul, I do not want to cry here," she said. "Let's talk about something else for now. All right?"

"Of course. For example?"

"Your drunken dinner with Barbara and Roger."

I had to laugh. "Roger's wife had to leave their children at home and come to the restaurant to rescue us. She drove us both home, because none of us was in a condition to drive."

"I can't picture Barbara drinking too much."

"She would prefer you didn't."

Grace put her fork down and dabbed at her lips. "You got through her armor, though," she said.

"Roger was the one who began the talk about dreams."

"That's interesting." She was watching me.

"Barbara said that you sometimes teach."

A little smile at the corner of her mouth. "Do you still dream of—how did you put it—*consummating* your love of music?"

"I'm not sure I can. I've lost a lot in seventy-five years."

"Maybe not as much as you think."

I was hearing double entendres in this conversation, and I changed the subject. "Do you still play?"

She waved her hand. "Oh, once in a while it's fun to sit down and finger a keyboard, but I'm past the point where I want to perform for others."

"I'd love to hear you finger a keyboard sometime," I said.

She smiled. "Would you? Maybe sometime."

"When you are playing for yourself—fingering the keyboard—what do you like to play?

"Oh, it depends upon my mood. Sometimes I'm sentimental, and play things I have memories for—Chopin. Sometimes I want to prove to myself that I can still do it."

"Then what?"

"Prokofiev. But I'm losing my taste for challenges lately."
She shook her head, and suddenly stood up and said softly,
"Lets talk again, please?"

"I'd like that." I collected my tray and we made our way
out. In the hall, she went immediately into the women's room.

I returned to the office feeling unsettled.

Several notes lay on my desk. Someone had a stopped-up
toilet, and another resident needed help with a computer. I
called the plumber and went upstairs to guide a resident
through installing Microsoft Office.

As I returned, Susie handed me a note. It was from
Barbara. *Please come to my apartment* was all it said. As I
turned away from her desk, I caught Susie glancing at me.

Barbara greeted me at her door with a smile. "Thanks for
coming up. I wanted a little privacy for my apology."

I shrugged. "Nothing to apologize for."

Seated at her dining table, she said, "I was inappropriate
last night."

"I enjoyed our talk with Roger. I haven't gotten to that
kind of depth with anyone in a long time."

"Nor have I," she said. "But you and I have to work with
each other, and I don't want personal issues between us."

I sighed. "I suppose you're right. I admit I was feeling some
things last night that I shouldn't. I'd like that admission to put
a lock on those feelings—my feelings—so they don't affect how
I am with you here. It's probably not possible, as I've learned
over the years, but I want you to know that's my intention."

"My God," she said, "is all of your life so deliberate?"

"I don't think so, but I value my job here and I value the
relationships I'm developing, and I don't want to jeopardize
any of that."

"Last night you said you had considered me 'uptight.'"

I hung my head. "Sorry. I didn't mean that."

"Yes you did. And you were right. I feel my responsibilities
here, and sometimes I need to make hard decisions. But I'm

also human. I don't get much chance to let out the other side of me. As a result, I don't gauge the circumstances well enough, and go too far. Last night I went too far."

I smiled. "So right now both of us are practicing being more deliberate, and calling on our superegos to protect us from getting into messy situations. Right?"

"Bummer," she said, and we both laughed. "Now, let's go back to work."

"Okay, Boss."

Eight

Barbara and I remained on good terms after that. Our interactions were business-like but friendly. Every once in a while, though, we'd exchange a glance that conveyed, ever-so-briefly, something more.

The group of women who had requested a support group following the reality TV showing began meeting regularly, and Barbara told me that most of them felt it was helpful to their own personal situations. Many were widows, and much of the dialog in their meetings revolved around the missing part of their lives—sex. "A few of them," she said rather mysteriously, are discovering how to be their own best friend."

I raised my eyebrows at that, but she didn't elaborate. "They do, however, want us to have a New Year's Eve party with a little more pizzazz, and try to get more men to attend."

"You mean, let the Barry Manilow impersonator go and hire somebody who plays guitar with his shirt off?"

She huffed at that, then said, "I gathered that the punch we have served is not very popular. They want mixed drinks."

"Want me to be a bartender?"

"You know how to do that?"

"I'll read up on it."

"Excellent."

I made a point of mixing with the men more often, sitting down to watch a game on television with them, contributing popcorn and occasionally bringing a dozen beers with me. I was never interested in sports, but gradually I learned some of the terminology and the names of local players. Those times were easier for me than the poker games. Competitive play left me feeling anxious, as though everybody knew something I didn't. And there were more conversations going on, often getting into sexist and racist remarks. Watching a football game with them allowed me to be more anonymous, yelling when everybody else yelled, and otherwise blending in with the sofa as I nursed a beer.

When I mentioned at one of these gatherings that we were planning a regular bar at the New Year's Eve party, there was general noise of approval from the men. "I'm going to be the bartender," I told them. "Remember, Mrs Robinson will be watching our behavior."

Someone began that old Simon and Garfunkel song, *"What's that you say, Missus Robinson ..."* and everybody laughed.

A few male residents didn't regularly attend the sports and poker gatherings. The library was usually a quiet spot where one or two people could be found, engrossed in reading or working at one of the computers. One afternoon I found Charles Duncan there printing out something, and sat down nearby. "Something you're writing?" I asked.

He turned his wheelchair so he could see me more directly, and held out a couple of sheets of paper. "First draft," he said, his baritone voice, now raspy, suggesting a man who might have been in the theater when he was younger. "I don't have a printer in my apartment," he said, "so I have to come down here to print."

I read his short story, a gem of composition with an ironic twist at the end, and smiled. "You have a real knack," I said, handing it back to him. "You have more of these?"

He admitted that he was collecting his stories for a book. "I figure I'd better get them published while I still have time."

"I'd like to read them all," I said.

"Come up to my place sometime," he said, gathering a stack of papers and rolling toward the door. "I'd like to hear what you think about them."

It was only when he left that I noticed Grace sitting in a corner reading, her feet up on an ottoman. She looked up and smiled. "He's really a good writer," she said. "His stories have a sweet poignancy about them.

I went over and sat near her. "I heard someone playing Gershwin yesterday. Was that you?"

"Yes. I like to play *Rhapsody in Blue* the way George Gershwin did. I have a recording made from his piano rolls."

"He made piano rolls?" I laughed.

"Of course! Before there were phonographs, that's the way people recorded their music."

"I remember a neighbor when I was a kid," I said. "She had this old player piano and hundreds of paper rolls for it. We had a lot of fun pumping the pedals and pretending we were playing."

"A lot of composers and performers made paper roll recordings. Gershwin recorded it with a faster tempo than in the orchestral version."

"The first time I heard it was by Paul Whiteman," I said. "I was about twelve. I fell in love with it. That clarinet opening just grabs me by the throat and pulls me up with it."

She laughed. "That glissando's hard to duplicate on a piano."

"I'd love to hear you play," I said.

"Usually I'm up in my own place, playing a keyboard with headphones—that way it doesn't bother others."

"How could it bother anybody?"

"Not everybody feels about music the way you do."

"Or you do," I said.

She nodded. "Or I do."

I was falling for that smile of hers.

When I noticed her glance down at the book in her hands I made an excuse to leave and went back to the office. As I worked that afternoon, I listened to George Gershwin on my MP3 player. After that, I checked the library regularly on my rounds, to see if she were there.

In my occasional one-to-one conversations with men, I brought up the reality TV episode that Roger played for us, and asked, as indirectly as I could, if they could be interested in a support group of some kind. Two or three said they might, but nobody seemed enthusiastic about a men's group. One, whom I knew only slightly but knew was single, said he'd like to be in a mixed group.

"I don't know much about such things," I said, "but I suspect there wouldn't be many people who would risk that. I've heard of separate support groups that got together for one or two sessions after they had been meeting for a while."

"Back in the seventies we did that all the time," he said. "I wonder why people don't do that kind of thing any more."

"I guess it was a thing of the times."

"Too bad."

One day, as I was finishing my lunch, I heard a piano being played in another room, a theme I recognized from Khachaturian. Thinking it was Grace playing, I hurriedly emptied my tray and went to investigate.

A young woman sat at the piano with one of the residents seated in a chair next to her. She was playing the incredibly sweet melody, and the old man was listening, entranced. I knew him only slightly; he suffered from Alzheimer's and was usually accompanied by an older woman, I think a caretaker.

Other people wandered in as she played. It was a short piece, and soon she sat, her hands in her lap, her face turned toward him. His expression didn't change. "Thank you," he mumbled.

"I learned that just for your birthday, Daddy."

"Thank you," he repeated. "Are you a professional pianist?"

"I'm your daughter Christie, Daddy. I learned to play that just for you. Happy birthday, Daddy." Her face was sad, but she kept smiling at him.

The sadness of the piece and the emotion in her voice left me with a lump in my throat. I took a deep breath and turned to leave the room just as a woman approached the two, asking the young woman if she knew how to play "Mandy." Walking down the hall, I was grateful not to hear the piano again.

Barbara was at her desk, and looked up as I entered the office. "You look like somebody stole your chewing gum," she said.

I told her what had happened. "Sometimes this is a very sad place."

"Yes," she said. "There are times."

Then she looked up. "You are a real softy."

"I have a daughter somewhere." I hadn't meant to say that, but I'd been thinking it.

"You never told me that."

"Haven't seen her since she was three years old."

"And she would be how old now?"

I managed a weak smile. "About that old. Maybe thirty."

We went back to the work on our desks for a while, and I thought about my life of a long time ago. It didn't seem possible she would be that old, but she had to be.

A few minutes later, Barbara asked, "Ever try to contact her?"

"No," I said. "It doesn't seem fair."

"What's her name?"

"Shirley. She's undoubtedly got a life, and now even a history. Probably kids of her own. She wouldn't thank me for intruding on that."

"Wanna bet?"

I looked up, and Barbara was looking at me. "Check it out," she said, and then went back to her work.

Thirty years ago seemed like eons. I was a different person in a different world. We had married hurriedly, with only her mother and a friend as witnesses. Our daughter, crowned with golden ringlets, came into a home wracked by discord and eventual separation. I had moved away and made a new life. *A long time ago*, I thought, but not so long that I didn't sigh about it occasionally, even now.

Nine

I was assigned the job of decorating the Center for the holidays. Barbara gave me the name of the florist she had used for several years. "You're not obligated to use the same one. They are just who we used last year."

I visited the company she had told me about, and they were helpful and knowledgeable. "We put up big trees in the cafeteria and the main hall," the manager said, "and smaller ones in the entrance foyer and the library. You also have a smaller music room, I think you call it. Do you want a tree there, or just wreaths and tinsel?"

He pulled his file from last year and showed me what they had done for the Center. I was a little shocked at the price. "Would you do it for the same price as last year?"

He hesitated, then said, "Okay. Trees are higher this year, but we'll install the same decorations as last year for the same price."

While I was out, I went to a liquor store to price beverages for the New Year's Eve party. After we talked for a while, they agreed to fax me an itemized list for approval.

When I received that, I made up a report for Barbara.

"Last year," she said, "punch was cheaper, and I know it's going to cost more for a DJ. You'd better line up the DJ right away—they book New Year's 'way in advance."

I hadn't even thought about reserving musicians for the party. I had no idea where to start.

"You might get Grace involved," Barbara said. "She's a musician."

I got the name of last year's DJ from Susie, and called Grace's number. There was no answer, so I left a message and went out into the public areas on the chance that she'd be around. She wasn't in the library or the music room or the big hall. I went back to my desk and began searching online for a DJ in our area. Every one I found either didn't answer their phone or had already booked New Year's Eve. I even called the one they had used the year before, the Barry Manilow impersonator, but he was also committed to another engagement.

The next morning after breakfast, Grace stuck her head in our door. She had a big grin on her face. "You should have done this six months ago," she said. "You'll never find one, at least a decent one, now."

"I was hoping," I said, "that you'd have just the perfect candidate among your associates."

"If you wanted a string quartet, I might be able to help. I don't know anything about the current pop music scene."

"I didn't realize that I would have to find a DJ," I said. "She sprung it on me yesterday." I pointed toward Barbara at her desk across the room, who looked up and smiled.

Grace came in and sat in my visitor's chair. She could have been the First Lady, dressed as she was. But the First Lady probably wouldn't have known how to find a DJ on such short notice, either.

"You are always dressed for an affair of state," I said, and she smiled.

Barbara spoke up. "Among all those aspiring musicians you've taken under your *wing*, so to speak, ..."

Grace drew herself up in the chair. "I beg your pardon!" Both women were laughing, and I was probably blushing. Even Susie, outside the not-quite-closed door, could be heard chuckling.

"I don't know what to suggest," Grace said. "unless you want to recruit one of the residents and ask around for music. We have a decent sound system, don't we?"

"We should have," Barbara said, "We spent a lot of money for one a couple of years ago. Radio mikes and all."

Grace looked at me. "You'd make a good DJ."

I laughed. "I'm already the designated bartender."

"I know where you can probably get a good collection of dance music," Grace said. "Mike Wilson, up on the third floor, has a huge cabinet full of CDs, all the old swing music, jazz, early Rock and Roll, even some from the seventies. He may not have anything recent—I heard him complaining about the contemporary 'noise,' as he puts it."

"I don't know him," I said. "Do you think he would DJ?"

"You don't want to ask him. He shakes too much from Parkinson's to handle the records."

"Maybe he'd help me pick out the music, and then we can get someone else to play it."

"Good idea. You want me to introduce you?"

"I'd love it."

She stood up. "Okay, let's go."

In the elevator, I caught her scent, just a hint of a very expensive perfume. I looked over at her, standing quietly, the epitome of aristocratic elegance. She sensed my stare, and smiled without looking at me. "I enjoy you, Paul," she said.

"Why is that?"

"You make me feel attractive, I guess."

"Thirty years ago, I would have made a fool of myself over you."

She turned to look at me. "Thirty years ago I would have wanted you to."

I had to say it. "But now?"

She put a hand on my arm. "Just—not now."

"I don't know what I'm asking," I said.

"I know."

The elevator stopped, and we stepped out into the hall. She led the way to Mike Wilson's door.

Ten

When Barbara came into the office, I told her, "I think we've got New Year's fixed up."

"Excellent! You have a DJ?"

I grinned. "Actually, I handed the bartending job off to Doug White."

"Susie's husband?"

"She heard all the talk about it the other day, and she offered his services. She said he has done that before, and she'd really like to come to our party instead of the bar they usually go to on New Year's. Mike Wilson has supplied us with lots of music that our folks would enjoy, and I can run a couple of CD players."

"Sounds like a winner." Barbara was shuffling through papers on her desk.

"You know," I said, "Grace has been a big help."

Barbara looked up at me. "She likes you."

"It's mutual."

She and I looked at each other for a long moment. I felt something going on in that silence, but I let it go.

"The decorations should be arriving tomorrow or the next day. The florist was trying to get a better tree for the big hall."

"Good," she said, and turned back to her work.

I told Susie that I'd be back in the storage room checking out the audio system. At the library, I poked my head in to see if Grace was there. No luck.

The electronic gear was not stored well. I found the amplifier and speakers, but the wireless microphone receiver was not visible. I'd been planning to use my own CD player, plus one that Mike Wilson offered. I thought I'd better put the system together and test it before Christmas, to give us time to get it repaired if necessary.

I felt better about being the DJ at the party rather than the bartender, because I wanted to be free to have a drink or two, and a drinking bartender tends to be noticed. If I'm busy spinning records, I won't be wandering around with a drink in my hand, either.

I found the janitor drinking coffee in the kitchen. He and I returned to the storage room and carried the equipment out into the big hall. Several women were sitting at the far end of the room talking.

"Ladies," I said to them, "we're going to be testing the sound equipment. I hope we don't disturb you."

"If you do, we can move," they replied.

It turned out that there was a CD player with the other equipment. I went up to my apartment and retrieved the box of CDs that Mike had loaned us. The janitor found the missing mike receiver, along with a fairly good mixer. I spent a fun hour putting everything together and testing it. One of the recordings we had was an Artie Shaw disc with all his favorite swing pieces, and I played that to test the system. "Begin the Beguine," one of my personal favorites, took me back to my youth, when I was still resisting the growing popularity of Rock and Roll. Recently I'd heard a completely different version of that song in a movie about Cole Porter, sung by Sheryl Crow—in a minor key, which I found both intriguing and awful at the same time. Not a version for our New Year's party!

The women who had been talking at the far end of the hall came over to watch me work. "Do you have any Count Basie there?" one asked, browsing through the box of CDs.

"I think so," I replied. "We tried to select a range of dance music, from the thirties up into the seventies."

"Disco?"

"I don't know," I said. "I guess I'd better make a list of what we have so I can answer questions."

"Are you going to be the DJ?" another one asked. "Can I bring some of my favorites?"

"I guess so," I said, "but I've been given strict instructions not to play any Barry Manilow."

"Aww."

"I wasn't here last year, but I understand you had quite a lot of Barry Manilow."

They laughed together. "That guy was pretty bad, wasn't he?"

"Remember," I said, "if you bring your own records, make sure they have your name on them. We don't want to get them mixed up."

"You're a doll."

"He is, isn't he?" It was Grace, who had joined the group without my noticing her. She grinned at me. "Hi, soldier."

"You've made my day," I said, returning her smile.

"Wanna buy me a cup of coffee?"

"Love to. Excuse us, ladies. And please don't touch the equipment."

They laughed, and we left for the cafeteria.

At a table in the far corner of the cafeteria, I said to Grace, "I don't know what it is about you, but I feel drawn to you like a moth to a flame."

She put a hand on mine. "Paul ..."

"I know, I know. You said 'not now.' I'll respect that."

"I said in the elevator, I enjoy your attention. You make me feel attractive. But I'm still grieving my loss, and I want to respect that, too."

"I'm sorry."

"Don't be sorry! Look around you at the people in this place. Every one of them is looking at the face of death—if not their own, then someone they love. None of us has a lot of time left."

I put my other hand on hers. "Ten years ago I didn't think I could ever love anyone again. I didn't want to *live*."

She smiled. "That's where I was three months ago."

"You sure seem to be alive now."

"Not completely. I have decided, however," she said, sitting up straighter in her chair, "to stay among the living, at least. I don't know for how long. I've had some medical problems of my own, and I am waiting to see what's going to come of them."

She was silent for a moment. "And I'm trying to come to terms with the consequences of that, because I don't feel as though I have anything to offer to anyone else."

I wanted to protest, but I sensed something more in what she said. "I'll be content with what is here, now," I said. "I'm not sure I have anything more to offer, either."

That smile again. "We're both too old to play the old games."

A thought occurred to me. "This is reality TV, isn't it? That happy ending in the program Roger screened here, aside from the embarrassment and the titillation, was still fantasy."

She sighed. "There was a song in the musical *Hair*—remember that?"

I nodded, grinning with my memories of that time.

"I can't remember which song it was now, but I'll never forget the last line—*The rest is silence.*" She stopped, emotion spreading over her face. Her voice broke as she said, "The rest is sadness, I think."

We sat there for a long time without speaking, eyes on our hands rather than each other. I sipped my cold coffee.

She pulled her hands from under mine and, slapping them gently, stood up. "I shall wear a red dress!" she said quickly, then turned and walked away.

Feeling discouraged, I went back into the big hall and dismantled the smaller pieces of equipment. As I picked up the CD player, I noticed that it still had a disc in it, so I had to plug it in again to extract the CD. It was a Beatles album, *Abbey Road*, and the first title I saw on the label was "Here Comes the Sun."

The irony of that caught in my throat. *I thought I was past all that stuff,* I reminded myself. *I'm retired! I'm old! How is this all coming back up again?*

Lois's face flashed through my memory again, lying pale and sad on the pillow ten years ago, saying goodbye to me. *I never wanted to hurt like that again,* I thought, *and here I am, setting myself up for loss one more time.*

I put the disc into its case and carried the equipment back to the storage room.

When I returned to the office, Barbara was sitting back in her chair, her hands behind her head. Seeing me, she sat back upright. "I hunch over too much when I'm working," she said.

"Looks like we have all the audio equipment."

"I could hear Artie Shaw clear up here," she said, smiling. "Do you have 'Frenesi'?"

"Yes."

"Those old songs still move us, don't they?"

"Wasn't 'Frenesi' before your time?"

She laughed. "My mother used to play all the old swing numbers. She thought Rock and Roll was terrible."

"What kind of music turned you on?" I asked, then stopped. "Uh, maybe I should rephrase that! What kind of music did you like?"

Barbara looked at me boldly and laughed. "I loved it all. I remember going to a Ramsey Lewis concert once, at the ball field because no other place had enough room for the crowd. I felt like I was the only white person in the stadium, but I could move with the rest of them."

"Are you going to the party?"

"I wouldn't miss it." Her eyes sparkled with mischief. "Will you dance with me?"

"I'll need a stiff drink first."

Susie had come into the office with a note for Barbara. "Tell Doug to make you his special martini," she said to me as she handed the note to Barbara. "It will do the job, believe me!"

"Maybe I'll have one of those, myself," said Barbara.

Eleven

Someone else organized the Christmas Carol singing. I took the evening and the holiday off and stayed in my condo. I always got depressed that time of year. I blamed it on losing Lois, which happened just before Christmas, but I suspected that it came from other things, long before that.

The Center was very quiet between the holidays. Many of the residents were away visiting relatives or taking a break from the cold weather, lying on the beaches in Florida. We set up a refreshment stand in the music room, where one could get eggnog or punch and cookies around the clock. The cafeteria seemed deserted. But there was a growing sense of excitement as New Year's Eve neared. Our announcements encouraged residents to invite guests. Even so, I wondered how many people we would see at the party.

We set the party to begin at eight o'clock—early, because some of our residents would not be able to last until ten, much less until midnight. They told me that New Year's parties at the Center never went more than a few minutes past midnight. "One year," Barbara said, "we sang 'Auld Lang Sine' at ten o'clock, because there were only a few people left, and the musicians wanted to leave."

I hadn't stayed up to see the new year in at all since Lois died. I was invited to parties several years, but didn't feel like going. I decided that this year I was going to do better. And I was anticipating seeing Grace.

New Year's Eve was a working day. I was in the office most of the day, checking now and then with the kitchen staff and the janitor, who brought out all the audio equipment. About four o'clock, Barbara called Susie into the office and retrieved several bottles from a small refrigerator. "Since we're working all night tonight," she said, smiling, "we need to enjoy the holiday while we can. What is your pleasure?"

After pouring the drinks, she held up her glass. "To a wonderful staff!"

"And to a great boss!" Susie said.

"God bless us, every one!" I quipped.

The door opened, and Grace appeared. "Ah, you made it!" Barbara said. "You are practically one of the team, and I wanted you to know how much we appreciate you."

Grace smiled shyly, and accepted Barbara's offer of a glass of wine. I caught Grace's eye and lifted my glass to her silently. As I looked back, Barbara was watching us. She smiled and lifted her glass, as well. "A very happy new year," she said.

Dinner in the cafeteria was light, with party food such as deviled eggs and a selection of cheeses with toast and crackers. I would have loved a glass of wine with my food, but thought it was probably better that I hold off until my duties were taken care of.

By eight o'clock I had everything set up, and Doug White was working behind the bar. I put on a selection of music, keeping the volume turned down for a while. Later, I knew, the sound level in the hall would rise as people gathered, and they would want it louder. The kitchen staff set out food to nibble on, including bowls of pretzels and chips on the tables, and were prepared to set up a hot buffet later. The florist had placed a colorful centerpiece with a candle on each table, and hung a "HAPPY NEW YEAR!" banner on the wall.

Doug offered to make me a drink, but I settled for a Bitter Lemon—"I have to run that system over there, so I'd better go easy at least until everybody else is feeling good," I said. "Then, Susie tells me you have a special martini."

"Sure do," said the young man.

Doug seemed a likable fellow. I noticed that he appeared to be very young, but decided that mixing with seniors every day had skewed my perceptions. Everyone outside of the Center seemed young to me.

Barbara arrived, looking gorgeous in a white evening gown with almost no back—but busily conducting business on her phone. She glanced at me, nodded, and sat alone at a side table, talking all the while. I went to the bar and said to Doug, "She was drinking gin and tonic a while ago. You might start her out with that."

He grinned and began mixing the drink. "For an old lady," he said, "she's a knockout."

"She is that," I replied. "You take it over to her. I'll guard the bar."

After he had delivered the drink, Barbara looked over at me, lifted her glass, and blew me a kiss. Within minutes, several women had gathered at her table.

I played an old Duke Ellington piece, "Take the A Train," and got a cheer from a table of women.

"Is it gonna be all women here?" Doug asked.

"I hope not," I said. "If it is, you're going to be kept busy dancing all evening."

He laughed. "I couldn't begin to dance to those old songs! Don't you have anything less than fifty years old?"

"Tell you what," I said, "when you're not busy, go over and ask a group of them to teach you the steps. You'll be an instant hit."

It reminded me how uneasy I was about dancing. I was never very good, and I dreaded asking Grace to dance with me because I was sure I'd be tromping all over her feet. I told Doug to give me another Bitter Lemon, this time with gin in it. Then I put on a Mamas and Papas record. Several people got up and began dancing. I even counted two men on the floor at one point.

I had just taken a sip of my drink when Barbara appeared at my side. "Take a big gulp," she said. "You're going to need it." She stood there with her arms up, waiting for me to walk into them, a big smile on her face.

I complied, but said, "I hope you have steel-toed shoes on."

She bent forward and lifted her gown to show me her silver straps and bright red nail polish. "You break-a these, I break-a your head!"

Barbara danced very close to me, even on these faster numbers. I could feel her body undulate against mine, but her feet were never close enough to mine to be threatened.

"How do you do that?" I asked.

"What?"

"Keep your feet safe from mine."

"Practice. I've danced in a lot of bars, with a lot of drunks."

"And that was not your first drink." I pulled my face back so I could see hers.

She had a wicked grin on her face. "You're in trouble tonight, friend. I'm off duty."

She must have sensed a hesitation in my body. "Relax, Paul, she said quietly. "I'm kidding."

Over my shoulder, she was watching someone. "Oh, oh. Now you really are in trouble." She spun us around so I could see the door.

Grace stood there in the threatened red dress, watching us. Her white hair glowed in the soft light. I eased out of Barbara's grip and together we walked over to greet Grace.

"You look like a Christmas candle," I said over the noise in the room.

"Candy?" She looked mystified.

Barbara shrieked with laughter. "He said candle, but I like what you heard! You look good enough to eat!"

I cringed, hoping no one else had heard us. Just then the music stopped. "I have to get back to my post," I said, and left them standing at the door. I hoped that Barbara would escort Grace to the bar.

Artie Shaw came next, and I cued up "Frenesi" to play first. I saw Barbara turn and look at me, smile and walk with Grace to an empty table. She retrieved her shawl and her glass from the table where she had been sitting, and the two of them sat and talked, heads close together so they could hear each other over the rising noise level. Grace went to the bar and returned with a glass of white wine.

I picked up my glass and went to their table. "Private conversation?" I asked, putting my hand on a chair.

"We were talking about you, actually," said Barbara. It was clear that she had had more than one drink before coming to the party.

Just then "Begin the Beguine" started. Barbara took my drink out of my hand and said, "Dance with your candy—er—candle."

"Yes, Boss." I smiled at Grace, took her hand and helped her from her chair. I got a whiff of that expensive perfume. We walked to a vacant spot on the dance floor. She turned and melted into my arms.

"You didn't have to obey your employer," she said teasingly.

"I was obeying my heart," I said, and she laughed.

We had to stop, a moment later, to find our steps. "It's a beguine," she said. "The steps are like this." She demonstrated.

"I should have warned you," I said. "I'm a klutz on the dance floor."

I felt her leading me gently for a while, and then it seemed that we were floating together around the floor. By the time the piece finished, I was enjoying it. We stopped, smiled at each other, and walked back to the table. Barbara was at the bar, and returned in a moment with three full glasses.

I managed to stay sober enough through the evening to keep the music going. I played whatever people requested, if I had it, and once played a CD that someone had brought with them. I kept the tempo up, although I would have preferred to dance to slower numbers. I was busy enough that I didn't have time to either drink too much or dance too much. But I was definitely feeling the presence of these two women. When I danced, I pulled them to me and enjoyed the sensuous pleasure of our bodies moving together.

Barbara moved easily and fluidly; she seemed to sense where I was going even before I knew myself. More than once, I wondered how it would be to sleep with her. Every time, I successfully resisted the impulse to say anything.

Grace in motion was just as her name says—she knew how our bodies should move, how our feet should travel. I had to learn what she was expecting. When I had learned it, our movements were perfect. That was not all the time. My joints began to ache, so I sat out more and more numbers.

"You're wearing me out!" I protested, taking a big sip from one of Doug's special martinis.

"I told you you were in trouble tonight," Barbara laughed.

"This is my last drink, though," I said. "I'm glad I'm not trying to play vinyl records. I'd ruin them all!"

"You are doing great," Grace said. "I'm getting weary, myself."

By ten o'clock, the crowd was beginning to thin out and the noise level had dropped noticeably. I cut the volume on the amplifier, and played more slow numbers.

Doug's wife Susie had joined us at our table, and occasionally Doug wandered over when no one was waiting at the bar.

"Did you get Guy Lombardo?" Barbara asked. "We may be playing 'Auld Lang Sine' a little early."

"Yes," said Grace. "Mike pulled that one out first."

"Paul and Doug, you both did a good job. Thank you." Barbara saluted us with her glass.

"It was fun," Doug said. "I only had to look in the bartender's guide once. Somebody ordered a Sidecar."

"I'm glad we had the ingredients."

"Yeah," he said, "there were different recipes in the book—one called for four ounces of cognac, plus an ounce of Cointreau!"

Susie laughed. "I hope you didn't give some little old lady one of those!" When the rest of us laughed, Susie blushed and hung her head. "Oh, I'm sorry!"

"It was funny, Susie," Grace said gently.

Barbara said, "I think we're lucky that nobody had to be carried out of here tonight."

I looked at her quickly to see if she were joking.

"Seriously," she said, "in the past we've served only punch on New Year's Eve. I didn't know what to expect tonight."

"We still have twelve bottles of champagne," Doug said. "When should I start serving that?"

"Just before the stroke of midnight," Barbara said, "Or when there are only six people left in the room—whichever comes first."

"We are five," I said, looking around. "Or is everyone at this table expecting to make it to midnight?"

"Will you be the last man standing, Paul?" asked Barbara.

"No, I think Doug could outlast me easily." Doug and Susie both laughed at that.

The five of us talked and laughed for a long time. Doug left the table occasionally to get someone a drink.

Finally, Barbara seemed to wilt. "I think I'm not going to make it to midnight. I seem to have overdone it." She smiled a weak smile, and laboriously got to her feet.

Grace looked at her, concerned. "Barbara, take Paul with you. You look like you might need help."

I stood. Barbara started to wave me off, then thought better of it. "Would you, please, kind sir?"

I offered my arm, and we moved toward the door. Barbara turned and said, "I shall return your man shortly."

Grace waved at her.

In the hall on the way to the elevator, Barbara said, "Thank you, Paul. I felt badly taking you away from your date."

"Grace is not my date, Barbara. And she's in good hands."

"I'm in good hands, aren't I?" She looked up at me and smiled. "I would love to be in your hands."

I was imagining something similar, but I said, "You'll be asleep the minute your head hits the pillow."

Riding up in the elevator, I was thinking about how Grace had smelled the day we took the elevator to Mike Wilson's. I'd had enough to drink that my imagination was running wild. I kept telling myself to watch my step.

At her door I helped her through, and started to turn back. She stumbled. "Oh, oh," she said, and I caught her. My heart was pounding, but I kept my head. Leading her into the bedroom, I helped her lie down, then removed her shoes.

"This dress will get ruined!" she said, fumbling with the straps. "Help me?"

We had to stand her up again to get the dress off. I draped the thin garment over the back of a chair, and she climbed into bed. Pulling the covers up to her chin, she smiled at me. "Sure you don't want to come in, too?"

I leaned over her and kissed her gently on the lips. "I don't want you to feel bad in the morning," I said, and moved toward the door. Just as I went through the door, I glanced back. She had the covers pulled down to her waist. I was shaking as I turned away.

"Coward!" she called after me.

In the hall walking to the elevator, I could still smell her woman scent around me. I took the stairway instead, and at the ground level I was completely out of breath, but I felt better. And completely sober.

A dozen people were left in the big hall. Doug had put on another record, and he and Susie and Grace were still talking. "We may be ready for champagne and Guy Lombardo," said Grace. "Is Barbara all right?"

"She may have a headache in the morning," I said. "I helped her out of her gown and made sure she was in bed."

Doug laughed, and Susie slapped his arm.

"Thank you, Paul. You're a real gentleman," Grace said. "You were gone—" then looking at her wrist, on which there was no watch, "—exactly thirteen minutes."

It brought laughter from all four of us.

Grace stood and addressed the room, "Folks, it's only eleven twenty, but some of us are ready to call it a year. What do you think?"

There seemed general agreement, so I went to the CD and put in Guy Lombardo, cued to "Auld Lang Sine." Doug got out four bottles of champagne and glasses for all. "C'mon up," he said, popping the first cork.

The small group stood around the bar and sang along with Guy Lombardo and drank to the New Year.

I watched Grace carefully. She turned her back at one point, dabbed at her eyes with a loose fold of her red gown, and turned around. "Happy New Year, Paul. Happy New Year, Susie and Doug. Happy New Year, all my friends in this wonderful place."

"Happy New Year, Barbara," I added, and Grace raised her glass one more time, looking directly into my eyes.

As the other people slowly drifted out of the room, Susie and Doug began clearing up the bar area. "Wait for me," I said to Grace, then told the young people to just put the perishables in the refrigerator, and leave the rest until morning.

"Good night," Susie called to us as we left the hall.

"Good kids," I said to Grace.

"Yes."

"Are you all right?" I looked at her as we walked.

She smiled. "I feel wonderful."

"Was it really thirteen minutes?"

At that, she laughed out loud. "Paul." She made her face serious again. "Paul. You'd be a fool not to want that woman."

I started to protest, but she stopped me. "And you'd be a fool to do it—right?"

I laughed. "Exactly right."

"Remember that old Judy Collins song, 'Send In the Clowns'?" And she sang, beautifully, in the elevator,

Isn't it rich
Isn't it queer
Losing my timing this late
In my career

I turned her around and kissed her passionately. She didn't resist.

When I let her go, there were tears in her eyes. The elevator stopped at her floor, and she took my hand and led me to her door. Turning to me, she said softly, "Paul, thank you for a wonderful evening. You are a prince."

She opened her door. "Now I'm going to cry myself to sleep. I will see you tomorrow, all right?"

"Good night, Grace. Sleep well."

I waited until I was in the elevator to blow my nose.

Twelve

New Year's Day was as quiet as we expected. I was at my post by nine o'clock—not really ready to work, but able to—and saw to the cleanup. I asked the kitchen staff to fix a breakfast tray for Barbara. I was pretty sure she would not be able to face the day for a little while, and I wanted to check on her to make sure she was surviving.

I hesitated a moment before tapping on her door. Eventually, I saw the peep hole go dark, and she opened the door wide for me, wearing only a towel and a wry smile.

"Room service," I said, setting the tray down on her coffee table.

"I notice you brought two coffee cups."

"Am I presuming too much?" It was hard for me to keep my eyes off the towel.

She laughed. "I'm not at my best, but I'd enjoy company."

"I hope you slept well. How are you feeling this morning?"

She sat down on the sofa, causing one leg to be exposed by the towel. Tugging futilely at it, she finally gave up and grinned at me. "You saw more of me last night than my leg."

"I did."

"Thank you for being our Jiminy Cricket," she said. "I did it again, didn't I?"

"You were very cute. And very tempting."

"Sorry." She looked down.

"I'm not complaining," I said. "Grace told me last night after I put you to bed that I'd be a fool not to want you, and I'd be a fool to do it."

"You agreed?"

"Yes."

"Paul, I hope we can stay friends. You are a good friend."

"I hope so, too," I said. "One of the benefits of advanced age is that the hormones are quieter, and that makes good sense easier to follow."

She looked at me for a long while. "I don't want you to take this the wrong way." She paused, choosing her words. "I'm jealous of you and Grace."

"We are also just friends," I said. "She is still grieving."

"I know. I also want you to know that I think you should take that friendship as far as it will go."

I shrugged. "I don't know where it could go."

"I love her," Barbara said. "She's one of my heroes. I'm suggesting that as much for her as for you—maybe more."

"I gathered that."

"You did?"

"You wear your heart on your sleeve, Barbara." I cleared my throat. "And I love you for that."

She smiled. "You'd better leave, before I tear this towel off."

I stood up. "Yes, Boss." Grinning, I left the apartment.

Going back down the stairway, I was aware that I was on very thin ice. It would be so easy—and the consequences so bad—to pursue Barbara. She seemed the most physical woman I had ever known. It was no wonder that her dream had been to dance. It was hard for me to understand why she was not married, or at least in an intimate relationship.

My feelings for Grace were of a different sort. I found her breathtakingly attractive, and I would love to be intimate with her—not merely physically, but in a deeper way. I admired her, I respected her, as one would admire and respect royalty. That she had been a concert pianist fit perfectly the image that I had of her. *Of course* she would perform before audiences. I could imagine her standing in that red gown to the roaring applause of thousands, bowing, smiling, stooping to accept the bouquet proffered by an admirer. She was as delicate as a flower—with a scent that aroused fantasies of sitting on a flowering terrace overlooking the Mediterranean, sipping wine and feeling the breeze and having nothing on earth to do but to be with her, perhaps read poetry to her.

I had to laugh at my daydreams as I made my way back to the cafeteria to eat my lonely breakfast on a tray, sitting at a Formica table listening to the clatter of dishes in the kitchen.

I, who for the past ten years had had no serious female relationships—didn't want any—and had considered myself done with romance and sex and mystery, had gotten myself caught up in two impossible situations. I, who was well past the age in which one might expect to fall in love, or whatever these fantasies might be called, was now entertaining thoughts of romance. I, whose aging body could no longer be depended upon to consummate a relationship with a woman, lived with curiosity and desire—not for one but *two* attractive women.

I had never even considered the purchase of a stimulant such as Viagra—it was one of those commercial products valued by men hoping to extend their powers in the bedroom, but I thought of them in the same class as breast–enhancement surgery or face lifts, fooling no one.

My physical life with Lois had been wonderful, and as it naturally declined over the years, it still satisfied us both. When she became ill, love making became simply holding and stroking and gentle kissing. We spoke of our past passion, but we did not mourn its passing. Only the sudden loss of her touch and her simple presence wrenched me terribly. I thought forever. Until only recently, she occupied my thoughts every day.

I don't think I felt guilty, looking into the eyes of someone who was not Lois. It was not even unexpected; over the span of a few months, my thoughts simply changed. I could identify with Grace as we toasted the New Year, who shed a few— perhaps a flood of—tears for her lost lover. It's what happens to people, and it had happened to me as well. As Grace reminded me earlier, all of us in this place are faced vividly with the presence of death, either our own or of someone we love, or both. Death simply stands over there, waiting, a ghostly chauffer with his practiced hand on the door of the limo, the motor running.

My reverie was interrupted by Her presence. "Good morning," Grace said. "May I sit with you?"

I had to smile. I was actually surprised that she wasn't wearing that red gown. "Please do, m'lady."

She set her tray down and pulled her chair closer to mine. "You look wide awake this morning."

"Mmm," I said, chewing a bite of English muffin. "Did you cry all night?"

Grace blushed and looked at her plate. "Only for a while. I fell asleep thinking of you."

She held my gaze. Her irises were an unusual color, light brown with a tinge of green. Without taking her eyes off mine except for an instant, she put a bit of scrambled egg in her mouth. I watched those lips revealing the movement of her jaw, and thought how wondrous was the simple act of chewing.

"You have my undivided attention," was all I could think to say.

"Do you have to work today?"

"Only to be on call, in case someone needs my help."

"Have you seen Barbara?"

I laughed. "Yes, rather a lot of her, actually. She's recovering from her fling."

Her eyebrows went up. "Explain, please!"

I told her about the towel—and about our mutual recognition of propriety. "I'm sure she will appear shortly."

"You went home last night, and came back already?"

"Yes," I said. "Seemed a shame, considering how much I had to drink and how all that alcohol affected me."

Her face showed concern. "Were you okay to drive?"

"Almost. Probably it would have been more prudent to sleep on a couch here, but I didn't have any problem."

"On New Year's Eve, there must have been a lot of drunks on the road."

"It was before midnight, remember? Not much traffic out there. Everybody was standing in a crowd waiting for the moment when they could kiss somebody."

"Or several somebodies," she laughed.

I poked at my breakfast. "I only remember kissing one somebody."

"C'mon. You didn't kiss Barbara?" Her eyes played with me.

"That was different," I said. "It was tucking a little girl into bed and bidding her goodnight."

One eyebrow went up. "I'll bet. Did you tell her a bedtime story, too?"

I laughed. "Only in my head on the way back downstairs."

"I so enjoy playing with you, Paul." She put a hand on mine.

"It's good to be this age and be able to joke easily about things most people are so serious about."

"Isn't it! I don't remember flirting like this as a young woman," she said. Then her face changed. "Paul—we need to— *I* need to talk about this."

I looked around. Nobody was in the cafeteria except one of the kitchen workers.

"No, not here," Grace said.

"The library?"

"Come with me to my apartment. I don't want any distractions."

"Sounds serious."

"It is," she said, rising from the table.

Thirteen

In her apartment, she took my hand and led me to the sofa. Sitting at the far end, she tucked a leg under her and faced me, her arm on the back of the sofa. Smiling, she began, "I'm not used to discussing such personal things with people other than my doctors." She looked down at the hand in her lap. "This may be premature. I know you are interested in Barbara, and this may even be irrelevant. But I need you to know, in case you have thought about our sleeping together ..."

"Of course I have," I said, "but ..."

"Please let me say this, Paul. I'm not able to have intercourse. Not ever. When I told you, the other day, 'not now,' I had an appointment with my gynecologist. And now I know."

"All right," I said. "It doesn't ..."

"Of course it matters. My husband and I had not had intercourse in years because of his own medical problems. I have not had intercourse in many years. Now, it's too late. I'm sorry, but it is. You need to know that."

I must have looked confused, because she went on, "This is very difficult to say." She paused a long moment. "My gynecologist says that my vagina has atrophied to the extent that intercourse would almost certainly be too painful to endure. The walls are too thin. I'm sorry."

I shrugged. "Okay," I said, through a flood of feelings.

Her eyes brimmed with tears. "When I sang to you last night, the Judy Collins lines about 'losing my timing this late' that is what I was saying. And then you kissed me, and I knew I had to be direct with you."

"I didn't kiss you because I wanted to have sex with you," I said. "Well, I wouldn't have objected." I laughed, lamely. "But that wasn't on my mind. You were. I'm not twenty any more, either."

"It's hard for a woman," she said, "to let go of those assumptions about her relationship with men, how she perceives her value to men. I never went through those young years of playing the field, enjoying the attention of men, basking in the feeling of being sexy. Craig came along while I was focused on my music and we connected intimately in that shared passion. I felt sorry for the women I knew at the time, always seeming to perform for an audience of men. To me, performance meant giving my music to others. I wanted people to want me for that. 'Sexy' meant revealing my musical soul. It was never about my body." She gave a wry smile. "Isn't that bizarre?"

"When I was young," I said, "I loved to look at female bodies. I enjoyed fantasizing about them. I'm sure I did my share of ogling. I married twice, the first time I think it was purely for sex. That didn't work very well. When I married Lois, we married for companionship—sex was the icing on the cake. I won't say I never noticed women after that. For me, feminine beauty—even in young girls—has always seemed reason enough to believe in God."

She smiled.

"But I was content with looking. The first time I really looked at you, I was humbled."

"Humbled?" She was watching my face.

"You have a grace about you—your name couldn't be better—a work of art, that inspires, somehow."

She blushed. "Paul, …"

"And if I noticed your body—well, I *did* notice your body, especially in that red dress you wore last night—it was an admiration of the perfection of my image of you."

"Oh, God!" She covered her face with her hands. "You're too much!"

"But you know something? With all this admiration for you, I have never heard you play."

She took her hands from her face. "You haven't?"

I laughed. "I've lusted for that, as much as for your body."

Grace suddenly stood and went to the keyboard standing by the far wall, a full-size Yamaha. Sitting down before it, she unplugged the headphones, turned the machine on, and played part of Franck's sonata for piano and violin, a piece that she had mentioned being a favorite of her and her husband. I was transfixed.

When she finished, she swung around on the bench and smiled at me.

My throat was full. It took me a minute to respond. "Thank you."

"Any time," she said. Her face was serious.

"That was wonderful," I said, smiling, "even though I kept wanting to hear the violin." Too late, I realized what that piece meant to her, and what it meant in how she was feeling about me. That music was her precious connection to her husband; now it was a gift to me, and I had clumsily reminded her what she had done.

She bent over, her face in her hands, and sobbed.

"Grace," I protested, "I'm sorry!"

After a few moments, she lifted her head. Her face was a mask of agony. She stood up. "Please," she said softly, "Let me be alone for a while."

I felt terrible. "Of course," I said, and started for the door. She caught my arm to stop me, and I turned to look at her.

"It's not your fault, Paul. It just triggered everything." Her hand gripped my arm a little tighter. "I just need time."

"I know you do, Grace. I can wait."

Leaving her apartment, I felt as though I had chopped off the flowing pleasure of the morning. Close to tears myself, I took the stairs to the main floor and escaped into the dark office. The blinds were closed, both to the hallway and to the outside. At my desk with my head on my arms, I let all the emotion pour out of me until my tears dried, leaving my barren face a desert of sand and dust and regret.

I heard the door open and then close again. I looked up, suddenly embarrassed, but there was no one there. I guessed that it had been Barbara, and that she had glimpsed my state and left me alone.

In a way, I couldn't understand why I had been overcome—Grace's revelation to me might be disappointing, but not tragic. It wasn't about sex, I knew. I wasn't sure I could perform, either, if our relationship got to that place. The physical part of my desire was simply to hold her, to cherish her. I had hurt her with my remark, and my tears were about destroying that moment of intimacy. My thoughtless blunder had merely reminded us both that she could not yet give herself to me emotionally, not even tentatively. It was too soon for her.

I thought she would surely never forgive me.

On another level, I knew that we had both been ignoring the obvious; that our age would allow us at most only a brief taste of the joys of companionship before presenting us—one or the other—with the invoice of irretrievable loss. And both of us knew, keenly, how that feels. I remembered thinking the day before, *I never wanted to hurt like that again.*

I got up and opened the blind to the morning sun. Wetting a paper towel at the little sink, I wiped my face. Then I sat back down at my desk and pulled out my calendar. On the last page, it read:

JANUARY 1 NEW YEAR'S DAY

Another year of my life, I thought. *How many more do I have? What do I need to do?*

My shaking hand scrawled an entry in the box JANUARY 2. "Try to locate Shirley."

The End

The Note

He pulled into the overlook at Drake Park and stopped. No other vehicles or people were around. The weak December sun, veiled by high clouds, cast light shadows across the pavement; the temperature was mild for the time of year. Across the wide valley they could see the Kentucky hills, but only a bit of the river curving before them. Everything was shades of brown and gray except an occasional evergreen tree.

"Still pretty out," Kathy said, looking out through the windshield and reaching into a bag to pull out her sandwich. She'd been chattering on the drive up to the park.

Mason mumbled something and unwrapped his own lunch. The knot in his midsection had been building since they had left the office.

She turned and gave him an impulsive kiss on the cheek; then, smiling, she took a bite of food.

He knew he had to do something. He had to tell her. "Kathy," he began.

She looked at him sharply. He didn't usually use her name when he addressed her.

"I'm torn up," he said. "I love you, but I can't keep this up."

She continued to look at him, her eyes questioning. "What's wrong?" she said almost in a whisper. She put the sandwich down in her lap.

"I don't know how to say this. I feel awful."

"I could tell something's going on with you," she said. "You've been quiet all morning."

He tried to keep facing her, but the knot in his gut kept pulling him away from her. He looked out toward the horizon.

"Mason," she said very carefully, "are you breaking up with me?" Her gray-brown eyes, clearly lighted by the low sun, glistened as tears welled up.

The lump in his stomach was rising into his throat. "I've gotten so I can't even look at Marsha," he said. "She would die if she knew!"

Her voice was suddenly loud. "Knew what?" Kathy demanded. "I'm not trying to steal you from your wife! I don't want to own you—I just want to *be with you*." Tears were now streaming down her face, and she reached in her purse for a tissue.

"It's too *much*," he said. "I can't keep it up. I feel like hell."

"We're not doing anything wrong!" she insisted. "We haven't slept together. We're just spending time together!" She held up her sandwich. "Having lunch together!"

"But I can't tell Marsha about all the conversations we have. I think about you all the time. I had to lie about how I took the Mensa test. She'd be crushed if she knew it was you that got me to take it." He took a bite from his sandwich, and almost couldn't swallow it.

"My god! She would blame me for *that?*"

"It's not just that. You and I have been getting closer and closer, and it's getting too intense. I have to lie to her about what I'm doing at work."

She was angry now. "You mean she won't let you have *friends?*"

He looked at his hands gripping the steering wheel. "You know we're not just friends," he said. "I spend time with you almost every day. We've been sharing stuff with each other that I haven't shared with anybody—not even my wife. I feel like I'm getting in too deep."

"Mason, we've kissed once," she protested. "We danced at the office party. What's the big deal in that?"

"I need space. I can't deal with these feelings." He looked away again, out over the valley.

She pulled his face around toward her. Her eyes were rimmed with tears. "Mason, don't do this to us! Please!"

"I have to, Kathy." He wanted to cry, himself.

Her face was contorted with angry tears. He wished he were somewhere else. He waited for her to stop crying, then handed her his handkerchief.

Eventually, she wiped her face and looked at him soberly. "Okay," she said, her voice hoarse, "what now?"

"I don't know. I want to be friends, but I have to back off."

Kathy put her sandwich back in the bag. After a moment, she said quietly, "Let's go back."

He started the car and pulled out of the parking spot. Neither spoke all the way back to the studio. Kathy tried to restore her makeup, but her eyes were puffy.

Later, in his own office, he closed the door and sat at his computer. Eventually, he wrote to her a kind of poem, trying to get across how he felt about her and what he was going through. He didn't blame her for anything. "I just can't," he wrote, "I just can't." A dozen lines, full of his torment and his guilt. Printing it out, he penciled some changes, and then reprinted it with the changes.

Downstairs, he folded the note several times and slipped it to her at her desk without saying anything. Just before he went back up the stairs, he saw her heading for the restroom. He felt sad and anxious, yet somehow better. He had taken control of a situation that had felt out of control. Still, he grieved for—something.

Later, she appeared at his door, stone-faced. She slowly tore the paper up into small pieces and dropped them into his wastebasket. He watched them flutter down, like petals of a flower.

At five o'clock he went out to his car, and sat there for a long time, thinking. He and Marsha had agreed to have dinner out that evening, just the two of them. He hoped he could get free of the tightness in his chest before he got home. Turning the key, he backed out of the parking space.

Marsha was bright and cheerful when he arrived home. "Susie said we can drop the kids off at her place," she said. She was wearing the silk dress he liked.

"It's been a long day," he said to her while he picked up little Nancy so she could kiss him on the cheek. Her brother was busy playing with a new toy, and just waved at him. "C'mon, kids," he said, "Let's go visit Susie!"

In the restaurant, half-way through their wine, Marsha looked at him. "You have had a long day, haven't you?"

"Yeah." He finished the glass of wine. "Some tough decisions."

"Well, now you can let it all go. Have another glass of wine." There was a familiar warmth to her smile that he had loved from the first time he'd seen her.

After they had been served their food, he thought of the note in his pocket—a copy of the note he had written to Kathy. He wanted Marsha to know that she didn't have anything to worry about, that he was and would always be true to her. He pulled the wrinkled paper from his pocket and handed it to her. The note, he thought, would explain everything.

He was mistaken.

.

The End

The Interview

"What's she want?" The woman remained seated by the window, a book in her hands. She didn't look up.

"She said you told her she could visit with you about a story she's writing for a magazine." The nurse waited patiently at the door.

"Why, for god's sake? I've told everybody everything I know. Nobody cares what I think anymore."

The nurse smiled. "Now, Missus Frederick, you know people love you and care about what you think."

"Well, all right, send her in." Madeline Frederick marked her place and closed the book, but as the nurse turned to leave, she raised her hand. "Oh," she said.

The nurse stopped and waited.

"Could you please, dear, bring us some tea?" she managed a little smile.

"Of course."

A few moments later a woman appeared at the door. Well-dressed, middle-aged, pleasant looking. "Thank you for seeing me," she said, entering and extending her hand.

Madeline touched her hand, then gestured toward the other chair across the little table. "I understand I agreed to talk with you about a magazine story."

"Yes."

"I don't remember, but since you're here ..."

"My name is Stephanie Brooks." The woman sat down and pulled a notebook from her purse. "I'm writing an article about people who have done a lot of good for people in East Africa."

"I don't know how much good I did. Looks like it's in as big a mess as it was twenty years ago."

"But you started a foundation that is still over there, helping people." Stephanie opened her notebook. "Stanley Mitcheson told me how much it meant to have you there, how dedicated you were."

Madeline slumped back in her chair. "It's overwhelming, actually. There's so much suffering." She looked at Stephanie, her eyes sad. "I cried every night I was there."

"Mrs. Frederick," Stephanie said, "I have admired you for many years. I used to have your picture—the one Joe Channel took in the Sudan, with that child in your arms—I had that on the wall in my bedroom."

Madeline smiled. "You know, Joe set that up? I mean, he saw me with little Aiko, and I'd been holding her, but I had put her down, and he asked me to pick her up again."

"It was a wonderful picture."

"Joe did us a lot of good with his photographs. I've seen them all over the world." Madeline struggled to her feet, but waved off Stephanie's gesture to help her. She went to a book shelf and returned with a book. "This book," she said, "brought more donations to our foundation than all our public appearances."

The cover photograph on the dust jacket was the one Stephanie had mentioned, and the book was full of other pictures, mostly of poor, dark-skinned women and children in barren settings, refugees from war and drought. A few pictures showed relief workers tending to the sick and feeding the hungry. Madeline Frederick's face appeared here and there.

Stephanie leafed through the book. She looked up at Madeline, her eyes glistening. With a little laugh, she said, "I'm choked up. I'm supposed to be a reporter, but pictures like this tear at my heart.'

Madeline carefully sat down again. "Like the rest of us, I guess you have to pay attention to your heart, but to get your job done you have to suck it up and keep going."

Stephanie drew a breath and let it out slowly. Smiling, she said, "I used to think I could do that. I covered a flood in Tennessee once, years ago, and I just lost it. My editor called me back home and sent somebody else in my place. Those poor people down there were a lot stronger than I was."

Madeline looked at her steadily. "You look familiar. Have we ..."

She was interrupted by a knock at the open door. "Here's your tea, Missus Frederick," the nurse said.

"Thank you, Minnie. You're a dear."

After the nurse had set the tray on the table and left, Madeline said, "I ordered tea for us. I hope you'll join me."

Stephanie appeared flustered. "Yes, thank you."

Pouring the tea, Madeline said, "You came here to ask me questions about East Africa?"

"Yes, I've been talking with people who have been there, and your name kept coming up."

"But you obviously knew about me, if you had my picture on your wall." Madeline sipped her tea without taking her eyes off those of the younger woman.

Stephanie looked down, and then leafed through her notebook as though looking for something. Then she looked up at the older woman. "I've known about you for many years," she said. I've always admired you—you're one of my heroes."

Madeline picked up a teaspoon and stirred her tea, even though she had not put any sugar or milk in it. "I'm flattered," she said, watching the gold-brown liquid. "Now—what do you want from me, right now?"

"I have a whole list of questions," the younger woman said, still leafing through her notebook.

"But you want something else—right now." Her last words were soft.

Stephanie looked up at her. She blurted, "I didn't want this to happen!"

"We know each other, don't we?" Madeline took another sip of tea.

Stephanie nodded, not meeting her eyes.

Setting her cup down in its saucer, Madeline said, "I'm an old woman, and in my long life I've met very many people. Some of them have been good people, caring people, kind people. Others have been not so good. I decided a long time ago that most people are good, even some of those who have done bad things. I'm not proud of some of the things I've done, either."

"You remember me." Stephanie said softly.

"Yes, I remember you." Madeline sipped her tea slowly. "I remember the first time I saw you, at an affair in our home. I think it was a reception to introduce my husband's new partner. I don't remember how it was that you were there, but I noticed you."

"I was a publicity attaché for John Wright, his partner. I was taking pictures."

"Beautiful young woman."

The younger woman blushed.

"You had no idea what you were getting into, did you?"

Stephanie looked up, questioningly.

"Charles took one look at you," Madeline said, "and I knew what was going to happen."

Stephanie covered her mouth. Her eyes looked haunted.

"He was always very determined. I'm sure you know that you weren't the first—nor the last. You lasted longer than most of them."

Stephanie shook her head, unable to speak.

"There are some men," Madeline said, "who exude power. They are like a narcotic to women like us. I used to hate such men, even though I knew it was not they who were the problem, but my helplessness around them. I hated that, too."

Taking her hand from her mouth, Stephanie looked at the silver-haired old woman through her tears, trying to hold her gaze. She whispered, *"I'm sorry!"*

Madeline smiled at her gently. "Yes, we all are. You were what—nineteen?"

She nodded, dabbing at her cheek with a handkerchief.

"I wasn't much older when he first saw me." She sipped her tea. "I used to wet my pants watching the jocks at the track meets. Most of them were such boors; I couldn't stand to be around them. But then once in a while, there'd be this Adonis in a business suit, who would touch me just so." She touched her cheek, smiling. "I'd melt."

Stephanie smiled through her tears.

"Charles Frederick was like that. JFK was like that. More tea?"

Shaking her head, she said, "He made me dizzy."

Madeline laughed. "He made a lot of women dizzy." She reached across the table and touched Stephanie's hand. "I wasn't the first, either. And I knew it."

"But you were—even back then—you were so poised, so self-assured!"

"I learned how to do it. It was a power game." She smiled again. "I remember the first time I slapped a man's face. It felt *so good!*"

Both women laughed. Then Madeline continued, "But I learned pretty quickly that I could get back in control by other means. Slapping a man's face is a dangerous game, sometimes, and not as effective in the long run."

"I didn't know what to do," Stephanie said.

"Of course you didn't. I didn't either. I saw him talking with you. You were fumbling with your camera and looking up at him, and I knew the two of you would disappear in a minute. For a moment I hated you, but I knew you were just another deer in his headlights."

They sat in silence for a long moment.

Madeline looked at her watch. "They're going to call dinner in a couple of minutes. I'd invite you to stay and eat with me, but this is a hospital, after all. The food is atrocious."

"Oh," Stephanie said, "I'm sorry! I had all these questions!" She flipped through her notebook.

"They'll keep," Madeline said. "We had to get through that other stuff first. There are more important things to talk about, next time."

Standing, Stephanie said, "You are so kind."

"You're young," the older woman said, laboriously getting out of her chair. "One of the good things about getting old is nothing threatens any more. Death is just on the other side of that door." She gestured. "He's the ultimate Adonis."

Stephanie looked puzzled.

"He has all this power," Madeline said, "and sometimes he reaches out to touch my cheek, and I just melt."

"Oh, not so soon!"

"Any moment, actually. I look around at all the people here, and I know that any day one of them will be missing at dinner." She reached for Stephanie's hand and held it. "We can make a date for our next session, but ..."

Stephanie hesitated, then embraced the other woman. "Oh, thank you!"

They separated, and Madeline took her hand again. "I'm glad we could talk," she said. "You needed that."

"I didn't mean to ..."

"Maybe not. Maybe you wanted to talk about my work. But that other thing would have been there, between us. Now, let me hold on to you and we can walk together as far as the cafeteria."

The two women made their way slowly down the hall. When a nurse approached them to help, Madeline said, "We're fine. We can lean on each other."

At the door to the cafeteria, Stephanie turned to her. "I can't tell you how much this means to me."

"Next time I want to tell you about East Africa. Be well, Stephanie."

An attendant stood at the door holding it open, and Madeline shuffled through it.

.

The End

Beware of Darkness

Beware Of Darkness (George Harrison)

Watch out now, take care
Beware of falling swingers
Dropping all around you
The pain that often mingles
In your fingertips
Beware of darkness

Watch out now, take care
Beware of the thoughts that linger
Winding up inside your head
The hopelessness around you
In the dead of night

Beware of sadness
It can hit you
It can hurt you
Make you sore and what is more
That is not what you are here for.
. . .

One

He'd been dozing for a while, and woke up looking at the road ahead, a gray runway fading into the night, nothing visible on either side—just that long triangle illuminated by their headlights. Glancing over at her behind the wheel, he wondered what she was thinking. In the soft glow from the instrument panel her face was as blank as the road ahead.

But she sensed that he had awakened, and smiled without turning her head. "You were tired."

"Where are we?" His mind was muddled from sleep.

"Same road, just thirty miles farther along."

"And still nowhere."

"And still nowhere." She smiled again.

"You want me to take it for a while?"

"No, I'm okay."

A pair of headlights appeared far ahead, approaching fast. In a moment the car was gone again. He could see its tail lights in his side-view mirror. The gray triangle ahead remained.

He turned the radio on, and was rewarded with static. Pushing different buttons resulted in a series of country music stations and evangelical preachers. "We really are nowhere, aren't we?" he said, turning the radio off again.

She reached down beside her feet into her purse and withdrew a little music player. "There's a cable in the glove compartment," she said, and pointed to the dashboard. "You can plug it in there."

He plugged the little instrument into the dashboard and turned it on. When no sound came, he turned the radio on again. The player was at the end of some rock music he didn't recognize at first. Then there was applause, and a guitar began a piece he remembered from a long time ago: "*Watch out now, take care / Beware of falling swingers / Dropping all around you ...*"

"George Harrison," he said, looking at her.

She smiled. "Beware of Darkness. That's Eric Clapton."

"*The pain that often mingles / In your fingertips / Beware of darkness ...*"

"Takes you back," he said.

They listened to the track without speaking. Then he stopped the player. He was about to say something to her when she spoke: "That's from the Concert for George, a year after he died."

"What does it say to you?" He turned in the seat to see her better. The greenish glow from the instruments made her lipstick look black.

She glanced quickly at him, then back at the long, dark gray road ahead. "The part I like is where he sings, 'Beware of the thoughts that wind up inside your head in the dead of night.' The hopelessness that holds you by the throat."

"You have those thoughts, too?"

"You don't?" She was smiling again.

"Sometimes." He looked away. "The sadness."

She looked at him again, this time longer. "Brian."

He didn't answer. He felt a lump in his throat, and he was afraid it would betray him. He stared through the windshield. Ahead of them was the dark gray pavement, disappearing into darkness.

She slowed the car and pulled off the road, switching on the four-way blinkers, and stopped. Turning to face him, she said, "Brian, look at me."

He looked down at his hands.

"Brian," she said again, "we can do this."

He watched the blinking lights illuminating the weeds alongside the road. A long-forgotten image returned to him, of a child in a back-yard swing. Leaning his head back against the headrest, he sighed and peered blankly into the darkness.

She reached for her door handle. "Why don't you drive for a while?"

"Okay." He opened his door to the dry prairie wind. His steps crunched in the gravel. Rounding the back of the car, he felt the warm puff from the exhaust against his pants leg. The sensory distractions of the moment helped to dissipate the feelings gripping his gut.

She appeared in the blinking amber light, coming around from the other side of the car. As they passed, she touched his cheek gently with a soft hand.

He paused when he reached the driver's door. The other door clicked quietly closed, and the interior lights went out. Unzipping his fly, he relieved himself onto the dry pavement. *Just this is real,* he thought. The wind was cold around his eyes. Filling his lungs with the prairie air until his chest hurt, he looked out into the darkness. Only the brilliant beams of the headlights pierced the black night, fading in the distance. He let out his breath and opened the door.

She was watching him intently as he climbed into the car. Just before the door closed and the interior light slowly faded, he managed to smile at her.

Gravel crunched as he pulled back onto the road. "What's next on that thing?" he asked.

She pressed a button, and a tinkling guitar intro began. The audience inside the player, recognizing Harrison's "Here Comes the Sun," burst into cheers and applause.

He looked at her and grinned. "That's not Eric Clapton singing."

"Joe Brown."

A deep bass air horn from behind them suddenly announced a truck approaching, startling him. The semi whooshed past them at a great speed, its Christmas tree lights disappearing into the distance.

"Little Darlin', it's been a long cold lonely winter ..."

She sang along with Joe Brown, "Little Darlin', it seems like years since it's been here ..."

And he joined her, "Here comes the sun, and I say, it's all right ..."

She strained against her seat belt to reach over and kiss him on the cheek while Joe Brown's guitar tinkled through the bridge.

Remembering the suddenness of the truck behind them, he glanced at his mirror. A thin streak of light marked the eastern horizon behind them.

"Here comes the sun, and I say, it's all right ..."

Two

The sun slashed through tall fir and cedar trees lining the road, a stroboscope of brightness that made it difficult to see as he drove. "It must be along here somewhere," he said.

She studied the paper containing directions. "Watch for a sign that says, 'Watch for fallen rock.' Then the road is just past the cliff on the left."

"I don't know what to say to her," he said.

"She invited you," she said, looking over at him. "I bet she'll be just as uncomfortable as you." Glancing ahead, she said, "There's the sign."

They came upon a curve in the road, and the trees on either side suddenly gave way to an open expanse of mountains on the right and a sheer wall of rock above them on the left. He slowed the car.

"There's the road," she said, pointing to an unpaved lane leading back into a kind of canyon. A decrepit sign leaned against a tree, with a barely visible name, "Adams."

He turned into the lane. Bushes brushed against the sides of the car as he slowly made their way into the forest.

"God, I hope we don't meet another car coming out," she said, "there's no place to pull off."

The car lurched and rolled along the uneven tracks. "She didn't say how long this lane is."

"No."

He peered up through the windshield at the trees. There was no sunlight showing, except at the very tips of the fir trees.

He remembered the vast emptiness of the prairie the night before, the intense blackness, without stars or moon. Now the forest seemed to close in on them, and the curving lane was visible only a short distance ahead.

Then it opened into a spring green meadow. "Beautiful!" she exclaimed.

A blue-gray mountain was visible across the open grassland and beyond more trees. The lane disappeared into the grass next to a rather old mobile home, planted near one side of the meadow and surrounded by flower gardens. An old car sat under a makeshift canopy attached to the building, and several small outbuildings clustered around. A retriever barked once, then came bounding off the little porch to greet them, tail wagging.

He stopped the car in a place that might or might not have been a parking area near the house, and they both got out. As they approached, the door opened and a middle-aged woman came out. She was wearing a too-big man's shirt and blue jeans. "Hi," she said, smiling, "I guess you're Brian."

"Yes. This is my fiancé, Jean."

"I'm Olive," the woman said, "Come in."

They followed her into a small, dimly lit room. The dog came in behind them, squeezing past the closing door, and lay down. Olive gestured toward an old sofa, and the three of them sat in awkward silence for a moment.

She could be attractive, he thought, *it's hard to tell.* He glanced at Jean, who was watching Olive. He took new notice of her quiet beauty.

"I have some things of your mother's that she wanted you to have," Olive said, not getting up. "Photographs and letters, mostly."

"Thank you," he said.

"Did you know she wrote quite a lot?"

The knot in his gut became more noticeable. There was a lot about his mother that he didn't know—some that he had made a great effort to not know about. "No, I didn't," he said.

"You were on her mind a lot. She kept journals, too."

Jean spoke. "Can you tell us where her, ah, ..."

"There's no grave," Olive replied. "I scattered her ashes all over this meadow, as she made me promise."

Brian frowned. This was more difficult than he had feared.

"I'm sorry," Olive said, "I know you didn't approve of her lifestyle."

The memory he had glimpsed the previous night on the prairie, of the child in the backyard swing, returned. There was a woman—not his mother—pushing him in the swing, smiling at him. In the years since then, he had concluded that the woman was his mother's lover, and he came to hate her. But at the time, she was just a sweet smile. Now, looking at Olive, he knew that she was not that woman.

There were other memories, of his parents fighting, that still caused him fear and pain. When his father had left, he hadn't even said goodbye—just slammed out the door. A gaping hole in his life had remained unfilled, for many years. Blaming his mother for his loss, he'd been eager to go away to school, and never returned to her home. He hadn't even written her in the past ten years. Her letters to him were thrust into a drawer unopened. She had become a stranger, an unpleasant stranger whom he chose to ignore.

Her death resurrected feelings he'd thought he had overcome. When Olive had written him asking what she should do with his mother's belongings, at first he wanted to tell her, "Just burn them." But Jean, who knew him, insisted that they go and get them. "You'll never get closure with her if you don't," she said, holding him in her arms as he cried.

Now, Jean sat and watched him, saying nothing, her face questioning but not insistent.

"It's been a long time," he said simply, trying not to reveal the turmoil inside him.

"But you came," Olive said.

It felt like a challenge to him. He suddenly blurted, "I don't know why! She means nothing to me!"

Olive put her hand out toward him, but he withdrew from the gesture.

"She always loved you," said Olive, her voice shaking. "She was a good woman, a good person." She paused and took a deep breath. "She was a wonderful person!" She dabbed at her face with a sleeve.

"What do you have for him?" asked Jean, softly.

Olive stood up and went into another room. In a moment she returned with a large cardboard box. "This is one of three," she said. "I'll get one more, but I can't lift the box of manuscripts."

Brian followed Olive to the other room. She picked up another box from the floor. "You may need help to get that one." She squeezed past him in the doorway, meeting his eyes. Her eyes were filled with tears.

He was surprised at the weight of the third box, but managed to pick it up and carry it out of the room.

Jean offered her hands to him. "Can I help?" she asked.

"I've got it," he said, heading for the outside door. The dog scrambled out of his way.

"Do you want to see what's in them?" Olive asked.

He stopped, and looked at Jean.

She nodded. "We can at least open them," she said.

He placed the box on the floor and sat down. With the three of them sitting around, the three boxes seemed to fill the little room.

He sat unmoving for a moment, then pulled a box toward him. Olive handed him a small kitchen knife. Cutting the tape on the box, he opened it.

Lying on top was an envelope he recognized. It was an invitation, the last thing he'd read from his mother. Jean motioned to him, and he handed it to her.

"An invitation to a wedding—yours?" Jean asked Olive.

"Yes."

Jean read the invitation. "It's sweet," she said, handing it to Brian.

"I read it," he said flatly, taking it and replacing it in the box.

"She kept copies of all the letters she ever sent you," Olive said. "She told me that some day you might want to read them."

"I still have them—some of them," he said.

Jean looked up quickly. "You do? Brian, you didn't tell me!"

He glanced at her, but waved the question away. Then he went through the other letters and papers in the top of the box, not opening them but looking at the envelopes and dates. Then he closed the box again and pulled the other smaller box toward him.

When he opened it they saw that it contained photographs, hundreds of them, mostly loose, seemingly just tossed in. Jean came closer, kneeling beside the box to see better. Brian dug a small album from the stack and leafed through it. "These are all old," he said. "Dad and Mom and me."

Jean looked over his shoulder for a moment, then picked another photograph from the box. "This is you," she said to Olive, holding it out to the woman.

"We had just met," Olive said. "That's Pike's Peak."

Brian was focused on the album. He held it out to Jean. "I remember that swing," he said. The photograph showed him in the swing at perhaps four years old. The legs of a woman were behind him. A great sob welled up into his throat, and he coughed, stood and left the room.

Jean and Olive looked at each other. "I'm sorry," Jean said softly. "This is hard for him."

Olive just nodded, and dabbed again at her cheek with a sleeve.

"Don't you want some of these?" Jean asked.

The other woman shook her head. "I have the ones I want."

Brian came back into the room. "Thank you," he said to Olive. "We'll be going." He closed the box of photographs.

Olive stood up. "Brian, I want to say something to you."

Brian turned toward the door without responding.

"We don't know each other," she said. "I understand that. But I loved Joyce with all my heart, and I know that she felt terrible that you and she could never reconcile. I hope that you will go through these things—they are all that's left of her, except what I carry in my heart. You may not understand why she did what she did. She was no less a mother because she chose a different life for herself."

Brian reached down and picked up the one unopened box. Jean opened the door for him. "I'll open the trunk," she said, then turned to Olive. "We'll get the others in a minute."

After loading the box into the car, they both returned. As he picked up another box, he looked at Olive. "I don't hate you," he said.

Olive burst into tears. Jean went to her and embraced her. Brian took the box out the door. The two women stood for a few moments, weeping together. Then Jean reached down for the last box. "I'm sorry for your loss," she said hoarsely.

"Thank you."

"He's a kind man. Give him some time."

"Does he have any contact with his father?"

Jean smiled. "A little. Maybe we can get them together to look through the boxes."

"He doesn't understand."

"No."

Olive touched Jean's arm. "Do you?"

"Yes." She smiled again. "I do."

"That's a start."

"What about you? Do you have any support?" Jean took Olive's hands in hers.

Brian returned and picked up the last box. After he left without saying anything, Olive said, "Yes, of course. We had a lot of friends."

"Do you need anything?"

"Thank you. No. I have this place—our home—and a lot of wonderful memories."

Jean took a slip of paper from her purse and wrote her phone number on it. "If you do," she said simply, handing it to her, then turned to leave.

Olive touched her arm, and the two of them embraced again. "Good bye."

"Good bye, Olive." Jean took a deep breath and went down the porch steps toward the car.

Through a window Olive watched the car turn around in the grass and disappear up the lane.

.

The End

Unnamed

Rosalind laughed. "Forget it, Ricky," she said, "she's gay."

My sister loved to tease me, especially about women I was attracted to. She was older than I by four years, and never let me forget her early advantage as we grew up. I was always her "little brother," even though I passed her in height when I was fourteen.

We were at one of those noisy holiday-season cocktail parties in which people mix their friends from different cohorts, with the resulting energy a little familiar and a little odd, where one could strike up a conversation with a stranger while not feeling that discomfort that comes from being alone in a crowd. I had noticed the sleek brunette as soon as she arrived, and was trying to get up the nerve to approach her.

"Do you know her?" I asked Roz, sipping my gin and tonic.

"I've seen her in town," she said. "She usually has a group of women around her."

"Want me to introduce you to her?" I asked, my way of parrying Roz's thrust. I'd had just enough gin to feel confident.

"She's gorgeous," she said, a half smile on her face as she watched the woman move through the crowd, "but I haven't had that much to drink. Thanks just the same."

Actually, I wished she had said yes, because it would have given me the advantage of a role to play. There are few things I fear more than introducing myself to a stranger. Roz and I have had many conversations since puberty about how to meet girls and what not to say to them.

Of course, in a little while my sister turned the tables on me. I saw her making her way to me through the press of people, accompanied by the brunette. "Richard," she said, "I hear you wanted to meet Ashley."

Ashley had a great smile and a low-cut dress that shimmered in the dim light. Her hand shake was soft and light, not at all what I might have expected from Roz's pronouncement about her earlier. "I'm flattered," she said, and then she said something else that I couldn't hear in the noise of the room.

I leaned closer to indicate that I'd missed her words, still holding her hand.

"She asked if you had seen her act at the Ark," Roz said, with a knowing grin.

Feeling foolish, I admitted that I had not. "I don't get down there very much."

"I hope you can make it sometime," Ashley said. "We have a lot of fun."

Just then, someone else came out of the crowd and spoke to her. She turned and greeted them with a hug, then as she moved away she said to me, "Come on down sometime."

I nodded, and turned back to Roz, who was enjoying the scene greatly. "Okay," I said, "you got that one."

"You should have seen your face!" she laughed.

"Did you know she was a performer?"

"I guessed."

"Singer?"

"I have no idea. Probably, I'd say." Roz picked up her glass from a nearby table. "Now, you have to introduce me to somebody I don't know."

I looked around the room. "Like who? Should I pick somebody gay?"

She scanned the crowd with me. "Preferably not," she said

"How can I tell?" Finishing my drink, I chewed an ice cube.

She laughed. "Well," she said, "that's just something you have to learn."

"I need another drink first."

"Okay, I'm going over to talk with Sally."

I watched her move gracefully through the crowd.

She was good, my sister. She'd been married briefly before going away to college, and now seemed happy to be single— making her way up the corporate ladder, dating a lot of men but none for very long. We moved generally in the same social circles, but didn't spend much time together—an occasional lunch or dinner, rather just friends. That we both ended up in Ann Arbor was mostly coincidence, although I wished at times that we could share a little more of our lives.

Growing up in a small town in southern Indiana, we both had been eager to escape to a big city. After college, she'd settled in Ann Arbor, and I got a job there a few years later. It wasn't a big city, but the university gave it a sophistication we liked. Although we had a few mutual friends, mostly we moved in different groups.

I refreshed my drink and stopped at the food buffet. It was hard to tell what was in some of the casseroles, and since I don't eat meat I stood there, paper plate in hand, studying.

"The fish tacos are really good," observed a voice at my elbow. I turned. It was Ashley, holding her own empty plate.

"I don't eat meat," I said, moving a little to one side to give her room to move in.

"Oh."

"These mystery buffets are always a challenge." I picked out some sliced cheese and garlic toast, then dipped a broccoli floret in the dressing and put it on my plate.

"Being an omnivore has its advantages," she laughed.

I looked at her while she scooped something out of a chafing dish. "You're a singer?" I asked.

"Yeah, and guitar," she said. "Our group is Lady Grace. We mostly do folk songs, but we like to experiment, too."

"I seem to remember another group with that name."

She laughed. "Yes, there's one in Seattle, and there used to be a couple of women in Cincinnati, a long time ago. But most people know the name from the clothing company—fancy bras and things."

I couldn't help but glance down at her dress, and she caught me. "No!" she laughed, "not mine!"

Roz was standing a few feet away, waiting to get to the buffet, and she looked up when Ashley laughed. Catching my eye, she raised her eyebrows and smiled.

I ignored my sister. "Sorry," I said with a little laugh. "I'm embarrassed."

"Don't be," Ashley said. "Why do you think women wear these things?"

"Okay. Let's talk about your music. How long have you been playing?"

"Singing as long as I can remember," she said, moving away from the buffet. "C'mon, let's go over there out of the way."

We found a quiet corner. I didn't look to see where Roz was. Setting my drink on a small table, I picked up the broccoli and took a bite. "So you wanted to perform for a long time," I said.

"Couldn't wait to get into the School of Music. But I still haven't finished." She laughed. "Been too busy doing gigs."

"You said you were having fun."

"I am," she said. "Now, tell me about you. Besides having a beautiful sister, what else are you known for?"

"Absolutely nothing. I work for an ad agency."

"Doing what?"

"Writing, mostly. A little design."

"You don't say that like it's what you want to do." She took a drink from her wine glass and looked at me. "What are you passionate about?"

I had to smile. "I did think it would be more fun than it's turned out to be. What I'd really love to do? I'm not sure. I envy people like you who do what they love."

She studied my face, sipping her wine.

I was feeling the gin. "I do love music," I said, "but I can't sing or play a lick."

"What music really grabs you in your gut?"

"Rachmaninov. Sebelius. Brahms. Samuel Barber. Philip Glass."

"A romantic. I knew it," she said, smiling. "Rodrigo?"

"Of course."

Just then Roz joined us, munching on a piece of toast topped with something or other. "I wasn't eavesdropping," she said, "but I heard Rodrigo."

Ashley turned her smile on my sister. "Another romantic?"

"I guess so," Roz said. "His Aranjuez Concerto makes me want to take off my clothes."

I shouldn't have been shocked, but I felt my face get hot. Ashley, however, laughed loudly. "I have an album ..." she began. I was glad for all the noise in the room.

Roz put a hand on her arm. "Sorry," she said quietly. "I've had too much to drink."

We all laughed, and I drank most of my gin and tonic while the two of them talked about music and nights in the gardens of Spain. I don't remember much about the rest of the evening. I never did introduce her to a man in the group.

Shortly after the holidays, Roz phoned me. We hadn't seen or talked with each other since the party. "How are you doing, Little Brother?" she asked. "Did you recover from the party at the Feldman's?"

"I must have," I said, "although I don't remember leaving there or driving home."

"You shouldn't do that," she said. "You don't want a DUI on your record."

"How did you get home?" I asked. "You had quite a bit to drink, too."

"Sally took me home. It was a good party."

"Yes it was." I didn't want to mention Ashley.

"You remember that gorgeous woman in the red dress—Ashley?"

"Un humn." Like I'd ever forget her.

"Well, we're invited—you and me—we're invited to her place to listen to some music."

"Lady Grace?"

"Lady who?"

"That's her group that plays at the Ark."

"I don't think that's what she had in mind," Roz said. "She mentioned Rodrigo."

For the first time, I felt uncomfortable. I remembered Roz's tipsy remark about taking her clothes off, and I also remembered that Ashley was a lesbian. While we were talking at the party, I'd forgotten that little fact, if it was a fact. I had really enjoyed talking with Ashley. Now, it felt complicated. Ashley was very attractive, but she was unavailable. Not "unavailable" as in "married," but *really* not available to me. What was she thinking of, inviting both me and my sister to listen to romantic music (classical, but still romantic)? Roz had always been up front with her straight orientation, but none of our family was homophobic. We just didn't see many homosexuals in our little home town—that we knew of, anyway. I couldn't imagine what Roz would do if she were approached by a lesbian. As good looking as she was, I suspected that she probably had been. No doubt people of both sexes had hit on her. But that's not the kind of thing that a brother would think about very much. It made me uncomfortable.

"Do you want to go?" I asked.

"Might be interesting," she said. "You don't get many invitations to go to somebody's home to listen to classical music."

I tried bravado. "Are you going to keep your clothes on?"

"Richard! What a cruel thing to say!"

"I was kidding, Roz."

"I nearly died when I heard that coming out of my mouth at the party. Especially ..."

I broke in, "Especially if she likes women."

"I was so embarrassed."

"To say nothing about saying that in front of your little brother."

"Oh, I'm sorry, Ricky! Were you mortified?"

"I'm kidding, Roz. We were all smashed by that time."

Her voice got quiet. "Ricky, I'm sorry."

"Forget it. We're adults. I'm not your little brother anymore."

"It was inappropriate. I'm ashamed."

"It's okay," I said. "Let's forget it, okay?"

"Ricky, can you come over? I want us to talk about it where I can see your face."

I smiled. My sister and I kid each other a lot. It never means anything. But it was feeling like a line had been crossed somehow. "Sure," I said. "Now?"

"Yes, now."

"Okay. Bye."

By the time I got to her apartment, I'd forgotten why we were getting together. She seemed to need to clear the air about something, her remark at the party, or something.

It wasn't to be in her living room. She set out a bottle of red wine and a couple of glasses on the kitchen table. I thought about all the family discussions around our old kitchen table back home. I'd never realized how matter-of-fact a discussion stays when it's there. There can be intimacy, but there's always a level of respect, an equality—even when it's with our parents. Hands on the table, cards up, very little hidden from each other, an honesty, somehow.

Roz poured wine into our glasses and then looked at me. Her eyes were troubled.

"What's going on, Roz?" I asked.

"I'm not sure," she said, her eyes on her glass. "I think I shouldn't be talking with you about this."

"You want to go to confession? I'm sure Ann Arbor has such people."

"Please—I'm serious!"

"Sorry. I'll keep quiet."

She put her hands on the table, palms up. "I used to be able to talk to Mom, about anything. But that's ten years ago. I don't think I can do that anymore."

I felt a sudden warmth toward my sister. I'd never seen her be—or try to be—so vulnerable. I put my hands over hers. "I'm here, Roz," I said softly.

She took a deep breath. "Sex anymore is so *ordinary!*" she said. "I've had ..." She stopped and looked into my eyes. "I've had lots of men. At first it was really exciting."

She stopped again. "And now it's not."

"Overload?" It's the first word I thought of. I couldn't imagine actually *being there.*

"Maybe."

I shook my head. "You could fool me," I said. "You always flirt with everybody."

"That's all bullshit. It's like the face I put on in the office. There, I know I'm wearing a mask, and I do it because I have to. I've gotten really good at it."

I took a drink of wine, trying to think, trying to put myself into a different place with my older sister. It was as if I were hearing my mother talking about her sex life.

"Roz—can I be really honest with you?"

"I need that," she said. "You're the only person I know that I can trust—truly."

"When I was in high school, I watched the really attractive girls, and I kept thinking, 'They've got it all. They can have their pick of any jock in the school. They never have to sit home while other people go to the parties or the prom.' Sometimes I hated them."

She had a wry smile on her face.

"And I ached for them." I finished my wine.

"I remember," she said. "You told me about it."

"And you said I needed to stop thinking about them—as if I could!"

She nodded. "I knew girls like that, too," she said. "I hated them too."

"But you were beautiful! You *are* beautiful! They don't have anything you don't have."

Smiling, she picked up her glass and saluted me. "Thank you, Ricky."

"You are one of them."

Her smile disappeared, and she swirled the wine in her glass. Finally, she said, "At the party at the Feldman's, I watched you with Ashley, and I saw how enchanted you were." Looking up at me, she said, "I was jealous."

I shook my head. "I don't understand."

"I guess it was just the situation. The two of you were so—caught up in it."

I had to grin. "I was having a ball," I said. "I didn't even think, until later, about her being a lesbian. It was just this gorgeous woman, playing with me."

She nodded. "Yeah. I know."

"You've been there."

"Yes."

She put her hand over mine. "Ricky, I don't want you to take this the wrong way."

I was aware of getting tense.

"I was jealous of both of you."

"What do you mean?"

"Okay." She put both hands on the table, palms down. "You're my brother. I watched you running around the house with your diapers hanging down. I wiped your nose and put band-aids on your cut arms. But since you've grown up I've seen you as some kind of model man, somebody I compare all the other men to."

My face got hot. Then I had to laugh. "That's mutual, Roz."

"Wait," she said. "That's only part of it."

I poured another glass of wine for each of us, wondering what she was getting at. Something in my gut was growing.

"That remark I made to you and Ashley? I know now that it wasn't just the alcohol. It was like—I don't know, like it was to both of you, like I wanted to be part of what I was seeing between you."

I didn't know what to say. She was looking into my eyes as if she needed something, as if I could make everything all right. But my gut was tight, and I had the feeling I needed to run out of there, to run from something I couldn't deal with. "Roz," I began.

She burst into tears. I put my handkerchief in her hand, and she wiped her face. She didn't look at me for a long time.

"It's okay, Roz," I said.

"No, it's not!"

"Roz, when we were still at home and I was fantasizing about girls—you think I didn't fantasize about you, too? But you were just as unavailable as any of the cheerleaders I couldn't have."

She looked at me with wide, red-rimmed eyes. Then she smiled, and in a very small voice, "You did?"

I held out my hand to show her it was shaking. "This stuff is really hard to talk about."

She blew her nose in the handkerchief, then held it up. "I'll wash it," she said, stuffing it into her pocket. We both laughed.

I plunged on. "I knew guys at school, guys I didn't like anyway, who had sex with their sisters. It gave me the creeps, but I knew that I was just as bad . . ." I tapped my chest, "in here."

Roz mirrored my gesture, very slowly, her sad eyes clinging to mine.

We sat there, lost in our own thoughts, long after the wine was gone. I finally got up to leave.

"Ricky, don't drive," she said, her voice hoarse.

"I'll walk. It isn't that far."

She walked with me to the door.

"You going to accept the invitation?" I asked.

"Should I?"

"Yes."

We hugged each other, very carefully, a tentative gesture that betrayed both our mutual anguish and our profound need for comfort.

.

The End

That . . .
Sense of History

Turning off the main road onto the little blacktop—a lane, almost—I felt immediately as though I had passed through a portal of time. In the distance was the river, barely visible through the trees, and hills rising beyond it. The bottomland was broken up into little plots, some planted, some gone fallow, some overgrown—taken over by nature to do her own thing. Everywhere was this sense of history, of things and places that once had been something different. A field with little clumps of young willow trees growing here and there, a couple of dead corn stalks leaning against one another in a corner near what used to be a fence line, a rusted pickup truck with no wheels or glass, almost hidden by vines and brush.

I stopped my bike and stood there for a while taking it in. I'm a city boy. I've never touched a plow or a rake (other than the garden kind, with a painted metal handle and foam rubber pads to keep a city boy's hands from blistering after an hour of work). I could imagine this valley a hundred years ago, busy with people working, growing food for the county. On Saturday mornings there would be trucks heavy with vegetables gear-grinding up the steep grades out of the valley, headed for little outdoor markets in villages and towns nearby. My city boy's imagination gave it a romantic glow. I pedaled on, smelling the late summer life, a thousand unnamed scents of trees and plants, all those spores that give people with allergies such discomfort and pharmaceutical manufacturers such joy.

Here were a couple of small farms, sitting side-by-side between the road and the river. The one on the left was apparently a working farm. In the field behind the house grew something low and green, maybe soybeans. In the little patch between the house and the road was a vegetable garden, heavy with produce. It was too steep to work with a tractor, its rows of plants following the curve of the land, like the stripes of a slowly furling flag. Two people stooped near the center of the garden, unmoving.

I turned my bike down the dirt driveway, thinking to speak with them when I got close enough. But then I realized that they were praying. Standing together, heads bowed, they reminded me of a Renaissance painting, perhaps something named *The Vespers*. I rode silently past them down to where the driveway simply disappeared into indifferently mown lawn at the side of the house.

Around the house and the nearby barn were relics of farm life. A foot-powered grinding wheel, obviously not used in many years. A cistern pump, one of those sheet-metal once-modern-looking things with rounded top and a crank on one side to turn the sprocket wheel inside that lifted little buckets on a chain from the water below. A rusted child's wagon, missing its back wheels. Off to the side, almost in the bushes, sat an ancient automobile, sans wheels, sans hood, its running boards almost hidden by grass. The engine stood proud, even in its silence, reminding me of brown stone monuments to pioneers that one sees on the prairies west of here. Three clotheslines stretched between a pair of tee-shaped poles made from steel pipe. Bright purple morning glories bloomed over a fence.

A medium-sized dog trotted around the corner of the little barn toward me, her tail wagging, followed immediately by a young woman in shapeless jeans and a man's shirt. "Howdy," she said. "Help you?" She carried a bucket filled with some kind of plants.

I let go of one handlebar to reach down and let the dog sniff my hand. "I don't want anything, really," I said. "I was about to chat with the folks in the garden, and then saw they were praying, so I didn't want to disturb them."

She smiled. "They do that every day of their lives. They wouldn't mind an interruption." She set the bucket down. There was water in the bottom of it, but the plants didn't look too healthy. I didn't ask what they were.

"Actually," I said, "I stopped because this place just pulled at me, for some reason. I don't know." I felt foolish.

"You grow up on a farm?"

"No. But it just feels *solid* here." It wasn't the word I was searching for. "Most places I know don't look as though they've been lived in more than a couple of years. This is like a museum."

"My dad used to call places like this 'fender farms.'" She gestured at the old car. "My grandparents had this place forever. When they passed on, Mom and Dad moved down here from Eaton to retire. They don't make any money on it, but they don't care."

"You moved down here with them?"

"No, I just come down to help 'em out once in a while. I live in town, but I like the quiet here."

"I don't mean to intrude." I turned my bike around.

"It's a real museum. Nothing much has changed in fifty years. Want to see the inside?" She picked up the bucket of plants and started for the house. The dog, which had lain down in the grass nearby, got up to follow.

"Sure," I said, setting the kickstand under the bike and falling in line behind the dog.

The screen door spring squealed when she pulled the door open. A rubber ball swung from a little chain near the top of the door. The threshold was worn round from countless feet crossing it. I let the door close gently behind me, remembering the sound from long ago of screen doors banging behind children flying from the house in their play, followed by cries from inside, "Watch the door! Close it quietly!" The little swinging ball was there for an old reason, to prevent the slamming of the screen door, because kids never learned.

The smell of the kitchen was right out of my nostalgia—the faint scent of kerosene, of burned sugar, of bacon fat, of a thousand different foods. A linoleum rug covered most of the floor, and cracks separated the boards around it. In the center stood a heavy table with turned legs, and three old ladder-back chairs. A huge stained glass chandelier hung directly over the table. The white enameled cast-iron sink was brown with rust under the twin faucets on the high backsplash. A soap dish hung on springs between the faucets. Over the sink, the wooden double casement window stood open, and I could see past the soybean field to the trees lining the river. The dog nuzzled my hand.

The woman set the bucket on the drain board and moved toward the opposite door. "I spent a lot of time playing on these floors," she offered.

Following her into the parlor, I smelled pipe tobacco. Two overstuffed chairs and an old sofa dominated the small room. A library table stood against the front wall under a big window, adorned by a crocheted doily and another stained-glass lamp. A rack of smoking pipes hid on one back corner of the table, and a thick book dominated the other. Opposite the chairs, a small television set on a stand made of bent brass-plated tubing looked out of place with the rest of the room. An old rug covered the floor to within a foot of the walls. Next to the kitchen door stood a china cabinet with a curved glass door and carved feet. Inside were dishes and teacups, and a tall silver tea pot. Each of the shelves was lined with a white linen doily with crocheted edges, and dotted with porcelain Hummel figurines.

"Looks like what you'd expect down here, doesn't it?" She gestured toward the cabinet. Her voice had just the slightest Midwestern twang.

Just then, the older man and woman stepped up onto the front porch and kicked off their boots. As they entered the parlor, each carrying handfuls of vegetables, they smiled in greeting. Both of them wore old bib overalls and wide-brimmed hats. "Howdy," he said. "We saw you come in."

"I don't mean to intrude," I apologized. "There's just something about this place that—I don't know, reminds me of home, or something. And I never lived on a farm!"

"It's old." The man seemed well beyond retirement age, but had that sunburned look of a farmer. "I grew up here, and I hated it as long as I can remember, till I finished high school. I bought a car and got a job and only came back on holidays. N'then, when my folks died, I couldn't bear to sell it."

The woman set her vegetables on the kitchen table and took off her hat. "I talked him into moving back down here." She raised her voice as she moved about the kitchen. "I always loved it."

"How long have you lived here?"

"Seven, eight years. When I retired from the company, I didn't know what to do with myself in town." He handed his load to his wife, wiped his hands on his pants, and took off his hat. His close-cropped gray hair rose out of pale skin just above his hat line. He shook my hand.

"We used to come down on weekends," she said, "and kept a little garden here." She returned from the kitchen, wiping her hands on a towel. "One day we just decided to stay."

The young woman was watching them, her arms folded in front of her. "I tried to get them to fix the place up, like at least put in a new kitchen."

"Heck no." He grinned at his daughter. "Everything works. Even the oven. Why throw stuff away, just because it's old?"

"Okay, okay," she gestured with her hands. "It's your place." Turning toward me, she added, "Truthfully, I like it, too. Like you said, it feels like home."

"I don't keep up the place the way my dad did. All that brush along the fences? He kept it tidy. I don't mind nature doing her thing with the place. She's doing her thing with me, too." He laughed.

"How old is that old car out there?"

"That was mine. Bought it when I was in high school. I always intended to restore it. It's a twenty-nine Hudson. Used to be a real car—even a curtain you could pull down between the front and back seats. Had those big spare wheels in the front fenders, like in the old gangster movies."

He paused, thoughtful. "Some things just don't get done in life."

"Ain't that the truth?" His wife shook out her long gray hair, twirled it again and tied it back up on her head.

"Mom's a musician," the daughter offered. "Taught it in high school."

I looked at her in a new way. "Do you play?"

"Not any more," she said simply.

I began to feel the time. "I'm sorry. You all have things to do. I really enjoyed meeting you." I moved toward the back door.

"Stay for supper?"

"No, but thank you very much."

My bike had fallen over in the back yard. As I picked it up, the man stepped out onto the porch. "Come on by anytime."

"Thank you. I'll do that."

I walked the bike up the steep drive. Looking back, I saw the man and his daughter, an arm about each other, watching me go. I waved, and they both waved back.

It was almost dark by the time I rolled up the walkway alongside the house where I lived near campus. Locking the bike to a pipe that carried electric wires into the basement, I climbed the outside stairway to my little apartment on the second floor. I hung my bike helmet on a nail next to the door and looked around.

This was old, too, maybe not as old as the farmhouse but a lot older than I was. I lived here because I could afford it. Meg, my ex, had been talking about getting remarried, and that would mean I wouldn't owe her anything more. Maybe I could move to a better place.

I dug a frost-covered frozen meal out of the refrigerator, wiped off the outside, and stuck it into the microwave. Five minutes, the box had said—just enough time for a cold beer.

I walked with the opened bottle into the combination living room-bedroom and turned on the stereo. Ravel's *Daphnes et Chloe* emerged from the speakers. It was right at the part that I had always thought was a chase scene from an old Western movie. I could picture the dozen riders, galloping around a big tree and passing close to the camera, one at a time, raising dust. I wondered, for the thousandth time, what Ravel had in mind when he wrote that.

As I ate my dinner I thought of the little family out by the river. They wouldn't be eating frozen dinners. Vegetables fresh from their garden, maybe a small roast. The three of them would do the dishes together, the old man with his hands in the dishpan and the two women wiping and putting away in the old cupboards. They might be singing together.

Her mom had taught music, the young woman said. I wondered what she did for a living. She said she came out from town on weekends. I grinned to myself picturing her in town, walking down the street in bib overalls. She was not at all like Meg, with her weird hair, miniskirt and black fingernails.

Since we'd split up, I was a lot more relaxed. I could listen to my own music and not have to put up with the awful contemporary pop that she listened to.

I scraped my plate into the garbage can, rinsed the plate quickly under hot water, and turned out the kitchen light. Sprawling in the one overstuffed chair in the other room, I listened to Schubert in the dark. The old lace curtain at the window cast an intricate shadow on the wall from the streetlamp across the street.

I couldn't remember what color her hair was. All I remembered were the too-big jeans and man's shirt. She was attractive, with an open face and big, wide-set eyes. Her smile came slowly, as though she had to think about it.

I kept thinking about her in the days following, and a kind of curiosity grew. I needed to go back down by the river again.

So it was a shock to actually run into her on Maple Street one lunch hour. I saw this pretty woman coming toward me and give me a nice smile, but I almost passed her before realizing who it was. "Hello!" I said, and she stopped, looked me in the eyes and smiled broadly. My face felt hot. "I didn't recognize you!"

"I recognized you from a long way off," she said. "But you look different in a tie."

"And you look different without the bib overalls."

Her face changed, and I regretted my joke. "I'm kidding," I said. "You weren't wearing bib overalls."

"Farm clothes," she said, the smile returning. "I like to get out of these." She looked down at her skirt and blouse, then lifted a foot to show me her patent leather heels.

"You work around here?"

She pointed to some second-story windows across the street. "I'm a legal aide in a law office."

"You're in law school?"

"I finished last year. I wanted to stay close to Mom and Dad, and there weren't many openings for new lawyers."

Her brown hair had a bit of curl to it, and she was wearing just a little makeup around her eyes and conservative lipstick.

"I've been thinking about you and your folks," I said. "It's like I'd like to live like that. I don't know, back to the earth or something." I was fumbling for words.

"Tell you what," she said, and her eyes were sparkling with mischief, "why don't you come on down this weekend. Spend a night or two in that old farmhouse with us. See if you still think it's how you want to live."

"You serious?"

"You bet. Dad will put you to work clearing brush in the side field."

I stood there, a stupid grin on my face. She had called my bluff.

"Well?"

"Okay!" I blurted, feeling trapped and giddy at the same time.

She took her phone from her purse and pressed a key. "Mom," she said, "you remember that nice young man who came to the farm last week on his bicycle? Well, I just invited him for the weekend."

She paused and looked at me. "She wants to know your name."

"Ryan James." My ears were getting hot.

"Ryan James," she said into the phone. "I think he's from the University." Looking at me, she asked, "Right?"

I nodded, wondering how she knew that.

"Yeah, Mom. Okay, I'll tell him. Bye."

"How did you know where I work?" I asked as she put the phone back in her purse.

She grinned again. "A lawyer has to size people up quickly. So, what do you do, Ryan James? Teach?"

I looked down at my tie. "Is all that written all over me?"

She laughed. "I just guessed. Actually, your tie doesn't go with teaching, does it? At least not on a young guy like you."

"I have an appointment with the dean after lunch," I said.

"You're bucking for a job."

"Yes. Boy, are you quick!"

That slowly emerging smile again that I remembered from the farm. "Y'all want me to slow down?" she drawled.

"I told you my name. Now you tell me yours."

"Therese Edmunds."

"They call you Terry?"

"Some—those who don't know me."

"You prefer Therese."

"It's a good name. I was named after my aunt, who was a singer I always admired."

"You have a musical family," I said, circling her a little so she didn't have to squint in the sun to look at me.

"Aunt Therese was a folk singer."

"That fits with my image of your family," I said. "I have to run now—when do you want me out at the farm?"

"Supper on Fridays is late, because I stop for groceries on my way. About six?"

"I'll see you there. Thank you."

"Good seeing you."

I hurried back to Adams Building for my appointment with the dean, who I thought sure was going to ask me about my plans for the future, and I dreaded it. I didn't have any.

On Friday, I stopped and picked up a couple bottles of wine on my way to the farm, although I realized that I didn't know if the Edmunds family drank at all. That I had first seen Therese's parents standing in their garden praying gave me doubts, but I took the chance that at most they would politely decline without spoiling their easy hospitality that I had encountered.

I needn't have worried. Therese immediately brought out wine glasses when she saw my gift. "Dad can't drink because of his liver," she said, "but he's said that he had enough alcohol in his lifetime anyway."

She had apparently just arrived herself, because two grocery sacks still stood on the kitchen table. I was put to work at once, washing and cutting vegetables for salads.

"Therese tells me that you're a teacher yourself," her mother said as we worked side-by-side.

"I do teach a couple of classes," I said, "but it's not my first love."

"Ah," her father said, "and what is your first love?"

"You know," I began lamely, "I really don't know. I'm getting my master's in philosophy, but I can't see spending my whole life in that field."

Therese said, "You were on your way to the dean's office when we met in town. What was that about? Or should I ask?"

I glanced at her. She was smiling at me.

"I think the dean was asking me that same question," I said. "And I don't think she was pleased when I gave her the same answer."

"We have to find ourselves in our own time," her mother commented. Then she and Therese got into a discussion about the veal roast that was in the oven, and I was relieved to be off the hot seat.

Truthfully, I didn't know what I wanted to do with my life. Part of the reason I was still in school was that I didn't know what else to do. I'd inherited a bit of money from my parents, who had both died when I was a kid. That enabled me to live and pay tuition, and I'd become a teaching assistant just because my advisor had recommended it. The dean had suggested to me that if I went on for a PhD, I could expect some day to have a permanent position in the department. The idea didn't appeal to me.

At the dinner table, we paused briefly for a silent prayer, holding hands around the table. After a few moments of passing and dishing food, I asked Therese's father, "What kind of work did you do before you retired?"

"I was a mechanic," he answered.

"He was the factory superintendent," corrected Therese.

"But I was still just a machinist. I wanted to work with my hands. They kept shoving me into an office."

I laughed. "The extent of my mechanical ability is to tear down my bicycle and put it back together."

"Have any parts left over?" he asked.

"No."

"Well, then, you're a passable mechanic."

I turned to Therese. "What made you want to go into law?"

"She has a strong sense of right and wrong," her mother said. "She wants to save the world."

"Mom, that was me in high school. I'm more realistic now." Therese had a way of looking directly at people when she spoke, reminding me how much I look someplace else instead.

I made an effort to look directly at her mother when I asked, "Miz Edmunds, why did you go into teaching—which was more important, teaching or music?"

"We're not Edmunds," she corrected me. "That's Therese. Our name is Hauptman. I grew up loving music, and took a couple of years of music school. I discovered I wasn't very good, though, so I transferred to teachers' college."

"I didn't have a chance to tell you," Therese said. "I've been married."

"So have I," I said.

"Children?" her mother asked.

"No."

"Do you want children?"

"Mother!" exclaimed Therese.

"Simple question. I was just curious."

"I just *met* Ryan. That's not appropriate!" Therese turned to me, a helpless look on her face.

I smiled. "No problem," I said. "The only thing is, I don't know yet."

Her father was suppressing a grin. "First thing a mother wants to know."

"All right, Daddy, what's the first thing a father wants to know about a young man *who has been in our home for an hour?*" There was a hint of defiance in her voice.

"Well, let's see," the old man said, leaning back in his chair. "Show me your hands."

"He wants to know if you can work in the fields," Therese said sarcastically.

"Well," said her father, "you asked."

I held out my hands, well aware that there was not a callous on them. "Sorry," I said, more amused than embarrassed.

"Ryan," Therese said, "take a walk with me?" She pushed her chair back from the table.

I followed her out the door. Just as we left I glanced back. Her father still had a grin on his face, but her mother's face was grim.

Outside, she said, "I'm sorry. I didn't invite you out here to be evaluated for anything."

"That's okay," I said. "When I was married, we were both students, and we weren't ready to think about a family. It was just as well, because we hadn't grown up yet ourselves."

"I guess that's my story, too."

"Actually, I respect a man's callouses," I added. "Something honest about working with your hands."

It was just getting dark, and the night insects were tuning up. I couldn't see any lights around except from their kitchen. When we walked around behind a shed, even that light was gone. Living in town, I had forgotten how dark and peaceful the country is at night.

"I hope being interrogated by my parents didn't offend you," she said. "They're good people."

"Are they worried about you?"

"Yes, of course." She turned toward me, but I could barely make out her face. "Mom wants grandbabies, and I'm not making any. Dad wants security for me—he doesn't think I can get that for myself."

"And you bring a young man home for a weekend, they want to know how I measure up."

"Ryan—I'm sorry. It's too soon to be asking personal questions."

"Well, it's probably better that we get acquainted this way than in a bar. It's real, at least."

She laughed. "In the bar scene, it's all about finding out things indirectly, because everybody lies."

"Out here in the country," I said, "it seems like being honest is part of what it's all about."

"You said when you were out here last week that it felt like home to you."

"Still does. When I was a kid we went to my grandmother's house sometimes, and she lived on a farm. She and my granddad didn't farm, but they liked being out in the country. Like your mom and dad."

"Yes." She walked on down a path that I could no longer see. I followed her, feeling less and less secure. When she stopped, I bumped into her.

"Sorry," I said. "I was blind."

"I know this path like the back of my hand. Actually, better, because I don't at this moment know the back of my hand at all."

I laughed. I could see well enough to know that she had turned to face me, and was standing very close.

"If I know my parents," she said quietly, "they are thinking that we are out here making love."

I had no idea how to respond to that.

"This is not a bar," she said. "Tell me what you are thinking—really."

"In a bar, I would consider your last statement an invitation."

She laughed. "Yes, I guess you're right. That's not what it was. It was an observation about my parents."

"But the thought was there."

She put her hand on my arm. "The thought was there."

We were silent for a few moments. Then she said, "This is not a good place for it, though. There's poison ivy all over out here."

We both laughed. "I'm enough of a city boy that I prefer clean sheets."

"Me, too." She took her hand off my arm. "If we should choose to do that, let's wait until we're back in town, okay?" Something in her speech sounded lawyer-like.

"Okay." I found her face with my hands and kissed her. She responded with enthusiasm, and then stepped back.

"That," she said, "was an invitation."

We walked back up the path holding hands until we got into the light from the kitchen windows.

"I take it," her mother said, standing at the sink, "that the mosquitoes aren't out tonight." Her voice sounded flat.

"Didn't notice," Therese said, smiling quickly at me.

"Your father is ready for his ice cream."

Therese got a carton from the freezer. "Ryan, would you dish this out?" she asked, getting dishes from the cupboard. "It's too hard for me."

I dug out the rock-like ice cream, and we carried the dishes into the parlor. Her father was in his chair alongside the big table, reading a magazine. He looked up and smiled as Therese handed him a dish and a spoon. The rest of us sat on the sofa. "By rights," he said, "ice cream should be soft when you eat it. But we can never wait that long."

"The lightning bugs are beginning," Therese said. She turned to me. "Last year there were millions of them! I've never seen so many."

We ate the ice cream in silence. The only sounds were of spoons clinking on the dishes. Then her mother said, "Ryan, I'm sorry if we were rude."

"That's okay, Miz Hauptman," I said honestly, and smiled at her.

"Mom, do we have Aunt Therese's record here?" Therese was browsing among a small collection of vinyl records next to an old stereo cabinet that sat next to the television set.

"No, I don't' think so. I haven't seen it in a long time."

"I told Ryan that we had a folk singer in the family." She gave up searching and returned to the sofa to collect the ice cream dishes.

"My sister loved Therese," her mother said to me. "She even wrote a song about her."

"She was a very special person," Therese said from the kitchen.

"She had MS for years," Ms Hauptman said. "She died recently."

"I've heard that's an awful disease," I said.

Therese sat back down next to me. "She was a real trooper. She did what she could and never complained."

We sat and talked about nothing much for a while, until Mr. Hauptman got up from his chair.

Therese stood up again. "I'll get Ryan's room ready," To me, she said, "Come on, I'll show you where you'll sleep."

I followed her up the narrow stairway into an attic that had been made into two small bedrooms. In one of them, she turned down the spread on a twin-size bed. "The bathroom is at the bottom of the stairs," she said. "You said you wanted 'down home'—well, this is it."

I can't say I slept soundly. I thought of Therese sleeping in the other upstairs bedroom, and during the night fantasized about her.

Morning light came early through the little dormer window, accompanied by country sounds. I lay awake for a long time. Eventually I heard movement downstairs, and got up. At the foot of the stairs, the bathroom was occupied, so I sat with my Dopp Kit on a step until Therese emerged, smiling. "Good morning!" she said. "Did you sleep well?"

I nodded. "It's very quiet out here."

"What do you like for breakfast? I'm the short order cook on weekends here."

"I'll eat whatever you want to fix."

"Pancakes, then. You'll need lots of carbs in you for mowing the south field."

The aroma of fresh coffee greeted me from the kitchen, along with maple syrup heating on the stove. The sun was pouring cheer through the kitchen window. Therese's parents were already outside working. "They like to be outside early in the morning," Therese said.

I went to the door and breathed the country air. "Smells wonderful," I said.

"Come and eat with me while they're hot," she said, and gave me a quick peck on the lips before she sat down.

"Good pancakes," I said. "Good company."

She smiled. "What you didn't hear last night about my Aunt Therese—she was a lesbian. Dad had a real problem with that. In fact, I knew it before he did."

"It used to be a taboo subject."

"She was a great person, as well as a good singer. She and her partner were together for thirty years, until she died."

"I've never been close to anyone like that," I said. "I've known a few gay people in school, but never had much contact with any. I'm sure I could use some consciousness raising."

"I grew up," she said, "knowing that Aunt Therese was gay, but to me she was always Aunt Therese and I loved her and I never thought of her as strange."

"My ex-wife was strange," I said, grinning. "But that's not why we split up—or maybe it was."

"Why did you split up?"

"Different ways of looking at the world. Different priorities about what we wanted to do and where we wanted to go. In the end, we got on each other's nerves."

"Last night you said you didn't know what you wanted to do for the rest of your life, and whether or not you wanted children." She smiled at me. "I'm not judging; I'm just curious about whether those things had an effect on your relationship."

I thought for a moment about that. "Maybe it did for her, but she didn't bring it up. For a while I kinda followed her around most of the time because she knew what she wanted to do—and then I didn't want to do that anymore. When I began telling her what I'd rather do, we'd end up in a fight."

"Tim and I got along great until we got married." She grinned. "An old story, I know. We had very different ideas about the roles of husband and wife, and we just never thought to check it out beforehand."

We ate our pancakes without talking. I wondered how different our ideas of roles might be. I hadn't thought about that while Meg and I were married.

Soon her father came into the kitchen from outside. "Therese said you'd be willing to do some things around here," he said to me.

"Sure. Whatever you need done, I'll sure try."

"We got a little riding mower that you could use to start on that pasture out there." He gestured outside. "Probably can't finish it, because it's been let go too long, and it'll go slow."

I got up from the table and looked at Therese. She grinned again and waved me off. "Show me how to work it," I said, "and I'll give it my best."

Out in the tool shed, he painstakingly demonstrated how to start and run the mower. It was clear that he was used to training people in mechanical tasks. I didn't have to ask him anything, until ten minutes into my first row when the blade became clogged with wet grass. He had been watching me from the shed, and recognized the problem immediately. Walking out to where I was stalled, he showed me how to tip the mower over enough to pry the grass out of the blade housing. "Just don't tip 'er too far, or you'll dump all the gas out of the tank."

The ground was uneven and the grass was high and a little wet, so the going was slower—and harder—than I expected. The time, however, seemed to go by quickly. I was surprised when Therese came across the field to tell me to stop for lunch.

"You're doin' good," she said. "Daddy said you figured it out pretty quick."

"For a city boy," I said, smiling.

"Yep." She led me back to the house.

By the end of the day, I'd mowed about a third of the field. My body ached from the constant rocking and trying to keep the mower going in a straight line. I'd never done such physical labor before. But Mr. Hauptman complimented me on my work during dinner. "You stuck it out," he said.

"That field has needed mowing for a month," his wife said. "Thank you for your work."

"You're welcome." Actually, I was a little proud of my sore muscles.

Therese spoke up. "Ryan and I are goin' over to Wal-Mart after dinner. We need some things." She gave me a little smile as she passed me the mashed potatoes.

Later, in the car, she said, "We don't really need anything. I just wanted to give you a break from family talk."

"Where we goin'?" I asked, trying to mimic the country speech she had been using with her parents.

"To the roadhouse, of course." She grinned at me. "You got to see how country folks relax."

Sure enough, she pulled into the gravel parking area in front of a tavern called The Roadhouse. Several other cars were parked there, and a couple of motorcycles. "Don't worry," she said, "These are good folks, live in the neighborhood. You won't have to defend yourself—or me."

Loud country music greeted us inside. Therese waved and said hello to several people, and we sat at a table at the end of the room. She held up two fingers when the bartender called her name, and in a moment we had bottles of beer sitting before us. No glasses, but a bowl of peanuts in the shell. I soon found out that peanut shells are to be tossed on the floor.

Another young woman came over and greeted us. Therese introduced us, and they chatted for a minute before the woman returned to her table.

"Colorful place," I commented.

"It's not really my kind of place," she said, grinning, "but I thought you ought to have the experience while you're out here in the country."

A group of people were laughing at the far end of the room, and the bartender was having a serious conversation with a woman in very tight jeans and a low-cut blouse. We finished our beers and got up to leave. I gave a bill to the bartender and waved off the change. "Thanks," he said. "Come back, hear?"

Back at the farm, we pulled into the side yard next to my car, but Therese made no move to get out. "I'm glad you came out," she said.

"So am I. I'm having a good time."

"You worked hard today. Tomorrow's Sunday, and Mom and Dad will go to church. We're not expected to go with them."

"I can get some more of that mowing done."

She turned in the seat. "That field will wait. I want to spend some time with you while they're gone, okay?"

I leaned over and kissed her gently. "Okay. Only this time I get to make breakfast. Okay?"

"Wonderful," she said.

"You know." I said, "we've known each other only a week, and I feel really comfortable with you."

She pushed a bit of hair behind my ear. "You're sweet," she said softly. We kissed fervently, and our conversation pretty much ended there.

A while later, I noticed that the house was dark. "Looks like your folks have gone to bed."

Therese sighed and sat back. "Mom still thinks I'm sixteen," she said. "One of the disadvantages of being here."

"You want to go in?"

"I love my mom very much, but sometimes I feel like she lives in a different world."

"I've heard that complaint a lot at school," I said, opening my door.

We went into the house as quietly as we could. The floor boards squeaked all the way to the stairway. Therese went into the bathroom and I went on upstairs.

A few minutes later, I heard her come out, and I started toward the stairs to use the bathroom when I heard voices. Her mother was whispering something to her. I waited.

"Mother, I'm not sixteen any more!" Therese said in a frustrated stage whisper.

I couldn't hear what her mother was saying, but Therese was obviously upset with her. They argued for a few minutes, then a door closed and Therese came up the stairs.

The stairway was narrow, so I waited until she was at the top before starting down. She caught my sleeve and said softly, "Ryan, I'm sorry!"

"No problem," I whispered, and went on down the stairs to the bathroom.

When I returned, she was waiting for me. "Sit with me for a minute," she whispered.

We went into her bedroom and closed the door. Sitting on the edge of the bed, we talked quietly about parents and "the old days" when we were younger and still held in the thrall of parental authority.

"I understand," she said, "that they develop this sense of responsibility for us when we're kids, and it's hard to let that go when we grow up."

I chuckled. "I had an aunt who got divorced at sixty and moved back into her mom's house—mostly to take care of her—but she had her own friends, and liked to go out at night. Her mother had fits if she stayed out past midnight. They finally had a blowup and she moved out again. The rest of us in the family joked about it, but to her it was not funny."

"I was so glad when they moved out here so I didn't have to stop in to visit with her every day."

"You said she lives in a different world. That goes along with this place, doesn't it?"

"What do you mean?"

I thought for a moment and then said, "I've been feeling some kind of nostalgia for the kind of world this farm suggests to me, where life is simpler—like, 'tomorrow, we mow the south pasture,' and twenty other things don't intrude on the peace and quiet."

"And the family is the whole world," she said. "Kids grow up and rent a house in the neighborhood and stop by every day to make sure Mom and Dad are okay, and they never experience the real world, and some day they have kids of their own, and the same thing happens all over again."

Sitting beside her I hugged her with one arm. "But you've tasted the honey of independence."

She smiled. "I love it that they both love me—I can feel it in my bones—but I have to be able to choose things, like staying out late or sleeping with a friend." She turned and kissed me on the cheek, then pushed me up on my feet. "Okay, I'm feeling calmer now. You go to bed—alone."

I lay awake for a long time, dreading the morning, because I thought there might be more conflict. I felt caught in the middle—in the middle of my ambivalence about life. My own world, the swirling excitement of the university environment where no idea is carved in stone but is constantly buffeted by competing ideas and values, allowed me unlimited choices. The life of the country, of family and neighborhood and summer mornings smelling mown hay and barnyards and burnt coffee and pancake syrup, pulled at me. I missed my mother and father, although I had barely known them. The thought of them gave me comfort and stability, as though through them I could know who I was. But they weren't around to tell me.

The farm felt like home, the home that lived in my fantasies, the home where I was wanted. That want brought tears to my eyes, even as I knew it was just dreaming. I didn't really want to live a country life. It just seemed simpler, and on the surface it seemed easier than the life I'd been living.

I must have slept. I awoke with Therese tapping on the door. She opened it enough to stick her head in. "You were going to make me breakfast?" She was smiling. "Mom and Dad have gone to church."

"C'mere," I said, moving to one side of the bed.

"That was an invitation," she said, coming to the side of the bed. "But this is as far as I come."

"I'm not comfortable," I said. "When they get home, I need to be gone."

She sat on the side of the bed. "Ryan, they are my problem."

"Maybe. But I don't know how to handle it."

"They won't be blaming you. We've been through this before."

"But I haven't, not with them. Yesterday, I felt welcome and appreciated here. Even if they don't say anything to me— or to you while I'm here, I'll feel like I'm not welcome anymore."

"All right," she said, her face sober. "Let's have a nice breakfast together, anyway." Then she went downstairs.

My stomach was still knotted up when I arrived in the kitchen. Somehow, the smells I had so loved the day before now reminded me of her mother's angry voice the night before.

"Do you still want to make me breakfast?" She was looking at me guardedly.

I tried to smile. "Of course. This isn't about you and me, but right now I feel a little like I'm a fox in somebody's henhouse."

Therese laughed. "A good, country expression."

"Okay, how do you like your eggs?"

"Speaking of henhouses!" Both of us laughed, and I felt a little easier.

"I like 'em anyway you want to fix them," she said. "I'll make toast and coffee, okay?"

When we finally sat down to eat, the knot in my gut had eased, and I could feel for her the way I had last evening in the car. "I'm sorry," I said. "I don't handle conflict very well."

"Don't be sorry. I'd probably feel the same way if it was your family."

The sun was shining through the open window over the sink, and I could hear birds outside. We talked about other things, my position in the university and her job in the law office. Both, we agreed, were temporary. I knew I had to make some decisions about my career path, and she knew she would not be content as a low-paid legal aide for very long.

"My ex-wife is planning to remarry," I said, "and I'll be able to afford a better place to live."

"You're paying her alimony?" She seemed surprised.

"She had never worked, and didn't have a place to live unless I helped her out."

"She's what—sixteen?" That slow smile on her face.

I laughed. "No, she's twenty. She has a job now, but I had agreed to contribute."

Therese leaned back in her chair. "I think you need a good lawyer," she said.

I put my hand on hers. "No, I just need a friend."

One eyebrow raised. "Okay," she said, tentatively.

The pickup truck pulled into the yard.

"Oh, shit," I said. It was too late to try to escape.

"Relax," she said. "Just smile." She demonstrated. "Really."

When her parents came through the kitchen door, I tried to look pleasant, but my heart was pounding in my chest.

"How was church?" Therese asked them.

"Comforting," her mother answered. Her father nodded to us, and went into the front room without saying anything.

"We just had breakfast," Therese said. "Can I fix you anything?"

"No."

I could think of nothing to say.

Her mother came around the table to stand next to me. "Young man," she began.

"His name is Ryan," Therese broke in.

"Ryan, we don't know each other very well ..."

"Mother. Stop—please. This isn't about Ryan." Therese had stood up to face her mother.

"We don't know each other very well," repeated her mother, "but you need to know that this is a moral household."

"Mother!"

I wanted to flee out the door. I knew I should tell her that I would respect her rules, that Therese and I were just getting to know each other, and that we would not do anything ...

Therese interrupted my thoughts. "Mother, just stop. Ryan is a guest, and he has been a perfect gentleman, to me and to you. He does not deserve this!" Anger showed on her face.

"I'm just making things clear."

"No, you're not! You are assuming things that you have no right to assume. We are not children!"

"I will not have immoral behavior in my house," her mother said, turning to her.

At that, Therese burst into angry tears. "If you don't respect me, then I don't belong here!" She disappeared suddenly into the hallway to the stairs.

"Missus Hauptman ..." I began, but the woman turned her back on me and went into the front room. I stood there, frozen by fear and bewilderment.

A minute later, Therese appeared again, her face distorted with fury. She had a suitcase in her hand. "Ryan, I'm sorry. Better get your things so we can leave."

I collected my clothes from upstairs and followed her out to her car. She threw her suitcase in the back seat and opened the driver's door. "Please, would you follow me to my apartment? I live on Middleton."

I felt caught up in a maelstrom. "All right," I said. "Can we talk then?"

She closed the door, opened the window and smiled up at me. "Yes, we need to talk. But let's just get away from this place!"

I threw my duffle into my car and followed her out to the road. Driving back to town, I was torn by mixed feelings. This situation was not my fault, but I didn't know how to handle it. I felt that I should try to make things right with her parents, but it was clear that nothing I could say would change the relationship Therese had with them. Obviously, they had been through this kind of conflict before. For all I knew, it might simply blow over in a few days. I didn't have the kind of family history that could prepare me for this. My relatives who had raised me after my parents died never raised their voices at me or each other. If we had a disagreement, it was always resolved in a calm, rational way, and I always felt respected.

When I pulled up behind her car at her apartment, I could see that she was talking on her phone. I waited until she finished before getting out of my car.

She met me on the street. Her face betrayed the emotion she had been feeling. "I'm finished," she said. "I won't go back into that house."

I was as unnerved by her anger as if it were directed at me. "Therese, do you need some time?"

Her face softened. "Dear Ryan—this is quite an introduction to my life, isn't it? Yes, I need some time, but I'd like it to be with you. We both need some time to sort through all this and get ourselves together. Come on up—lock your car, though. This is a campus neighborhood." She kissed me lightly on the cheek and went toward the front door.

I wasn't sure I wanted to go inside. What I really wanted was a drink. Since Meg, I hadn't dated anyone, partly because I wasn't sure that anyone would find me interesting to be with. Therese was a fluke. I had felt really comfortable with her ever since we met at her parents' farm, because I wasn't looking for a relationship. What we had just sort of grew from a seed. Still, I couldn't help but feel at least partly responsible for the trouble at the farm. Maybe I secretly wanted to be outrageous, to push the limits of propriety. I had led a pretty ordinary life. What would it feel like to walk down a city street naked? I'd dreamed of such situations, but never consciously entertained the idea while awake. A couple of times I'd been sufficiently stoned on some chemical or other that I wouldn't have batted an eye to find myself on said street in said degree of dishabille, but that wouldn't count as *wanting* to.

All these thoughts ran through my mind, not necessarily in that order, as I dutifully followed Therese up into her apartment.

"Nice place," I said as she ushered me in.

"For a country girl."

I laughed, and noticed how sore my abdominal muscles were from the tension of the morning. "Part of me wants to run away from all this," I admitted.

She looked at me, concerned. "From me?"

"No, from this feeling I've been harboring almost all morning."

"Want a drink?"

"Yes."

What?"

"Anything—preferably over eighty proof."

"I have vodka." She turned and went into the tiny kitchen. Lifting a bottle off a high shelf, she asked, "Straight, or with something?"

"Straight."

She returned with the bottle and two empty glasses. "Pour your own."

Fifteen minutes later, we were sitting on her sofa smiling at each other. "Now," she said, "what was it we were upset about?"

"You said you'd never go into your parents' house again."

She sighed. "I probably will, but never again will I trust them with a friend."

"I could have handled that situation if you hadn't been so upset," I said. "I felt like I should protect you, but I had no idea of how I could."

She leaned over and kissed me quickly. "And I was furious at her for attacking you."

"She didn't really attack me," I said. "She said she wanted to be clear about what she could tolerate in her house."

Therese looked surprised. "That's how you remember that?" When I nodded, she said, "I was expecting her next words to be 'fucking' and 'prick.' She's used the 'slut' word on me more than once."

"I heard 'immoral' a couple of times. I did feel a bit misunderstood."

That brought loud laughter from her, and I had to join in.

"Your parents," I said, trying to be serious, "have old-fashioned ideas, and that goes with the feelings I had about that old farm."

"You're a sentimental man." She tenderly touched my cheek. I had an impulse to grab her hand and kiss it, but then I thought it would look ridiculous.

She went back into the kitchen and returned with some crackers and cheese. "We need to eat something," she said.

I became aware of my body responding to this woman. "I need to say something," I said, stumbling over my words.

She sat with her hands in her lap, back straight, as though she were a school teacher waiting for a first-grader to recite a poem.

I had to laugh. "I am in no condition to drive," I said. "That was a very big drink."

"You poured it yourself," she said, smiling sweetly.

"That I did. But I forgot myself."

Her brow furrowed.

"I mean that I am getting turned on."

"And?" Her brow was now smooth, and that slow smile was forming at the corner of her mouth.

"We haven't talked about this yet."

She stood up and took my hand. "Come."

Standing up so quickly was a mistake. I sat back down on the sofa. "I'm embarrassed," I said. "I can't stand up."

She looked at me for a moment, then picked up my legs and placed them on the sofa, arranged a pillow for my head, and said, "Don't move."

I closed my eyes for just a moment. I remember vaguely having a blanket laid over me at some point. The next thing I remember was that she was sitting on the floor next to me, stroking my forehead with a damp cloth. When I opened my eyes again, she smiled at me. "One minute he says he's turned on and the next minute he's asleep!"

"Sorry."

"I've been sitting here watching you sleep, as though you were a little baby. It was sweet."

I made an effort to sit up.

"Are you all right?" She stood up and helped me to my feet.

"I need to pee," I said, laughing with embarrassment.

She walked with me to the bathroom, and then let me go in alone. I felt steadier, but still moved carefully. She was waiting outside the bathroom door when I returned. "How are you feeling?"

I gathered her up in my arms. "I am now awake," I said.

We turned in the direction of the bedroom.

About midnight I had recovered enough to remember that both of us had to work the next day, so I got up from the bed, kissed her one last time and drove to my own apartment. We hadn't eaten since breakfast except for crackers and cheese, and I raided my refrigerator before collapsing in my bed, totally in love.

The next day I phoned her and we arranged to meet for lunch on Maple Street.

Both of us were grinning as we sat down in the restaurant.

"That was something else," I said.

"Yes it was. This morning I went to work completely relaxed."

"Amazing, how a few little endorphins can change the whole world."

"I talked to my mom this morning," she said, touching my hand on the table. "She apologized to both of us."

"I'm glad you patched things up."

"Only in part. I'm afraid, Friend Ryan, that you won't be able to mow the rest of that field. I won't give her another chance."

"My feelings about farm life have changed some, anyway."

"How so?" That slowly growing smile again.

I thought for a moment, then said, "It was all fantasy about a simpler way of life. Life is not simple, wherever I am."

"So right now we can start all over again, and forget last weekend?"

"Yes and no," I said. "Last weekend was not all bad. I don't have to forget that. I just have to let go of my illusion about the simple life. And for me, last night began the starting all over."

We agreed to see where life might lead us.

Back in the university library, I thought about life. Whatever one's life, there are decisions to make, often difficult decisions. I was sure that even though I respected hard, physical work and country air, it wasn't how I wanted to spend my life. I'd never even gone in for sports—the thought of pushing my body to its limits didn't appeal to me. What did pull at me were the questions of the mind. And the heart.

Philosophical clarity was beginning to seem a worthwhile goal. The university environment offered me those questions and the tools for pursuing them.

I'd go back to the dean next week and sit down with her and plan my future. I hoped—but I couldn't know yet—that my future would include Therese, the lawyer.

The End

Where Never Lark

But never by laments or prayers shalt thou recall thy sire from that lake of Hades to which all must pass.

—Sophocles, *Electra*

1. Small Things

He pushed the throttle forward slowly, counting, "One, two, three," to pace the time of the movement. The little aircraft rolled over the rough grass, picking up speed with each second. He held the stick centered. The fat tire just beyond his right foot bounced a little, and the landing gear strut whipped through the taller grass. At first, he had to steer assertively. He was a bit breathless with excitement but his hands and feet responded surely on the controls, steering the craft straight toward the end of the field. In a few moments he could feel it want to fly, so he nudged the stick toward his belt buckle. The bouncing suddenly stopped, and he was airborne.

He watched the ground move away beneath him. All motion appeared to slow. Now seemingly suspended over the line of trees marking the end of his landing strip, he looked around him at the exposed structure of his plane. Wind, the only thing reminding him of his motion through the air, roared past his helmet and whipped his clothes. The steady growl of the engine reassured him. The wings were level with the horizon, and the nose a little high. When he judged that he was about 300 feet up, he took a breath and let it out, and eased the throttle back a little. He had passed the critical altitude, below which if the engine failed, he'd have to try to land straight ahead, into the rough terrain, avoiding trees and rocks as well as he could to set down without breaking his neck. Now he was high enough that he could turn the ultralight aircraft back toward the field, if necessary, and probably glide safely there without power. He kept climbing until he was about 500 feet above the terrain, then adjusted the throttle just enough to maintain level flight. The wind curled around the edges of his helmet faceplate, cooling the perspiration on his face. Reaching into the little foam cooler strapped next to his seat, he took out a plastic bottle and squirted some water into his mouth. He looked straight down between his knees at the tops of pine trees. Small ponds dotted the landscape, reflecting the sun that was shaded by the wing over his head. He turned slowly toward the west. The sun touched his neck with warmth. "Now, this is *flying*," he said aloud, barely able to hear his own voice. It reminded him of being on a motorcycle years ago, feeling the wind whip his clothes and yielding his hearing to the sound of the engine. When he turned, it felt a lot like turning a bike, leaning into the turn and keeping his weight pressed into the center of the seat.

The mechanic turned the little engine upside down on his bench, and inserted the two piston assemblies into their cylinders. Then he retrieved a crankshaft from a pallet behind him and assembled it into the engine. Bearing caps came next, each one secured with bolts. Through holes in the bolt heads, he threaded a wire and twisted it with pliers to make it tight. When he clipped the end of the wire, it flew from his fingers. He peered into the cavity of the engine, but saw nothing. Then he installed the bottom cover of the engine.

"Watson Tower, this is Cessna alpha bravo three-five-one. Permission to leave your nice little airport." She slipped the bows of her sunglasses under her headphones and tugged at the bill of her cap. It never quite went away, this little nervousness at the beginning of a flight. The anticipation of flying always brought damp palms and that peculiar nudge in her midsection. The engine ticked over quietly, her patient servant Cessna, forever ready, never nervous like her, but competent and steady.

"Cessna alpha bravo three-five-one, Watson Tower. Proceed to runway two seven."

Leaning forward to scan the parking and taxi ramps, she eased off the brake pedals and let the aircraft inch forward until it was at the edge of the runway. Setting the brakes, she advanced the throttle and checked both magnetos. Glancing at her other flight instruments, she said, "Watson Tower, three-five-one. Ready for take-off."

"Three-five-one, you're cleared for takeoff. No other aircraft in the vicinity. Heading north again, Jen?"

"Three-five-one. Yes I am. Request right turn-out."

"Permission granted. Jim was up there north of the power lines yesterday. The snow is gone now, and visibility is good."

"Thanks. I'll stay south of that today. I figure I've got four good hours."

"Good luck."

"Thanks. Three-five-one out." She breathed in deeply and let it out.

For several weeks, she had been flying every day out of this little country airport, and had talked with the people who ran the place, the control tower operators, the pilots, and the "locals." A relationship had developed, a common hope.

The Watson runway was streaked with tire marks from hundreds of student pilots practicing touch-and-gos. As the little Cessna turned to line up with the runway, she adjusted the bill of her cap to shade her eyes from the sun, and pushed the throttle forward with a practiced hand. The seat pressed into her back and carried her quickly down the runway. Moments later, the plane was airborne. She turned north when she was clear of the airport traffic pattern at five hundred feet, then straightened her cap and with a crooked finger pulled her hair up over the adjustment strap in the back.

The late morning sun was high enough that she could see the shadow of the Cessna down to the left and ahead of her. As she gained more altitude, the shadow became smaller, but still raced with her across the roads and farms and trees.

A representative of the kit manufacturer had checked over his new airplane just last week, and this was the first time he'd had a chance to take it out for more than a few minutes at a time. Before, he'd been paying all of his attention to the operation of the aircraft. Today, he was just going to enjoy flying. *Real flying!*

Over open land now, he could see acres of cultivated farmland showing vestiges of fall harvest. Here and there were rectangular patches of woods, tiny remnants of the vast hardwood forests that used to cover this part of the country. A few minutes later, nothing but forest flowed by under him, miles and miles of hardwood and pine, green on green, just a few hints of yellow and red. Occasional small lakes broke up the solid cover, brightly reflecting the clear sky. Now and then he could see a road slicing through the forest, appearing and disappearing. He always knew where he was, however, by a huge power line that led directly back past his landing strip, and by the city off to the south, crowned by a thin brown layer of haze.

Flying was in her blood. She still remembered her first flight, sitting next to her father with those huge earphones perched on her head threatening to topple her five-year-old body over in the seat. She couldn't see over the window sill without straining, so most of what she saw was sky. But the feeling of flight! Like those elevators in the big buildings downtown, scary and fun. And when her father banked the plane, she clung to the panel and the framework and looked *straight down* at the ground!

Back home, her mother couldn't stop her gushing about the flight all through dinner. "Dad says I can get a license at sixteen!" The glances between her parents were not friendly at that point.

All through the "bad years" after her mother and father separated, she lived with the same dream, even though she saw less and less of her father after he moved away. By the time she reached the magic age, he lived far away, and they saw each other only occasionally. She spent a week with him during summer vacation one year, but he no longer flew then, and finances didn't permit flying lessons for her. "Some day," he promised, for the twentieth time.

A flock of geese crossed his path, untroubled by this noisy silver bird that shared their sky. Several honked as they disappeared behind him.

Suddenly it became quieter. The engine had stopped. Even though it was obvious, he twisted around to see that the propeller, too, was motionless. After a moment of panic, he went into a familiar routine: keep the wings level, keep the nose down to maintain flying speed, and think. He pulled several times on the starter cord that hung beside his head, but the engine was locked. Okay, he thought, let's set her down someplace smooth. He looked around below him, especially straight ahead, where he could glide farther. Tense as he was, he noticed that the little craft still handled smoothly and easily. He maintained airspeed by dropping the nose slightly to extend his glide as much as possible.

In college she joined the student flying club and paid for her lessons by tutoring other students in whatever subjects she happened to be taking at the time. When she soloed, she wrote to her father the same night. A month later, he replied with appropriate congratulations. He hadn't flown in years, but when she visited him she noticed a photograph on the mantle of him standing next to his old red Taylorcraft. "Too busy lately to go up," he told her. She felt an emptiness in him.

And a distance. This god of her childhood was old now, and too busy to fly. The thing that had kept him alive in her as she grew up without him—flying—seemed not in him anymore. She kept her old image of him, though, and when she finally could afford to buy her own airplane, she named it after him. One weekend, when she flew it to where he lived and asked him to go up with her, he said no. Her heart wilted.

A large lake lay ahead of him, and at the far end a little farm interrupted the continuous surface of treetops. Sighting carefully over the little instrument panel to gauge his angle of descent, he estimated that he could glide just that far. A quick glance around told him that it was his only clear shot. If he couldn't make it across the lake, a water landing was preferable to smashing into the trees. His mind was too busy just then to think about how he was feeling, about the impending loss of his brand-new aircraft, about the months of work it took to build, the late nights of frustrating effort to make parts fit together, the phone calls to the kit manufacturer, all the time lost to his family. An experienced pilot, he didn't dwell on the possibility that he, as well as his aircraft, might not survive the next few minutes.

A few years after she had bought her Cessna, her mother had written to her that he had bought an airplane kit. He lived alone out on an old farm and commuted an hour each way to work. "It's an ultralight," her mother wrote, "Looks more like a toy. I hope he never finishes it, because he'll just kill himself in it." Her mother had remarried, but she exchanged occasional letters with her ex-husband. Their daughter felt both gladness and further isolation, especially that he had not shared his news with her.

As much as she had told him of her passion for flying, he seldom took her aloft while she was young. The air was his own private place, his retreat away from the dullness of work and the stress of an unfulfilling marriage. To share it with others changed the experience for him. She came to know all that after she grew up. She thought she understood, but it remained a keen disappointment, an undigested lump inside her.

They were past the farms now, and below the Cessna she could see nothing but forest. "A small plane could go down in there and *never* be seen from the air." She'd told herself the same thing twenty times since she arrived two months ago to help search. It seemed a hopeless effort, but she couldn't just quit.

The lake rose ever closer. His glide-path sightline now showed only water ahead. At a few feet above the surface, he pulled back on the stick, raising the nose and slowing his descent, but only momentarily. When the wing could no longer support the weight, it stalled, and the nose dropped suddenly. He took a deep breath and reached for the buckle of his seatbelt. Then he hit the cold water, that seemingly soft surface that now felt as hard as concrete. Something smashed him in the face, and he no longer saw or felt anything.

He didn't know that the great wing floated on the surface of the water for a long time, his head just inches below. He couldn't feel the tangled aluminum structure slowly tilt to the left and, gracefully as a mallard side-slipping down from the sky, drop ever so quietly, ever-so-slowly, into the dark, deep lake. A trail of bubbles followed them down.

Minutes later, far overhead, an osprey glided across the lake. Something in the water caught the bird's attention, and it folded its wings and dove. As soon as it grabbed the piece of plastic, it released it and once more flew skyward. A multicolored oil slick began to spread out over the surface of the lake, catching the sun in a flat rainbow broken only by a steady stream of bubbles. The faint swish of pines in the wind whispered the only sound for a long time.

At three thousand feet, she could see for miles, but the ultralight would be just a speck on the ground, so she alternated her passes between higher and lower altitudes. The low winter sun cast dark shadows between the trees. A warm spell a week ago had melted the snow that had covered the area for the past two months.

She no longer hoped that he was still alive. Other pilots in the area had helped search for a couple of weeks, but eventually, one by one, they went on with their lives. A downed plane reminded them of their own mortality, and they hoped it would be found. It could have been them, each one was aware, and the longer the search went on, the more they felt the need to move on, put the incident behind them, forget it. She got to know several of the local pilots, and every so often one would phone her to report on where they had recently scanned.

He had loved flying so much when she was young. It seemed to be most of what he ever talked about. She remembered a lot of arguments between her parents about the money his airplane had cost the family. The old Aeronca finally took too much to maintain, and he sold it to a young man who thought he could restore it. That happened about the same time they divorced, and her father seemed to change afterward.

She wrote to him after she found out that he was building the ultralight, and reminded him of those dreams they had shared. He confessed that he might not live long enough to finish the aircraft, or might be too old to fly it if he did. He'd let his pilot's license lapse years before. It was a hobby of nostalgia. He finally brought her in to visit the craft a couple of times while it was under construction, but she couldn't see much progress. He did finally agree to go up with her in her Cessna, but he seemed distracted in the air, and refused to take the controls. She glanced at him, but he had looked away, off to the side, where the wing skimmed over the blue-gray horizon.

The sun traced its autumn arc across the blue sky and eased itself into a line of high clouds in the west, setting them afire. Bursting bubbles glittered on the darkening surface of the lake. The light gradually faded into blue, then purple, and then black.

The next day, even the oil slick had gone. A few small pieces of plastic foam slowly drifted away and disappeared.

In the depths of the clear water, the tangle of aluminum, sailcloth and trapped air finally reached a point of equilibrium where the density of the water exactly balanced, and it floated quietly, a strand of fabric tugging toward the surface, undulating in a slow, twisting dance of a water nymph. The stout nylon belt still held the body of the pilot in the midst of the wreckage. It all hung there, halfway between the surface and the bottom, drifting inch-by-inch with the glacially slow current of the lake.

The air today looked crisp and clear with visibility at least twenty miles. She watched condensation trails from high-flying jets criss-cross over her, and once she saw a small twin flying about a thousand feet above her. Otherwise, the sky belonged to her. She banked the Cessna into a slow three-sixty turn, and looked almost straight down at an old farm beside a long lake. Leveling the wings again, she watched the ground through the left window, sometimes banking a little for a better view without changing the general direction of her passes over the forest below. A well-used chart lay on the seat next to her, divided into blocks with a felt-tip marker.

Ordinarily, this would have been a time of quiet joy for her, suspended like this over the landscape, identifying roads and buildings, keeping her bearings so that her back-and-forth passes covered every acre of the green and brown forest beneath her. Flying gave her a sense of relationship with the land that she never got on the ground. When she drove on the highway, she didn't feel any connection with another car in passing—it was just a vehicle that she needed to avoid running into. From the air, a car on the road seemed alive—or perhaps it just symbolized life to her. It was going from *this* someplace to *that* someplace, carrying human beings who were like her. She pictured the occupants anticipating getting *over there* or remembering having been *back there*, two different times as well as two different places, while from her vantage point she could see both places at the same time. And in her mind, a house seen from the air was always occupied. A woman tying the shoes of her four-year-old before sending him out to play, a farmer sharpening his tools in the garage. A little girl watching her father tinkering under the hood of the family car. Or the family airplane. A familiar knot formed in her stomach.

While the pilot's last sensation as he crashed into the water was one of cold, actually the water was quite warm after a whole summer of sunny days. The fish who lived in the lake stayed near the bottom, or in areas cooled by fresh springs that fed the lake. No people came near here. The farm that the pilot had struggled to reach was overgrown and deserted, now used only as a hunting cabin by city people who came bumping over the rutted lane from the distant highway during deer season.

For several days after the crash, other airplanes flew back and forth over the area, people searching for the downed craft in a vast wilderness. Finally, even these flights became rare.

As the temperature of the lake changed with the season, the craft became more buoyant, and gradually— over weeks—it floated to just beneath the surface.

More time passed, and a hollow wing strut developed a leak and slowly filled with water. This disturbed the delicate balance in the wreckage, and the wing tilted ever-so-slowly downward. At first, surface tension of the water held the opposite wing on the surface, but eventually the air trapped inside the wing became warmer from the sun, making it lighter, and the wing lifted clear of the water. Freed from the surface tension, the wing rose slowly, and water that had entered small places found its way back out, lightening the wing even more. There it stayed, sloping upward with its tip a few inches above the surface.

Then one bright winter afternoon, the aircraft slowly rolled over in the water, and the wing lifted gracefully into the air like a dancer's slender arm, reflecting the low sun.

Off to the southwest the sun sagged lower in the sky. "One more pass up high," she decided, and throttled up for the climb. At three thousand feet, she headed straight west, and peered into the growing gloom below her, feeling defeated. "He was *never there*," she finally said aloud, and burst into tears. *"He has never been there for me!"* Then she quickly removed her sunglasses and wiped her eyes, glancing at the sky around her before returning her attention to the land below.

At the end of her final pass, she held the westerly heading for a few minutes, watching the low winter sun over some gathering clouds on the horizon. Even in her grief, the scene before her touched her deeply. Then, in a slow, sad bank to the left toward the airfield, she looked backward at her day's search area, just visible under the left wing. The power lines were all but invisible, and the long lake loomed nearly black, reflecting the eastern sky where night waited just beyond the horizon.

A flash of light came from the Center of the lake. Startled, she stayed in her turn so that she could see better. A brilliant light, something reflecting the late sun, pulled her back toward the lake. She throttled down to lose altitude for a better look. As the Cessna got closer, the light wavered a little. She made out a tall shape, like a sailboat. She'd not seen any boats on that lake, and she had flown over it time after time.

An airplane wing, standing straight out of the water! Heart pounding, she went down to a hundred feet, watching the fabric and metal wing grow larger and larger. Her mind held no doubt about what this was. She switched on her radio. "Watson Tower, this is Cessna alpha bravo three-five-one. Can you hear me over there?"

The tower answered immediately, "Three-five-one, Watson Tower. You're broken up a little, Jennifer. Where are you?"

She ignored radio protocol. "Over Long Lake just south of the power lines." Her voice was tight. "I think I've found him."

A hundred feet above the surface of the dark lake she turned the Cessna in a wide circle around the ultralight and looked down at where her father finally was, *for her*, and she sobbed.

2. First Flight

Sometimes, things look smaller from a distance, charming but without threat. At other times, distant things loom over us like thunderclouds, and we run and hide.

He lifted the little girl up high enough to get her legs through the doorway of the red Aeronca. "Okay," he said, "climb in."

She let go of his hands that she had been clutching as he picked her up, and quickly reached into the airplane to grab the back of the seat. Thrust into the little cabin, she first stood on the seat and then turned around and slid down into it, almost hidden below the instrument panel. Her heart pounded. She was leaning far back, and she couldn't see anything and almost couldn't move, cradled as she was in the big seat. "Watch your hands." The door next to her slammed shut. The cabin smelled of leather and oil and other things she didn't know.

He walked around the tail of the plane and opened the left-hand door, securing it open with a latch on the strut. Inside, the face of his five-year-old daughter, flushed with excitement, peered at him from the other side of the cabin. Stepping up onto the little metal step that protruded from the bottom of the fuselage, he reached across the near seat toward her. "Hand me the end of the seat belt. Yes, that."

Clicking the seat belt into its socket, he continued to climb into the airplane, finally leaning back in his own seat and fastening his belt. He turned to look at her. "Okay?"

Her eyes wide, she blinked and nodded. He reached behind the seats and retrieved a pair of radio headphones that he used when flying in controlled airspace. They weren't needed at this field, so he adjusted them to a small size and placed them on her blond head. She grinned at him, the weight of the phones causing her head to bob until she learned to hold still. She sat upright (as upright as she could, with the plane tilted back on its tail wheel) and looked straight ahead. "Hello, tower," she said seriously into her fist.

He adjusted the throttle, worked the rudder pedals and turned the yoke back and forth, watching the ailerons moving on the wings. Turning the magneto switch, he pushed the starter button. The engine caught immediately, filling the cabin with noise and vibration. He throttled back, watching the tachometer settle. For a moment, they sat there in the noise. Wind eddied around the open door and explored the cabin. Blond hair scattered across her upturned face. A tiny hand gripped his leg through his trousers. He grinned at her. "Noisy, isn't it?"

With his toe he released the brakes. His palm pushed gently on the flat throttle knob, and the clattering engine noise grew into a smooth roar. He peered around outside, looking for other aircraft. They started to move. The little pink hand tightened on his leg.

She wanted to see outside, but couldn't lift her head high enough to get her eyes over the sill of the window next to her. In front, she could see only the blur of the propeller against the sky.

He taxied slowly across the grass, pulling the door closed beside him. The roar of the engine was just as loud, but the wind stopped whirling inside the cabin. They rocked gently as the fat wheels mushed over the uneven ground. At the end of the grass runway, he leaned forward and scanned for other planes. There wasn't much traffic at their airport, no control tower, and no radio contact. Just an occasional light plane taking off or landing, a single rather dilapidated hanger and a gas pump.

It was bumpier in the airplane than in their car, she thought. And a lot noisier. Her insides were tight. She knew that she was holding her breath, but somehow couldn't let it out. Her feet couldn't reach the floor of the plane. The front edge of the seat pressed hard against the backs of her legs. She watched her father lean forward and peer out the windows, one after the other. He wasn't saying anything. She wondered if he were as scared as she was, but she couldn't yell to him over the roar of the engine.

She had seen this airplane once before, when her dad had just bought it. All three of them—her father, her mother and she—had driven to the airport and walked around the red machine, admiring it and running their hands over the smooth surfaces. They made her sit in the grass while her mother and father climbed into the plane and sat talking. She finally got tired of waiting and called to them. Eventually, they both climbed down and her mother came and picked her up. "It's Daddy's new airplane!" Her mother sounded excited. Her dad did some things at the airplane, then joined them as they walked toward the car. He sounded even more excited than her mother did. "It's old, but it's in good shape!" After that, she heard them talk a lot about the airplane. Her mother didn't always sound excited.

Now the seat pushed against her back, and the rocking of the airplane got worse. Then suddenly they tipped forward, and the jolting stopped. She felt as though they were going to tip clear over. The belt across her lap got tighter. She drew in her breath even more, and grabbed at her father. She looked up at him. He had a big smile on his face as he turned to look at her. "Here we go!" he shouted.

Now she could just barely see out the window beside her. The trees and grass were speeding by, faster and faster.

And then the bouncing stopped. The ground outside drifted downward, and everything slowed. She felt very strange inside, the way she felt when her mother had taken her to the big store and they rode in an elevator.

"Breathe!" her father shouted to her. "Just relax! It's fun, like Coney Island." But she didn't let go of his leg for a long time.

After a while, the elevator feeling went away, and she looked around. Outside, the big red wing shaded her eyes like a porch awning. They weren't moving at all now. She could look down over the window sill and see a little play town, with tiny houses and roads. She pounded on her father's leg until he looked at her, and then she pointed out the window, trying to point downward. He laughed. She felt better now. She could breathe, although somehow she still couldn't let all her breath out. It was like the time when they took her to a swimming pool and held her head above the water as they walked her out into the deep end. She couldn't breathe right then, either. But it was fun!

It was scary again when he turned the airplane over on its side. She was afraid she was going to fall, but somehow it didn't feel like that. The seatbelt held her tight. It was as though the ground were tilted instead of the airplane. Even so, she held onto her father with one hand and something on the airplane with the other. She looked straight out the window at the tiny houses tilted up even past the end of the wing. "We're flying!" she shouted, reaching up to adjust the headphones that had become skewed on her head, but even she could not hear her own voice.

He leveled off at three thousand feet, and maneuvered the aircraft through several lazy S-curves, dipping the wings first in one direction and then in the other. The Aeronca recovered easily from the turns, without losing altitude. *It was going to be a fun little plane!* Older than the planes he had learned to fly in, the Aeronca rattled a bit, and air leaked in through panel openings, but it was stable and reliable, they said—and cheap. He watched his daughter as they flew, wondering how much she saw, whether she could tell how high they were, and if she were nervous. Yes, he decided, she's nervous. But she's a real trooper. Not afraid of anything.

He remembered a few weeks before, when he had taken her to the amusement park. On the little kiddy rides with her, he got dizzy and nearly threw up, but she laughed and laughed, enjoying the motion and the noise and the bouncing. She kept begging him, "One more time, Daddy, *please!*" Until finally he could take no more, and staggered away with her, to sit on a bench while she ate ice cream and he recovered his equilibrium. Later his wife had said he was "already an old man," and laughed.

His wife hadn't laughed a little while ago, however, when he told her that he and their daughter were going flying. "I don't feel good about that," she complained. "What if something happens up there—you're going to have all you can handle without a five year old girl to worry about."

"Nothing's going to happen." He would rather have taken his wife, but she had long ago adamantly refused to fly with him. "It's just like riding in a car," he protested, but she shook her head.

"You go. I'm not going to sit out there in the car waiting for you to come back, wondering if you're both dead in a field somewhere."

And here they were, droning over the countryside in a flivver of an old airplane, looking down at the world and all its scurrying and rushing around and worrying about bills and plumbing and patching roofs. Here he could relax, because here the world slowed down. "Next time," he said to his daughter, "we'll get something higher for you to sit on, so you can see out better."

She never heard him, though, and continued to look down at the fields and roads, her nose pressed against the glass and her chin hooked on the narrow windowsill. Now she had both hands on the door next to her face, craning to see everything. He rested his hand on the leg of her jumper, and she turned her face toward him. They both laughed. She made a tilting motion with her arms, and pointed at him. "You want more turns?" he yelled.

She nodded vigorously, causing the headphones to fall into her lap, and made the tilting motion again. So he turned the yoke and did some more S-curves, watching his beautiful child swinging her arms back and forth as though she were dancing on the playground, every once in a while looking out the window at the world far, far beneath them.

3. The Cessna

"After midnight the moon set and I was alone with the stars. I have often said that the lure of flying is the lure of beauty, and I need no other flight to convince me that the reason flyers fly, whether they know it or not, is the esthetic appeal of flying."

Amelia Earhart

"He won't believe this," Jenny chuckled as she sat in the left-hand seat, hands on the yoke, looking out past the still propeller at the expanse of the flying field. An old memory took control of her thoughts, of sitting in the right-hand seat, a huge pair of headphones perched on her head, of holding her breath while her father started the engine of the old Aeronca. And of sucking in even more air a few minutes later when the tail came up and they left the ground. That first flight!

Checking the throttle and the magneto switch, she set the brakes and pushed the starter. The little Lycoming started instantly. She let it idle while she put on her headset and turned the radio to the tower frequency. A Lear bizjet was negotiating for a landing. Check controls, flip several switches up, look around for other craft on the ground. Behind the airplane, she could see her rotating beacon flashing across the hanger door.

Buying this airplane was more exciting—much more exciting—than buying her first car. For one thing, her father had taken her out to shop for the car, and she didn't know enough to choose it for herself, except to pick from three or four that he had decided were "appropriate" for her. Not wanting to incur one of his bad moods, she had resigned herself to having the car he wanted her to have. Not that it wasn't a good car. She had driven it all through high school and college, finally trading it in when she got her first real job. But this beautiful white airplane, this was *hers*. She had flown in a lot of different planes while she was learning, and rented others as she built up her hours. She had decided what she wanted two whole years before she was ready to buy it. The Cessna 152 was reliable and easy to fly. They built them for years with only small changes in all that time. The main thing was that it was cheap to run, only about twice the cost of running her car. Flying was her only extravagance. Nearly every weekend she went up for at least a few hours. She felt at home in the air, like her dad used to say.

And she was comfortable in this little Cessna. She'd had it long enough to know it didn't have any bad habits. Now it was time to show off to him. As soon as the bizjet was down and off the runway, she got clearance from the tower to taxi out and take off. Once clear of the pattern, she turned south.

Flying alone like this was like a meditation. One has to be alert for other traffic and pay attention to the instruments on the panel, but another part of the mind is free to wander. Although one notices things on the ground, they seldom take up much space in one's consciousness. The rest of one's life gets played back and forth, feelings from earlier encounters and conversations, dreams for the future, regrets from the past—all the stuff that comes up for a person when they are alone and quiet.

She was pretty satisfied with her life. Her job was challenging enough without keeping her stressed out. She had friends she could count on and with whom she could have fun. She dated occasionally, and thought that some day she'd meet someone who would feel like *the one*, that man who would allow her to be herself and still offer her a sense of adventure. The perfect relationship. It was still a little hazy to her, just what this perfect relationship would be like. But she'd know it when it appeared. At the very least, he'd have to love flying.

She and her mom had come to an understanding a few years ago. After those tumultuous teen years, when almost everything she wanted to do made her mom mad or scared, they had settled into a mutually satisfying friendship. She moved out after she finished college, and her mom moved into a condo.

It was her dad she couldn't figure out. When she was young, he loved flying, and he infected her with the bug. After that first flight, he took her up with him once in a while despite her mother's protests. Those were the times she felt closest to him. After he got laid off at work that summer and had to sell the Aeronca, everything seemed different. She was twelve, and was keenly aware of the problems her parents were having. Eventually, he moved out and got a job up in Middletown. She got to see him only on occasional weekends, when he'd drive down and pick her up, and they'd try to figure out what to do together. It never included flying. He said he got to go up every once in a while, but he couldn't afford it much. She felt sorry for him, but he seemed so distant! They went to movies, and once he took her to King's Island. He didn't talk about himself much. In his apartment, she noticed a photograph of him in front of the old Aeronca. She decided right then that as soon as she could, she was going to get her license. And then she was going to get him back into the air. She wanted him to be that old Dad that she remembered!

Watching the big cumulus clouds ahead on the horizon, she thought about the name—her father's first name—that she had painted on the cowl right after she bought the Cessna. It felt strange, writing his name, instead of "Dad" as she always thought of him. Once, as a teenager, she had addressed him by name, playfully. He acted surprised, but he didn't say anything. Her mother would have said it was "inappropriate," but she wasn't around. Somehow, it didn't feel right, though, so she never repeated it. Later, alone back at home, it had made her angry. Why couldn't she call people by their names, instead of "mister" or "daddy?" She was a woman, fully grown, an adult! But every time she wrote his name on school documents, she remembered that uncomfortable feeling, a tinge of shame, a line crossed.

She followed the interstate most of the way down, swinging west just south of Troy to avoid traffic around the Dayton Airport, and then straight south again to the Middletown Airport. When she made contact with the tower, they cleared her to enter the pattern and land on runway 23 behind another Cessna, probably a student. She found a place to park and walked into the terminal building, removing her cap and shaking her curls, combing them out with her fingers.

Her hand began to shake when she picked up the telephone to call him. He hadn't known she was coming today, except that she had told him, "One of these Saturdays." He answered the phone immediately. "Hi, Dad!" she said. "Guess where I am!"

When he was obviously fumbling for an answer, she said, "I'm at the airport, Hook Field. I came down to see if you'd take a ride with me."

"Well, now," he replied, "we could at least have lunch. Want me to pick you up there?"

"Would you? I have something to show you."

"Okay, lets see—give me fifteen minutes. In the terminal?"

"Right. I'll be waiting."

She hung up and began pacing. *Maybe my timing is off. He didn't pick up on 'taking a ride with me.' He's probably busy.* As she paced, she kept watching for his car out front.

The terminal was busy. Pilots stood around in little groups, talking. A city bus arrived, discharging a group of people who were evidently traveling together. A woman approached them and greeted them warmly. "Our plane is due in at any minute." The group huddled around her.

Outside, the bus pulled away, and was replaced immediately by a taxicab. A man pulling a case on wheels pushed through the doors and climbed into the cab.

A few more minutes passed before his car pulled up at the curb. She dashed down the steps and pulled the door open to greet her father. He smiled and reached out his hand. In the back seat, a woman sat, hunched forward, her arms crossed on the front seat back. "Jenny," he said, "this is Holly. She works with me."

"Hi, Jenny," said Holly, warmly. "It's good to meet you."

"Oh, hi, uh, Holly. I was just in the neighborhood," she lied, "and thought I'd look up my dad." She looked at her father, feeling helpless and inept.

"Well, get in. Where would you like to have lunch?" His tone was just a little too cordial, as though he knew this would be a shock. He had never before shown her that he had women friends. She had always assumed that he dated, at least, but the reality hadn't sunk in until this moment. She got into the car and closed the door.

"I don't care, really. Where do you usually eat?"

"They have good food at Randolph's," he said, pulling away from the curb. "Let's go there."

At lunch, Holly sat down opposite her father in the booth, and invited Jenny to sit next to her. "We can keep a better eye on your father," she laughed.

She was young for him. *Of course,* Jenny thought, *that's what they all do, isn't it?* But she sat down next to Holly. *Clever. She doesn't want to give me her place next to him, so she offers a compromise. Oh, I shouldn't be feeling this way. He has a right to have his own life. I'm glad he's not just sitting home brooding. Mom has gone on with her life. He should, too.*

The lunch went well enough, considering. Holly wasn't an air-head; in fact, she was pretty sharp. She didn't let the man control the conversation, but gave both of the others plenty of opportunity to participate. She asked about Jenny's flying, but nothing was said about the new plane. She called Jenny's father "Richard," instead of "Rich" (which was the name painted on the cowl of the Cessna). By the end of an hour, Jenny was feeling more relaxed.

Rich finally looked at his watch. "Wow," he said, "You're on the clock, aren't you?" He turned to Holly. "She's renting an airplane by the hour, and we're costing her some money."

"No, I'm not," Jenny said.

"You're not?"

"No. That's why I came down here today."

He was genuinely puzzled. "You phoned from the airport that you wanted me to go up with you."

"Okay," Jenny said patiently. "Come back to the airport and I'll show you."

Holly said nothing through all this, probably thinking that the game was a family thing. Rich picked up the check and the three of them left the restaurant. On the drive to the airport, he made small talk, letting Jenny have her little surprise in her own way. Jenny led them through the airport terminal and out onto the parking strip. In front of the Cessna, she turned to face them and gestured at the plane. "It's mine," she said simply.

Holly gasped and gushed. Rich smiled broadly. "No kidding!"

"I came down here to take you up as her first passenger." The statement wasn't as easy as she had wanted it to be. There was an edge in it that she sensed, but the others didn't seem to notice.

"Gee," he said. "I would love to, but ..."

"Richard, go!" Holly pleaded, catching the importance of the moment—the importance of the whole trip down here for Jenny. "I can run some errands and come back for you in an hour or so—how much time do you want, Jenny?"

Rich was uncomfortable. "I don't think it's a good time, Jenny. We were working on some contracts. I'm sorry. I wish you had let me know beforehand."

Jenny turned abruptly and walked around the plane, checking the control surfaces—obviously trying to hide her feelings. "Okay, Dad. Another time. Holly, it was nice meeting you."

The other two stood by the wingtip of the gleaming white and blue Cessna, watching Jenny climb into the cabin. She waved at them, and started the engine. Holly looked at Rich and said something that was drowned out in the noise. Then they backed away a few steps, clear of the airplane. They could see Jenny talking on her radio, and in a moment the airplane began to roll. As it turned away from them, they turned their backs to avoid the prop wash.

Jenny didn't look back. As she turned onto the taxi strip, she caught a glimpse of them standing by the fence, watching her go. She took a deep breath and let it out. "Hook Tower, Cessna alpha bravo three-five-one at the terminal. Request permission taxi to the active."

"Cessna alpha bravo three-five-one. Proceed to runway two-three. Barometer two nine point nine six. Wind southwest at seven to ten."

The two were silent while they watched the white airplane taxi to the end of the runway and then turn and take off. Then Holly said, "She was *so* hurt."

Rich looked down at his hands on the wire fence. "Yeah."

"Why didn't you go with her? That was a big thing for her."

"I just wasn't ready to deal with that now." He turned and walked toward the terminal.

Holly followed him. "Deal with what, Richard?"

They walked silently through the terminal and got into the car. Rich's face was a thin-lipped mask.

Holly sat sideways in the seat, facing him. "Talk to me, damn it!"

He looked at her, and then down at his hands on the wheel. "Flying used to be a passion for me, like it is for Jenny." He paused, without moving. "At some point, I don't know exactly, after I lost my family and my airplane, it just all turned around. I didn't want anything to do with airplanes anymore."

"Not even just to go up with her in her new plane? She was obviously wanting your approval. Did you see the name on the nose of the airplane?"

He looked out the window, away from her. "Yes."

"Hey, this is your problem, Richard. I'm not in it. But it feels to me like it's about something more than just flying."

He drove silently. Holly finally turned around abruptly and fastened her seat belt. Neither spoke until they pulled up in front of his apartment.

"Richard," she said, "I love you. You know that. But I'm scared. It's been ten years since your divorce. I wish you could let go of that life so we might have one of our own."

His fingers tightened on the steering wheel.

Her voice softened. "Okay, I hear you," she said. "I'm sorry. I just don't like to see you shutting down, that's all. And that's what you did back there."

There was another silence, until she finally spoke again. "Let's forget the contracts for today. I'm not in the mood for that. Okay?"

"Okay."

"I don't want to see you go inside and just sulk for the rest of the weekend, either. C'mon." She was pleading again, her hand on his arm. "Let's drive down to Cincinnati and try to get tickets to a concert."

He leaned over the steering wheel and rested his forehead against his knuckles. "Okay," he said.

4. The Bird

Nothing stands alone. All things, all events, are both individual and parts of something else. Sometimes small things portend large consequences.

--unknown

Three times, he started dialing her number, and each time hung up before the connection was made. He poured himself a brandy, and walked around outside the old farmhouse. Finally, he tossed off the drink and went back inside to make the call.

"Hello." His daughter's voice was like honey.

He choked a little (from the brandy), and said, "I've been puttering here on this bird, and thought you might like to see her. Got a way to go to finish her, but she's taking shape."

Jenny was obviously delighted. "I'd love to, Dad! When?"

"Well, tomorrow's Sunday. If you don't have other plans."

"I'll be down first thing in the morning. I'll call you from the airport, okay?"

"Okay."

He hung up, aware of the tension in his gut. *Why is this always so hard?* He thought of calling Holly to talk to her about it, but decided not to. Instead, he poured another brandy and went out to the barn to look at his new ultralight aircraft, or as he called it, his "bird." It was all just framework, without any clear shape, aluminum tubing with guy wires holding it together. He sat down in the pilot's seat, for the hundredth time, and moved the stick back and forth, looking out the barn doors at the rolling field outside. Propped against the wall was the almost lacy framework of the wing, looking 'way too big for this little craft.

There was no cabin in the airplane. The pilot sat exposed to the wind and elements, nothing in front of him but a little pylon with a tiny instrument panel. The rudder pedals were out in front of that, the very front edge of the airplane. The little engine, which sat temporarily on a wooden stand nearby, was to be mounted behind his seat. It would start like a lawn mower, with a rope that ran through pulleys over the pilot's head. It reminded him of the instruction sheet for an outboard motor he had bought a long time ago: *To start, pull sharply on the rope. Repeat until the motor starts.* In those days, starting a small engine usually took many pulls.

Finally, he went into the house and went to bed.

The next morning, he had been lying awake for almost an hour, watching the sun play on the leaves of the maple tree next to the window, when she called. "Okay," she announced, "I'm here. Where are you?" It was as though she were perpetually happy. Her voice was always bright and cheerful. *Maybe that's why it's so hard,* he thought, but he said, "I'll be right over to pick you up."

"Bye, Dad."

Her smile, when he spotted her standing at the curb in front of the terminal, was as cheery as her voice.

Even though his gut was tight, he tried to match her cheerfulness. "I haven't had breakfast yet. Are you hungry?"

"Starved. How about some pancakes? Isn't there a place on the way?"

As they drove, she chattered on. "I can't believe I'm going to see your new airplane! I'm so excited!"

He gradually relaxed over breakfast. His daughter was no longer a girl, but was even more beautiful than when he had left. He wondered why she wasn't married yet. She must have hundreds of men pawing after her. He almost said that out loud, but changed his mind. Instead, they talked about the ultralight.

"How will you get it to an airfield?" she asked.

"Actually, I don't have to. There's a pasture right next to the barn, and it's plenty long enough if there's just a little wind from the west."

She looked concerned. "You're going to fly out of a pasture?"

He laughed. "People used to do it all the time. There weren't any airfields for years!"

"But what happens … " Her voice trailed off.

"If I crack it up?" He was now enjoying himself. "Maybe I can hire a crash truck to stand by."

"You're teasing me! I'm serious!"

"Well, the manufacturer's rep is going to check it out before I get cleared to fly it. He's the one who will find out if the pasture isn't big enough."

"You mean, he'll fly it first?"

"Yep. If he doesn't think I've done a good job on it, he's not going to risk *his* neck."

They paid the check and got back on the road to the farm. Somehow, glancing now and then at his daughter sitting there beside him in the car, he felt a little of the old joy, the way he used to feel before things all came apart. But she was changed, this young woman. This wasn't the sweet, coy little girl who used to charm him out of anything she took a liking to, whom he could pick up and throw up over his shoulder while she squealed with delight. This was almost a stranger to him, yet one that he felt tied to by a thread stronger than he could break. A thread that terrified him.

As they pulled into the rutted lane back to the farmhouse, Jenny said, "You know, this is only the second time I've been to your new home." Then she looked over at him, cocking her head the way she used to, and put her hand on his arm. "I'm sorry. That sounded like a complaint."

He started to protest, but she broke in, "No! It *was* a complaint! I don't see enough of you!"

"I'm not very good company these days."

"You don't *have* to be good company. You're my Dad!" The thread tightened.

He parked the car next to the old house and they got out. "Well," he said, "You ready for this?"

She linked her arm through his and they walked across the yard to the barn. He swung the big doors wide to let the morning light into the dim interior. Jenny walked around the aluminum framework, studying it. "Will it have any covering?"

He laughed. "Only the wing and tail surfaces."

"And you sit out here, without anything between you and ..."

"Yep. You'll notice that there's a good, solid strap here, to hold me in. They furnished some clothesline for that, but I had some webbing left over from a lawn chair."

"Daddy!" She was nine years old again, loving being teased by her father.

He showed her the wing and tail assemblies, and pointed out how they attached to the fuselage. She examined everything. This was not a nine-year-old any more. Then they walked out of the big doors to the pasture. The sun on their backs felt warm and comforting.

She turned to him. "How soon will it be ready to fly?"

"I don't know. I can't seem to put much time on it these days. I just thought it was finished enough to show you that she's a real airplane, anyway."

"There's only one thing I don't like about it."

"What's that?"

"There's only one seat. How am I going to ride in it with you?" She was squinting in the early sun, watching his face. When a smile began to appear, she laughed and grabbed his shirt front with both hands. "I want to fly with you!" She shook him vigorously by the shirt.

He grinned, but slipped from her grasp to turn around and pull the barn doors closed. "It's going to be a while," he said.

Inside the big old farm kitchen, they talked and drank coffee. It was mostly small-talk. He asked her about her mother.

"She's doing great. She's still working at the farmers' market in Batavia, and loving it. It's funny, both of you ending up on farms, after living most of your lives in the city."

"I like the quiet here. I go out when it's beginning to get dark, and just walk around with a brandy in my hand and look at the trees."

She cocked her head to the side. "Aren't you lonely?"

"I think I was born lonely. But no, I'm in town every day, almost. And Holly and I do things together." He poured himself another cup of coffee, and held the pot over her cup.

Jenny waved the offer away, and rested her cheek on the palm of her hand, with her elbow on the table. "Are you going to get married?" Her eyes were serious.

"No."

"She's not the one for you?"

"She's great. She puts up with a lot."

"Well, then, why ..."

"She deserves better than me." It was a simple statement of finality.

She lifted her head off her hand. "Daddy, what is it? What's gotten you so down on yourself?"

He stood up and picked up a pair of binoculars from a shelf. "C'mon, I want to show you something." Leading her out the kitchen door, he pointed down a path. "I just noticed 'em the other day."

The two walked down the path to a large pond almost hidden in the forest. What seemed to be a kind of island at the far end of the pond was overgrown with large trees. "Look up at the tops of those trees," he said, handing her the binoculars and pointing.

Several of the trees were topped with nests, and a number of large birds could be seen in them or on branches nearby. "Blue herons," he announced.

"Wow," she said softly. "They're gorgeous. Oh, look, one just flew!"

"Wish I could get pictures of them."

The large bird spread its wings and glided, circling the pond and finally dropping gracefully among some reeds at the far side.

"I've never seen one so close up." She continued to peer through the binoculars. "Isn't it awesome, flying like that! And I know how it feels!" She lowered the binoculars and grinned at her father. "And so do you!"

They stood by the shore of the pond for a while, until they began to be found by those other flying creatures, mosquitoes. After swatting a few, they both turned and walked back up the path.

At the farm house, Jenny said apologetically, "I should be getting back. I have to do some things at home tonight for work tomorrow."

"Let me turn off the coffee pot." He went into the house, and returned a moment later. Jenny watched him, silently, and then followed him to the car.

On the drive back to town, she said, "I'm worried about you, Daddy."

He looked at her and grinned. "I'm okay."

After a few moments, she replied, "I don't believe you."

When they pulled up at the airplane terminal, she opened the car door, and then turned. "Will you take that ride with me—now?"

He hesitated.

"C'mon," she laughed, "you afraid to fly with me?"

"Okay. Let me park the car."

She stood on the curb until he parked the car and joined her again. They walked through the terminal and out to the white Cessna. "You want the left seat?" she asked.

"No, you're the captain."

She thought he looked awkward, climbing into the cabin. She walked around the airplane, checking the control surfaces, and then climbed in.

"Are you being careful because I'm here?" he asked, grinning.

"Actually, I do that all the time." They both buckled up.

"They taught you well."

"Yes, they did." She put on her cap and then her radio headset. *Very professional,* he thought, watching her ready the plane's instruments for flight. She contacted the tower, looked right and left, and started the engine. As they started to roll, she slipped on her sunglasses. "There's an extra pair up there," she said, pointing. He put them on, feeling strange. It had been years since he last wore sunglasses. "Flying glasses," she used to call them.

Rolling down the runway, when they reached fifty knots she eased back on the yoke to lift the nose wheel, and in a moment the airplane rose gently from the pavement. She looked over at him. "We're flying!"

They both laughed at that reminder of her first flight. Her words had become a favorite family expression for years.

After they left the airport pattern, she turned west, away from town. "You want to take it?" she shouted. He shook his head. She removed her hands from the yoke and put them into her lap, watching him. He shook his head, and she took control again. Turning the plane once more, she headed for his farm.

It was easy to spot. In fact, she had found it once before, flying over and returning home without contacting him. The pasture that was to be his landing field looked much too small from here. She banked the plane so he could see better, and pointed out the pond where they had watched the herons an hour before. He nodded.

After a half hour of flying, he motioned that he was ready to return. The noise of the engine and the wind discouraged conversation, so they were mostly silent until after they landed and she pulled up at the gate, letting the engine idle. They said their goodbyes, and she leaned over and kissed him on the cheek before he climbed out.

"See you soon," she said.

"I'll let you know when I finish the bird."

"I love you, Dad."

He waved as he closed the door, and then walked toward the fence.

From the gate, he watched her taxi out again and take off. He didn't see her remove her sunglasses and wipe the tears from her face.

5. The Aeronca

Into the distance, a ribbon of black
Stretched to the point of no turning back
A flight of fancy on a windswept field
Standing alone my senses reeled
A fatal attraction holding me fast, how
Can I escape this irresistible grasp?
Can't keep my eyes from the circling skies
Tongue-tied and twisted Just an earth-bound misfit, I.[1]

It was something he had always wanted to do—fly. As a boy, he built model airplanes out of balsa wood and tissue paper, and tried to fly them in the park across the street. They were powered with rubber bands that he wound up with his finger, turning the propellers until his hand ached. Most of his models would fly, but they always crashed within a few flights, and so he kept building until his teen years, when other things seemed to demand his attention.

No airplane, large or small, could fly over without his craning his neck to see what it was. He learned to identify nearly all of them, and often on a Saturday morning he rode his bicycle to the airport to watch the planes take off and land.

Once, a man noticed him hanging around and asked him if he wanted to go up for a ride.

"I don't have any money," he replied.

"No sweat. My plane is back there in the hanger. Help me roll it out and we'll take 'er up for a spin."

His dream had come true! Eagerly, he followed the man back along the line of hangers and into an open door. In the rear of the dark hanger sat an old Aeronca Champ, its red paint stained with oil and chipped from the metal fittings. His

---

[1] Pink Floyd, "Learning to Fly"

new friend pointed to a handle on the bottom of the fuselage near the tail. "Lift it there when I tell you, and we'll swing her around and just walk her out backwards."

The airplane was surprisingly light. The two pulled it out into the light at the door to the hanger, then turned it around again to face the airfield. Rich stood back and looked at the old aircraft. To him, it was beautiful.

The pilot checked the gas tank and the oil level, then opened the door on the side of the plane. Inside were two seats in tandem. "Get in the back seat," he told Rich.

Heart pounding, Rich climbed clumsily into the strange little plane, twisting his legs in order to get them around the control stick protruding in front of the seat. He peered down to see where he could put his feet without interfering with the rudder pedals. He already knew what most of the controls were for, but he'd never touched any.

"Pull that strap over you and connect it to the buckle." The pilot made sure Rich was secure before going around to the other side and reaching through the window to move the throttle. He then turned a rotary switch on the panel, and ducked under the wing struts to grab the propeller. Swinging the prop through a couple of revolutions, he returned to the window and made more adjustments. Then, standing in front of the airplane, he pulled hard on the propeller. The engine popped. Once more he pulled the prop, and was rewarded by a cloud of blue smoke and a loud clatter as the engine took hold and began idling.

He walked swiftly around to the right side of the plane, pulled on a rope attached to wheel chocks, and climbed into the front seat. Adjusting the throttle until the engine sound smoothed out, he peered out the windows on both sides and craned his neck to see ahead. The nose of the plane, with its whirling propeller, blocked a direct view in front. Carefully, he advanced the throttle and the plane began to move. He reached out to close the open door.

Zigzagging across the apron so that he could see where they were going, he taxied over to the end of the asphalt runway. After pausing to look around once more, he flashed his running lights on and off, and waited until a bright green light appeared in the control tower. He pointed the nose directly down the runway and pushed the throttle all the way forward.

Rich held his breath as the seat back pushed against him. He couldn't see anything ahead of them, but watched the ground move past at an increasing rate. Then, smoothly, the tail of the plane lifted off the ground, and the bumpiness of their movement over the pavement lessened greatly. He could see the fat tires rolling ever more swiftly, and then suddenly they lifted clear of the ground. Flying!

Once more, the plane nosed upward as it gained altitude, and Rich couldn't see ahead. But beside them, he watched the ground drift away. They crossed over a road where a car passed by. Then there were buildings and houses and water towers and electrical power poles. He had a slow-motion view of the earth, as though they were an eagle soaring on the wind.

Rich had never experienced anything like this before. He tried to relate the sensations to the model airplanes he had built as a boy, but it was impossible. Watching something fly, whether a bird or an airplane, was nothing like *being there, in the air, really flying!*

The pilot flew them over a section of the city. Rich could see the Ohio River meandering along, and even make out boats and barges.

Then, without warning, he realized that they were descending. The airport runway was straight ahead, and the noise of the engine had dropped to a whisper. In another minute, they touched down. The ride was over.

He made a decision: as soon as he was able, he was going to fly, and he was going to fly in his own airplane. All his visions of the future, all his dreams about what he would do when he grew up, suddenly faded into that one promise he made to himself that Saturday morning over the farmland of Southern Ohio.

Years later, he could still remember vividly that first flight, especially that instant when the wheels left the ground and they were airborne.

In the next few years, he had only a couple of chances to fly again. School and work and romance took all his time and money. That first Aeronca was his icon, and he pinned a picture of it over his bed so that he could go to sleep looking at his future. It was ten years before he would be able to begin flying lessons, and twenty before he finally realized his dream of owning his own plane. By that time, he had a wife and daughter, and the expense of the airplane was a serious consideration in family finances.

There was no doubt about what airplane he wanted: an Aeronca. The plane he finally bought was red, like the one he first flew in, although a newer model with side-by-side seats.

And here he was, finally, where he had always dreamed he'd be. A secure job, a good home, a wife and daughter, a bright future—and his own airplane. Like most of us—at that age, anyway—he assumed it was forever.

6. Holly

Holly drove up the old lane to the farmhouse, expecting to find Richard in the barn working on his new airplane. The afternoon autumn sun played hide and seek among the veils of high cirrus clouds. The air was still. The old sycamore tree in the front yard was beginning to turn yellow. She loved the country, especially this time of year. Maybe he would leave his project and go for a ride with her. He'd been preoccupied with that funny-looking airplane lately, and she had hung around every weekend, watching him work, but she wanted more of his attention. Opening the door of her car, she reached behind her and pulled out the cold six-pack.

Her footsteps crunched in the gravel. She took the clip out of her hair and shook her curls free. Rounding the corner of the barn, she saw the big doors standing open.

The ultralight was gone. Holly was stunned. For a moment she thought he might have removed the wing again—the last time she was here he was installing it, and the tangle of aluminum tubing and wires had begun to look like an airplane. But the barn was empty. No airplane, no Richard.

He knew she was coming out this afternoon. He would have called if he weren't going to be here. She walked into the barn, feeling disappointed and a little bit angry. Turning around in the doorway, she looked out at the pasture. Faint tire tracks led away from the barn. "Oh, Richard!" She stamped her foot in frustration. She had wanted to see him take his first flight!

Sitting down in the open door, she took a bottle from the six-pack and tried to twist the cap off, managing only to scrape her hand. Getting up and finding a tool in the barn, she opened the beer and took a large swallow. Then she returned to the doorway and sat down to wait.

The only sounds were several crows calling in the distance. In a few minutes she would hear the little engine, probably coming from over there across the pond, and the strange little aircraft would grow in her vision over the trees. Richard said that the ultralight couldn't fly very high, nor very fast.

7. Passion

At sixteen, flying became an addiction to Rich. After that first flight, he continued to haunt the little airport. Other private pilots came to recognize him, and occasionally took him up, either on short sightseeing flights or trips to other nearby airports that they had reason to visit. He didn't see the fellow who had given him his first ride, until one day he was sitting on a bench by the terminal, eating ice cream, when the same man recognized him and stopped. "Hi," he said. Remember me? Ralph Underwood? We went up together sometime back."

"Sure, I remember you," Rich replied. You have that Red Champ."

Ralph sat next to him on the bench and they chatted about airplanes and the weather. Rich felt warmly toward this man just a few years older than he. They seemed to have a lot in common—certainly a shared enthusiasm for flying. Ralph invited him for another ride, "next week, when I'll have more time."

The following Saturday, Rich waited by the terminal all morning, his heart racing. He watched planes take off and land, imagining himself in them, at the controls. Finally, Ralph arrived, and the two of them walked down to the hanger and rolled out the Aeronca. "Would you like to take lessons?" Ralph asked.

"From you?" Rich was incredulous.

"I can teach you, but I'm not certified as an instructor yet, so you can't apply for a license. Just keep it between us, though, okay?"

"Heck yes!"

That Saturday was his first lesson, when he learned what the stick felt like in his hand as the wind buffeted the control surfaces of the airplane. He kept his hands and feet on the controls feeling their movement while Ralph performed gentle maneuvers. For a few minutes, he even had the Aeronca under his own control, making it sway gently from side to side as the wings dipped first this way and then that. By the time they landed, his knees felt like rubber. He thanked Ralph profusely.

Ralph laughed. "You really get off on that, don't you?"

"Can't remember ever having that much fun."

"I didn't eat lunch yet. Want to come up to my place and have a bite to eat?"

"Sure." Rich had indeed found a new friend.

They drove up to Mount Adams, where Ralph had a small apartment in an old brick building that had once been a large home. Wooden stairs had been added on the outside of the building to his third-floor rooms. Inside, he bustled around making sandwiches, while talking all the time. Rich sat at the little wooden table, watching and listening.

Ralph asked him about himself, where he lived, what school he went to, and whether he had any girlfriends.

"Oh, I used to have a girlfriend, but she dumped me for some guy," Rich admitted.

"Did you get any?" Ralph was grinning at him.

"Naw." Rich blushed. "She said she wasn't going to do that until she got married."

"That's what they all say at first. You got to keep the pressure on 'em. They'll all do it, though. I know."

"You got a girlfriend?"

"You better believe it. You want to see some pictures of her?" Ralph retrieved a pack of photographs from a drawer.

Rich looked at the first one and turned red. All the photos were nudes. As Ralph handed them to him one by one, Rich was too shy to look at them closely. He took each one, glanced at it quickly and turned it over in a stack on the table. He didn't want Ralph to think he hadn't seen his share of naked girls. "Wow," he said simply.

"Some knockers, eh? I use these pictures to beat off every day."

"How'd you get her to pose for you?"

"She loves it," Ralph replied. "She wants to be a model, and I told her I'd get her some jobs with these." He laughed.

Rich was aroused by the photographs. He picked up the stack and looked through the pictures again.

"Hey, you want to do it now?"

Rich looked up. "Do what?"

"Beat off. Go ahead, get your jollies. I'll do it with you."

His heart pounding, Rich swallowed. "Here?"

"Why not? Nobody here but us."

His excitement was crowding out his embarrassment. Ralph picked up one of the photographs and turned it around so Rich could look at it. "Look at that. Wouldn't you just like to get inside that? I can probably fix you up with her."

Rich unzipped his pants and allowed his erection to stick out. His hand shook as he began masturbating.

"Here, let me help you with that," Ralph said.

After that, things changed for Rich. He still went down to the airport on Saturdays, but he hoped he wouldn't run into Ralph there. What had happened in Ralph's apartment on that Saturday kept coming back to him, like memories of a scary scene in a movie that both repelled him and pulled at him. Sex had been something private to him, what he thought about when he was alone in his room at night. It was never talked about in his family, and it embarrassed him to hear his friends discuss it at school. All his mother had ever said to him was, "Someday, when you're older, you'll understand." He had spoken cryptically of his nighttime fantasies to the Father in confession, but never went into detail—nor was any asked for. Those fantasies felt dangerous to him, and he guarded them from the daylight.

Now, it was as though they were released into the world where he could no longer control them. Those troubling dreams of finding himself naked in public became somehow real. He never told the Father, nor anybody else, about Ralph.

Twice more, they went flying together, and then went up to Ralph's apartment "for sandwiches." The second time, Rich changed his mind at the last minute, and left Ralph standing at the foot of the wooden stairs to his apartment. He walked swiftly to the street car line and went home, feeling ashamed. He spent the rest of the weekend in his room. He tried to pray, but somehow couldn't.

Rich stopped going to the airport on Saturdays. Flying was still what he thought about the most, but it was always accompanied by something uncomfortable, a feeling that he kept pushing away.

8. Karma

Eventually, and gradually, his yearning to fly, as well as the discomfort, faded. He finished his schooling, and met and married a young woman who admired his gentleness and quiet manner. He was handy with mechanical things, maintaining his own cars and fixing appliances. His competence in his work produced a comfortable level of living. After a few years, he began to think again about flying.

Not long after his daughter was born, Rich started flying lessons. It was a way for him to occupy himself while his wife was preoccupied with motherhood. The few hours of instruction by Ralph had given him some confidence, and it didn't take long before he was ready to solo. That reduced the cost of the lessons somewhat, which pleased his wife.

"You're renting an airplane every week—it's like renting a car," she complained. You're just buying an airplane for somebody else."

"You're right," he replied. "And one of these days I want my own plane."

"It's an expensive hobby!"

"Well, as soon as I get my license I can start taking you and Jenny up with me."

"Oh, no. You're not getting me up in one of those little things."

"But I thought you liked the idea, when we used to talk about it."

She was quiet for a minute. "It used to sound like fun, I guess. Now that we've got a child, I'm not so sure I want to take the chance."

Before he could respond to that, she added emphatically, "And you're not taking Jenny up, either!"

"But ..." He watched her back disappearing into the kitchen.

Eventually, however, he got her to admit that, while she was scared and would not fly with him herself, if Jenny wanted to try it once, she could. "But if you scare her, you'll never get another chance!"

Rich didn't bring up the subject again for a long time. Meanwhile, he got his pilot's license, and took a part-time job in a hardware store to pay for his flying.

Alone in the air, he seemed to let go of tension and uncertainties. For a short time, problems at work and at home just floated away. Some people walk around a golf course for their regeneration. He flew. Part of it was the solitude. He liked to be alone at least sometimes. He loved his wife Margaret, and he adored the little girl that greeted him at the door each afternoon.

Jenny was active and bright. When he talked to her about flying in the air, she listened to him, fascinated. He took her to the airport to watch airplanes come and go. On the first of these visits, however, he felt a vague discomfort. As much as he loved airplanes and flying, something about that place made him feel—*something*.

After that day, he took her to a different airport, where he said there were more interesting airplanes and there was a deck on the roof of the terminal where they could see better. The first time a big twin-engine plane turned away from the terminal to taxi out to the runway, the blast of wind engulfed the two standing by the rail. She cried out, and he turned her around with her back to the wind, and shouted in her ear, "It's just the wind, it doesn't hurt you—but always turn your back so you don't get dust in your eyes." After that, she simply did what he had told her, adding one more bit of information to her inquisitive mind.

When she was about five, he bought his own airplane. They all went out to the airport to see it, but he didn't say anything about either his wife or his daughter going up with him. A few times he took a friend up with him. Mostly he was satisfied just to enjoy the solitary pleasure of flying on his own.

One day, his wife said to him, "You've been talking to Jenny about her flying with you, haven't you? She's starting to bug me about it."

"Well," he answered, "I think she's getting old enough. She's five, and she won't wet her pants, and she'll do what I tell her while we're up."

Jenny agreed. "Daddy, when are you going to take me flying?!!"

His wife turned to the girl. "One of these days, Jenny. When you're older."

"Soon," Rich said.

And "soon" finally came.

Jenny had flown! Afterward, Rich stopped at the counter in the airport office and bought her a little pair of wings. He helped her pin them on her jacket, and she paraded around the room showing them to everyone in the place.

Jenny was sold on flying. Nearly every weekend she asked Rich if he'd take her with him. His wife was plainly concerned. "I read every day about plane crashes. I don't like it. I don't want to lose both of you in one accident!"

"You don't object when I take her with me in the car."

"That's different."

"She's probably safer in the airplane. You don't have all the crazy drivers to worry about."

It was an endless argument that occasionally got more intense, depending upon how well Rich and his wife were getting along otherwise. He chose times to take Jenny up when his wife seemed more relaxed. Sometimes, the family could talk about flying without the conversation ending in another disagreement, or worse.

Flying with Jenny was a real joy for Rich. She sat still when he told her to, and she learned the jargon and the procedures needed to prepare the airplane for flight. She walked around the plane, wiggling the rudder and the elevator surfaces, and looked at the tires, pronouncing them "okay." He even built a little stairway that she could roll up to the plane herself in order to get into it, and stenciled her name on it. It was still fun to watch her scrambling to get from the stairway to the seat. Behind the seat he kept a small pillow that she knew to get out and put under her so she could see outside. Once inside, she closed the door and fastened her seat belt without being told. She insisted on wearing a heavy pair of headphones so she could hear Rich talking on the radio. Everything that happened was an adventure and a delight for them both.

The bond between them grew through the next few years. He took her to work with him one day when his company organized a special "kids' day" for the employees. While the atmosphere in the office on that day was unusually light—there were seven or eight children to entertain at the same time their parents were trying to be productive—Jenny was a perfect little "secretary," reading his mail and writing memos to her mother and school chums. He made up a little nameplate for her "desk." After that, to her it was "our" company.

She was as shocked as he the day "our" company announced that his department was being eliminated in a cost-cutting reorganization. She was twelve at the time, old enough to wonder why such a thing should happen. His wife was furious, and at times seemed to blame him for what happened. For a while, he kept his confidence that he'd find another job immediately, and began sending out résumés.

When the severance pay ran out, he had no choice but to sell the Aeronca. His wife found a job in a produce store, and they all tightened their belts. But sitting at home alone all day, trying to follow up on ads in the newspaper and trade magazines, calling people who never returned his calls, and facing down the women he ran into in the grocery stores who wondered why he wasn't at work, he finally hit the bottom. He went for days without shaving. He began to drink, but even that didn't seem to help. Besides, it was too expensive. His wife kept their finances in her control, and she didn't allow for such extravagances.

She also began coming home late from work. He would fix dinner for Jenny and himself, and flop down on the couch to watch television.

Jenny, on the other hand, watched him closely. When she saw him moping, she brought him something she had been reading and ask him questions about it. If she thought he was watching too much television, she took the remote from him and insisted that they talk instead. Their conversations were mostly about her school. She took the little plastic airplane model that she had assembled herself down from the fireplace mantle and stored it away someplace.

One night his wife came home late and told him she wanted a divorce. She had obviously been drinking. She moved her clothes to the guest room. Soon she was staying out all night.

On one of these occasions, Rich went to bed early, deeply depressed. He lay awake, thinking about all that had happened in the past year, from living a satisfying and easy life to being completely without personal resources, without love. He cried uncontrollably in the darkness.

In the midst of his agony, he heard the door open quietly, and Jenny came in and lay down next to him. He reached over and pulled her close. She was the one person in the world who still cared if he lived or died.

After a while, his sobbing quieted, and he became aware of her scent and the smoothness of her body under her thin nightgown.

That night he dreamed about flying. He and Jenny, alone in the sky, holding each other, ecstatic with the freedom. Even the airplane seemed to evaporate, leaving them soaring effortlessly in the air. He was quoting to her a poem as they flew, one that he had read years before and that had stayed with him ever since:

Oh! I have slipped the surly bonds of earth
And danced the skies on laughter-silvered wings;

And she laughed that laugh of hers, and kissed him. And then she spread her arms wide and tilted them to one side and then to the other, and cried, "We're flying!"

One morning, he got a call from a company in Middletown. They wanted to talk with him about a job. At the end of the interview the next day (he accepted their offer, of course), a great leaden lump was gone from his gut. He found an apartment in Middletown, and drove home to gather his clothes.

Jenny cried. He promised her that he'd be back every weekend to see her. His wife was silent, except to wish him good luck in his new job.

Moving out of his home was a relief, in a way. He began a new life—spare, simple, and lonely. Somehow he felt he deserved it. He went to work every day—sometimes working late just because he didn't have anything else to do. He met some people in the new company, but they all seemed to be busy in their own lives. He talked with them in the cafeteria sometimes, mostly about flying. Nobody else had the passion for it that he felt.

And there was something more. An old feeling of discomfort, of dread, surrounded his thoughts whenever he spoke of flying or of airplanes. Especially when he talked about how it *felt*.

And he remembered the image of Jenny from his dream, her arms spread wide, soaring among the clouds, laughing and kissing him.

After a while, he stopped talking about flying, unless someone else brought it up, and then he spoke only of ordinary things, of stall speed and magnetos and crosswind landings.

But at night, he began thinking more about Jenny. The Jenny who had come to his bed, and the Jenny from his dream—they became one, a fantasy nymph who stroked his temples and kissed him in the darkness, as his heart pounded. They flew together, felt the visceral thrill of the elevator ride clinging tightly to each other, and smeared their lips together with the world thousands of feet below them, the world powerless to quench their passion.

Afterward, in the mornings, he showered the memories away, and ate his tasteless meal and drank his drab coffee and went to work full of shame and disgust. Among his coworkers, usually he was able to put it all out of his mind for the day. He made sure he always had a lot of work to do, anything to keep his mind present. Nobody, he was sure, could guess what he couldn't talk about, what he couldn't allow himself to think about. But he always knew that when he got home and closed his door against the world, *she* would be there waiting for him.

The hardest times were the weekends. He had promised his daughter that he would see her every weekend that he could get away. He could *never* let her know about his fantasies. Quiet by nature, he became taciturn around her. They went to movies, or out to inexpensive restaurants, occasionally to a concert if something she liked were playing. She bubbled and chatted about her life, telling him stories from school, even occasionally revealing her feelings about other people. He did not pry. Afterward, with the real Jenny safe at home, he extracted pieces of memories from their time together and wove them into the Technicolor cloth of his fantasies. The way she looked up at him and laughed that laugh of hers, the electric touch of her fingertips as she dabbed at a bit of food near his mouth, the smell of her hair when she leaned her head on his shoulder as they drove home. When she moved toward him to kiss him goodnight, he turned his cheek because he was afraid of what he might do if their lips met. Afterward, safe in his lonely bed, he played the scene again, and didn't turn away. His testicles ached the way they used to when he was a teen himself, teased by girls who wanted his attention but wouldn't go all the way.

One day at work, he found himself in a conversation with a co-worker named Holly. He had noticed her before, but she always seemed to be in the midst of other men, laughing and chattering. His loneliness was a magnet to her, as was the moat he kept around himself, denying others entrance to his castle. His castle of secrets.

He and Holly talked about things of the world, about music, about flying. She knew nothing about flying and, sensing something in him for which flying was a key, she pressed for more.

Aware of the dangerously thin membrane that was his face to the world, he allowed her to taste little spoonfuls of his feelings, carefully filtered. She licked the spoon.

Part of the thrill of flying, however often it is denied, is the awareness of the nearness to death. Only the thin skin of an airplane separates one from free-fall into oblivion. No matter how "reliable" the aircraft, failure can mean that this moment supplies the only certainty there is.

Holly knocked at his castle door, and he put his hand on the knob.

9. Waiting

Holly thought of going into the farm house and finding something to fix for dinner, but she couldn't leave that spot, watching for a speck to appear over the trees. She opened another bottle of beer.

The sun had moved around so that she was sitting in the shade, and she began to feel chilled.

Anger and anxiety grew in her, inseparable as Siamese twins. She took her cell phone from her purse and called his number. Back in the barn somewhere, she heard it ring faintly. "Damn it, Richard!" She snapped the phone closed. *Why hadn't he at least taken his phone with him?*

After an hour, she was frantic. She paced back and forth in the big doorway, pausing on every lap to search the skyline and listen to the birds. A cicada began its long, rasping call in the sycamore behind her.

Finally, the reality of the situation took hold of her. Trembling, she retrieved Richard's cell phone from his jacket pocket and looked through his call list. Tony was a neighbor who had helped Richard with some of the assembly work on the airplane. She punched in the number.

When Tony answered, she broke into tears, and finally managed to tell him between sobs what she feared. "Stay right there, Holly," he soothed. "I'll be right over."

In the growing dusk, Tony and his wife Judith tried to reassure Holly, and the three of them phoned everyone that they could think of who might know something about Richard's plans, about the probable direction of his flight, about how far he might have gone. Could he have landed at another field, maybe at a friend's to show off his new plane, maybe ... ? They even found the number of the manufacturer's inspector, who had been at the farm the weekend before. It was dark when they finally called the sheriff.

Holly stayed all night at the farm, alternately pacing and crying on the bed. When the telephone woke her, the morning sun was poking a blood-red finger into the room. A sheriff's deputy told her that search planes were getting ready to take off. He asked if she wanted to come to the office so that she'd know immediately if Richard were found.

Through the day, Holly phoned Richard's ex-wife and his daughter. Margaret asked that she be called immediately if there was anything to report. Jennifer told Holly she was flying down to help in the search.

Holly took off work the following day, but it was too hard to just sit in the sheriff's office waiting, so she returned home that evening and resumed her routine the next day. The sheriff promised to call her with any news. Days passed, and then weeks. Her tears became less frequent, but the tightness in her stomach remained.

Richard had come into her life ten years before, a new hire in the company that had been her home since college. He was quiet, and seemed forlorn. She had a steady boyfriend at the time, a jolly, outgoing fellow who made her laugh a lot. Eventually, she tired of Eddie's effervescence, choosing to sit alone at home in the evenings, listening to music and reading. One day she sat next to Richard in the cafeteria, and they began to talk. His usually solemn expression lit up when the conversation turned to flying. She had never flown except in a commercial jetliner, and was apprehensive when he offered to take her up in a light plane. But she went.

Holly came to love his passion about flying. She could feel him change when he talked about it, and she could see it in his whole manner when he was at the controls of an airplane. She wondered at the sadness she sensed in him. He told her about his ex-wife and his daughter, but seemed reluctant to say much about the separation. It wasn't long before he announced matter-of-factly that he was now divorced.

They saw more and more of each other. Both of them loved music, and they often drove down to Cincinnati for a concert. Gradually, their flying together became less frequent. Richard admitted that his finances were getting tight, since his daughter was entering college soon. And Holly noticed that as he flew less, despondency seemed to take over his frame of mind. She offered to pay for their flying, but he made excuses.

Their relationship settled into predictability. Sometimes she felt as though she were the only thing keeping him afloat, that if she weren't there he would drown in his own melancholy. Still, she told herself, he was worth it. When he moved out to the old farm and began working on an airplane kit, she was delighted. Perhaps this was the corner he had to turn.

When Richard's airplane was finally found and recovered, it was the sheriff's deputy who called her. Richard's daughter left a message on her answering machine about the funeral. Holly felt numb that whole day, as though she were sleepwalking. She slipped into the church and sat alone in the back. The people who spoke about Richard seemed not to know him at all. One person talked about his flying as though it had been a tragic hobby. After the service, Jenny introduced her to Richard's ex-wife, whom she had talked with on the telephone but never met face to face. Margaret was there with her current husband, both of them rather stone-faced. Jenny hugged Holly, and they both cried. But afterward, Holly got into her car and drove away, still feeling as though she were sleepwalking.

Margaret phoned her a few days later asking if there was anything at the farm that she wanted.

No. She wanted only to see that grin on Richard's face when he banked the airplane so she could see the world through his eyes.

10. The Pieces

Several weeks after the funeral, Jenny arrived home to get a telephone message from Holly. "Jenny, when you're feeling up to it, I'd like to have dinner with you or something. Anything, just so we can talk. Please?" She gave a Middletown number.

Jenny waited another week before calling back. Holly's voice sounded warm, as it had at the funeral. Jenny felt awkward talking with her, but she agreed to meet with her.

"I changed my mind about dinner," Holly said. "I don't want to talk in public, and I'm not sure we'll be hungry anyway. Let's make it some weekend, maybe during the day?"

"All right, Holly. I appreciate your support at the funeral. Thanks for being there."

"I'd have crashed the party if I hadn't been invited."

"Can you make it this Saturday?"

"Yes, anytime."

"It will take me two hours, a little more, to get there."

"Would you rather meet somewhere half-way?"

"No, I'm flying. You'd be driving. If you can pick me up at the airport?"

"I will, Jenny. Thank you."

They agreed to meet before noon, and hung up. Jenny thought about Holly, and remembered the first time they met. It had been awkward, but Jenny was so involved in what she wanted from her dad that she had barely noticed Holly. Her father had not talked much about his relationship with this woman, and yet she seemed committed to him. Jenny was so hungry for *something* about her father that she would have put up with anyone who had known him, even if she hated her.

Her mother wasn't much help. Margaret had decided long ago that Rich just wasn't the person she had thought him to be, and wasn't whom she needed in her life. After they had divorced, they continued to be in touch with each other, mostly to share information about Jenny. But she didn't know Rich the way Jenny felt she did—or had.

As she sat on the concrete bench in front of the airport terminal waiting for Holly, she thought about how distant her father had become. It was an old routine; the more she thought about him the more depressed she became. And, as always, she caught herself, removed her sunglasses and dried her eyes, and looked around her. In a moment, a familiar car rounded the circle drive and stopped at the curb. She took a deep breath and walked to the car.

Holly was prettier than Jenny remembered. And older. Odd, that Jenny had felt that she was so much younger than her father. A little, maybe. Younger than her mother. She had a way about her, a warm personality, unlike Jenny's mother. It was hard to think about Holly being to her father what her mother had been.

She told some of this to Holly, sitting in the older woman's living room, on the opposite side of the coffee table. She reminded herself that the only way she could expect Holly to be open with her was to be open herself. It felt safe.

Holly began. "Richard wasn't too kind to you these last few years."

"How about fifteen years?"

Holly frowned. "He practically worshipped you, you know."

"I thought he used to, when we were all together. He changed." Jenny was holding her sunglasses, opening and closing the bows. She suddenly stopped, snapped them closed, and laid them on the table. She put her hands in her lap. "Tell me about him," she asked softly.

"I first met him when he started to work at the company. We spoke occasionally. He seemed pretty somber sometimes, as though he had the weight of the world on his shoulders. I was dating someone else at the time. But I kept thinking that

Richard needed some TLC. It's probably my nature to want to comfort the afflicted, as they say." She laughed.

"Is that why you called me?" Jenny wasn't trying to challenge her, but she was curious. She smiled, as though to say, "I'm kidding."

Holly caught the gesture. "Maybe. I don't know. I watched you that time when you came down in your new airplane and Richard brushed you off. I felt sorry for you. I know how I would have felt."

"He told me one time that he didn't deserve you."

"There was something in him that I felt I could love, if I could just get to it. Oh, I did love him, just the way he was, but I wanted to see that other part of him."

"Yeah, I can identify with that."

"I know about his demon."

Jenny cocked her head. "His demon?"

"His flying demon." She paused, waiting for a response. "You don't know about it?"

"I don't have the faintest idea what you're talking about."

"It's what I called it. He had always loved flying so much. It was his passion in life. But some things happened that he couldn't separate from flying, and they haunted him. One night he had had a little too much to drink, and it all came spilling out."

"He scared me, sometimes when he drank," Jenny said. "Not that he got ugly or anything. I just couldn't read him. I remember when he and Mom were having problems, he'd drink and begin to cry. I wanted to cuddle him in my arms—and I was only twelve!"

Holly smiled. "Yeah. Me, too. He told me about the man who taught him to fly. Do you know about that? He said he hadn't told anyone."

"Tell me, please."

"When he was in high school, he met this young man who owned his own airplane. The man—not much more than a boy, himself—befriended him, and took him up in his airplane a few times and then seduced him."

Jenny was shocked. "I never knew that!"

"Rich was so ashamed that it contaminated his feelings about airplanes. For a long time, he lived with the guilt, thinking that he had done something terrible."

The two women sat quietly for a while. Finally Holly asked, "Jenny, would you like a drink?"

Jenny took a deep breath. "All those years, he thought he was bad?"

Holly stood up. "*I* need a drink. Anything?"

"What are you having?"

"Brandy. Your father's favorite."

"All right." Jenny sat lost in her thoughts until Holly returned. Then she said, "He ruined his life—and mine—because he did something as a teenager?"

Holly sat down next to Jenny on the couch. "Also ..." She stopped.

Jenny cocked her head, then turned to look at Holly. Slowly her face changed. She sat there without moving for a long time. "He told you about that?"

"Yes. He was so ashamed. It was killing him. I think it helped for him to get it out to somebody. I'm glad it was me."

Jenny's voice was barely above a whisper. "That was *my* fault. I knew it at the time. I never blamed him."

"But he did." Holly put her hand on Jenny's arm. Sweet Jenny, you were *twelve!*"

"Oh, . . . my . . . god." The words were one long, drawn-out wail.

"He even went into therapy about it, but he couldn't tell the therapist. That was just before he opened up to me."

Jenny threw her arms around Holly and sobbed on her shoulder.

Gradually, the sobbing softened, and she sat up and reached in her pocket for a tissue. "He never did anything but hold me and stroke me," she said. Her voice was barely audible. "It felt wonderful. I loved him so much, I'd have done anything if it would only make him feel better."

"Yeah, I know."

"He finally sent me back to my room. I thought I'd done something really bad. I felt terrible. But we never said anything about it afterward. It was like our dark secret—my dark secret. He stayed in that depression, and I thought it was my fault. I had let him down."

Jenny looked down at her hands, twisting the tissue. "Nobody—my parents—never talked to me about sex. I was pretty confused, but I couldn't ask. I thought I was a slut because I had feelings—*you* know."

"Can I ask you something personal?" Holly put her hand on Jenny's arm.

"You mean something more personal than that?"

They both laughed.

"Did it hurt you later on? I mean, …"

"You mean, like why I'm not married?" Jenny smiled wryly. "Actually, I've been so tied up in knots over my dad, I haven't felt like I could, you know, really *be there* for somebody else. But did I feel like, uh, *damaged?* No. He never hurt me, except to stay away from me." Then, vehemently, "*Except to keep me at arms length!*"

After a moment, she continued, "I have always understood, more these past few years, that I was living in a fantasy world about him. At twelve, at fourteen, I'd have married him in a minute." Jenny, her hands over her face, bent over and sobbed.

Finally, she straightened up and wiped her face. "Well," she said, trying to control her voice, "all that went away." She glanced at Holly and smiled weakly.

A few minutes passed. They each sipped the brandy. Jenny smiled again. "I recognize this." She cleared her throat pointedly.

"Oh?" Holly pretended surprise.

"When I used to visit him on weekends, I'd sneak a sip now and then. I felt very grown up. Then I spoiled the taste by running into the bathroom and brushing my teeth." She sipped again.

Her face became sober once more. "It's hard to believe that all these years he'd been carrying that around."

"I think he felt better after he told me. But he still felt so awful about it. It was like he had done to you what that guy did to him. But he even felt guilty, after all those years, about that time, too."

"You were right about 'demon.'" Jenny's face screwed up again and she began to cry. Holly pulled her over onto her shoulder and let her cry.

Then Jenny abruptly pulled away and looked at Holly. "Do you think ... do you think his accident was deliberate?"

"C'mon. The coroner's report said the engine had failed. It was mechanical."

A bare whisper, "Yeah."

Jenny slumped against the back of the couch, exhausted. "You know, we should have eaten something. This stuff has gone right to my head."

"No flying for you anymore today. Let me fix us something." She got up and went into the kitchen. Jenny followed her. "I must look a mess," she said.

"You look like you've been crying. I don't call that a mess."

"Holly, you are something. You must have taken on a lot of Dad's stuff on your back, too."

The woman stopped tearing lettuce and looked at her hands. "I thought I could help him, too. Isn't that our job as women?" She looked at Jenny and smiled wanly.

"Who takes care of us, then?"

"I guess we have to take care of each other." She continued making the salad.

Jenny sighed. "It's such a waste!"

Holly nodded. "There was somebody wonderful in there. I could see it, every once in a while." Then she stopped. "No. I saw it a lot. I kept getting tangled up with trying to get him to open up, so I wasted a lot of our time together, too. I wish …" She stood there, a knife in one hand and a tomato in the other. Then tears welled up in her eyes. She put the knife down and steadied herself against the counter.

Very softly, she said, "There was a passion in him. I could feel it, like when he talked about flying. I wanted to share that passion." She turned and went out into the living room, then returned with a framed poem. "This was him, under that armor he wore."

Jenny read the poem and the inscription at the bottom. "To Holly, the angel of my wings."

The poem was titled "High Flight," was written by a Spitfire pilot during the early days of World War Two. He was killed in an accident soon after.

Oh! I have slipped the surly bonds of earth
And danced the skies on laughter-silvered wings;
Sunward I've climbed, and joined the tumbling mirth
Of sun-split clouds – and done a hundred things
You have not dreamed of – wheeled and soared and swung
High in the sunlit silence. Hovering there,
I've chased the shouting wind along, and flung
My eager craft through footless halls of air.
Up, up the long, delirious, burning blue
I've topped the windswept heights with easy grace
Where never lark, nor even eagle flew.
And there, with silent, lifting mind I've trod
The high untrespassed sanctity of space,
Put out my hand, and touched the face of God.[2]

---

[2] Pilot/Officer J.G. Magee, Jr. RCAF No. 412 Squadron, 1941

Jenny choked back a sob. Then she handed it back. Holly placed the poem carefully on the table. "I've only flown a few times. I haven't felt it as intensely as he did, but I could see what he meant. What pulled me to him was that intensity. Whatever it had been about, it was something that he felt in his soul, so deep, I wanted to drown in it with him. And then sometimes it was like he just slammed the door. On me, on himself. I think that's why I called you. I thought you knew that part of him. We had that in common."

Jenny moved close to Holly and put her arms around her. "Thank you, for giving him back to me. I'm going to have to learn to live with his demon. I hope, better than he could."

They ate and talked, and eventually Jenny curled up on the end of the couch and immediately fell asleep. Holly got a blanket from the bedroom and carefully put it over her. Then she went into her bedroom, leaving the door open, and crawled under the covers.

Both women dreamed of flying.

11. The Lake

As soon as she left the pattern and turned south, she began reciting her letter.

"Dear Dad,

I know this is coming too late for you. I don't know if it would have made a difference in how things turned out if you had been able to read it. But I need to say some things to you, for me, so that I can let go and live my life instead of wishing.

Holly told me about your 'demon,' the feelings you lived with for so many years, and how you tried to avoid them by avoiding me. It still hurts, because it was so unnecessary. If only we could have talked about it! If only—

I don't know what kind of world you grew up in. Well, maybe I do, a little. Uptight is the word that comes to mind. I grew up in a different world, even though I grew up with you and Mom. I can't imagine carrying such a load of guilt about something that happened when I was a teen-ager."

She smiled to herself, remembering her own first encounter with sex after a high school dance. Scary, yes. Regrets, yes. Traumatic, no. *He was such a dork. But at least he wasn't rough with me.*

The sun was low on the horizon and partially obscured by red clouds. Already the ground beneath her was darkening. She scanned the air ahead of her, watching for moving lights.

"And for you to lump that with what happened with me that night—it's so sad! It's sad that I didn't know what I was doing, and it's sad that you blamed yourself all that time. I thought you were angry at me. I went back to my bed knowing that I had spoiled something for us, and sure that you would

never speak to me again. But for those few minutes, I was in heaven.

And the worst thing is what it did to your feelings about flying!"

She burst into tears, and struggled to suppress them. Taking a deep breath, she reached for her handbag on the seat beside her. The Cessna was trimmed well enough that she could take her hands off the yoke to blow her nose.

"It's hard not to think that I took your joy of flying away from you. But I'm not going to do that. I can't do that to myself.

At least now I don't have to wonder anymore what happened to us. It's weird, thinking now about all these years I've thought you didn't like me anymore. I can see now that it was too important to me. I guess I've grown up some."

She had no trouble finding Watson Field in the dark. Their tower was closed, but the runway lights were on. She entered the pattern after making sure there weren't any other aircraft in the vicinity, and switched on her landing lights.

On the ground, she taxied to the apron and shut down the engine. Outside the Cessna she stretched her legs and opened her cell phone to call a cab.

They knew her at the motel—she'd been a regular there for a lot of weeks while she searched for the ultralight.

At dawn, she was back at the field, doing a preflight inspection of the Cessna, shivering in the cool air. Thin layers of fog hung over the low places in the field. An old Aztec twin landed and taxied noisily over next to her. When it stopped, a middle-aged man in a suit got out.

"Good morning," he greeted her.

"Morning. Early start, eh?"

"A meeting. I understand there's a cab near here."

"The phone number is on the booth, on the side of the building."

"Thanks." He walked toward the terminal.

Jenny pulled the chocks from her wheels and climbed in. From behind the seat she took a metal container and placed it on the floor in front. Then she buckled herself in and started the engine. The light was still dim enough that her navigation beacon flicked repeatedly across the face of the terminal building. Releasing the brakes, she taxied out and took off, heading north.

Long lake was a silver platter in the middle of the forest. She'd never forget that lake, looking dark and ominous, with that shining wing sticking straight out of it, like Excalibur.

"Well, Daddy, I'm not the lady of the lake. I'm just a girl who lost her father. It's better that you go back down there than sit on my mantle all my life."

She dropped down to a hundred feet above the surface of the water. Reaching down, she opened the can at her feet. With one hand she untied the wire on the plastic bag inside and replaced the lid loosely. Then she opened the window next to her. The cold wind whipped her hair. In a quick move, she thrust the can out the window to let the wind remove the lid and suck the ashes out. Fine dust eddied around her face. She dropped the canister into the lake.

"Goodbye, Daddy. I love you."

Those few moments of inattention had allowed the Cessna to drift downward, and she pulled back on the control just before the wheels touched the smooth water. "Oh, no you don't!" she cried. "You don't get both of us!"

Throttling up, she went back to a hundred feet and turned, making a full circle over the lake, watching the faint spot of ash disappear.

Then she closed the window. The sun was just appearing in the east as she climbed and turned north, toward home.

The End

www.ingramcontent.com/pod-product-compliance
Lightning Source LLC
Chambersburg PA
CBHW060139260626
47160CB00001B/44